CIVIL BLOOD

by Chris Hepler

"Americans... are as much disposed to vice as their rulers,
and nothing but a vigorous and efficient government
can prevent their degenerating into savages,
or devouring each other like beasts of prey."

—Dr. Benjamin Rush
Signatory to the Declaration
of Independence
1788

1 - INFINITY

August 4th
A generation from now

I don't like vampires, underhanded politics, or the idea of being put down like a dog, but the little stick in my hand tells me I can't avoid any of the three. I'm never supposed to say the word "vampires." No one on the team is. But we're not supposed to get infected, either, and I'll choke before I call myself a newly minted "disease vector." I've got a year's supply of names we made up, but all I want to use right now is profanity.

The last ten hours have been a string of freakish dreams, night sweats, and aches that feel like every tendon is stretching farther on the bone. The thought of food is gag-worthy. The light from the bathroom window stings my eyes. I want to break something. Throwing up is the last of the early-stage symptoms. I can check off food poisoning, and it's not the flu. Now that the pregnancy test is negative, it's obvious. I have VIHPS.

I flush the toilet and brush my teeth. The stink is bad, but the scents of toothpaste and the smoke in my hair help cover it. The test stick was a last-ditch hope; not that a positive result wouldn't *also* be a kick in the gut. I've gotten used to the idea of my twenties ending, but I always thought I'd have something more permanent to show for it than a three-year car lease. Temping gave way to modeling, which gave way to jiujutsu, which gave way to Forced Protection.

F-prot, as we call it, is responsible for the Band-Aids on my hand. On Monday night, I was the bait for the Los Angeles team, crashing in on some San Fernando fuck-pad with a spectacular ganja-to-air ratio and a cultie vipe who thought the infection made him a sex god. We went in expecting a pair and found three more of his chew toys in the house.

One went for my gun, so I split my knuckles across his teeth. Then, Louis and Jared were on top of him, cracking him with Mag-

3

Lites until he stayed down. The rest of the team asked if I was all right and took me at my word. Saliva-to-blood isn't supposed to happen this way.

The previous Friday wasn't much safer. I'd gone clubbing and caught myself a visual effects artist. In answer to your next question, once on the balcony, once on the bed. Then, I found out he was a Darwin-lifer, and that's the kind who poke holes in condoms. That's L.A. for you: every dick is out to screw you in at least two ways.

The door shakes. My boyfriend Aaron.

I decide at that moment that I prefer karma when it's subtle.

"I think I'm coming down with something," I announce.

"Fantastic," I hear through the door. "Is there, like, medication for it?"

"Of course," I say real low. "Take one dose of hollow-points through the ear cavity."

"What?"

Louder, I try, "I'm going to take a shower." I need time to think.

The water is hot enough to scour away everything but the black dye in my hair. I attempt to formulate a plan and only succeed in repeatedly grinding the same few panicked thoughts into my head. First stop, the confidentiality agreements I signed with the Benjamin Rush Health Initiative when they recruited me. Next, the security clearance which is my only real shot to stay hired in a shitty economy. Finally, the extreme unlikelihood that if I tell anyone at work what happened last night that they will ever again let me walk free.

That's the thing about EBL-4, the virus that causes VIHPS. There is no cure, no vaccine. There are handcuffs and high-capacity magazines and a mental hospital that has been converted to a research lab. I'm not supposed to see the inside of that place when we drop off the vipes, but oh well.

One tough night when we brought in a cold one, and Jared was sporting a broken rib, I asked whether the bodies were taken to the county morgue and what kind of permits they need to bring them back. I was immediately assured that another staffer knew all that, I period, E period, don't worry your pretty head about it. I didn't, until today.

The shower stops, and yesterday's underwear goes back on, as does any clothing that can get me out of the apartment quickly. I open the door into Aaron—last week's haircut, designer blue contacts. He's two years younger than me, an amusingly cynical hedonist with a band and some talent who hasn't yet realized that in L.A., there are two hundred thousand people with exactly that much going for them. Realizations often come to him slowly.

"Hey, sweet knees." Aaron's nose crinkles. The vomit. "Still not feeling good?"

I inhale to tell him the truth. He smells odd. Not sweaty but sharp, warmer somehow, and I swallow. I've started salivating.

I've thought about telling him. The fantasy in my head starts with *Sit down*, moves on to *I actually capture and kill vampires: P.S., they exist*, and then, *you can't ever tell anyone*. Today I'm feeling a Kids Story Time vibe and want to start with *I really need to tell you about my special friend, European Bat Lyssavirus-4. See, he causes VIHPS, and someday when you won't freak, I'll tell you what that stands for, 'kay?*

"It's bad," I say.

I have a stash of four hundred dollars inside a sock in the drawer. A visit to the ATM will get me another thousand as a daily maximum. Only at times like this do I realize how little that is. I have to get moving. I don't have any good answers yet, not for Aaron, nor for the phone calls from my supervisor, Darcy, who'll ask why I didn't file my after-action report last night. I have to focus on the essentials, what I'll need to survive.

Toothbrush, toothpaste, not the half-empty one but the spare box, pads, razors, cosmetics and towel. I also grab jewelry; my credit cards leave an e-trail, but a pawn shop won't care.

I have a chipped passport and most definitely a birth certificate: Lilith Infinity DeStard. Even in Hell, new employers want two forms of ID.

"Is this what I think it is?" Aaron has the pregnancy stick in his hand.

"Yeah, we dodged a bullet."

"Okay... so why are you packing like you want to get out of town?"

Because otherwise I'll have to dodge fifty of them, I don't say. "It's work."

"A conference?" I shake my head. "A stakeout kind of thing?" I hesitate, deciding whether to say yes. It would be easier, but I have to pick words carefully. If I stay, I am well and truly fucked. In about an hour, I'll need an answer for Darcy about when I'll report for my next assignment, and oh, by the way, remember to be at Epidemiology by five for my monthly blood screening. Because just to put the cherry on top, the calendar says it's time.

If I don't stay, I might live, but Darcy's team will be here checking on me, and Aaron will be answering the door. He'll say everything I tell him, one way or the other.

I snag my Glock from the holster at the side of the bed. Aaron never likes arguing with me while I wear it. But he really doesn't like my preoccupied silence.

"Look, can you let me in just a little?" he implores. "I know I don't get to ask about work. But I get to know if you're worried. And this..." he waved the test stick, "...this is all us, right?"

I stop throwing high-capacity mags and sweat socks into the suitcase. The sensible thing to do, the normal thing, is to stay here in bed and let Aaron hug my worries away. Vipes do that all the time. They tell people about their symptoms and cry and get fed and cuddled. And when their loved ones survive the first attack, the next stage is more shock and reconciliation and an invariable resolution that they should at least go to the emergency room to get stitches. From there? They get flagged. From there? Downhill.

"There's a lot of things I'm not ready for right now," I say.

"Me neither," Aaron says. "But we face them head-on together. That's the deal, right?"

I wince. My words, recycled and weaponized. Sticking to straight talk is how Aaron lasted longer than any of my previous bed-friends. On a good day, I can call our relationship open and be satisfied with it. On a bad day, it's like ground glass in my mouth, making me wonder if it's no better than the mountain of coping strategies that came before it. The thread by which it all hangs is the honesty. It gives the illusion of progress so I can think I'm wiser now.

"Okay," I say, "the truth is I didn't follow procedures, and my boss is going to call me on it. So now I'm... volunteering. To get brownie points so all that goes away." There. Euphemisms are better. They are how F-prot rolls. If your EBL-4 gives you Virally Induced Hematophagic Predation Syndrome, you're a "vipe." Our operations are all about "disease vectors" and "isolation complications" and people "retiring for health reasons." Even the name "Forced Protection" alleges that we confine vipes for their own good. Which we do, provided they don't resist. I'd resist.

"Is that all? How long are you going away?"

"I don't know, so I'm packing for five days."

"We should say goodbye." He has his euphemisms, too.

"I just got clean."

"Then you'll taste nice." Aaron leans in, and my senses flood. He smells like a steakhouse. I can feel the heat of his face as it gets close. His mouth opens, and I realize that his tongue, full of blood, will soon be between my teeth. I could chatter them like an addict or deliberately latch on, hold him in place with strength and leverage.

But no. I keep my teeth clenched, my body as unresponsive as a wooden doll. His lips mash against mine but make no headway. He pulls back, frowning.

"That's... different." It's one of the better things about him. He likes enthusiasm. When I don't have any, he stops.

"I can't do this," I blurt. I hug him, sticking my face way out so I don't have his neck pressing against my mouth. His whole body is warm where our torsos touch.

"There's things I can volunteer," he says. I know them all. Massage, fingers, oil, tongue. But my heart is in fight-or-flight, beating against my rib cage as I realize he has nothing with which to defend himself. This boy couldn't break my grip with a hammer, and his idea of how to deal with me is extra foreplay.

My cell phone rings, with its tinny Beethoven music no one will

7

ever dance to. It rings, eclipsing the silence. I keep holding and smelling Aaron, keep thinking of highs he's given me and songs he's played, and the phone keeps screaming at me with its Fifth Symphony electronica remix that there is nothing rational about this situation because I have to run, they will lock me up. I don't do well locked up. I learned that pretty young.

I pick it up and see the number.

"Who is it?" Aaron asks.

"Louis and Jared. They're going to be by later." I don't need to answer to know that. I set it to block, first Louis, then Jared, then Aaron.

"But you said you're not going to be here...." He doesn't see the screen, but he's putting it together.

"They're worried about me," I say. "And to tell you the truth, they have reason to be." Time to spin. "I pissed some people off this week. For a few days, I shouldn't be at my home address. You shouldn't act like you know me."

He's incredulous. "These guys know where we live?"

I have backup. "I don't know for sure, but it's my name on the lease," I say. "Louis and Jared will find the bad guys. It shouldn't take long." I try to imagine what the F-prots will tell him when they knock on our door. They are pros. If he doesn't know what a vipe is, they sure aren't going to tell him.

As he mulls that over, I pack. He has more questions, all about what the bad guys might look like if they loiter around the house, but I bat those away by sounding experienced. He should be vigilant, everything is under control, the baddies aren't known for hurting civilians, garbage garbage garbage.

"Wait," he says after a few more reassurances. "You said you're sick, you didn't follow procedures, and there are people looking for you."

"Yeah?" My oh-crap senses fire up, but I have to stay cool.

"So, how is that not changing your story?" he asks. "I just wanna say, if we don't have the truth, we don't have anything."

I stop packing. He's right, and the terrible thing is, it won't matter. "What would it take to convince you that I'm coming back?" I ask. "Calls every day?"

His face drops its guard. "That... it'd be a start, yeah."

"All right, then we'll do that," I say, "but to be safe, I'm going to need a burner phone, and we should get you that privacy app I told you about. I'll call through there."

Aaron nods. "Show me which one." I do. It takes only a few minutes, sitting next to him on the bed, and by then, he is calmer.

"Why do you need a burner if you have this?" he asks.

"If my office caught me using that app for personal business, they'd freak," I say, continuing to spin. "So, I'm thinking a cheap second phone and, poof, no panicked firing of Infinity. You want me to go get it, or do you want to be my hero?"

"I can get it," he says, and I see I've calmed him. "Back soon, but first..." He tries a kiss again. If I freeze him out now, I'll be explaining it forever. I open my mouth and taste him. All nausea is gone. He's more than delicious—he has an energy, a vibrancy to him, that I want inside me in all kinds of ways. When he starts to pull back, it's my teeth squeezing his lower lip that keeps us together. At first, I don't even realize I've done it. After a guilty glance, I let go.

"Well, now," Aaron says, face flushed. "Don't go anywhere."

He leaves the room, and I can breathe again. I was stupid. If he'd had a bad floss that morning, the cuts in the mouth could have done him in. As soon as I hear the front door click, I scramble to the wall over the bed. I get my black belt off its hook and the last portable piece of my life.

It rests on the dresser: a little tablet of cherry wood. I look at the god carved into its face, then throw it into my bag. It was a god to me once, or at least a goal, when I had none. I couldn't see any future with me alive in it, but making this was something I could do.

It's coming with me.

I consider waiting for Aaron, but by the time my suitcases are full, twenty minutes are gone forever. My nerve breaks.

I go out the door and squint in the hot, unfriendly L.A. sun. Will Aaron be mad? Of course. But on that day far in the future, in which

I take his calls again, I'll figure out what to say then. Hurrying down the apartment complex's steps, I make it into a cool, dim parking garage.

The last choice that lies before me: cycle or car? The cycle can handle my bags fine and gets more kilometers to the volt, but once I'm out of SoCal, it'll be toast in any kind of rain. If I'm trying for distance, the car will be more comfortable. And if I need to sleep in it because I can't afford a motel, well, three strikes and you're out.

I drop my cases and roll the little blue Zero out of the way of the Dodge Atlantis. Its kickstand is still too loose; something that Aaron has been meaning to fix forever. The cycle has been with me for eleven years, which beats Aaron and any of my other boyfriends. Doesn't it?

I have no trailer to bring it. And the day a cycle, even a small one, fits in the back of an Atlantis will be the day the angels break the seals and all that shit. So, I kiss my hand and touch it to the cycle. If I get reincarnated as a machine, I hope someone does the same for me.

Then, I throw the suitcases in the trunk of the car, climb in, and start it up. What I am doing is wise. It spares Aaron a nasty fate. If I had a real choice, I would have been loyal.

Somewhere around San Bernardino, I find out I've forgotten to pack tissues.

2 - RANATH

August 4th

Tonight, I have to lie a lot. Good evening—it isn't. Glad you could make it—not really. Traffic wasn't bad—please. The petty deceits are practice for a larger fiction: that every conversation is normal, and everyone is safe.

The Folger Shakespeare Library is within a rifle shot of the Capitol, tucked behind the Supreme Court and a half-dozen other Masonic stone buildings with killer *feng shui*. Here, I have to lie about many things but mostly about what I do for a living.

"I'm in marketing," I say, this time to a socialite-for-life sewn into a black dress. She doesn't ask for details, and the lie slips away with the empty martini glasses. I handle her long enough to find out she's funny, vivacious, and a waste of time.

"I work at a travel agency."

I have a little game I sometimes play. I question my companion and commit their story to memory so I can recycle it for the next inquisitor. I take the socialite's job now.

"I'm in human resources."

I am at the Folger to find Simon Walter Davis, height one point eight meters, weight ninety-five kilos, born forty years ago to Gary and Meredith Davis. Simon has never been married, never been in jail, and is a registered member of the Solar Citizens Party, all of which he blathers about on social media.

It would not be difficult to become Simon Walter Davis. Davis has never lived outside Maryland and got his master's in business administration from UDC. He's overqualified for his accounting position, but he's loyal. I've already spent the requisite time online to speak knowledgeably about Davis-like subjects for five minutes or less—more than that is rarely necessary. But Davis is the last person I want to be.

It would be very difficult for Simon Walter Davis to become me.

"Where do you work?" A businessman this time, starched collar and tight tie with a jacket already over one arm because D.C. humidity can make you stink.

"At a desk."

I move on. The Elizabethan Great Hall held one hundred and eighty-one people when I arrived and studied the guest list a rented receptionist was checking off. One hundred and eighty people are not enough for Simon Walter Davis to hide behind.

The lights blink over the Folger lobby. Cue audience. Well-dressed adults walk to the theater past the display cases of Shakespearean memorabilia. Under glass are two swords: not the domesticated fencing foils used by actors but Elizabethan-era rapiers, wild and long and with an edge that can flick off an ear. I finger the container of needles in my left jacket pocket. Weapons change over the years: intent, never.

Simon Walter Davis tested positive for the antibodies for European Bat Lyssavirus-4, the virus that causes VIHPS. The syndrome is not listed in any disease directory, and the epidemiologists that run the tests at the Benjamin Rush Health Initiative have never heard of it. I have committed the symptoms to memory: overwhelming hunger, violent urges, bone ossification and muscle attachment, significant synaptic plasticity and phenomenally accelerated cell regeneration. As for the blood, and their consumption of it, that's a separate lecture.

I see a balding pattern, Davis-like, not far from the exit. It would not be out of character for Davis to be a wallflower—he was allegedly infected eleven days ago, and headaches and nausea often put a damper on vectors' sociability. Another percentage—I honestly forget how much, as it changes so often—are uncomfortable seeing people from their pre-infection lives.

The man in the corner is not my quarry. I turn on my heel and hurry to the Reading Room. Oak bookshelves, balconies, chandeliers. No cover but desks.

I spot an unkempt beard. Most vectors have trouble concentrating in the first weeks after infection, and Simon Walter Davis is neither well-dressed nor well-groomed. He probably has no clue what he's infected with, but he knows something is wrong. He's concentrating so much on acting normal that he misses it completely.

I am practiced at acting normal.

He moves through the stragglers, eyes downcast. Then, he looks relieved: he sees a familiar face. His conversation partner has a sport coat and the short limbs and muscular build of a wrestler. They head off together. Not to the theater.

Vectors like isolation. It takes no imagination to figure out why.

I try not to run, try to keep the coldness from my face and eyes. If Davis knows the building, he might be headed for the gardens. Though vectors are often too nervous to do anything within shouting distance of a crowd, "often" is a very thin shield. Vectors and criminal masterminds have little in common.

Three people block my way. Living static.

"—you should have been here for the First Amendment March. It had everyone from every adult film ever *made*—"

"—I was. That's that time I got hit on. We're nose-to-nose in the subway. I mean, like *here*, and not only was he a porn director, it was fetish, and then he starts asking what spas I've been to, and I'm not sure if I should take it as a compliment—"

"—it's totally a compliment—"

"—and then the Metro conductor's like, 'Next stop, Dupont Circle,' and the whole train goes, 'YAWHOO—'"

I glance over. Though I am tall and quite distinctive, Davis has no idea who I am and so does not flee at the sight of me. He is intent on his conversational partner. Their talk would be audible if it weren't for the theatergoers who have wandered into my face.

"—so, that's my experience with demonstrations."

"What about you? You ever been in a march?"

The three twenty-somethings look at me. I fake it. "Two. One for stimweb control, one for water rights." My politics range yellow rather than blue or red, but D.C. is deep sapphire on the electoral map, so the answer helps me blend.

There. Davis is leaving with his friend, a viral transfer in the making if I've ever seen one. But the three chatterers are drunk and interpose.

"God, another one who wants to get away from me."

"Yeah, why might that be?" says the woman, who is popping Vitamin C from a bottle. "Don't let him scare you, whats-your-name."

"Roland," I say. I have forgotten the last person I spoke to, so I use my standard alias. "I do sanitation."

She doesn't miss a beat. "So, I guess you can take a lot of shit?"

"I don't need public appreciation," I say. "If you'll excuse me, I'm with him." I point to a cluster of four men. I slip past the trio, smile and, as I reach the next cluster, clap one man on the back as he goes by, completing the illusion of a friend. While the man tries to place me, I make for the restroom, cutting across voices.

"—her statements are so out-there. She wants the Freedom Forever candidacy—"

"—but that's what actors say, right? Nobody's a villain in their own mind—"

The crowd thins as the audience flows slowly to their seats. Cold molasses.

In the restroom, I shut myself in a stall. Shadowing Davis directly is chancy. I have an alternative, if I'm fast. I pull the straps of my stimweb out from my sleeve and loop them over my fingers. I pin its baggy fishnet in place with the acupuncturist's needles I take from my jacket pocket. Unlike in Chinese medicine, here the needles go in the doctor, not the patient.

I was a doctor once. What I do now is not medicine, traditional or otherwise.

Two more needles go through the conductive web under my jacket collar and into the flesh of my ring finger. Touching thumb and ring finger together, I feel for the interrupted rhythm of qi flow.

Qi? It's life's energy. It was elusive for centuries, until Dr. Jessica Ulan finally tamed it with technology and biofeedback. Remember Jess. She's the famous one for a reason.

Thap-thap. My heart pumps blood, and I dial up the stimweb. Three-quarters of a volt circulates through my arm, a faster, pulsing twitch. *Thap, thap, thap.* I hold my right thumb and forefinger in a circle, making a ring of living qi. I concentrate: my thumb and fingers warm, signaling a dot of invisible energy growing in the center of the ring.

The circle spreads out, shimmering like heat on a desert road. It expands in an ever-larger donut. For a qi function to last and grow, you need to balance opposing positive and negative energies, spin them like a record with a carefully calculated drop-off rate. I increase the stimweb's voltage by squares to keep the energy's expansion steady despite its diminishing power. When it flows easily through my body and reaches the stall wall, I kick the cybernetics.

Roughly two dozen jolts go through my body from nanotech pulse-points. The effect on the biowave is like lighting an acetone fume, and the spiralling energy shoots out. I feel it flicker against a moving yang-within-yin field. My vector, outside the building but caught in the net. Davis has left by the street, not the garden. Going home.

Like a tide leaving behind seaweed, the wave marks Davis. I feel a gentle tug drawing me closer while the stimweb keeps the function sustained. The chancy part, the long-range part, is done. Now, it's time to allay suspicion. I close my eyes and stroke my fingers over them: they tingle. I push my hair back. It warms my skull. This biophysical field is easier, a familiar function that toys with other people's perceptions. I check my reflection in the chrome of the toilet: irises gray, hair a sandy blond. The truth has been masked.

A shudder runs through me. I am wet with sweat, and my saliva tastes like metal. Biochemical imbalance: hazard of the job.

Checking outside the stall to ensure no one is near, I pull at my shoe. I produce a four-round magazine that fits in a hollowed-out steel heel. From my breast pocket, I pull a thick pen with ends that come off, forming a rifled barrel. From my jacket, a box that I twist, releasing an all-plastic pistol grip. I rack an eleven-millimeter Glaser into the firing chamber.

The murmur of the crowd has stopped. I hear the chant of a chorus.

Two households, both alike in dignity,
In fair Verona, where we lay our scene,
From ancient grudge break to new mutiny,
Where civil blood makes civil hands unclean.

Anchoring my personal qi field, I alter the biophysical radiation emanating from my hand. It shimmers in the bright light of the bathroom stall, and the pistol vanishes. Yes, my hand still reflects the same number of photons per square centimeter and other such dross. But with a concealment field radiating out from it, humans nearby won't register it as anything other than bare and empty, which makes it ideal for my line of work.

I am a magician. I make people disappear.

*   *   *

The air outside is like a swamp's breath. Simon Walter Davis and his companion don't seem to mind sweating. They push a brisk pace down East Capitol Street, away from the eyes of his former colleagues. The streets are largely deserted, but my qi function is like a wire connecting us. I can fall back to a good shadowing distance. I dial the number for the hot van.

"Hello."

"I have a dog in heat." It's code. "Is this the number for animal control?"

"It is not." The phone clicks as if hanging up. I stay on the line, allowing the F-prots to cue up their finder program. The van now knows exactly where I am in real time.

Davis turns a corner, and I close the distance, staying only a block behind. Running three qi functions, I am in no shape to sprint for long, either toward or away. By all precedent, Simon Walter Davis will be nervous and irritable from the strange new senses flooding his brain. Being sick will only make him stronger, more capable of lashing out.

The hot van has restraints, but no one on my team believes in them.

I withdraw the last section of my pistol from my pockets; a disposable silencer. Last night I downloaded its specs off some eternally mirrored Net site, slid them into a forgebox, and one nasty smell of burning plastic later, produced a small assembly line of muffler-shaped, killer Tupperware. Now, of course, it smells like hand soap from the bathroom sink, a precaution for a vector's sensitive nose. I thread the silencer and thumb the slide lock into place. It'll be a quiet shot, but I'll only get one.

Simon Walter Davis hears none of this, intent on his companion.

Davis and his friend turn in to a brownstone on East Capitol, through a low, decorative iron fence. I pause in the shadow of a tree and key in the emergency number. With a civilian out of sight, I must assume Davis is aiming for infection. But the F-prot program is strict: never confront a vector alone.

My skin starts to sting a little from the functions as I wait the long minutes before the hot van pulls up. It's red and white with just the right amount of attention. The whole neighborhood will remember an ambulance but rarely any additional details.

"Is he alone?" asks the driver, a former prison guard named al-Ibrahim.

"No."

Al-Ibrahim circles his finger in the air, and two F-prots open the ambulance's back doors. One unloads the gurney. The other dons yellow gloves, the kind a novice might mistake for a surgeon's or a dishwasher's. These go up to the shoulder. Deer hunters call them gutting gloves.

That one, Breunig, comes with me to the door. I'm the specialist. Breunig leads the team. Hands-on, from the front. He has a touch-and-talk tablet ready. I remove my jacket and bind my long hair up in a fry-cook's net, then tuck it under a cap with a caduceus on it: EMT gear.

I ring the bell, wondering what I will be interrupting. Davis, smoking weed and playing Scrabble? Vectors are often surprised, and that's the safest. Davis, interrupted during feeding? Happens all the time. It's wet and messy, every drop of blood turning a suburban living room into a biological minefield. Davis, reaping the rewards of a proposition? Plenty of them don't even get dressed to answer the door.

There was an incident a year ago in Anne Arundel County where four vectors assaulted a jogger, Andrew Leyman, on the side of the road. One of them slashed Leyman's throat with a serrated plaster-saw and, using a Big Gulp container taken from a nearby convenience store, passed around a liter of his blood to the others. Not being direct from the wound, it didn't give them the energy they needed to live, but one vector later said under interrogation that it had a certain amusement value. When a young mother, Ani Sikorsky, saw the blood-splattered trio and sent her sport utility vehicle's brakes squealing, she froze in confusion for four seconds. In that time, two of the vectors tipped her SUV over with brute strength and tore the passenger door off. They then beat her to death within the confines of the vehicle because she screamed too loudly.

The last member recorded it on digital video, again for the amusement value.

Copies of this video are on file at Forced Protection's headquarters, where they have been used to effect several changes in procedure. The first meeting on the subject ended in a unanimous decision to show the video to all newly recruited F-prots. It was my suggestion.

"Who is it?" asks Davis through the door.

"Mr. Davis, my name is Doctor Albert Burks. We got a telephone call that someone was in distress here."

The door opens. There is nothing protecting me. "No."

"Really?" I see the vector's eyes flash to the gurney. "We received a call a half hour ago from this address, saying someone had chest pains. Trouble breathing."

Davis looks like he has a headache. "No, I don't know who could have called..."

I look behind Davis to the wrestler from the theater, now in undershirt and slacks. The man is on the couch, just reaching for a remote control. He looks unhurt. It's time to effect the second procedure change. "I'm sorry to take up your time, sir, but there are a few questions I have to ask everyone in the house as part of my job. Is there anyone here other than you two?"

Davis glances back at his friend, flushed. "No, just us."

I relax and let the locator function fizzle out. I have to be calm. Loose.

"Can you sign here?" asks Breunig. "We need a record that someone in the household said no exam was necessary." He holds out the tablet.

"I suppose..." Davis says. As he hands the tablet back, I step to where I can verify that Davis's friend is engrossed in the TV and shoot Davis in the face.

The unseeable pistol doesn't sound like a gunshot. The neighbors will hear something like a stone thrown against the floor. The bullet plows through the vector right into the apricot-sized brain structure that keeps him standing. He falls forward against the doorframe, and Breunig catches him and the tablet in one motion. I push in. Simon's friend turns to see, but the angle is bad. By the time he twists around like he means it, I'm on him.

I press my palm to his head. Behind the push is a yin qi-function, a straight line instead of a circle. My body comes alive with electrostim points. The man blinks, as if that will clear his vision, but the signals in his brain are cracking like popcorn. He can't think through this.

"Simon? Are you—whoa. Is Simon okay?"

"Problem, sir?"

"I can't... getting up is—" He struggles, but it's as if someone's pushing his brain down.

"It's best if you remain seated," I say. The man keeps twitching at the overstimulation but no more. He is foggy but awake, excessively so.

"Did you touch?"

"What?"

"Simon Walter Davis. Did you touch him? Did he touch you?"

"Is something wrong with me? I can't—"

"Sir, Mister Davis has been sick for some time. It's best if he is looked after in a hospital." The gurney clatters as the F-prots bring it up to the stoop. Everyone outside will see professionals doing their job. Reassurance is key.

"Is this about the virus?"

Great. I watched Davis to stop an assault, not to obtain a sidewalk confessional. But a well-placed question is more trouble to the Forced Protection Program than a whole neighborhood of vectors. The gun shifts in my hand; in all likelihood, the man is infected already—

I make myself let go, coiling my arms over one another. This man is Forced Protection's mission statement. Unless Davis has bitten him, until the minute he shows symptoms, he lives. He didn't even see Davis fall. He is an us, until he becomes a them.

My voice comes out pleasant. "Mister Davis may have said many things under stress, not all of them accurate. I'll need your contact information." The man stares. The flush in his cheeks might be from qi or fear... or fever. "Sir, have you been in contact with his bodily fluids?"

"No. He just... he hugged me. He said he was afraid for his life."

I give him my wearied stare, like an overworked orderly searching for a better bedside manner. I sit on the corner of the couch and use that sympathetic, low voice reserved for extremely bad news.

"Mister Davis has an infection that settled in his brain tissue. I advise you to take what he *said* with a grain of salt. Now, I'll need some ID and to know what he told you about the virus." The man reaches for his wallet without thinking about how odd this all is.

Shortly, the gurney is in the van. All that remains is for the F-prots to collect everything the vector might have touched. Simon Walter Davis's life goes into plastic biohazard bags; his pillowcases, his dirty dishes, his bedsheets. As for Davis's guest—Neil Berman, according to his license—I keep his brain spinning in neutral. All he can comprehend is that there is a voice of authority in the room, and it is a good idea to cooperate and wait.

After copying down Berman's address and phone numbers, I make as if to hand the license back. As Berman reaches for it, I touch his head.

For the rest of his life, Berman will never know exactly what happened next.

I, on the other hand, have extensive experience classifying the properties of qi, the most essential being that the effects generated diminish with distance. When I touch Berman's head, that distance is zero, and hitting Berman's brain so hard that his memories of this night can't form becomes very, very easy. After as many functions as I've thrown tonight, easy is good.

"You done with the surgery?" asks Breunig.

"Yes." I shake out my hand. It is more than fevered-hot. Berman lies on the couch, temporarily unconscious from the bioshock. I have his home address, in case I need to pay him a visit in three days and see if he exhibits symptoms. Breunig hands me a kit, and I take a blood sample. Berman will wake up a few hours later, and he might remember there was an ambulance, but he will likely think he called it himself.

Another F-prot pours lye onto the floor where Davis bled a few drops before being whisked onto the gurney. It won't kill the virus, but it masks evidence. I do one last sweep of the house before joining the others at the door. I leave on the electronics—when Berman wakes, it will seem as if he fell asleep in front of the TV.

The drive back is quiet. Davis's body, even though it took a bullet to the head, is held to the gurney by Kevlar straps. This much restraints can do.

We watch for signs of consciousness. The body jerks when we hit a pothole, and I flinch. The pistol is gone, and I have a long, thin knife we keep in the van. If the bullet has not done its job, I will direct the blade into Davis's eye.

This procedure has not emerged from a particular incident but by van consensus.

"Dispatch, hot van one-oh-three, coming in with a spayed dog and papers." The radio squawks back, and we make for the drop-off point. In a few hours, Simon Walter Davis will advance the cause of scientific research.

After a few kilometers, I turn off the stimweb, and the ongoing functions surrounding my hand and head cease. The others in the van see me as I am, knife-hand gloved, hair long and silver, still bound up to prevent evidence from falling to the floor. My eyes, green now instead of gray, are fringed by metallic lashes, changed in the same accident that colored my hair. I stretch my legs and lay my bare hand across them. Gradually, the hand cools to its normal temperature.

Without the adrenaline, exhaustion settles in. Breunig passes me a bottle of water, knowing I have run too hot. I glance every now and then at the collection kit and Berman's sample. A few minutes' work online reveals Berman is a personal trainer. If he turns out positive, a bereavement specialist at BRHI will call his clients and let them know he will not be keeping any future appointments.

Breunig catches me staring off into space. "Hey," he says, "buck up. We did a genuine save just now."

I shrug. "We'll find out in three days."

"You had Shakespeare and surgery in the same night," Breunig says. "It doesn't get any better."

I watch the body and try to recall the few lines I heard. Then, I give up. They cannot be as important as the cold face I see in front of me. His name was Simon Walter Davis, and he was a victim of VIHPS. I have to remember that.

3 - INFINITY

August 5th

I'm pretty sure I break my tenth commandment in Buckeye, Arizona.

I got eight of them when I was a young little thing and thought getting all of them would be hardcore. I mellowed a bit, then got adultery by accident. That just left number six, the one that graduates you from hot mess kinder-rebel to what-the-hell-did-you-just-do?

It's not supposed to happen like this, but then, very little in my life happens like it's supposed to. I'm not supposed to be stuck on the freeway when the Santa Ana winds whip up a wildfire. The world smells like smoke and ozone as the too-bright sun sits directly ahead, making me angry. I'm not supposed to have a stabbing, cramping pain in my gut, and when I stop to grab graham crackers and ginger ale with my meager funds, it's supposed to help.

I don't puke, for which I'm grateful. I sit in the car at the gas station, trying to keep body and soul together. When the asshole behind me honks, I nearly get out of the car and drag him into the street right there.

What I can see of him through the back windshield, I like. A teenager driving his grandfather's gas-guzzler. Young enough not to know how to fight back, young enough not to be on medication that would spoil the taste.

I shake my head. It doesn't clear up shit. Another honk. I pull out and consider options.

I take back every irreverent comment I have ever said about the stupidity of vectors. I've called them vipes, biteys, rabies babies—watching them make every mistake. How any of them managed to plan an attack when their body was shooting raw want through every nerve, I'll never know. That is, I'll only know when I do it.

The first hurdle is the no-brainer. Find a secluded place. Interstate 10 has its share of sprawl, but once you get far enough out in the desert, you get rest stops where people are few and far between. I pull off the freeway into two of them but chicken out each time. I need somewhere alone, somewhere I won't be digipixed. That rules out gas station pumps, ATMs, and anywhere with a drone corridor or stoplight camera. So, I get on the road again and find myself driving all the way to nowhere. Before I know it, I'm on the endless string of asphalt between L.A. and Phoenix. I scan the side of the road looking for broken-down cars.

The hunger builds. It grabs me. It squeezes me. I consider faking a breakdown myself, but what do I do if a cop pulls up to help? Instead, I tough it out with teeth-grinding denial and then stop dead in Buckeye, when I can't stand it anymore.

Behind the trucks of a Fuel N' Fix, I meet my mark.

How do you choose your first? Some vipes still have it confused with intimacy and see who responds to flirting. Some look for repulsive ones, to make the deed an act of hate.

Me, I can't think straight, so I pick a big man with a child's face, a long-rider doing a machine's job. Automated trucks are what make Cali go, but guys like him can still make an end-of-the-week stipend for riding along and checking the convoy every five hundred klicks. I make interested noises and find out he won't be missed for three days.

The proposition is easy. People come to Fuel N' Fix for the gas and the almost-spa. Some bright entrepreneur, whose name is a household word in other people's houses, stuck together a gas station, motel, and massage machines to work out long-ride backaches. My act is to play too-poor-for-the-rub.

He offers. I don't even remember his name.

I recommend we make a picnic of it, and we walk over the hillside and into the endless scrub. Deserts are living places, filled with dirt, dry grasses, and bugs. With some distractions and a blanket from his truck cab, we begin to massage, then make out.

He rubs my shoulders inexpertly. Instead of relaxing, I go cold. I get a whiff of his sweat, and my stomach stops stabbing me like it knows what's happening next. I turn and put my mouth on him, kissing his warm flesh on the cheek, the neck, even the places still covered with clothing. My buried fears come to the surface, of course, because this is one of those situations your sensei tells you never to get into. But I'm dead certain this won't end with my clothes off. I can't tell you why because there is no *I*. My body feeds all by itself.

My lips move down his bicep, close to the stained armpit of his T-shirt. I wind my arms around his, fingertips tracing his skin in a light touch. My left elbow cushions his. My hands wrap his wrist, coming together in a prayer as I lick the inside of his arm.

My shoulders jerk. His arm snaps. The open fracture is in my mouth.

I suck just a little, thinking I can swallow the way you drink a soda, but the blood fills my mouth in a warm, red, cocaine fountain. The guttural sounds he makes are distant and secondary, half-hearted attempts at a scream that comes in loud and clear once his blood hits my brain.

The trucker struggles, trying to push me off with his free arm, but I dig in with my knees and pretend it's a roller coaster. *The victim ride will make sounds shocking to small children. Your restraints will come over your arms, and there will be no exits once we begin.* My feet hook his legs, and all he can do is rock and roll without the leverage to get me off. Without leverage, all he has is strength, and I'm an anaconda in cycle boots.

He lurches one last time. I have a free hand and send his head into the dirt. The sound is like an apple dropped from two stories up.

Oh, shit. I watch him for signs of life. Assault and battery are one thing; cops don't try too hard solving that. Straight-up manslaughter can follow you around forever.

I take another lick, trying to think. My gut feeling is to stay and relax, because guts don't understand criminal charges. They no longer feel like a tube of needles, more like a warm flower just opening up.

At least my victim's brain is in neutral, so he isn't making noise anymore.

I sit up, wiping the drops from my chin. My hands are sticky, and in my first sober thought, I remember paper towels. I should have packed them. Did I say I was sober? No. I shouldn't *have* to worry. Why bother? I'm magic and can't even feel my right hand.

No. Plan.

He probably won't bleed out, not from an arm wound, right? It's the carotid artery that turns vipes into killers. They chomp down like they see in the movies, and when they're done taking a liter or whatever, the prey keeps on gushing. Here, I can fold his arm, apply pressure, wrap him in the blanket, hope the shock doesn't kill him.

I wipe my face on his shirt—which will leave skin cells behind—so I tear it off and take it. I wrap him a little, then I take out his wallet. Robbery. It'll look like a robbery, sort of. I make it a few steps away from the body before looking back.

A traitor's look. That's what my father called it. He knew whenever I'd try to lie that the remorse would give me away. So, I got better at lying and then better at running. Not that tonight is my best showcase. He's bleeding. Unconscious. In shock.

I go back, grab his phone using only my fingernails, and click it on. "Emergency," I say. The screen brightens—phones are cued to do this now. No password needed. "Call 911, ambulance." I turn and walk away before it connects and shows the dispatcher a face full of red. GPS will do the rest, or maybe it won't. I don't have a father anymore, and that means I can run. Freedom isn't fear.

I slide into my car seat. Makeup wipes get the stain off my chin, and I let my smile crest with the high. Little me would have frozen in fear when a man's hands were on me. Adolescent me would have stayed and gotten caught. The thought that carries me onto an endless strip of highway is that I can *do* this.

Phoenix, say the signs I follow, *30 mi/48 km*. As good a place as any to start over.

4 - KERN

August 7th

I'm not sure who brought the gift of pliers to the ten-dollar meeting, but I make a note to use them later. I know the safehouse has its own set somewhere; the F-prots believe in preparedness. Usually, I use one of those little blowtorches powered by a cigarette lighter, but you have to open a window or else deal with the smell of the torch doing its business on plastic.

"Okay, let's get to it," I say to the five people filling up the oatmeal-colored living room. Most of them are in casual wear; it is one of the few creature comforts they enjoy during brain sessions. Ranath sports long hair; others, neat beards, and one, Jackson Yarborough, has enough tattoos to outdo the rest of them put together. All the F-prots are in good enough shape to pick me up and carry me if they have to. They have never done so, but the day is young.

"I'll start by saying congratulations are in order. With the removal of the vector Simon Davis, our map is looking much better." I click a button on my phone, and the wallscreen projector flashes an image with a few animations to keep it lively. The green web of connections leading from Davis turns black and shuts down. "You just got our sanitization rate back up to a healthy eighty-eight percent, and you have officially finished off the Corus family."

"Is there cake?" asks Yarborough. He's the youngest and most irreverent.

I respond with a smile. "I resorted to praise in the quarterly reviews that determine bonuses. I didn't know how many candles should be on the cake."

"Wait, no joke. Don't you have a body count?" It's Mukhtar al-Ibrahim, our driver. He gets a chorus of boos. "It's just candles," he adds defensively. "It's not like evidence someone could see."

I'm patient by necessity. "I guess I have to say this again. This meeting is to give you need-to-know information on vectors you still need to isolate. The methods you use are determined by Dr. Cawdor and Mr. Breunig on an as-needed basis. I do not know what you do or how often you do it."

Al-Ibrahim holds up his hands. "I'm clear. Wrong words, that's all. Who's left? Did Davis get anyone?"

"Berman, the man with Davis, was just cleared. All test results negative."

Ranath is leaning against the counter separating the safehouse's living room from its kitchen. He straightens up. "Fantastic."

Softening up: achieved. "Davis had co-workers and relatives, though, and our lead says he had contact with a few. That means interviews." There are groans. I hit a few buttons, and icons with question marks pop up around Davis.

"Where are all the hermits and the basement dwellers?" says Olsen, the medtech. She scrapes the shaved part of her scalp with her fingers. "I swear we did twenty interviews to isolate that last girl, and Roland had to shut all of them up."

"We only know of three this time. I wish I could say they're not worth bothering, but I don't believe in deceiving co-workers."

Yarborough coughs into his hand. "BRSHRT!"

I only like humor when it's accurate. He gets a scowl. "Do you want to have a discussion? Because you can list your problems to me, and I will address them."

Yarborough's peeved but not confrontational. "Just saying, a second qi guy would help."

"Biomancer," says Olsen. She sounds tired of correcting with the technical term.

"Hitmage," says Yarborough. "Speak-and-spell. Whatever. Get one."

"I believe Roland considers memory altering a trade secret."

"I can speak for myself, thanks." Ranath regards me with a stare. This is normal. It's been Ranath's habit to stare people in the eyes as far back as our undergraduate years.

"Sorry, but a large portion of managing this team is based on me allocating what people know and what they don't know."

"Cushy," Yarborough says. "You got a list of all the shit he can and can't do?"

Eloquence fails me. "Not... written down..."

Ranath examines his fingernails. "This I want to hear."

A few smiles break out. The F-prots look at me expectantly. I can't freeze longer than half a second. If I fail to match up, I'll never control them again.

"It's basically 'hide, seek, heal, harm,'" I say, holding finger number one. "Hide. You can alter others' perceptions so they ignore you or forget you. But other biomancers can counter it." Finger two. "Seek. You can track a vector. If he's farther than fifty yards, it doesn't work without a DNA sample." A third finger. "Heal. You can speed up blood clotting, tissue repair, the works. Can't bring back the dead."

"And?"

I put up a fourth finger. "You've done research on hitting someone with pure yin qi, about which I know more than I legally should."

"Given how rarely he uses it on vipes, you're safe," says Olsen.

Yarborough frowns. "Way to sell him on our urgent needs. We're talking about lightening the load."

"He only listed four things. If we could get someone with those skills—"

Enough chatter. "Did I pass?" Ranath nods. "Okay, everybody visualize your candidate. If he or she's like most people, they'll talk a good game right up until you tell them what the job really entails. Then, when we have trusted them with that information, they will leave. If the new hire is a biomancer, it creates a degree of uncertainty when it comes to how well they resist the memory cramp. So, I hope you understand that without Roland's methods of making our new hire permanently silent, we will have to resort to yours."

The room quiets down. I might not have them all on my side, but for now, the questions stop. It's time to present them with a problem to solve.

"Now, it has come to my attention that an important date has slipped." I tap the screen and close in on the image of a fortyish woman, an all-American mix of Belarusian and Han Chinese. Her hair hangs loose, all the way down to her cocktail dress. She's smiling and giving a thumbs-up to the camera with her stimwebbed hand.

Al-Ibrahim shakes his head. "I still can't get over that choice of mug shot."

"Company ID photo," says Ranath.

I continue. "I know that we've been head-down in our work, but I felt this deserved acknowledgement. We are now in our fourth year since Dr. Ulan first got infected. The bad news is we've got no reliable leads going to her. The last vector that we know had direct contact was tied off in June. Roland took care of the information-gathering on that one, but the vector's family didn't know anything. The good news is that with the Corus family removed, we can now concentrate on Jessica more than before. If anyone has a brainstorm about how to locate her, you have my full attention."

"Didn't she write extensively on qi theory?" Olsen asks. "Are we not hammering her publisher to see where her royalty checks go?"

"We know her publisher quite well now. They're clueless. Other ideas?"

There is silence for a second. "All my ideas involve law enforcement," says Yarborough. "Not letting them in on it," he adds, "but like a bait and switch. Say she's wanted for theft of our property, ask for FBI help for an interstate search."

"If a vipe gets arrested," I explain, "the prison is going to see some very odd behavior. If two vipes get arrested, a cop or a prison doctor is going to ask questions, and those questions will uncover the symptoms of VIHPS. And given how good forensic folks are at genetic fingerprints and comparative techniques, that won't lead anywhere but this room. Are we clear?"

Yarborough is unfazed. "I didn't say they were great ideas."

Breunig, who has been sitting quietly as his talkative team monopolizes the floor, finally speaks up. "It seems to me that whatever routine she's got for feeding and hiding, she's perfected it. If we're going to find her, she'll need to make a mistake."

Ranath doesn't look pleased. "Jessica's self-discipline was... notable."

"Are we talking about the same witch doctor?" says Yarborough. "The first thing she did when she discovered there was magic in the world was to start bombarding viruses with the shit."

Kids. "You're off by about fourteen years, and the decision to modify viruses was actually quite conservative. They were the simplest forms of life, and we followed strict protocols—"

"C'mon, she could have magicked up, like, the common cold, not freaking bat flu."

"She did plenty of harmless ones, and if we could refrain from calling qi sciences 'magic'..."

Yarborough rolls his eyes. "One of these days, Roland is gonna shoot lightning out of his ass, and then you're totally going to stop refraining."

"I think the point is," says Ranath, "our current strategy to catch Patient Zero is flawed."

Olsen looks relieved. "Like the man says, any ideas?"

"All of mine are for alternative elimination of the virus," Ranath says. "Vaccines, cures, timelines of educating the public."

"Who are you, and where did you put Roland?" spouts Yarborough. "You've dropped the hammer more times than John Henry."

"We're trying to race viruses and rumors. We only win if we keep the game short. Here, I can draw a diagram so you can see the math..." Ranath starts toward the touch-and-talk, but I pull it away instinctively.

Something flashes across Ranath's face. There is no pity in his stare, and for a moment, I see what Davis must have seen. It is why Jessica, gentle and pragmatic Jessica, feared him and why I came to Ranath those years ago to cover our tracks.

I fake a smile. Media training is my lifeline on this job. "Hold on a minute," I say. "There's something all of you should know about this proposed path. It ends in education and prevention. That means culpability."

"Kern's right," says al-Ibrahim. "It's giving up. We're here to win the war."

At least I have one supporter. "Not only that, are any of you aware what our list of enemies looks like?"

None of the F-prots speak for a second.

"Isn't that what's on the screen there?" says Yarborough.

"Wrong answer," I say. I grab the opportunity to take control again. "BRHI dominates biomancy. That means everyone from all sides of the political spectrum hates us. The greens? They see the Initiative as a step worse than GMO. The fundamentalists? They think we're pagan sorcerers out of the book of Exodus. There's competing labs that want legislation to break us up. Last... way down, *dead* last with only a few individuals and not much money... are vipes. But let me tell you, if they knew what we know, revenge would be a fire in their brains that burns bright and hot. If they talk to all our other enemies, we have real problems. You aren't here because all the cool corporations have armies. You're here because we *need* an army."

Several of them nod their heads. Al-Ibrahim and Yarborough don't concern me. Ranath is the important one. Breunig leads the team, but he's the F-prots' heart. Ranath is the F-prots' soul, a fact that is not very pleasant to think about for more than a few minutes. Ranath doesn't ask for promotions or praise. He is content to do his duty, night after night. How he blows off steam, I'm not sure. All I know is, normal people get prematurely gray hair, so a man who's gone all the way to metallic silver has probably bottled up enough stress to sterilize Bikini Atoll.

It's been four years since I asked him to help contain the vipes. I'm the only one he talks to regularly. We do dinners and project management sessions, and he seems... stable. But whenever I ask about where he was during his time away from the Health Initiative, he changes the subject.

He has two rules: call him Roland Cawdor, and don't argue when Mr. Cawdor brings in a vector, alive or otherwise.

Right now, he looks thoughtful. "Are you saying to stay the course?"

I unload. "What I'm saying is there's a very big difference between a brainstorm and a grievance. I appreciate that you brought this up, but it concerns me that we're starting to lose heart in our current trajectory. It manifests in different ways for each of us. Sometimes, we may be tempted to confide in a family member..." I nod at Breunig, "...sometimes someone forgets to swap a barrel out..." I point at Yarborough, "...and sometimes, we just have second thoughts. The first two are problems. The last one is only a problem if we *make it* a problem."

Ranath regards me with that same stare. "Do you have advice?"

It comes out naturally. "When's the last time you took a vacation?"

Ranath considers. He hasn't come up with an answer when Breunig chuckles at him. "Roland, you know there's some jobs you're supposed to like and some jobs you're not. We can handle a few interviews without you."

Thank God. I can play the senior F-prots off against each other. "I think he's got you there. Enjoy yourself for a couple of days. Keep your phone ready, but the main thing is to be rested. We can talk fresh approaches then."

I close the windows on my touch-and talk and kill the projector. I pull the external drive out and put the pliers next to it. I focus on Ranath. "Do you want to do the honors for the meeting?"

Ranath hesitates, and I can't say what's going on behind his eyes. Is this an affront? He was the one who suggested making the team actively participate.

Then, Ranath walks over, picks up the pliers and the drive, and pitilessly crushes the casing. He exposes the memory chip inside, wedges it between the pliers' teeth. Now, it too is in pieces. I think the rest of the team breathes with relief as much as I do. We can't lose Ranath.

"Ten dollars gone," announces Yarborough. "Come back next week, same bat flu time, same bat flu channel."

"It's really bat rabies," says Olsen.

"If you got no poetry in your soul."

The F-prots begin to file out. A few clean up the bottles and cans that litter the area. But the hitmage doesn't move.

"When we do this again," Ranath says, "I want to talk about sustainability."

"I'll be ready," I say. "We've got this under control." And because I believe it, it's true.

5 - RANATH

August 8th

Everyone relaxes in their own way. Mine involves venomous reptiles. North-central Virginia is not home to any particularly spectacular varieties, unless you count the ones in zoos, herpetoculturalist trade shows, and my basement.

I've hung a sign on the door to Ena's room. It's not much, just the word RESPECT. I hung it there as a reminder never to be forgotten. I open the door slowly, as always, with a grabbing stick around ankle level, just in case today is the day Ena has gotten out of her tank. She hasn't, in all the time I've known her. But I cannot take that for granted.

The room has no TV, no radio, no table lamps, no phone hookup. To the casual visitor, it would give an impression of old-fashioned tranquility, a clinical escape from the pressures of modern life. But... and you may think this weird... I've never *had* a casual visitor in this room. The lack of electronic devices is to keep distractions, interruptions, and sudden movements at an absolute minimum. The walls and floor are plain white, so anything out of place can be easily seen. Its chairs, when not in use, are up on the table, so there is no awkward reaching under.

I approach the enclosure. It's Plexiglas, three meters long by almost two high. Its humidity gauge is low, as I feared. Ena is out of sight, no doubt in her hide box. I start my preparations. Work has eaten into the month; I've neglected her, and now it is time for maintenance.

I unlatch the door and slide it aside. Almost immediately, the snake sticks out a gray, coffin-shaped head. I've tried not to open the door only when she's being fed, but I haven't been good enough. She pours out of the box, meter after meter, flicking a black tongue.

Her eyes are milky white, and tufts of skin hang off her in unsightly patches. It's my fault. Bad humidity leads to a bad shed, and she won't eat until she can see again.

I bring the grabbing stick up, and instantly, Ena gapes, showing the dark mouth that gives the black mamba its name. So, she can see, a little, and she can still strike like a flickering flame. I slowly move my hand to adjust the stimweb.

With the stick, I hold her body at bay, gentle enough that she reacts as if to a crawling surface, not a threat. I make a circle with the fingers of my free hand and cue up a concealment function. When I let go, her movements get much less frenetic—she's ignoring me. I ease the stick's mouth up to grasp her neck and keep it far away.

Patience is key. I run her body through her water dish and gently slough off the stuck skin, rolling it down toward her tail. When everything is stripped off and thrown away, I use my hand to hold her squarely behind the head. Ena twitches, but for such a touchy breed, she's downright sedate. Then, with a long, calming breath, I put the stick down and go for her eyes.

The skin sticks a little, and her reaction is immediate—thrashing, squirming to bite. With a pop, it's over, and the eye caps come free. I move to the beaker and put her fangs through the plastic film topping it. I let her bite, pushing on the venom glands to yield an almost-clear fluid. As her long gray body reflexively coils around my arm, the wallphone rings in the living room.

I let it ring as I milk Ena. This is our time together. Also, I need to keep my antivenin supplier stocked. I have a freezer-full, which goes bad at a slow but inevitable rate. You really need a horse farm and medical equipment to produce the goods or a top-notch meat vat. The alternative is not living with her. She's a worrisome, stressful vice sometimes, but she's worth it.

Some twenty minutes later, when Ena is safely sulking in her hide box, and the venom is packaged up for mail delivery, I emerge from her room. The doorbell rings.

I go upstairs and check the camera to see who it is. It's Parvati, who is the greatest neighbor I can imagine, in small doses.

I open the door for her. She's holding Indian donuts.

"Roland, I was wondering if you could do me a favor. Take these, and don't give them back no matter how much I beg. If you can't eat all of them, maybe bring them to your office."

"Um..." I say, "that's lovely. Thank you." Parvati is very easy to talk to, which means for me, she's not easy to talk to at all. Over the course of the last year, she's noticed my stimweb and gotten Breunig's name out of me.

The conversation ranges over hill and dale, including how skinny I am, whether investing in robots is wise, and about her spare Stowaway concert ticket, which I politely decline. I tell her to e-mail me at one of my decoy accounts. When she finally leaves, I don't remember what I was about to do. I check the e-board on the fridge.

Raking the leaves? No, I need daylight. Checking the tire pressure on the car can wait. The last note reads STAIRS. I kneel at the base of the steps to open the panel I built into the side.

Behind this secret panel is a small fire safe. Inside are my many identity records, the mortgage, financial documents, a spare license to carry a concealed firearm and a small stack of papers.

The papers are my long-term project, a series of observations and experiments. I can never publish them; they are a course in how to use qi to disable human biological systems. The only other hardcopy of this work exists in the United States Patent Office, where I sent the early drafts in case of theft. I flip through them but decide against editing tonight. Neil Berman's reaction was nothing special.

Next to the safe is a Kriss submachine gun, my quiet pistol, and a pair of Damascus-steel butterfly swords. All need oiling. I fetch a can before I see the light blinking on the phone. I dial the last caller.

"Hello," I say. The screen lights up with Marcus Kern's image, video-receive-only. I aim never to show my face or send my name. "Is my vacation over?"

Kern doesn't return the greeting, jawline locked tight. "Turn on your TV."

6 - INFINITY

August 8th

I wake up in the back of the car, feeling sore and cold. It's raining in Phoenix—yet another thing that's not supposed to happen—and I'm stiff and raw all over like I wrestled a gorilla for fifteen rounds. No, it's worse. Even my face and jaw and fingers ache, and those can't be leftovers from the struggle yesterday.

I sit up, pushing off the towel and jacket I was using as blankets. When I try to rub out the pain, I pinch myself without meaning to. I've got strength like a crab's claw. It's the virus, re-forging me into a predator. I just wish it didn't have to make me feel like I've been steamrolled.

As if on cue, I feel my neck relax. The crick in it from sleeping in the car is gone, before I've even had time to complain about it. How fast will this pain in the rest of my body be over?

I attempt to remember all the briefings I've been in and don't come up with much. Vipes really live on the qi of their victims, Darcy once explained: straight-up life energy they can use to stay alive and heal like something out of comic books. But the energy falls off with the square of the distance from the prey. If you want qi from their body, you have to drink directly from the wound, or it's no good.

I sniff. Old sweat. Everything smells stronger today, another of the signs. I'm feeling pretty rancid, but staying in a hotel seems like an even worse option than the car. That's how vipes get caught—burning through all their cash until they use credit cards or ATMs. Once you get a paper trail, eventually cops are on you and F-prots after that.

I always wondered why we never heard of smart vipes staying off the grid. A good bite on a victim can sustain them for a week, creating calories to burn without the malnutrition you'd expect. So, why not sell their possessions, live a nomadic existence on the road?

I get it now. Nobody wants to live on bread or blood alone. They want their central air conditioning, their clean, pressed sheets. In my case, I want something salty and hot.

Fortunately, I bedded down in a grocery store lot. Once inside, I go for the survival foods aisle, less for the trendy cachet and more because self-heating meals are cheap. I make for checkout, where the lines are clogged like a pork farmer's artery. I end up behind a mother with a small child and a cart that looks in danger of turning into a burial tomb for Pharaoh.

The checkout stands have little flat-panel screens up over the magazine rack. They're presumably a riot-control measure in case the customers in an over-long line are too illiterate to pick up a tabloid. It's twenty-four-hour news. I've avoided political television ever since they started asking for donations in the crawl beneath the screen. I mean, I wade through California's endless series of propositions like everyone else, but now I just want to ignore the ratings-grab ranting and focus on which downloadable magazine promises the most laughable sex quiz this month.

"—a lot like a vampire—"

I look up and freeze. The camera cuts away from the anchor who gave the story's intro, and now the words VAMPIRE VIRUS scream across the bottom in bright white letters. What follows is a badly lit, homemade video of a man in a black muscle shirt, ready with a barbell.

"This is not the face you expect when you hear about a new disease," narrates some reporter or other, "but the video uploaded by poster 'MorganLorenz' features individuals claiming to be infected with a virus brimming with active qi." I watch as the man lifts the weight first to his chest, then over his head. "The weights are supposedly two hundred kilograms, the virus, a kind related to rabies."

"Mama, can we have Frootsweets?" interrupts the blonde four-year-old a few centimeters in front of me and totally not on the same planet. I'm too stunned to even try to shush her.

"No, you're going to have ice cream at Heather's party," says her mom pleasantly. "Can you put the groceries on the belt?"

"—would seem like a hoax except that Morgan Lorenz sent tissue samples to eleven media outlets, samples that have now been confirmed to have unusual DNA. They do appear to be infected by a virus that has active qi. Mr. Lorenz has not made a public appearance, citing safety reasons."

With a sting of music, the newscast cuts into the digifile of Lorenz himself. I stare at the image of a man in what I guess is his early thirties. He has styled sandy hair, not yet gray at the sideburns, and dark brown eyes. Lorenz's face looks strained, as if he hasn't slept, with the same pale, queasy look I've seen on many vipes, most recently in the bathroom mirror.

"The rumors you've been hearing are true," he says, in an earnest, plainly-spoken voice. "I and an unknown number of other people are infected with a virus that makes us consume human blood. I say there is an unknown number because someone doesn't want us to know."

"—Honey, don't squish the bread. Hand it here—"

I stand welded to the aisle, half my mind screaming that it's a damn good thing I got out of the F-prot program *now*. The other half stares at the man on the screen, wondering how long he has to live.

"This is not a natural disease," Lorenz continues. "Lower-order life, viruses included, does not naturally turn its host's qi active. Someone *made it*, and I am going to find out who and when and why. I am offering a reward for any information about the creators or origin of this virus, and I will provide a safe haven for any of its victims."

"Mama, can you read the TV?"

"It doesn't say anything you need to worry about," says her mother.

The girl turns to me. "Can you read it?"

The video has cut back to the anchor, who's introducing the panel of Robert Rightwing and Laura Lefty, and they argue about the validity of the vid or the virus or why the other's political party is somehow going to get a bump from this.

"It's not a good idea to depend on me," I say. "I'm a stranger." I get a smile from the mom but not the kid.

As they go back to the mound of groceries, I take out my phone. There are ways to track people using their phones, and the F-prots know them all. But it will take them time to get people on the ground here, and I will be long gone. My phone doesn't have spyware from work on it—if it did, I would have been called into Darcy's office a lot earlier than this due to practical jokes involving turkey porn. So, it's a calculated risk when I access the Net for videos by this Lorenz person. I put in my ear buds and cue up what I can.

By the time I'm out the door, I've gotten a head full. Lorenz has made five video posts with the most recent getting about three million hits. The reward is ten thousand dollars, which hasn't raised any eyebrows in the media, but it sticks a little smile on my face. He doesn't have any contact info beyond what is no doubt an overflowing e-mail account. All I can do is fire off a message and hope he, or whatever friends and filters he has, will mail me back.

I sit in the back seat of the car, watching the phone's tiny screen. Morgan Lorenz is crazy—he's painted a target on his chest for any lunatic with a tent peg, to say nothing of Forced Protection—but F-prots never had to deal with someone this brazen. Maybe the vipes need a leader, a fixer, a man who jumps into the spotlight in the hope that it will preserve him.

He also lives over four thousand kilometers away.

I make a short mental list of who I know on the East Coast. I'll need somewhere to stay because I'll be sick of the car by the time I get there. Around the time I dig out contact info for an ex of mine named Owen Fargo, I realize I've already decided to go.

I look at the self-heating food packet, still unopened. I toss it to the floor. I might as well get started resisting temptation now. I'm out of practice.

7 - RANATH

August 9th

I sit alone on a bench in Rock Creek Park, watching the sun dwindle and the fear set in. In the early twilight, I stop seeing lone joggers and hikers; instead, they travel in packs. Though I left room on the bench, no one stops to sit beside me. Whether it's attributable to Lorenz's videos, I can't say—my stare keeps civilians away, too, and I'm not in a smiling mood.

When Kern arrives, he looks small outside his office, short and lean in a tailored coat bought more for fashion than for comfort. The wind whips his light caramel hair back, making it obvious how far it has receded. His eyes look puffy.

"Let me guess," I begin. "Not much sleep."

Kern flops on the bench next to me. "I wanted updates, so I didn't shut my phone chime off. Every minute of the night, another ping. *Washington Post, Boston Arrow,* One World Network. Their guys are working around the clock—"

"What do they know?"

"At the moment, they just want Dr. Kern, the talking head, saying qi isn't black magic. As the facts come out... that may change." Kern's phone chimes. He checks it.

"Surely, not so fast..." I say.

Kern doesn't look relieved. "No, it's Shelia. Says we have to talk alimony again. My life, it's comedy. So, I bet you're wondering why we're in the park and not the office."

I can guess. There is zero chance that the company is going to sin no more. Instead, Kern will rely on the tried and true, which means meeting to give the verbal go-ahead. The park is better than offices or vehicles. Those can be bugged by some cop or FBI agent tipped off to the Forced Protection Program by a vector's relative. Here, we can spot a tail, and the trees make it a little more difficult for drones.

Kern never utters the words. He doesn't have to. His pitch is, "It needs to look like a fanatic. It should be easy to come up with people who could watch that video and decide they're doing God's will."

I watch the wind caress the trees and make time with a question. "You want me to sign it 'The Van Helsing Squad' or something?"

"Would that be a problem?"

"It's a little pulp-adventure, don't you think?"

"People pull the trigger for dumber reasons." Kern is trying to look confident, but it's hot, and he looks flushed. "Lorenz made himself a public figure. Public figures never know where the shot is coming from."

"That makes some aspects easier and some harder," I explain. "Motivation isn't everything. Consequences are what concern me. We've never done someone tracked by media."

"Everybody's tracked," Kern scoffs. "You got that writer girl one time. What did she have, like ten thousand friends on her little social thing? And when she died, it was a bit of news, but it went away."

"It's not the same. Her death was the story, and then it was gone. If she had a cause, a phenomenon such as vampirism, then the death is just one aspect of the larger story, and the larger story never goes away. We have to avoid that like it's cyanide."

Kern waits a moment as a bicycle goes by. "He's not martyr material, not yet. No one really gets his cause yet. Once the deed is done, the best anyone can do is find out the details of how, not why— and that's only if you're sloppy."

"If he's smart, this is what he'll be expecting. He'll have made provisions. More video, stashes of evidence."

Kern's mouth goes crooked. "I'm unconvinced that is the case."

"Tell me we have a file on him and that our plan is not to assume our opponent is stupid."

Kern warms to the subject. "Lorenz works with a private insurer. He's never been to our hospitals, so we didn't have blood work on him. We've been tracking police reports, but everything I've found indicates he's shown no sign of aberrant behavior—"

"Who is he? Is he connected?"

"We don't know about connections. It takes a little time to access tax records, political donations, that kind of thing."

"Who infected him? When?"

"That we narrowed down," Kern says, and he looks grateful to have something that stops the questions. "His vector was in the Kovar family, D.C. locals we isolated a few months back. We missed one, maybe six months or a year ago. I don't know."

I nod. It makes sense. Marie Kovar had been a busy vipe. A cute little nightclubbing waif who fed at will, no remorse. She'd topped four exposures a night.

Kern's pocket chimes again. He checks the screen. "Edison Field." He frowns. "He needs a report." He taps a few keystrokes in reply.

"It'd be nice if every now and then he checked your meeting status," I say.

"It's not a report on Lorenz. It's a report on you."

So much for my confidence. The Health Initiative's executive VP is not supposed to want anything from me. As Kern's superior, Field has only an inkling of my role. He keeps ignorant of the details to avoid liability. For him to take a personal interest is trouble.

The amateur panics, I tell myself. *The professional knows.*

"The two of you had a meeting. Give me the highlight reel," I say.

Kern shakes his head but not in refusal. "He wanted to know if anyone had left F-prot. Morgan Lorenz will be looking for a whistleblower. I explained how you put on the memory cramp to keep a quiet team, and his words... well, they were, 'This hoodoo shit, will it stand up to some tabloid offering them fifty grand to tell their story?'"

It is earthy, and that sounds like Field, but I don't laugh. Kern continues. "Anyway, I said the cramp's batting a thousand, so he called *your* loyalty into question. You know, are you and your family financially comfortable, do you have a drug habit—?"

"Yes, can I pass my own background check?" I'm not mad; I just sound like it. I've asked similar questions of all incoming F-prots. "What did you say about my family and friends?"

Kern shrugged. "I wasn't sure you had any. You don't like people, Roland. It's... sort of your personal skill."

"If that comes up again," I say, "please tell him this is the only job in the world in which you let me do what I'm good at. Then, remind him that in this profession, a manager flexing his power is a bad reason for any sort of... action."

Kern's phone chimes again. He looks, and from his face, I guess it's the worst news yet.

"He wants you to solve the problem before it gets worse," Kern says, obviously striving to stay calm and focused. "Hell, *I* want you to solve the problem—"

"It isn't that simple. A pack of reporters can bring us low. We're not congressmen or celebrities. They get to survive in humiliation, go to white-collar prison. Us... we can't get nailed even once."

Kern shifts gears. "Okay, let's roll with that. Can you make it look like an overdose or an accident?"

I take a long breath and choose my battles. "Not an overdose," I say.

Kern gets it. Vipes shrug off most drugs. It's too risky. "Right."

"Accidents, unlikely. They tend to heal. You'd need massive trauma, plane crash or something similar."

Kern looks contemplative. "How hard is fake suicide?"

"Well, unlike the real thing, you only get one crack at it." That gets a smile. I continue. "If we were to go that route, we'd need surveillance on Lorenz. You can't do a passable fake note without knowing the man, and you've got to execute at a time when you won't be interrupted. The first enemy to put in your sights is Murphy's Law."

"But you could do it?"

I don't want to commit. "With surveillance, possibly. But there's no guarantee on a time frame. You can have it tight, or you can have it now, not both."

"Stop me if this is the stupidest thing you've heard," says Kern, easing in. "All Lorenz has is his own tissue for comparison to any found at our site. How hard would it be to create a fake lab? One that he could find, and boom, case is closed. This is where it came from."

"Stop," I say. "We could make a lab. People who staffed the lab, hell no."

"I thought maybe you could—" Kern waves his hand. The memory cramp.

"Virginia has a district magister now for forensic qi investigations. If something goes wrong while we're sanitizing, it just gets worse."

Kern has a look on his face like a man walking up gallows steps. "You're telling me Field wants the impossible, aren't you?"

I want to be kind to him, so I am gentle as I say, "Lies are for targets." It is our rule. We need honesty to plan accurately. And, left unsaid is that if there is ever mistrust between the two of us, it will create leverage on the day that we finally get caught. That way lies prison. "If you have another solution—"

Kern's sweating. I can smell it. He breaks, words coming out too quickly. "Our only other option is full disclosure, once we have a treatment or cure in progress, so we might be able to bargain with the infected directly. Disclosure would mean the end of the Forced Protection Program." Kern looks into the distance as he speaks. "Field's already consolidating records. It wouldn't be hard for them to paint us both as rogue troublemakers with histories of instability. They could say the whole cover-up was our idea. It wouldn't take them a second to decide to throw us out there."

Kern glances at me hopefully but doesn't quite meet my eyes. I can't help but remember the first time BRHI threatened me with expulsion. Kern wasn't able to look at me then, either. At the time, I didn't resist; I had been ready to move on. Now, as I listen to the sounds of the park and the road, I find myself wondering.

"Strange," I say. "It sounds as if Field knows exactly what I do, but he's more scared of Lorenz than he is of me."

"That's about the size of it."

I examine my assumptions. "Just how dangerous can one vipe be?"

"Roland," Kern says, "put yourself in Field's shoes. There's two things he knows for sure. This is America, and Morgan Lorenz is a fucking lawyer."

8 - INFINITY

August 12th

Just outside D.C., at a cute little Japanese restaurant, Owen Fargo makes me feel sane again. Which is good because, by now, the admissions staff at any mental health facility would have clucked their tongues at me.

"And on *Ilion Morris,* their opening skit was about the Lorenz guy." Owen's new girlfriend Didi prattles while I inhale another ginger ale. "He goes, 'I'm infected with a magic virus that gives me immortality and superhuman strength. I will now find those responsible and make them pay. Furthermore, I will find anyone who ever offered me a job and wreak a terrible vengeance. Then, I will go after every teacher who gave me A's. And just in case you smile at me in the elevator, I got grenades.'"

I laugh, despite everything. Half an hour ago I was alone, eavesdropping on the couple two tables down. They were talking about the vid, of course, blathering about how someone should put Lorenz's whole household into quarantine until the virus is analyzed. Everyone has an opinion. Everyone gives a damn. But for a few minutes, I don't have to.

Owen leaps in. "No, the Tyler show had the best. They had this guy, he goes, 'I'm petrified, hearing about these vampires living in the sewers 'cause they hate the sun. But I know how we get them. We get a priest to bless our toilets so they're full of holy water. Then, we'll flush 'em out.'"

I wince. "That's terrible."

Owen's made me feel normal before. He was an uninspired lover but a good friend, so I'd opened up to him about my less-than-ideal adolescence. He took it in stride and never, not even in the worst arguments, thought of me as anything less than an honest, if hurting, human being. Whether or not I deserved it is a debate for those sleepless nights with nothing to read in reach.

Last night had been one of those. I've driven hard for the past few days, autopilot off and straight into the rising sun when I had to. By the end, I felt like a flagellant whose back had outlasted the whip. I dug out Owen's number from the depths of my phone and curled up in the reclined seat with my jacket over my head. Just talking to him was blessed banality. I wasn't a fugitive or a runaway. I was just overnighting in my car because I was calling on an ex who was going to make it all better.

That hope disappeared as soon as I saw him enter the restaurant. It's not that Owen doesn't help people; he's a programmer and is used to picking up the check for his unemployed friends. What threw my hopes out was one-point-six meters of significant other, walking unannounced into the Yakiniku Grill.

No forewarning means the girl is someone he habitually thinks of as part of the package; no Owen without a Didi. That means I'll be lucky to get leftovers, let alone a couch for the night, given the stories he's probably told about me.

"So, how long will you be out here?" Didi asks casually.

I finger the necklace in my pocket. The gold can get me fifteen hundred, the silver another five. In my wallet are my three remaining twenties, a flimsy shield against the temptation of Owen's condo.

"I'm moving the rest of my stuff in a month," I lie. "Where, I don't know yet."

"Was it bad? I mean, it always is, but are you at least amiable?"

I cover as best I can to score a little sympathy. Lying isn't good for the soul, but the truth isn't good for the body. "We're not speaking to one another."

"Oh, how awful," Didi says. It's the strangest thing to *smell* her worry-sweat, but there it is, like lemon in a glass of water. Her fear will taste good, and that's the last thing I should be thinking right now.

"Do you need somewhere to crash?" Owen is watching me, not Didi, and I smile back. Didi is right to fear me. It could be really nice—sitting up nights, chatting with an old friend until I get back on my feet.

But in my trunk are bloodstained clothes that I will have to slip into the wash, and if I stay, I will be introduced to more warm, good-smelling friends of theirs. There is no safe way that will end.

"I can't do that to you," I say. "I can get a motel."

"Are you sure?"

I make certain to address Didi. "I can find a place. It's not like I'm a wanted criminal or anything. What I need, really, is a smaller favor."

I have to get to Lorenz. I don't know much about the upper echelons of BRHI, but I know the Baltimore-D.C. sprawl was where the virus began, and they aren't shy of personnel here. There is no worse place for Lorenz to have broken his silence. There will be meetings all across the city, task forces set up to silence him before he releases another vid.

Have I been thinking a lot about Lorenz? Honestly, I'm one step away from writing our names in a diary with little hearts over the "i's." Now that he's opened the possibility of VIHPS going public, I'm dreaming of this spot five years from now with Owen and Didi. Maybe they'll be married, maybe with kids, and I'll just casually follow up the teriyaki with a pill. And they'll be like, *oh, I didn't even know. How is that?* And I'll shoot back with *eh, a little dry mouth, but it beats the alternative,* and none of this will ever happen if BRHI keeps their secrets.

"It's this Lorenz guy," I say. "Does anyone actually know anything about him?"

Owen smiles and wags his phone at me. "I did my homework, Ms. DeStard."

My eyebrows go up. I wasn't sure he was listening when I babbled over the phone at him. But here he is, thoughtful and responsible.

"No one knows where he is, do they?" I ask. His grin doesn't fade. "You're not serious."

"As the clap," he smirks.

"You made him stay up all night talking to those criminals on the Deep Web message boards," Didi says.

"I'll have to go to the next meetup wearing a pickle hat and a T-shirt that says, 'Pedophilia Is Accepted in Some Cultures,' but I have your damn address," says Owen.

I don't laugh, for multiple reasons, but I say automatically, "You're the best." Then, after a second, "Dish."

"Okay, we found out he does like privacy, so it wasn't easy. He did a lot of basic tricks like uploading from a cybercafé and using an anonymizer."

"How'd you catch him? I know people who are practically cops, and they don't know where he is."

"Cops hire clickers who are clean, not the ones who are effective."

"Seriously?"

"Well, do you consider Lorenz a smart man?"

Good question. I'm still a little apprehensive about stepping into the crosshairs with a vipe, but somehow, he's gone in my mind from a possible friend to the leader of the new world order. This guy has to have spacious housing, a car with heated seats, and human blood on tap in the guest kitchen. "He doesn't seem like an idiot," I say.

"Lovely, I won't tell you so you can maintain that illusion. Let's just say his real name is indeed Morgan Lorenz, his Social Security number isn't as hard to find as he wants, and he's got his mail forwarded to a house that isn't his."

"So... wait, he's staying with a friend?"

Owen turns his phone over to me. It has an e-mail with hasty, lowercase notes—as well as an SSN, phone number, address.

"Like I said, he likes privacy, but he's not hardcore. He can afford to pay rent, though. Besides the lawyer thing, his parents died, and he's an only child, so... ka-ching."

"Apparently, he's Batman," Didi pipes up.

"Yeah, he's not married, lives alone... or used to."

"This is great stuff," I say. "I should totally pay him a visit."

Didi looks at me strangely. "You don't think the guy is full of shit? I mean, it's like every week someone says active qi can make you lose weight or shoot fire from your brain. Vampires, it's just so *obvious*."

I brighten up. "Shit or not, it will sell glossies." At their blank looks, I ease into the lie. "I'm doing a 'Most Eligible Bachelor' spread for a magazine called *Love and Leather*. Just the type, you know? I'm thinking I talk to him, bring a camera, get some shots of him and Castle Dracula."

Owen leans forward and taps his phone in my hands. "Castle Dracula's on the next page, hon. I got his ass on Street View. Now, you want to tell me how many backrubs you owe me?"

"This is worth more than I can say," I tell him, dead serious. But that brings up the uncomfortable specter of payment.

"I'm going to the bathroom," Didi announces, all sugar before she turns to ice. "Try not to fuck her until we get the dessert menu."

As she walks off, I watch Owen's face. He's without a comeback, and I'd guess he was hurt. "How deep is the shit I've just gotten you in?" I ask.

"No deeper than it's been for the last two days," he says, but that is far from reassuring. It's going to be another night in the car.

"What's really going on with this guy? You have some kind of business with him?"

He's on to me. Owen isn't the type to go to the cops, but that doesn't mean I'm ready for my true situation to be part of his and Didi's pillow talk.

"I've got no job," I say. "I don't have the overhead to start up a jiujutsu school. If I can sell to a magazine, that's food for the week. If not, I'm ess oh ell. If Lorenz dies of this vampire thing, or someone whacks him or throws him in witness-pro, my best idea is gone. I want to talk to him before any of that goes down."

"Are you sure you want to get involved in this? I mean, it's dangerous."

"I promise nothing'll happen that can be traced back to you."

Owen looks confused, then laughs. "I meant dangerous to you. Jeez, Fini, you sound like you're about to beat the guy up." I don't laugh, and his smile fades.

"I should check on Didi," I say.

"Why?"

"Because women can read minds," I say, and I stand up. Just to cement the point, I take a dessert menu from the waitstaff and plunk it down in front of him. His face becomes even less mobile—disappointment freeze.

I walk to the bathroom, where Didi's booted feet are visible beneath one stall. I knock softly. "It's Infinity," I say. "We were getting worried. Are you okay in there?"

There's a sniff that I try not to feel bad about, then a flush. "I'll be out in a sec," comes Didi's muffled voice.

As I wait, I look in the mirror. Black waves of hair hang across my shoulders, roots a dark enough brown to blend. I've got smoldering purple for eyeshadow—what I remembered Owen liking—but that's a strike against me now. I don't want to look pretty—right now, the word I'm looking for is harmless.

I bare my teeth. Nothing and no one stuck in them.

"It's fine," I mouth silently to my reflection. "There's nothing between us." Convincing.

"I need to borrow some money. I'll pay it back once I get a job." Mostly.

"I can last three more days without drinking blood." Not.

The stall door swings open, and Didi is there, eyes unswollen, mouth still lipstick-pink. "So, whaddaya think?" She says it like an accusation.

"About..."

"The new Owen. You haven't seen him for four years. Hasn't he lost weight?"

"I didn't notice." I had.

"He still thinks about you, you know. At first, I thought he was bringing me here to show me off to you. Now, I think he's angling for a threesome."

I shoot for the sympathetic smile. "That's not going to happen."

"He says you once broke into a church and had sex in the bell tower because you considered the altar too cliché."

"Uh..." I say, "in his defense, that was my idea."

Wrong answer.

"I'm just saying you lost your boyfriend, now you show up on his doorstep... you drove across the continent." I realize she's getting something off her chest rather than listening. "And he jumped to help you out, and I mean *jumped*, like you were his boss or something."

"I don't know how clear I need to be," I say. "He's probably got fantasies, but he hasn't changed. He doesn't stand a chance." Just the act of drawing the line eases my mind a little. If I'm going to be homeless, let it be because I wouldn't give up being cool.

Didi considers. She washes her hands and talks into the mirror. "Can I ask why?"

"He's afraid of me," It's close enough to the truth. "I'm a hassle to keep. I've got more issues than Marvel Comics."

"Well, that's a reprieve. So, am I duty-bound to help you? He sleeps on the couch, and we share the master bed? Platonically."

Didi turns and is almost in my face now. She still smells good, and I let my mind wander into the temptation of drinking my fill, right here over the sink or later when Owen is asleep. It's then I realize that it's not just Aaron I need to worry about. It's anyone with a pulse. But I was an F-prot before I became a criminal, and the two aren't the same thing. Not really, anyway.

The words escape my mouth. "I can find a hotel."

"Are you sure? We could try cushions on the floor."

"There's nothing you have that I want," I lie, and the Infinity in the mirror looks good.

9 - INFINITY

August 13th

Despite my exhaustion, I can't rest that night. I toss and squirm on the superfoam motel bed, which rejects me like a bad kidney. If vipes are supposed to heal so fast, shouldn't some of that mojo keep me from feeling like crap when I get no sleep?

I give up sometime around two in the morning and turn on the wallscreen. Soon, I'm watching the Lorenz video for the too-many-ith time. The hookup is nice and fast—I guess the telecom companies reached a peace agreement with each other—and it better be good because the room took the last of my cash. A long stare out the window makes me think of pawn shops I hit earlier. The jewelry's gone now. Impulse buys, gifts, now all turned into a mattress.

The e-mail Owen sent me beckons, but I keep my eyes on the vid. Every time I watch, I notice different details. Morgan is left-handed. His eyes don't do the left-to-right dance like he's reading a cue card or teleprompter, so he probably rehearsed what he had to say. On close examination, he looks a lot more presentable than I saw in the checkout line. On high-def, I can tell he fed before he made the video. It's not the healthy pink complexion or the short, neat hair. It's the relaxation, the presence focused on what he's talking about instead of being a scatterbrain with no idea where his next meal is coming from. Says she who would know.

I talk to the remote and open channels on the screen. I need news. Usually, my surfing only stops on some celebrity being charming or a fighter getting trashed in a combat sport. Consequently, it takes me longer than other people might, but a half hour later, I feel satisfied that Morgan hasn't blown up the world since last I checked.

It's naïve to think the F-prots will let him get away with his stunt. It's a matter of time before their own tech-savvy operatives tip off the door-kickers, and then Lorenz won't have a chance.

There's nothing I can—

Wait.

I open the mail attachment. I can control this. What I have in my head isn't so much a plan as it is a scheme—there will be a lot of improvisation and even more risk. There always is.

I go to my jacket in the closet and get my keys, bringing them over to the keyboard on the bed. On the key ring is a fob, displaying random numbers that change every minute. They're half of a security code, my personal identification number being the other half. A few key punches later, and the screen changes to BRHI's Web page.

Here's the first risk—entering my passcode and hoping I haven't been locked out. I've been gone for—what is it, past midnight?—nine days now. But the code works, and with it comes a little hope.

I root around the D.C. directory and find "Additional Numbers." Forced Protection is way down at the bottom of the list, with no corresponding link explaining its purpose or photos that can identify the employees. The program director is someone named Dr. Marcus Kern.

"Hi," I say to myself. "My name is Infinity, and as a matter of fact, I do know what time it is. Please hear me out."

Screw that. I dial Darcy's desk number. It'll be three hours earlier there, and knowing him, I might catch him at work. No dice. I don't leave a message and try his home number.

"Yes?"

I nearly drop the phone. I keep it audio only, part of the scheme. "It's Infinity," I say. "I know I fell off the map for the past week, but I spent it doing something important."

"Infinity! Are you all right? We were worried."

"I'm surviving," I say, honestly enough. Now, I need a lie that he can't check out or at least won't want to. "I got a little scared when I broke that vipe's teeth and stayed at home the next day, but if I were infected, I'd know it by now, right?"

I've gotten him scattered and agreeable. "Yeah, your muscles would be changing. It'd hurt like hell."

Stay perky. "Well, nothing to report there. But I have news. Big news. You know how whatsisname, the cultie vipe—"

"Andrews."

"Right, how I was playing bait with his human friends? One friend tracked me down."

Darcy exhales audibly. I hang, waiting for his words, which are only, "Shit. How bad of a breach are we talking?"

"No breach, but it took me a few days of playing totally vanilla valley girl and staying away from work. He's got my number, but he thinks I work in a diner."

Darcy laughs. "You're good."

I almost take a moment to savor the irony, but things like this work best when I talk fast. "Anyway, I got a hold of his phone and sent his contact list to mine so I could figure it out, when suddenly this vipe comes on the TV—"

"Yes, we're aware—"

"—and it turns out the guy on TV, Lorenz? His phone number's on the list."

"It what?"

"I know where Morgan Lorenz lives," I say. "It's in Virginia, and right now, I'm at the baggage terminal, and I'll safely deliver this phone to our D.C. office."

"You're in an *airport?*"

"Is that bad? I realize I should have checked with you first, but this guy needs to be—" I stop myself. There are things you don't say over unsecured lines. "Well, I'm going to present it to the branch here to make sure no one else touches it. But I have a favor to ask."

"Tell me what you're thinking."

"I need you to call Dr. Marcus Kern, who runs the head office here, and tell him that I'm at least minimally competent, and I want to be in on whatever Lorenz project he creates."

"Well," Darcy says in his best truant officer tone, "I'll have to see some evidence of minimal competence before we can go forward with this."

"Ha. Love you, hon. So, you'll call him, sometime when it's a reasonable hour on the East Coast, right?"

"I just want to confirm," he says. "You can guarantee you will be able to deliver Morgan Lorenz's home address?"

"I can send it to you now, but I thought it'd look better if you made it sound like I'm your trusted courier, and I'm already en route. Like you anticipated his needs and had a plan and shit."

I can hear Darcy chuckle. "Send it to me just so we have a duplicate in case you get hit by a truck. I'll make the call in the morning."

I consider. It goes against the grain to give it over before getting what I want. He could cut me out of the loop, and he's being far too nice to an employee who bailed on him. But if I score face time with this Kern guy, I can probably finagle something even if Darcy turns snake on me, just by virtue of being in the loop on Lorenz's location.

I read Darcy the address from Owen's info, and immediately after doing so, I think of altering it by one number just in case everyone decides to move without me. But if they cut me out, and I disappear into the cracks, that's a double win. I'll have the L.A. F-prots off my tail without ever getting on the radar of the D.C. crew.

"Oh, and you'll need to get tested," Darcy says at last. I try not to freeze.

"Right," I say. "I'll bring that up with this Dr. Kern before I do anything else. Let me get it right. We want a standard blind for European Bat Lyssavirus-4, yes?" I jab with the yes or no to make him forget about my taking the responsibility.

"Yeah, a fluorescent microscopy. He'll know what it is."

"Cush. So nice to deal with professionals. Okay, see you some time in the far future."

"Yeah, this is pretty crazy. Keep checking in, and take care."

I hang up, and the sane part of me catches up with what I've just done. I've traded one pack of hunters for another. But to hell with cash. I've made currency.

I turn off everything electronic and sleep like a stone.

* * *

The downside of being a double agent, of course, is that you have to keep stalling and lying even when, by all rights, you should be dead to the world. Marcus Kern is on my phone at five-thirty-eight a.m., which is most definitely not "the morning." That's still night or pre-dawn or something out of bounds. And he's talking fast.

"I'll break it down. The meeting spot is the Everything Asparagus in Crystal City. That's Jefferson Davis Highway and 20th Street. You'll be meeting one of our people, a Dr. Roland Cawdor. He's tall, his hair is long and silvery gray, and he'll be in a navy coat. You got all that?"

"A doctor?" I ask. Has Darcy said something? "Am I getting an exam?"

"No, no, he's just our biomancer."

"Am I getting spelled up?"

"No, you're delivering the information we discussed to him. He'll make the decision to move forward. Can you make it to Crystal City by seven?"

Warning bells beat themselves against my eyelids. I'm awake now. "I was on the red-eye," I say. "There's no way I can do anything before noon."

"Noon it is, then. But I want to move today. We've got at least three people who know about this. By the end of the day, it'll be twenty, and if I know anything about secrets, security will be compromised a day after that. That'll put our people in danger, which I absolutely do not want. You understand this all, right? You were F-prot in L.A.?"

"Yes."

"And I wrote down you want to be in on... uh... Roland will discuss with you the particulars if your intel is actionable." Well, at least he observes phone discipline. "Sorry to disrupt your morning, Ms. Stard. Get some rest. You're going to need it. Talk to you soon." By the time I have the opportunity to correct him on my name, he's hung up.

No time to waste. I boil myself in a scalding shower, and I doll up—I'm out to make two first impressions today. The hair, however, goes in a braid, which takes valuable minutes but is the least likely style to come loose and get in my face if I get into a tussle. I save time by avoiding breakfast and going straight to my car, packet in hand.

I enter the address into the car and set the pilot, hoping the automated instructions are right. The map of the D.C. suburbs looks more like a web spun by a spider on crack than the evenly spaced grid of a normal city.

I wind up in someplace called Vienna. It looks all right—there are still a few trees to give the illusion of nature. The house's wall encircles the property with about a meter of stone topped by another meter of steel-picketed fence. The building itself is up a slope, allowing for a full view of the street and no places for an intruder to do their work unseen on a door or window. I can see at least three bedrooms on the second level, curtains all drawn, even in a large, round globular room that is studded with windows.

I park a short distance away and approach the gate to the driveway. I press the intercom button. Nothing happens for half a minute. I press again.

"Yes?" comes a male voice.

"I'm here to see Morgan Lorenz. I need to tell him his house is no longer secure."

Big pause.

"Who the hell is this?" A different voice, also male. It sounds like Lorenz.

"My name is Infinity. I'm a vipe."

"A what?"

Of course. He doesn't know the term. "I'm infected like you."

"Use the P.O. box."

"You can't stay here, and if you let me in, I'll explain why."

There's no answer, but after a few seconds, the gate swings open. I head up to the front door. I don't even have to knock.

An imposing man I would have pegged as an Irish beat cop in some TV drama stands in the way: crew-cut red hair, his chest all barrel, and his arms able to pass for thighs in a dark alley. With vipe strength, I might take him, but the look in his eyes says I'd pay for the attempt. If he's a vipe himself, even worse.

"You want to see him, you get searched," he barks.

I unzip my jacket and let his hands on me. I tense up, and I'm ready to smash him at any moment, but he doesn't try anything. The thorough pat-down fits with my idea that he's law enforcement or at least former. He stands aside and follows me into a spacious receiving room with sectional couches.

For a second, I think I have a clear path to Lorenz if I want to do something desperate, but no. There's another two men between him and me. The one on the left looks like he eats barbells with breakfast. The one on the right is regular size, but stripped down to a muscle shirt that shows off a revolver in a shoulder holster. From the size of it, he probably uses it for elk hunting. Virginia has elk, right?

The door slams and locks behind me.

"Sit down," says Lorenz. I take a seat. "Now, please explain how and why you are here."

There's no way to say I'm not intimidated by the bruisers surrounding him, but my eye falls on Lorenz before it casts down to the floor. He's in his socks. The two others near him are in bare feet. Only the one who answered the door has shoes on. Everyone else is either sticking to a house rule or has thrown on clothes since it's early in the morning.

I snort. It's like picturing them in their underwear, except for the guy with the gun, who, if clad only in his underwear, would probably look more threatening.

"I know everything you need about the people who are after you. It's not just a few guys. They've got a whole program, well-funded. Procedures in place, qi-actives, trained hunters."

"Are you one of them?"

Um. "Well, that depends on what you mean."

"Am I going to wake up murdered like a friend of mine did after she got infected?"

"Not if you listen to me." He looks doubtful. "The disease you have is called Virally Induced Hematophagic Predation Syndrome. We shorten it to VIHPS."

"Who's we?"

I hesitate. That kind of information is worth something. I make a hasty decision—I need a friend more than I need money. "The Benjamin Rush Health Initiative. They owned the lab that made it."

The gunman shares a look with Lorenz. "And Morgan gets another one right," he says. I remember Lorenz yelling about finding the culprits on the vid. Is F-prot really that easy to find?

Lorenz is still hard in the face. "How do I know you're telling the truth?"

I crinkle my mouth. "Honey, before I signed up, I couldn't spell the word hematophagic, let alone tell you what it does. I don't come up with bullshit that fancy." I look for a smile among them and get none.

"Maybe you can, maybe you can't," he says. "Talk motivation. Why help me?"

I bite back the obvious answer. It's never a good idea to advertise when you're vulnerable. Saying I'm on the outs with F-prot means he could threaten to tell them. "Because it's right," I blurt. "Because you deserve to know who got you into this mess and whoever bit you and whoever bit them and so on back to the first vipe there ever was. I've seen what this shit does to people. It gets their whole lives."

Lorenz is quiet for a moment, obviously lost in thought. Then, it disappears. "And in return, you want what?"

"You did mention a reward or something, right?" I say gently. "Am I a sucker for believing that?"

"That's for people who contact us by the P.O. box. We haven't yet discussed what we're going to do with you. You know where we live."

"Hey, I'm trying to help you—"

"You also are in possession of a large quantity of blood," he continues. "And we don't get it delivered to our door very often."

He stares at me, but I stare back. He wants his moment to scare me. It does but only because if he's not someone I can run to, I have to figure out another plan. As for threat, I don't care if he's a predator; he can join the club.

"No," I say quietly after a few seconds. "I don't think you will. You went to a lot of trouble to make that video," I say, growing in confidence as my words come out. "You believe in what it says. You want to make a change so you and everyone else like you don't have to go through the killing, the hiding, the... I don't know, the injustice." It feels lame that I can't think of the right words, but Lorenz seems to soften a little. "What I don't get is why you think you can win."

Lorenz stands so still that I wonder if he is paying attention at all. Then, I see the tightening of his hands, his stare, and I know that inside him, there is a will. It's what brought him through that broadcast when all he wanted, like anyone else with the disease, was to say, *I give up. Nothing is worth this.*

"I lost my friends," he begins. I say nothing, out of respect. "It doesn't sound like much, compared to some. But the alcoholics say we all have our 'moment of clarity,' and I had mine with this guy who let me stay over when I was first sick. I don't have much in the way of family, so..." he trails off, focusing on a time long gone. "Mathias, this old university friend, he's got kids... well, just one."

"Just one... *now?*" I ask.

"Yes." Lorenz lets out a heavy breath. "Pretty much says it all, doesn't it?"

I'd like to maintain a polite silence, but after a moment, I realize he hasn't quite answered my question. "I guess I'd want someone to pay, too."

Lorenz makes eye contact again. "Until that day, I never knew I could be so completely controlled. Not even by a person. By a virus, a shell of protein. It's like, here's everything that I am... and every few weeks, none of it matters."

"How do you feed?"

"I try not to."

For the first time, I look at the marble and carpet and teak. It's not the softness of an easy life. It's everything Lorenz tries to hold onto. Is VIHPS easier for me because I have so much less to lose?

"I don't know much about the biology behind this," he finishes, "but I know the law. And I know I can't be weak, or this will keep happening."

No one in the room speaks for a moment. I clear my throat.

"Then, your first step should be getting out of this house," I say, "because there's something I have to do over lunch."

10 · RANATH

August 13th

My first impression is that the woman at the counter is dressed oddly for a corporate minder; I've been stuck with two over the years, and neither has dressed like she sleeps in Joan Jett's closet. Her coloring is punk Snow White: ivory skin, black pleather, deep red lip gloss. She has the air of a teen who dresses older for a turn-on or an F-prot who takes a corporate check with one hand and gives the finger with the other.

"Doctor Cawdor?" she asks and slides off her stool. Standing up, she's tall enough to seem five years older. Her forehead comes up to my lips; I've been a lanky one-point-nine meters since the U.S. went metric.

"Kern told me I'd be meeting you," she says with a smile, and I do a quick check to inspect my white linen shirt and gray slacks. Everything is in order but a few stray silver hairs I pick off one sleeve—my telltale signature.

The woman starts toward a table, but I shake my head. I keep my voice tight. "I don't want to stay here. We need to discuss matters in detail."

She shrugs. "You got a car?"

We leave the restaurant. I'm pleased to notice she hurries, perhaps from the heat, perhaps from impatience. It's a good sign—maybe she's young and hungry rather than young and lazy.

We reach the underground parking structure, which blocks the heat. My zero-em Chevrolet will be adequate cover from eavesdroppers. We sit inside, and I turn down the seat temperature. She has black gloves on—probably electric coolers, given the weather.

Screw preambles. "Kern said you have Morgan Lorenz's address."

"Yes."

"Have you scouted it?"

"Not yet."

"Why don't you start by telling me everything you know about him, his environs, and any observations you made about his personal security."

I don't think it's my imagination when she tenses at those words, but she instantly turns it into a charming smile and blinks thick lashes. "I thought you might have some questions about me first. There's plenty I want to know about you."

"I vet the F-prot team concerned with Lorenz as a vector," I clarify. I might as well answer the questions I know she's going to ask. "You are under my supervision and do not need to ask Marcus Kern further questions. If asked, he has no knowledge of this particular activity. No F-prots on my team will be logging hours. We are going dark. Do you understand?"

The woman's cheeks quirk, and she gives a little nod. "Sure."

"Humor me, and explain what you think that means."

She ticks things off on her fingers. "Don't talk anywhere we can be recorded. Comm-apps, phone, e-mail, whatever, they're restricted to messages about when and where to meet, and those will be in code. Nobody and nothing sanctions us, everything goes in the burn bag, on the street we'll pretend not to know one another, but in our hearts, we'll always have Paris."

She meets my gaze, face all seriousness and innocence. I fish about for what to say. I'm not sure if this is disrespect or just wide, blue eyes and unblinking, deadpan humor.

I had assumed when Kern called that the new addition to the team was handed down from above, a kind of corporate insurance against any intention I might have to let BRHI swing for ignoring my warnings. But somehow, I doubt this woman would be any easier for them to control. She's a shit-disturber. The question is, which kind?

"What else did Kern tell you?" I ask.

"That he trusts you. That you're the top guy in the field, however one gets that title." She leans toward me. "Now, I'm dying to hear what he found out about me in the last few hours."

"He said you were on the team in L.A.," I begin, fishing. "And that you'd pulled off some fancy tailing to get Lorenz's address." Her expression is skeptical. "Is there something else I should know?"

She gives an amused smile, and my shoulders tighten. I'm not sure what I said that she found funny, but I don't mind having done it.

"Well..." she drawls, "I'm still a bit shaky on whether you know my name."

I freeze momentarily, and she laughs. I've walked right into it, and for a moment, I am no suave professional. I'm a ninth-grader alone with a crush, missing every opportunity and babbling irrelevancies. But when the joke's on you, it helps to smile.

"Hello," I say calmly. "I'm Roland."

"Call me Infinity."

Now, normalcy returns. It's back to the dance I've done a thousand times. Extroversion is the hallmark of my adulthood. "Mathematician parents?" I ask. "Or car enthusiasts?"

"Middle name, actually. My real name's Lilith."

"I revise my guess. Pagan parents."

"Kind of the opposite," she says briskly. "My dad was unhealthily religious, and by the time I came around, my mom hated my dad pretty badly. As a result, he wasn't present at my birth, and she named me what she wanted."

"I'm sorry. I didn't mean to bring up family drama."

"You got a story about your name?"

"I do," I say, "and one day, I can tell it to you. But today is all about Mr. Lorenz and paying him an unexpected visit."

I lose a moment, watching her. Her features are sharp, her skin smooth and Eastern European-pale. The pleasant face is made more interesting by the fact she's meeting my gaze. She doesn't seem polite, but that's better than fearful. Most people would have looked away out of habit. She breaks her stare when she has a purpose.

"Here's the address," she says, pulling a folded-up piece of hotel stationery and putting it in my hand. "I trust it's not going to be just us?"

"Our standard team is five."

"Not a lot of backup, don't you think?"

"Biomancy gives us certain advantages. And we are going to keep knowledge of the operation to a very low number of people."

She puts a cool, gloved hand on mine. "You still haven't said if I'm going."

I consider my response and choose to test her. "You're not."

"And why is that?"

Part of me doesn't want to upset her, but if she gets petulant when denied, I need to know. "Guess."

She regards me, concealing anger well. "Well, if you're anything like my old team, unit cohesion is a big deal. I'm the new girl, and you don't want me fooling around when you've got weapons free. I can assure you I won't, but without seeing what I do rather than what I say, I could be a liability.

"Then, there's the fact that the Kern guy said you're the top in this field, so ten to one you've got exacting standards, even for the people who pass 'cause you don't get real improvement without constant testing. From your attitude, I'm guessing you want to move on Morgan fast, and you don't have time to give me a proper trial run. How am I doing?"

She keeps her head in the face of contempt. I give an acknowledging nod.

"Now, tell me what I haven't hit yet. That little nod isn't telling me much about your leadership style. And let me tell you, I can critique those plenty."

"Infinity..." I need to get used to her name. "I'm sure you've had an adequate number of high-risk, successful missions. Kern would never risk your presence otherwise. But this would not be like any capture you've performed. This Lorenz has notoriety. To the masses, he's the world's first vampire."

"If we're successful, first and only vampire," she corrects.

Her humor falls flat, but I try not to let it show. "Have you ever had an enemy?"

Infinity hesitates. "There've been men in my life who were pretty evil."

"I mean, someone you have tried to *destroy*." Infinity gives an odd little shrug—perhaps there have been, and she doesn't want to get into it now. "Morgan Lorenz is now our enemy. If we cannot put a bullet in him, we must make his life such hell that he cannot under any circumstances pay attention to discovering the source of his virus. There will be no mercy toward him, his friends, or anything he owns. Understand?"

The mischief disappears from her eyes. She seems wary. "Is this like, a crusade for you?"

Usually, I aim for dispassionate, but clearly, I've flubbed it. She deserves a disciplined answer. She needs to understand me. I need to see if she will scare. And why is that?

"No. He's not a monster, just... the enemy. He's a very important objective." Her expression doesn't change. "I'm sorry. Am I talking like a robot?"

The mischief returns. "Beep beep be-deep."

"The point is, Lorenz is smart, he's charismatic, and he can recruit. He could be the leader of a movement and motivated to infect others."

Infinity's lips are parted, about to respond with something wry, when her black leather waist-bag suddenly buzzes. "Phone," she says, and I wait. She listens for a moment, thanks someone named Owen and hangs up.

"Who was that?" I ask.

"A friend. I've been looking for somewhere to stay while I'm in town."

"We can compensate you since it's a business trip," I say, and that gets her to put the electronics away.

"Thanks, but doesn't that break up my alibi?"

"We have ways," I say. "Now, we'll do a covert photography session this afternoon, and tonight we'll rehearse how to enter Lorenz's building."

"When's the real dance?"

"That depends on how the training goes. I'll meet you again at seven." I wait until she untangles herself from the car. "Oh, one bit of dress code when we meet in public. If you're worried about fingerprints, add a little rubber cement. None of us wear black gloves."

She stops to stare. "Why?"

"It makes you look like a hitman." I give the final smile and get one back.

* * *

The assault, which was what it is, does its usual thing. It makes me feel alive.

We train just as long as is necessary. On the ride to our facility out in Chantilly, I quiz Infinity on all the F-prot calls and hand signals. Her training has been nearly identical to ours. Our practice runs in The Block, a school-like structure and some beaten-on house mockups, are short and high-adrenaline. We spatter wax training rounds against steel targets. It all confirms what I suspected from the girl with the stare: Infinity is deadly, not dangerous. She has more experience being bait, but she's comfortable kicking in a door and identifying friends and foes even in an unlit house. The decision is unanimous—we will move tonight.

Infinity and I ride on one bench in the back of the main van, with Olsen and Yarborough opposite us. Each F-prot is clammed up in body armor, taking up enough space with our gear that it behooves Breunig to ride up front.

He confers with al-Ibrahim to send messages over wireless to guide a second vehicle. It's just a backup, a self-driving machine that is there solely in case the first one breaks down, or we have to split up.

There is no fancy fake ambulance, no disguises. Getting close to one target works for an isolated vipe like Davis, but taking on a house-full means we wear bullet-stoppers. Speed and shock will have to get it done.

If you care, we're packing M12 carbines, chopped-down versions of the M20A1 rifles American troops used in those central Asian cash-wars. We've got enough ammunition to make Lorenz's living room awfully drafty the next time the wind picks up. The rounds can have overpenetration problems, but too much is better than not enough. Breunig is convinced we'll face professional security, and even one vipe with a spider-silk vest like ours is serious danger.

I gave Infinity brief introductions to the team, but far more important are our call signs. We have colors and numbers assigned to the sub-groups, so no witness will be able to say to a cop that one of the guys with guns called another "Roland" or "Infinity" or anything identifiable. Breunig is Black One. I am Black Two, Yarborough is Three and Infinity is Four. Olsen is Red One, and the drivers, human and robotic, are White One and Two. Easy enough to yell a color under stress, and the numbers are not so important.

The van slows, giving us a clear view of the house. Shielded by tinted glass, Yarborough gets binoculars on the front entrance. Spotting nothing unusual, we then drive half a block down as Ibrahim checks in with the other van. Everything is go. The van circles around, comes to a stop in front of the gates, and the doors swing wide.

It's fast. Breunig is first out and puts his skeleton key fob against the sensor on the iron gate. I have my stimweb firing in no time. I inhale and send a concealment signal radiating out.

Almost immediately, I regret it. A wash of feedback fires my adrenaline, and my mouth goes dry. I lost it at the tail end; it's not easy concealing auras that aren't mine. What should be as easy as throwing a punch is like throwing a hundred. I can still function, but precision is gone.

The rest of the hardasses hustle up the driveway, covering each other with their fields of fire. Infinity and Yarborough go for the back door to cut off any escape; I follow Breunig to the front. We stack up to the sides of the door as I make minor adjustments to my stimweb, making an effort to focus. I try the left hand and go slowly and carefully.

Finding little success, I dig my right knuckle into the center of my breastbone, just a hair off from the acupressure point called the Heavenly Pillar. I feel for the rhythm of my heart and lungs and let them slowly decrease. Qi flows freely as I relax, and I try to conceal us again. Not forceful—this time, it's a persuasion.

It doesn't work. I'm not exhausted, but I played it too safe.

"No go," I say. "Ram it."

Breunig unlimbers the SWAT ram from his back. I cover him as he bashes the door off its hinges in two clean swings. Noisy as hell, but it gets us inside. A wood-and-metal bang sounds from the back door. "Rear door down," we hear, just as we announce our own.

We go in fast, flooding the dark interior with our bodies. We don't use underbarrel flashlights like the police—it just presents a target if someone is lying in wait. Instead, we're all in night vision goggles; consequently, as I run through the rooms and up the stairs, weapon at the ready, everything is grayish green. And that's what is wrong.

There are no lights on. Vipes are sensitive to lights, true, but they rarely break the habit of having some around the house. And judging from the room-temperature bulbs that the goggles pick up, these lights haven't been on for hours.

The house is big, but we clear the rooms quickly. No gunfire. No shouts. No enemies. "We've got nothing," Breunig reports to al-Ibrahim. "Starting to toss."

"Police band is quiet," comes al-Ibrahim's voice. "Do it now."

I search. Yarborough and Breunig prop up the front door so it isn't obvious to some passing jogger that the place is being sacked. Infinity meets up with me in what appears to be a study.

"Look for mail and paper," I order. "Confirm it's the right place."

"Way ahead of you," she says, presenting a pill bottle. "Lorenz, Morgan R. has bugged out without his..." she pauses to pronounce it, "al-praz-olam?"

"Anxiety meds."

"You got the computers?"

"We'll bag them," I say, "but first, I need to take a look."

I run my hands over a keyboard that I assume is Lorenz's. *There.* I pull a fine brown hair from around two keys. "Go to the kitchen," I tell Infinity. "See if he has any yogurt or yeast." She frowns but goes without question. I now sweep the floor clear of clutter, with total disregard for Lorenz's possessions.

Infinity returns, arms filled with a bundle of blue Dannon containers and a half-gallon of milk, incongruously domestic considering she still has night vision goggles strapped to her head.

"Two packets of yeast, three quarts of yogurt, and last week's milk, which pretty much qualifies." She dumps the lot on an office chair. "Now, I think you'll tell me why you made the woman go to the kitchen in the middle of a vipe hunt."

Story time. "I need to create a ring of living qi. Usually, I use my fingers," I say, holding them up in an OK sign. "But my hands are shaking, and I need the function to be rock-solid stable. Think of it as a crutch, except it's a culture of living bacteria." She still looks quizzical. "That's basically what yogurt is."

"I got that. Just saying you lose points on style."

I paint a circle of yogurt on the carpet with a basting brush. Then, Infinity shakes the packets of yeast on top, like tiny brown sprinkles. It's strange, it's smelly, and when the cops eventually come to investigate this break-in, they will be extremely confused. It's living qi. Passive, sure, but alive.

I grasp the hair I found, with its tiny parcel of DNA at the root. With my other hand, I pull two tack needles from a pocket. One goes at the top of my head, and I slip one under the vest, just above my navel. Infinity looks peeved.

"Can we do this in the van? We are totally not secure if a neighbor calls cops."

"It makes it harder," I say, "and I'm zero for two right now."

She sits outside the circle; I'm inside. I start with the easiest work, casting a function within my own body. A dot of energy grows at my core, balancing yang within yin as if they were on a gently rotating disc. I calculate its strength and dial up the web's electric charge to expand it, feeling it weaken as it leaves my body until it hits the ring of passive qi around me.

The unseen energy stabilizes, and there I stop it, poised.

"What exactly *are* you doing?"

"If this is Lorenz's hair, his DNA will act as a focus for me to recognize his qi pattern."

"Like if you see him in the future?"

"No, right now." I prepare the search function. It's getting harder to talk as the yogurt-yeast paste begins to glow white. I'm fighting a wave of nausea: it's what you get when you build power in your gut, and your bacteria pay the price. Infinity sits up a little straighter. Though she's no doubt seen qi functions on TV, she probably hasn't been close enough to see them crackling in the air or smell the frying dust as everything gets hot.

"When my qi wave intersects him, it will map to his pattern and resonate. I should be able to sense where he is."

"How? With vipe blood, there's no range at all."

I really don't need these questions now, but I encourage knowledge on my team. "I'm not altering him. I'm altering my perception. His DNA is in contact with my skin so I know what to look for. This ring makes the function stable enough to expand. My web and my tech maintain my altered state so I can keep it up... hours, maybe."

Infinity frowns. Then, the pulse inside me crests. I push gently. This function doesn't respond well to heavy hands. It's as subtle as the feeling of standing in the sun versus the shade. I finally trigger the cybernetics, adding the jolt that spreads the circle of detection beyond the doubled ring and through the walls of the house.

The wave washes out in a blink. If one thing is clear, it is that Lorenz isn't in the house or environs. Nowhere near. The circle expands at the rate of quantum information, but there's only so much I can pay attention to at a time; therefore, my consciousness follows more slowly.

The search is not quite as simple as I put it to Infinity—the hair makes it *possible* for me to locate Lorenz, but it doesn't guarantee it. If I push too hard, I could mark a false positive and chase a stranger for days. If I don't push hard enough, Lorenz's pattern will slip through the net, and the function will be wasted. My skills have failed the other F-prots before, and every time, I have loathed it. I depend on them, and they depend on me. In my work, I give no charity or pity, and I want none in return.

I note the defensive biophysical barriers around the White House and Capitol building a few kilometers away. The government's protective blanks cast long shadows throughout the D.C. aura-scape, but this function expands like a gas filling its container, seeping into the gaps.

Then, I feel it. Like a hair falling on my hand. I whisper Lorenz's name, and the search image locks. The prey, a dozen klicks off, will feel a momentary spark, as if they think someone just spoke to them when no one was in the room.

Back in Lorenz's house, Infinity meets my gaze, goggles off. "Looks like I'm out of a job," she says.

"Far from it." My own face must look wild—my goggles are pushed into my hair, which is crackling with static, and my blood flow has turned my face red. I let the function cool down until only the stimweb sustains the pulse in the nano-thin niobium wires beneath my skin. I breathe deeply and regularly, trying to cool off like those dinosaurs with sails on their backs.

"Why don't you just sit in your bedroom and find every vipe in the world?"

"First, I need the material link or anything beyond a few meters is blurry." I stand. "Then, there's the fact that vipe signatures are inherently tricky. When they feed, they link with the victim's qi.

"Until the physical symbol, the blood, is completely digested, the ratio of elements in the signature changes. Fire, wood, water, metal, earth... some swell, some shrink. It's like crossing a river to confuse a bloodhound." I step out of the circle, careful not to leave a shoe print in the yogurt. "We're lucky. Lorenz is in hiding, which means he hasn't fed in days. But he's getting hungry; I felt it. We'll lose him if we don't go tonight."

I stride for the door, still locked to Lorenz and wanting to finish it. Infinity hangs back.

"That's still, uh, pretty incredible." I stop to watch her. She has none of her saucy confidence from earlier. Instead, she looks small in the high-ceilinged room, lost, a little pale. "I heard stories that the home office had people like you."

There aren't any people like me. I arranged that pretty carefully. But when I meet her eyes, I don't feel cocky. I'm just grateful I haven't let her down. "Thank me when we've got him," I say. She gives me a thumbs-up, but her eyes are directed at the floor.

11 - INFINITY

August 13th

The van bumps along the pothole-ridden roads to somewhere called Stafford. Al-Ibrahim says that's what you get beachfront to the Chesapeake Bay: freezing winter rain and an underfunded county that can't even patch the roads by August. Maybe the low property values are how Morgan has traded up while fleeing—the new safe house is high up on what passes for a cliff here. The long but steep sloping lawn ends in gritty sand and surf.

The chatter doesn't distract us from the real topic: Lorenz knew we were coming. The F-prots have no idea how, but I can't be grateful when I'm afraid of what I've wrought. The team is snapping at each other, which is a really bad place to be when people have sidearms.

"This fucker will be lying in wait," says Yarborough. "He knows we're onto him."

"He doesn't know it's going to be tonight," counters Olsen. "And he doesn't know what we can do."

"People who bug out—"

"He's gonna think he's safe." Olsen seems hot on the idea.

"People who bug out stay twitchy for days," insists Yarborough. "I'm not saying we don't go after him. I'm saying we wait until he cools off."

"We can't wait. He's gonna feed, and Roland's gonna lose him. Right?"

"Yes," says Roland. He's sitting up front with al-Ibrahim, conferring over the van's GPS screen. He's looking for the nearest neighbors or something. He hasn't found any, which is great.

"But if we know where he is—"

"He could move again."

"Why would he? He thinks he's safe."

"Because we've got a leak," interrupts Breunig. "He will know. I don't know how, I don't know when, but until we plug it, we have nothing. And that's why I'm making the call. We do it tonight, before anyone knows we've got a bead on him, or we're never seeing this guy again. And that is not an option."

Yarborough seethes. Breunig doesn't take passive aggression. "You got an opinion. It's welcome. But it's got to be tonight."

To his credit, Yarborough stays focused. "I say we get the C-4."

I try not to gape. We don't have high explosives in the L.A. office. I infer that there aren't any in the van, but I wouldn't swear to it.

"And your reasoning is?"

"I say we just bring the whole house down on him. Fuck walking into a trap. We don't let him touch us or shoot back or anything. We plant, and we go."

"That is the craziest thing I've ever heard," I blurt, and now everyone in the van is staring at me. I double down.

"I mean, shit, we just tossed a house. That's cool. That looks like a robbery. Shooting, we know that can be done 'cause no body, no case. But a bomb? That gets the FBI on your ass. They check the explosive residue for tags or whatever."

"Homemade," Yarborough says. "No taggants."

"Okay..." I allow. "I like homemade explosives even less."

"We've tested it. I know it works."

"No, I mean, if some lab like, compares residue from this bomb to all other bombs in the area, are they going to figure out who you are because you're the one guy with no tags? 'Cause unless there's a hundred other no-tag bombers, I gotta say, I have problems with that plan."

"She's right," says Olsen. "No American Jihad shit. Stick with what we know."

"This is FUBAR," Yarborough insists. "We don't have surprise. We don't have overwhelming force. We don't have a plan."

"You gonna stay in the van?" asks Olsen. "Let the new girl take the bullet?"

Yarborough is silent for a moment, obviously tempted to say yes and get it all over with. I try to figure out what's going through his head. Kern wants Morgan dead, and the order came from the top. It could very well be Yarborough's job at stake if he jumps ship entirely, which looks like what he wants to do.

Then, he comes back. "Your asses'd be bitey chow without me."

"On point!" Olsen says, bumping fists. "We got a real F-prot here."

"But I bet you a bottle of Jack that this guy is ready and fucking waiting."

"We're in business," Breunig announces. "Black Two, can we do a silent approach?"

"Yes," Roland says. He's been swigging Gatorade on the ride over and resting in the seat. I thought he'd be on the floor from keeping up his spell thing or whatever, but no such luck.

"Good," says Breunig. "I don't want to use the ram. The first bang anyone hears should drop a target. Understand?" We murmur assent. I check the battery charge on my night goggles—they don't do much for me, but the other F-prots don't need to know that—and wonder how the hell I ended up here.

We drive the last kilometer with the headlights off, slow as a driver's-ed student on his first day, and pray no one strays lanes. Al-Ibrahim is goggled up like the rest of us and cruises on the electric engine. We glide into place, as close as he dares to the long no-man's-land of the lawn. The side door slides open, and we descend, five bulky shadows in plate-and-fiber suits.

There is no way around it—a vipe's sensitive eyes can see us coming across the yard if they are waiting at a window. We can either do it in a bum rush or creep slowly on our stomachs, trying to cut down our silhouettes. We go with the second option. I scrabble in the wet grass after Roland, who leads from the front as we approach the house. Looking up to an unlit third-floor window, the biomancer nods and signals as he locks onto Lorenz's position.

We circle around for the beachside door, stacked three high as Breunig adjusts his skeleton key fob and presses it against the plate. The door clicks. Then, everything happens.

12 - RANATH

I feel Lorenz's presence, like a hot nail prodding my skin. I have to turn down the web to avoid the feedback distracting me, but the early signs are good. Lorenz's signal isn't moving as we enter the house—all that remains are a few flights of stairs. Breunig and I are up front, gliding back-against-the-wall whenever we can. Infinity and Yarborough cover the other direction, but we all stay in a clump for fear of friendly fire. Olsen takes up the rear. When the split comes, she follows Breunig. The first few rooms are all silence and patience. We slice the pie of angles around the second doorway and try not to stumble in the unfamiliar house. The goggles don't help. They have little in the way of peripheral vision, so we all frantically scan ahead and behind.

Then, Yar takes a door noisily. I can't fault him for it—he turns the handle and shoves, but the door is lighter than it looks, and it swings back into a hollow wooden closet loud enough to bring voices from upstairs.

We barely acknowledge the loss of stealth. We must go smooth and swift, and there is no time left to think.

We wash like a flood through the house, an endless clearing of rooms. We leapfrog and kick aside furniture as first one of us takes point, then another. We try to cover each other, but the house's layout isn't cooperating. Breunig and Yarborough each want to be the first ones through. Me, I run to stay even.

We stumble into the stairwell, me first. Breunig uses me as a shield as we go up together, aiming at the narrow slit above where we can see railing as the stairs double back on themselves. Something moves, and we burst the air with our carbines. The rifle rounds can tear right through wood and plaster, possibly the whole house. If someone is in the way, so much the better.

But there is no thump of a body, or at least I can't hear one after Breunig's carbine goes off next to my ear. The first thing that comes back is dogs barking somewhere. Infinity's team comes up behind us, taking it slower, and I push out into the second-floor hallway.

The locator function is weaker now, changing directions. Lorenz is running, looking for an escape route. He's due west of me, but it would be folly to chase the signal and walk straight into someone else's sights. Instead, I lead Breunig toward the barking, seeing an indoor fence blocking the kitchen where a German shepherd and a pit bull mix are held in more by training than by plastic. They are making noise, irritating WAU WAU WAU barks that cover the sound of anyone sneaking up on me. Breunig pulls a trigger. The carbine spits three bullets into each, sending one down instantly. The other twists up with the bullets in its chest. This is no mercy mission.

I kick down the gate. Even without the barking, the house is a cacophony—yells and shots and falling furniture. I run on light feet across the kitchen and buttonhook to the right, near the sink. Breunig follows, then splits left, and I see him slip and fall as a shape appears in the archway to the hall, a gun with a man behind it.

Everything narrows down to my finger, yanking away as the M12 keeps kicking. I have no clear shot at the head. I just keep shooting, riddling the vipe's body as the pistol in its hand fires away. When the silhouette in the hall finally collapses, I see a shell casing bounce on the floor. It isn't ours. We use caseless ammo to leave less evidence.

"I'm hit," says Breunig, trying to stand in dog shit—the dogs have actually shit all over the kitchen, either in excitement or death—and here he is, looking for the pistol round in his chest armor, hoping it hasn't snuck in behind the trauma plate. A lethal wound feels just like a punch to the ribs, and no one will be the wiser for the ten godawful minutes we need to catch our breath. The silk is good, it's stronger than Kevlar, but plenty of guns can match it now.

"Stay." I signal to Olsen, who takes the lead and steps over to Breunig. Meanwhile, I'm by the fallen vipe, doing a burst to the skull. Olsen doesn't see an exit wound on Breunig and props him up by the kitchen counter. We don't need to say any more—Breunig waves us on. Triage, surgery, healing functions, everything must wait. We have to secure the area. We have to kill vipes.

13 - INFINITY

I go up the stairs two at a time, aiming high and kicking down the third-floor door. In that same motion, I take to the side, and so Yarborough runs ahead of me.

I hesitate, not freeze. All the training pays off. But I'm slow, and Yar wants contact, so he runs ahead. He turns a corner high, expecting me to back him up by going low, but just as I'm about to, he comes barreling back, stumbling over his feet as a vipe catches and tackles him. They collide with me but brush off as they fall, and I recognize the Irish cop as he lands on top of Yarborough. They struggle over Yar's carbine.

The vipe is stronger, but Yarborough clings for dear life. The vipe one-hands his grip and slugs Yar across the face. The sound is a pumpkin hit with a baseball bat. The F-prot goes limp.

Dangerous as the vipe is, he's violated the first rule of ground fighting—never try it when there are multiple opponents. Before I think about it too much, I step up behind him, put my rifle to his head and pull the trigger. Blood, brain, and bone exit the front of his face, and he collapses onto Yarborough.

He was going to kill him, I tell myself. I'm going to make this come out even somehow.

I check on Yar. His goggles are skewed on his face, and as far as I can tell, he's out cold. From what I know of mixed martial arts fights, knockouts don't last very long, unless they're very bad ones.

My chance is now. I can do this, while there are no eyes on me.

Think, girl. I can't call out to Morgan or his pals—the F-prots might hear. So, I pull the goggles off my face and hold them under my weapon. There aren't that many vipes in the house, are there? And they didn't see me do what I just did, right?

There's gunfire from the floor beneath me. Roland and Breunig. A few seconds later, there's an answering shot. Yarborough and I missed a vipe.

I run through the next door and the next and the next, trying to figure out where the remaining vipes are hiding. If I were one of them, I'd be huddled down behind a gun safe or some other hard cover, lights off, using my night eyes to pick off whomever made the mistake of coming through the door.

But they're not me.

One door left at the end of the hall. I go to the side before trying the handle, just in case. No bullets come. I whip around the jamb, weapon up, only to see something I'm not expecting.

There are two of them, Morgan and some man I've never seen before—probably the owner of the house. They have a window open. When I enter the room, the stranger ducks to the floor as if it will help. Morgan raises his hands. He stares as I shove my goggles up.

"I know you," Morgan says. "Must've been a hell of a lunch."

"They're tracking you with qi," I say, shutting the door behind me. "If you want to escape, you have to feed."

"Say what?"

"Feed. It cloaks your signature. Cut him, feed, and then get out that window."

"Hold on, cut him? With what?"

"Oh, for fuck's sakes." I pull a utility knife free and snap it open, tossing it on the bed. Morgan and the other man look at each other, wondering what firehose of crazy I've been sprayed with.

"He can't heal," Morgan says. "He's normal. He could bleed to death."

The words knock the room silent.

"Okay," I say, grabbing the knife again. I pull down my long glove. "It'll be me."

"Did you come here planning this kind of—"

"Bite me, or they will kill you in less than one minute."

I lay the blade across my wrist and try to cut. My newfound strength is no help. It begins to hurt, and instinctively, I shy back. Instead of a cut with rich red blood, I get less than a cat scratch across the skin. Hesitation marks.

Gunfire pops from downstairs. Roland and Breunig. The other gun is silent.

"I'll do it," says Morgan, and I see determination in his eyes. "Give it here." I hand him the knife. We have no time for anything else.

He grabs me by the arm, brings the blade up and slashes my throat.

At first, I don't know how bad it is. There's a little pain, and I know I've been hit, but by the time I try to put a hand up to stop the blood flow, Morgan is on me. His mouth has somehow moved the clothing aside. For a terrifying second, I feel myself blacking out, vision fading to a small, bright pinpoint. Then, the fear leaves.

Drinking blood feels great. Being the drink feels weird. I relax like a dropped marionette, my whole body heavy and unresponsive. I try to move and feel my arms flail in great, dull swings. Each limb crackles with tingles and then my torso as well. There is no part of me that reacts like the Infinity I know.

On some level, I can feel blood flowing out of me and into Morgan's mouth, and my body throbs every time he sucks. In the haze, it makes sense to me that his aura would change. I become convinced that I can feel bits of me dispersed in him, like droplets of ink spreading out to tint a glass of water.

Then, he's gone, pulling out or pulling back—it's hard to tell which. Suddenly, I am lying on the floor, feeling warm wind from the window and wondering what the hell happened since I don't remember falling. The left side of my neck is on fire, and as I clasp it, I sit up. I have a great view of the spreading bloodstain on the floor. I have just enough time to realize the stain is the size of my head before the dizziness kicks in and the carpet comes up to slap me.

14 - RANATH

I'm confirming the kill on the second floor when I feel a sudden cold sensation. It's disorienting because the vector in front of me is in a bedroom, using a waterbed as cover. This isn't as stupid as it sounds—two meters of water actually stops bullets better than anything else in the house—but when he pokes his head up to shoot, Olsen has better timing. As the firefight is over, my boots are squishing the soggy carpet, and my first thought when I feel the cold shiver is that I'm being dripped on from somewhere above me. But nothing's coming from the ceiling, so I guess maybe my stimweb has malfunctioned. Instead of Lorenz's signature burning into my brain, I get an injection of ice water before the sensation fades.

"You all right?" asks Olsen, who notices my inattention.

"Upstairs," I say. "We're losing him."

Olsen doesn't need to be told twice. She runs for the stairs. I hurry after her, losing all hope of reorienting the function in the back of my mind. Breunig limps behind us.

"Black Three, location, respond," I say. I get nothing.

"Black Three and Four, we're coming upstairs. Watch your shots." The words go out into the void, and again, nothing comes back.

"Black Three is wounded," barks Olsen from up ahead. I'm at her side almost instantly and see Yarborough, on the floor with his goggles in one hand, propping himself up with the other. Olsen never loses focus, covering the hallway while I give Yarborough a hand up.

When we are nose-to-nose, Yarborough yanks his balaclava away from his mouth, and I can see the man's jaw is hanging at an angle. He stumbles into a wall for support, and Breunig is there, giving him an arm to lean on.

"Where's Black Four?" Breunig asks, and Yarborough only voices a gargling sound in response. Of course, he can't speak.

"Stay here. Not far now," I say and sight down my carbine again, following Olsen to a door. We stack up, and Olsen gives the signal—

three, two, one. I kick at the lock, but it has already been broken. The door bangs open and then rebounds shut again. An air current is going through the house and out an open window in this room. But I see no hostiles. I shove inside.

Infinity is on the floor. Her face is exposed, and even through the muted colors of the night vision goggles, I can tell the hand clamping down on her neck is covered in blood. Olsen clears the closet, and I go for the window.

Two floors below us, in the great unfenced back yard, a man is limping off toward the bay. I can't ID him, but it doesn't take a genius to guess he jumped. I know what to do—either this is Lorenz, or it's a witness. I aim for center-mass and pull the trigger. The carbine rips the night air, and three bullets cut straight through the target. He jerks and stumbles. The second time, I aim for the head.

As the body falls, I see another warm shape, this one far off in the tall weeds. It must be six hundred meters if it's an inch, and it flickers like a mirage in the ghostly green vision. Is it someone who's gotten a head start running? A neighbor? By the time I settle my sights on it just in case, it's too obscure to fire.

Olsen reports in behind me. "White One, we've got three injuries. Status."

Al-Ibrahim is refreshingly calm. "Nothing yet on police band. Stabilize on site."

The words jolt me back to what's important. I shut down my function—it's useless now—and kneel beside Infinity. I clamp my hand onto hers and dial up the stimweb to fire a gut-punch of yang-within-yin. If that doesn't jump-start her own yang to keep her alive, not much will. My hand burns and crackles with white energy, and Infinity spasms. Her body stretches out rather than curling up in a fetal position. Olsen gets her arm under Infinity's shoulders and injects a gel into the wound site. It starts to seal.

Infinity's eyes flutter, then turn to me. "Ow."

I pull my balaclava away from my mouth. "Stay still. You're going to live. We can carry you out of here."

"Okay." Coherency is not her strong suit.

"Were you bitten?"

"Cut."

"Did he bite you after he cut you?"

"No," she creaks out.

"Hold still," I repeat and pour more energy into my hand. As it pools there, her palm and fingers get hot, and I can feel her wound open like an iris, even as a clot begins to cover the cut itself. Her neck relaxes, and for a moment, the room smells like cooking flesh. I wipe the sweat from my upper lip with my free arm.

"Did... did he get away?" she asks numbly. "He had a knife..."

"There's a lot of people down," I say. "We don't have enough to go after Lorenz. Can you stand?" Infinity gets to her feet. Not bad.

"This is a goatfuck," says Breunig, supporting Yarborough in the hall. "Do you still have a lock? Can you find him?"

I put an arm under Infinity. Olsen and I lift her together.

"He's gone," I say. "We've got to get them to the vans. He's gone."

15 - INFINITY

August 14th

Breunig carries me over the threshold as Olsen keeps the gauze pressed to my neck. Roland gets the door and the lights, and down I go on the couch. If it wasn't for the throbbing and burning, I might mistake it for my high school friends taking care of me when I'm trashed.

The trio scurry around me while I squint into the recessed ceiling lights. Roland said it was a house of theirs, and I immediately agreed to go. If Roland can work on my wound, it's a far better choice than a hospital with their questions and insurance and metal detectors.

"One second," Roland orders. "Lift." Breunig and Olsen pick me up again, and he rolls a plastic tarp over the couch beneath me. I go down on it again, trying to make sure the gauze never moves from my throat. I'm not sure if I have Roland or VIHPS to thank for the sudden recuperation. I must have lost two liters of blood, but already my vision has stopped swimming.

"Get her vest off," someone says, and the Velcro straps rip. A hand goes over my neck, and my arms briefly straighten to let the armor by. I feel the cramp developing in my right elbow briefly before it goes back into place.

"Talk to me," Roland says. "Stay conscious."

"Right," I agree, watching Breunig and Olsen exit. I don't remember them talking about where they are going. "Are they coming back?"

"I can't have distractions. They wouldn't be much use."

"Olsen can do stitches," I say.

"They'd just pop out when we're done," Roland points out. "I'm going to heal you."

I'm lightheaded enough to think I'm stupid. "Didn't you just do that?"

"That was an emergency treatment. This is more."

Roland gently puts a hand under me to sit me up and then gets beside me. "I'm going to have to make physical contact with you, and I'll need your full cooperation to get well. Can you turn your head to the right for me?"

I try. A few degrees shy of forty-five, and the pain cinches in its claws. Roland frowns.

"All right. I'm going to have to reduce the distance to zero to maximize the function. Can I put my hands on you?"

I wince. "Not if it's in the cut."

"It'll have to be close. I'm going to touch either side of it." The fingers of his left hand work under mine, and then I jump. His other hand is pulling up my shirt. His right hand curves around me, and it's large enough that he can touch a point over my liver with his thumb and caress my kidney with his fingertips. Awkwardly, I look away, then back at Roland's green eyes, fixed on my neck.

"Okay, let me know when you're going to—hhhh," I say, just as warm pools of pleasure spread from his hands. The sensation of being heated up feels odd, but also right, as if the pain had just been me making some kind of mistake. I'm not feeling it anymore.

The pain has been replaced by a strange impression of being inflated. My posture straightens, and only then I realize I've been hunched. Likewise, my fingers point straight out, as if their new fullness prevents them from curving naturally. And there's the weirdness. With this new flow of something-that-is-more-than blood throughout my body, my nipples become erect, and my eyes water. I blink the fluid away, trying not to stare directly into Roland's face. I breathe through my nose rather than exhale onto him.

Roland, for his part, continues his focused gaze on my neck, and his dilated pupils remind me of a cat about to pounce. His long, slow breath catches my attention, and I decide to ease the awkwardness by focusing on it. I bring my breath in time with his. I draw my hand away from my wound, letting him hold me.

The first few inhalations are all right, but then I smell his sweat, and it has a musky scent that makes my stomach growl.

"Interesting," he says. "I'm getting yin-within-yin from your stomach meridian. Did you not eat tonight?"

"Uh... I don't remember," I fumble. "Maybe it's because of the blood. When you lose as much as I have, aren't they supposed to give you some apple juice?" I can't lose my shit now. His brain is practically plugged into mine. He's going to figure me out in three, two, one....

"Your heart rate's up," he says quietly. "Slow it down. Breathe with me, like before."

I try again. I stare into his eyes, and after a few seconds, he stares back. I feel a tickle in the side of my throat, which I guess is my flesh starting to knit. I blink first and attempt to smile. "Guess I lose."

"You're doing fine," he says. "Do you need something to concentrate on?"

"I've got something." I sync my breathing and close my eyes.

When Joram saw Jehu, he said, "Is it peace, Jehu?" He answered, "What peace can there be, so long as the whoredoms and sorceries of your mother Jezebel continue?" Then, Joram reined about and fled, saying to Ahaziah, "Treason, Ahaziah!"

"Whatever that was, it seemed to do the trick," Roland reports. "I'm done with the vein. I'm going after the cut in the muscle tissue."

I try to remember the rest. The book of Kings isn't hard—not like the endless lists from Chronicles. Jehu, son of Jehoshaphat, waging his war against his former master, Ahab, and his Jezebel. Ahaziah shot with an arrow. Jezebel, hurled into the street to be eaten by dogs. The pulpy stories soothe me just as they did when I was an adolescent, and it's not long before my neck feels hot to the touch.

"What are you thinking about?"

Explaining this one might be tough. "I thought you couldn't have distractions."

"It helps if you concentrate, too."

"Sorry," I say automatically. Then, after a second, "Bible verses."

A smile crooks the corner of his mouth. "That's not what I thought you'd say."

"Yeah, me and the book are at odds most of the time."

"I've heard you say, 'Oh, Lord.'"

"That's not for Yahweh," Explaining my god makes me feel like an idiot. "Anyway, my dad made me memorize them."

"Was he a preacher?"

"No." I look down. "Just nuts."

"How many verses do you know?"

"Practically the whole thing."

"The whole *Bible?* Is that even possible?"

"People used to memorize the *Iliad* and recite it. No problem. The letters of Paul are a bit fuzzy, but ask me something Old Testament, and I've got it."

"Exodus twenty-two, eighteen."

"You shall not suffer a witch to live. Give me something hard."

He seems momentarily quiet, but it's thoughtful. "Job," he says.

"Got a number?"

He adjusts his grip slightly. "You'd know it better than me. Start where you want."

I know which one I'm going to say, but I don't know if I'm going to choke up saying it. "Fourteen, eleven," and here we go.

"As waters fail from a lake,
and a river wastes away and dries up,
so mortals lie down and do not rise again;
until the heavens are no more, they will not awake,
or be roused out of their sleep.
Oh, that you would hide me in Sheol,
that you would conceal me until your wrath is past,
that you would appoint me a set time, and remember me."

No tears. No choking. But my heart's in my throat as he acknowledges it all. "Well, I'm not sure if that's right or wrong, but since I don't have the book here, we'll say you win."

"I said that at my mom's funeral. It's accurate." He looks ashamed, and I know he's off the scent. But there's more distance between us now. Metaphorically, anyway.

"Is Roland your real name?" The warmth shifts, and for a moment, it becomes tingles. My neck flesh prickles, awakening. My fingers dig into my palms.

"Why would you think it isn't?"

"Kern," I say. "He was a little weird when he talked about you. Like he was covering for something." The flesh cools, and I feel a pulse slowly synchronize with my heartbeat, a gentle *tap-tap, tap-tap*. I wonder if I should go for it and, as usual, do. "You don't tell your co-workers?"

"Breunig knows. No one else." Strikeout. I take another long, slow breath, and he adjusts to keep in time with me.

"How'd you... you know, pick it? Wow, that's—my heart's starting to—"

"The muscle is stable. We're going to accelerate your cell growth."

His grip tightens, and I freak a little. Being grabbed brings back my fight-or-flight reflex from the old days, and my hand slaps down to cover Roland's. Immediately, I let go because my strong grip could give me away. I'm just beginning to think of myself as a clever girl when my heart goes into overdrive. It's like I'm climbing a mountain.

I pant and feel a flush of fluid trickle down from my wound. Blood? Sweat? The junk from cells? My breath heaves, and I catch a glimpse of Roland's eyes again. It's intent, yet comforting. *I'm right here*, those eyes say. *We're doing this together.*

Then, bang, my neck stings, and just as quickly, it fades away again as Roland moves his hand from my side to my spine. Both of us are slick to the touch, now, but whatever he is doing, it's taking the pain and adrenaline away as fast as it builds up. It's like he's fighting my body to its limit... and then, it finally concedes.

My heart stops its desperate knocking at my ribs, settling down for a regular rhythm, and the easing pressure lets me once again breathe slowly and surely. His hand leaves my back. With a gentle wipe of his fingers, Roland sweeps the gauze away from my neck and crumples it up.

I feel the side of my throat. It's whole. "Wow. Is it always that fast?"

Roland stands and washes his hands in a basin I only notice just now. "No. Your body is very well attuned. And the wound wasn't as bad as it first looked."

I stretch and turn my head, finding I have full range of motion. "Beats the hell out of stitches." I pick up a small mirror and check for a scar. All I see is a little white flesh, like I got a paper cut three days ago.

"To answer your other question," he says, "I picked the name because I liked the knight."

"Lancelot was taken or something?"

"Lancelot screws his boss's wife. Roland is a stubborn son of a bitch who dies on a hill facing impossible odds. Did you have anything else?"

I smile. It isn't parity by a long shot, but at least I got one thing out of him. Then, a disturbing thought takes over. "Hey, with all this cell growth, isn't that how cancer starts or something?"

"It can be," he says, going over his fingers with a towel.

"Uh... then how is it you didn't just give me cancer?"

He looks at me strangely and replies, "Because I like you."

16 - KERN

August 17th

It's quiet in the second-floor office wing of the D.C. laboratory, and I'm getting worried. Ranath hasn't called in this morning, and I've rung his number three times. His last communication was brief, in code, and suitably chilling.

Check in, please, I texted him three days ago. *Coming into the office this morning?* It was casual, it was humdrum, it was the sort of message anyone intercepting it would skip over, hackles unraised.

The reply came several hours later, a worrying sign in itself. The team hates phones on sanitizing missions because they're distractions. A sudden vibration from your breast pocket, let alone a ring, is the last thing you want when keyed up behind a gunsight. Ranath's reply said: *In late. Don't know when. Dog got loose.*

I messaged back: *Anyone bitten?*

Unknown. The word hung in space, letting me imagine all sorts of terrifying scenarios. If Ranath didn't want to talk, he could have said so, unless something had happened to him. Perhaps he was cut off. Perhaps his phone died. Or perhaps the truth was something he didn't want to tell, and that level of hesitation in Ranath would be, in the nearly twenty years I've known him, unprecedented.

"—didn't get that memo, that's for damn sure—"

"—dude's got Band-Aids on him like he's covering zits—"

"—aren't vampires supposed to heal fast?"

Voices drift in from the hall, but I don't absorb them. I drink my coffee slowly, caffeine settling in a fluttery band around my heart.

I tell myself they just haven't finished. Maybe Ranath is simply taking extra care. He could be following the plan as we discussed it, framing Lorenz's death scene to be scandalous and incriminating. If he's good, he'll sell more news than any dry scientific report Lorenz was going to wave around as proof of something or other.

"Is Dr. Kern in his office?"

There's a knock at the door. I let them wait as I sip. The coffee is hot enough to sear my tongue, sweet with three packets of xylitol. Down the hall, the TV plays, low and indistinct.

I heard this theory once, back when I was considering a history minor, about how coffee started the Enlightenment. The idea was that once it was taken to Europe, someone developed the salon, where people passed around ideas instead of drowning their troubles in a tavern. Other theories included the potato starting the Industrial Revolution and the washing machine, women's suffrage. I thought it was all amusing crap that only smelled of enough truth to catch the gullible. I said leadership and marketing changes minds, not technology.

Then, I met Ulan and her little stimweb.

"Come in."

Brianna enters. Her face is pinched and tense, and it hits me with instant dread. Brianna is about as subtle and shy as her fire-engine-green hair. Brianna works in payroll, and if you argue with her, you'll find she's right about everything and everyone. That's why Admin chooses her to deliver bad news.

"You need to see something."

I follow her down the hall. The offices are empty, and only when we get to the break room do I understand. Everyone is in it, gathered around a phone serving as a wallscreen projector. The crowd parts, as if every person wants to give me the best seat.

Lorenz rants from the screen. "This virus has been loose for four *years. Thousands* of people could have been infected in that time, and BRHI *knew.*" He looks like he's gone from polished lawyer to mental case. He's disheveled, talking in front of a concrete wall. But his words are no less dangerous than before.

"They have no vaccine for it, no cure. All they have is an engineered strain of European Bat Lyssavirus that was deliberately irradiated by biomantic scientists at the Benjamin Rush Health Initiative, *against* the protocols decided by the FDA, *against* the EPA's guidelines on qi safety, against all common sense.

"Why? We may never know. But because of their hubris, human beings are now at risk from a plague. It is crueler than cancer, crueler than AIDS, a disease that makes its victims into villains."

I try to swallow and can't. Lorenz is wearing gray fatigues on-screen, his left hand wrapped and flesh-tone Band-Aids stuck up and down his left side as if he'd used up an entire box. But his skin has the rosiness of a vector who is freshly fed. That's when I know the vid is recent. The team failed. Lorenz has either infected, or he's killed someone.

"What else has he said?" I ask.

"Enough to get him committed," Brianna says. "His suit won't get anywhere."

"His... yeah," I say. "Why am I not surprised?" It's the maxim of the modern age—if it makes it to television, always believe the worst.

"My attorneys have already started action against the Benjamin Rush Health Initiative's Advanced Biophysics Experimental Lab. We are filing in civil court for wrongful infection, willful and wanton conduct, and reckless endangerment. If you have been wronged by their actions, contact the law offices at this number. Your pain and suffering are why we will be seeking damages."

I barely see the screen. We're too late. Even if Ranath reaches Lorenz now, our name is out there, and the truth will follow. Brianna touches the screen and opens a window to track BRHI stock. I can see the restlessness in the room as everyone watches the numbers after the minus sign get bigger and bigger.

My phone rings, and I let it because I've got to take control. They can't see me bleed. "Okay, everyone, back to your offices. You've got lots to talk about. We've known about this for some time and have a legal department that is ready and able to deal with nuisances."

"He said something about an attack on his life?" someone asks. My phone rings again, and I don't have to look to see who it is. The broadcast has ended; Edison Field is on the line. I answer.

"I'll be right there," I say. "I know what we have to do."

17 - TRANSCRIPT

From "Diatribe," with host Evelyn Vassa, National Crowdfunded Radio (ExtendCast), Monday, August 17th, 8:33 p.m.

VASSA: This is Diatribe. I'm Evelyn Vassa. My second guest tonight is former judge Robert Franco, legal advisor here on Diatribe. With the Morgan Lorenz case pending, America's attention has turned to the plight of those infected with Virally Induced Hematophagic Predation Syndrome, pronounced as either "vipps" or "vipes." Judge, we have heard a lot of speculation over the past twenty-four hours about the damage the infection can do, to Lorenz's life or potential victims. Can you tell us now what his chances are for prevailing in his lawsuit?

FRANCO: Well, the strongest argument is for medical negligence. If the virus originated at BRHI, and they failed to contain it, that could be easily provable. But it's a slap on the wrist to just make BRHI improve their safety procedures. Lorenz's team is trying for "willful, wanton conduct" and "wrongful infection." After reading the public filings, it seems the heart of the case is to punish the Health Initiative and give restitution to the less fortunate victims. It's an uphill climb— they'll have to provide evidence linking the infections to a specific outbreak from BRHI and willful intent, which can be tricky for something estimated to have started years ago.

VASSA: You see that as a difficult case to make?

FRANCO: Well, (*laughs*) the counter-argument BRHI presents, that's even more difficult. That's the precedent-setter.

VASSA: Let's cut right to it, then. They claimed that Lorenz and all the co-plaintiffs, quote, "lack standing to file a lawsuit in the USA because they are no longer human." Do you think they'll start walking that back tomorrow?

FRANCO: If they were politicians, perhaps, but the weird thing is, they didn't come to this strategy overnight. When Lorenz filed his suit, BRHI immediately moved for a dismissal based on it. At a guess, I'd say they can't stand the thought of a class action. They can't stand the idea of settling with who-knows-how-many wrongfully infected, so they're saying Lorenz has no right to sue, actually, no rights at all.

VASSA: Is this a novel idea? I mean, claiming Lorenz is not protected under the Constitution, et cetera. One is reminded of the war on—

FRANCO: —war on terror. Excuse me—

VASSA: Go ahead.

FRANCO: This, of course, differs. The rationale for Guantanamo prisoners being unable to sue was that it was a military tribunal, and this is a civil matter in federal court. But in a strange way, the Health Initiative has a legal argument based on precedents that have been around for some time. You're going to have to bear with me because I'm going to talk about the rights of chimpanzees, and I've put listeners to sleep with that before.

VASSA: I like to give our audience credit, but summing up is always good.

FRANCO: The thing about defining what "human" is, is that it's been such a self-evident category for so long that nobody really irons out a legal definition until something is close but not quite there. Then, we ask, what does "human" really mean?

VASSA: Well, a DNA test would answer the question, wouldn't it?

FRANCO: DNA, DNA, of course. The holy grail of what makes us human, DNA. Here's the problem with that. It's a case called *Cagersheim v. Simmons*, in which a custodian named Simmons set free eleven knockout-gene chimpanzees on a game preserve outside Atlanta. He was an animal-rights type and wanted them to live out their lives free, but his company, that's Cagersheim, saw the chimps as an investment worth hundreds of thousands of dollars. At first, they sued him, claiming larceny and wrongful appropriation of private property. But he had memos authorizing him to dispose of the animals if some funding didn't come through, and it hadn't. So... the interesting part... when plan A failed, they asked the authorities to charge him with criminal kidnapping.

VASSA: How did they reason that?

FRANCO: They argued the chimpanzees were nearly human. They said an ordinary chimp, genetically speaking, has ninety-four percent of the same genes that humans do, plus these had human DNA inserted into their genome before birth. Simmons was, in essence, kidnapping eleven human beings, whose only substantive difference was low IQs and inability to give consent to be transported.

VASSA: Did that argument get anywhere? DNA or not, they still look like chimps.

FRANCO: Looking like and acting like are very different things. They communicated with sign language. They showed signs of reasoning. When they were asked about traumatic events, they hesitated as if they didn't want to talk about it. But as you might expect, the appellate court ultimately ruled against Cagersheim. They said it was too far a reach to rule something as human just because of DNA percentage.

VASSA: Okay... let me see if I follow... that would create a precedent, of course, but a VIHPS-infected individual... aren't they completely human?

FRANCO: You just found the ace up BRHI's sleeve. No. They are somewhat different. When I asked a doctor friend of mine, not BRHI-affiliated, what the word on the genetic and epigenetic changes are with this EBL-4, he didn't say, "Oh, the genome's exactly the same. Don't be ridiculous." His reaction was, and I quote, "Um." The qi-activated virus inserts itself into the DNA of host cells like it's endogenous—uh, sorry, like it evolved alongside humans. Anyway, it plugs in, and the infected, their brain changes. They interpret smells better, they heal faster, they're wired to do things normal humans just don't do.

VASSA: Wait, but to categorize a person in the same class as the monkeys—chimps, I mean—you're categorizing them as corporate property.

FRANCO: Again, not completely without precedent. Monsanto's been arguing for years that because they patented GMO pig breeding, they get to own the pig's litter. Technically, if BRHI modified European Bat Lyssavirus enough to be a truly integral part of the genome, they'd have a claim to any nonhuman organisms carrying their virus.

VASSA: Excuse me, did you just say—

FRANCO: I said technically. I can't imagine they're going there. Cagersheim already got into trouble when they had to explain how they treated their human-chimps. The last time Americans put a claim on owning other people, we had a civil war.

VASSA: Let's talk about the arguments they're more likely to use. Can't we say it's like citizenship? Say, "if you have a human mother or a human father, you're legally human?"

FRANCO: I know companies that can make a human in a dish, grow them in an artificial womb. Are the babies not human just because the method was different?

VASSA: Well, but they had to have the genetic material from—

FRANCO: You're back to DN—

VASSA: DNA! (laughing) This *is* trickier than I thought. What about intelligence?

FRANCO: Very thorny. Are the mentally challenged considered nonhuman? Of course not, but we've got GMO chimps and AI that can surpass some of them in standardized tests, so watch what you say there.

VASSA: Well, you can get "incompetent to stand trial." What if you rule "if they're capable of understanding charges for or against them, they can have legal rights?"

FRANCO: I mentioned AI. Legal-assistant AI could understand that, no question.

VASSA: Well, what scientific basis do we usually use? I mean, what's the line between... like, a housecat and a wildcat?

FRANCO: You *could* use subspecies indicators, as is the case with livestock, which makes the test "are the infected people still capable of breeding with human stock?" We don't know that for certain, and (*laughs*) it sure would be an interesting test.

VASSA: Okay, let's talk practicality. There's the safety issue. We've heard the word "vampire" used more than once. The name BRHI uses, VIHPS, has the words "predation syndrome" in it. Do you expect the defense to play on our emotions, play on our fears?

FRANCO: They would be stupid not to.

VASSA: But the chance of a vampire attack on an average citizen is remote, isn't it?

FRANCO: Well, your chances of being eaten by a shark are incredibly low, too, but the psychological impact is far out of proportion. We don't know how many of these infected people there really are. There could be ten, or ten thousand, and active qi scares people. You want four words that explain why this case is going to be impossible to predict, remember those: active qi scares people. Even people in the judiciary.

VASSA: I understand the judge, Param Bayat, he's known for hearing qi-related cases.

FRANCO: That's true. What I hear from the people who know him is that if you could pick your judge for this, you could do a lot worse than Bayat. He tries to keep current with technology, including stimweb technology. This makes him a sort of rare bird in the legal system, which is usually hopelessly behind the times. He had a quote we dug up, "When the laws of physics no longer apply, the laws of man must then serve at the highest level."

VASSA: We did some digging of our own, and interestingly, we came up with video. He apparently is unafraid to have cameras in the courtroom.

FRANCO: Yes, that would be his controversial side. He's been outspoken, saying that if you can't defend your ideas in public, they must be lacking somehow.

VASSA: Do you think he'll allow the proceedings to be televised?

FRANCO: Yes, and very soon. Bayat's known for running a rocket docket, in quick and out quick. Unfortunately, with the cameras, we can probably expect theatrics on behalf of both sides.

VASSA: And can we expect the defense to play the qi card and say the infected are subject to powerful and unknown forces? To call them dangerous?

FRANCO: Again, absolutely. BRHI is going to beat the drum that these are monsters and should be locked up. They've evidently had a program in place to do so for some time. Of course, if one really wanted to lock up threats to the welfare of others, the defense might recall the case of *Kelly v. Seven Star Health and Hospice*—do we have time?

VASSA: I'm going to have to cut you off. We've run over even our ExtendCast time. My guest has been Robert Franco, Diatribe legal expert. Thank you very much, Judge Franco.

FRANCO: Pleasure to be here.

18 - INFINITY

August 18th

I have no idea what to do.

Morgan is gone. The F-prots aren't idiots. I'm surviving on the grace of the gods, and gods are famous for revoking said grace. I'm back on my feet, but Yarborough isn't. For lack of a better plan, I bring him soup during visiting hours.

He's on bed rest at the Stafford Medical Center. I bum a ride from Roland when he visits the safe house. He fills me in on the details since I slept for more than twelve hours, healing all the while.

The F-prots survived—the spider-silk vest stopped the rounds that hit Breunig, and he only got ugly bruises. It hurts for him to breathe, but no ribs or internal organs are screwed up. Yar is in worse shape. The vipe slugged him so hard that his mouth is a mess, all broken bone and cuts from his teeth inside his cheek. Breunig and Olsen took him to the contingency van and got him to the hospital. Then, they put deception upon deception. Stripping down to civilian clothes, Breunig claimed that he'd gotten into a fight with Yarborough and was checking him into the clinic out of guilt. All Yarborough had to do was shake his head when the doctors asked him if he wanted the police to come by so he could press charges, and the matter was dropped. Roland visited after the surgery and brought down the swelling in his jaw—more thorough healing will have to wait until after he is discharged, to avoid questions.

Avoiding questions is something I can get behind. I've been wondering why Roland didn't catch on while he was mucking about with my body or notice that my wound was closing fast. But I don't know the exact difference between vipe-fast and stimwebbed-fast, so I babble to keep his mind on other topics.

On the drive down, we have a pleasant conversation about cooking, in which I discover he's vaguely competent in the kitchen and has a connoisseur's taste for various yogurts. I never thought of that as a thing, but apparently, biomancers spend a lot of time with the stuff. When they generate energy in their core, sometimes it kills off digestive bacteria, so it's yogurt to the rescue. My own culinary confession is my loathing for recipes that require homemade sauce since a sauce's role is to help rather than become a project in its own right.

I also discover Roland lives alone.

As we enter the door to Yarborough's room, it's all smiles and a chorus of heys. I'm gratified to see that my guess was correct. The whole team has turned out—none of them is going to abandon a brother in arms. I take my sunglasses off. I have to blend, bright lights or no.

"I may be wrong," I say, "but I believe someone owes someone a bottle of Jack Daniels."

"Been there, said that," says Olsen. She indicates a brown paper bag on the table with a bottle neck sticking out. "He tried some to kill the pain. Bad idea."

"Stitches in my cheeks," says Yarborough. "It's like a mouthful of bees."

"Isn't your jaw wired shut?" I ask. "You said that really well."

"Can still talk with my teeth together. Try." The Y comes out a little buried, but I have no problem understanding him.

"Can't believe I'm doing this," I say, teeth clenched. "Howzat?"

"Like sweet poetry." I set the soup down. Roland, who has been the pack mule, hands me the bowls and ladle. Soon everyone is thanking me. It's a tactic I learned early, dealing with my father—feed him, and I have a little bit of power. I could change his mood, change his focus. If I fed him, we had something to talk about that didn't involve punishment.

Punishment had practically been his way of talking.

"You made this while recovering from a knife wound?" asks Ebe. "I feel like a slacker."

"I thought anything that involved chewing would be painful, so it's just canned tomato. How's the chief? I heard you got banged up."

"My back's the worst part," says Breunig.

"You got hit in the back?"

"No," says Olsen, "but his back's got all the muscles that have to compensate keeping him upright. So, they're strained."

"I need a week lying on a beach in Tahiti."

"Jasper, baby," says Yarborough.

"What's that?" I ask.

"Yar's gonna take us skiing in Jasper when he wins the lottery," says Breunig. "Not the jackpot. That's stupid. But he's got this system to win ten grand or so."

"You get good skiing in Virginia?" I say, once again feeling too new.

"Canada," says al-Ibrahim. "Roland discovered it. Go to Montana. Take a right—"

"—drive north for eight hours," Yarborough and al-Ibrahim finish together, obviously having said it a hundred times before.

My eye catches Roland, standing by the door, looking out with his arms folded and hands empty. "You sure you don't want any?" I call.

"I'll have some in a minute," Roland says, attention on the hall.

"He's letting us relax," Breunig confides. "He does that."

"Did something happen?" I ask. From the looks passing around the room, something has.

"Roland's been with the company longer than us," explains Breunig. "He knew some of the original people who, uh... turned. So, whenever we're social, and he thinks a vipe might show up to retaliate, he volunteers to watch. It's no big thing."

I try to avoid looking alarmed, but before I say anything, Olsen jumps in. "Looks like he did a job on your neck," she says.

"Yeah, it was pretty incredible," I say, wondering if Roland has been so intimate when healing Olsen or the men. Surely, they've been wounded before?

"Was there saliva contact?"

"Please, I just met the man," I blurt, and everyone laughs. Olsen turns red, and knowing that she's going to follow up, I prepare.

"The vipe who cut you," she says. "I'm still not clear on the details."

"There were two of them, a human and Morgan," I say, adding "Lorenz" at the last second, just before it sounds unnatural. "Morgan must have bitten the guy, then had him lie in wait for me with the knife. It all happened really fast."

No sooner is the lie out of my mouth than I know it won't hold up.

"How did you know he was human?"

"He leaked like a human," Roland says, and I can breathe again. Roland closes the door so we can talk freely. "I saw two shapes fleeing the scene. I took out the slow one. A single burst, and he went down. The rest was just insurance."

"And the vipe didn't try to feed?"

"No," I say. "He was practically out the window."

"This may sound harsh, and I don't mean it to," says Breunig, "but we have a policy about engaging vipes alone. You were faced with a bad choice once Jackson went down. If it had been the vipe holding the knife, you'd be infected right now."

"Right." I nod and wonder when he's getting to the harsh part.

"This isn't the place to talk about the details, but we're all going to have to give an after-action report. And my report is going to say your partner was taken out, and you had no choice but to continue against your better judgment."

"Sure," I say. "We went to great lengths to pursue, yadda blah."

"Kern may come down on you, but we're on your side, and we want you to know that."

"'Specially me," adds Yarborough, and for a second, I'm not sure why he's said it. Warning bells are going off that they're all being too nice to me, but then I think, why not? Yarborough went from a vipe sitting on his chest to waking up with that vipe shot in the back of the head. Acting on instinct saved me... instinct and a phenomenal amount of luck.

"Well," I say, "feels good to be part of the family."

"Everyone give Mom a hug," calls al-Ibrahim, who leads by example. The sudden movement makes me tense. I want to throw him. I *should* throw him; but I allow it.

"Respect, Ebe," warns Breunig.

"I'm being respectful."

"You totally couldn't do that in Qatar, could you?" says Breunig.

"She's from L.A. They hug in L.A.," al-Ibrahim declares, then confides in me. "It's his hang-up. Breunig doesn't even hug his kids."

I fake a smile, and just as I wonder if Breunig is going to take that, the others leap to their leader's defense.

"Ebe, you are so full of shit," says Olsen. She sounds as if she speaks from long experience. "He's jealous 'cause Breunig actually gets laid, while he's waiting for some webcam princess to dump her boyfriend. It's a very tragic tale."

"It's only tragic if it never happens," retorts al-Ibrahim.

"So, you have kids?" I ask Breunig. "Do they know what you do?"

"Not all the details," he says. "I tell them the police can't catch all the bad guys themselves, so our company helps out."

"Huh," I say. My F-prot team in L.A. had happy people, married people, and people with offspring, but I've never seen all three in one. "Is it hard?"

"Nah, it's good motivation," Breunig says, as the others dig into their soup. "I want them to grow up in a world without vipes and whatever else." My heart kicks up a notch, but I know this dance. Pretend to agree. Words aren't literal poison. You can smile through them, no matter the dose. He fills space. "You figure people have been messing around with active qi for what, twenty years, give or take? This is the tip of the iceberg. When something else comes down the pike, it's going to be bigger and nastier and stronger."

"And we're gonna be there," says Olsen.

"Giving some!" says al-Ibrahim, and they bump fists. The others pass it along, and Olsen even walks over to reach Roland. I return the gesture, escaping into the moment to feel the vibe. As the conversation carries on, I look at each F-prot. They feel closer to me than I do to them.

I can live with guilt—I know this from experience. It makes me tougher when I feel it and freer when I don't. If I just forget about what's right and what's wrong for a little while, I can feel loved by good people. And if it takes a double life to get that feeling, then at least I've managed to increase my chances somehow.

But I can't forget forever. And when I see Roland by the door, waiting for some vipe to try something, I know he's waiting for me.

19 - INFINITY

August 19th

Kern emerges from the fitness center pool after one lap and strides over to a towel he's tossed on a white plastic chair. I hardly recognize him out of pinstripes. I wouldn't be surprised if he's selected the meeting place just to show off his body, which looks pretty good for someone his age. He's not triggering my appetite, though—all I smell is a nose full of chlorine.

"Have a seat," he says, working the towel. "I guess you don't have a suit."

"Fresh out." I'm fully dressed and jacketed with little plastic booties over my footgear because the swim area likes hygiene more than recycling. "You pick this place for a reason?"

"No listening devices," he says. "And it clears the head. I could use some circulation. That conference room was deadly."

"When you called, I wasn't sure I'd still have a job. Or you either. I thought in our company, failure means you wake up with a horse's head in your bed."

Kern smiles, which is not what I expect. "Not everyone in our structure is a staunch ally of the F-prots, but it'll take a lot more than Morgan Lorenz to bring me down." Eye contact, easy posture. Is he clueless? "You don't believe me."

"When someone says they're invincible, that's when I start measuring the coffin. They've got to consider having you resign—I mean, if everything goes public, it just takes one guy in management or one F-prot to roll on you."

Kern shrugs. "The F-prots' hands are dirtier than mine. People up the food chain are more dangerous, but there's a more likely scenario than whistleblowing."

"Which is?"

"Everyone's giving contradictory strategies, and no one's respected enough to be in charge."

I absorb that. "Okay. But the news said we're having a hearing soon..."

"Our legal department has more coordination than management does."

I don't give a damn. I focus on playing Little Miss Wide Eyes. "I heard Lorenz can't technically have a class-action suit in Virginia or something."

Kern makes a face. "That's why it's federal. The damages he wants are over five million dollars, so strap in, and say hello to the honorable Param Bayat."

"Were you the one who suggested the defense? Because it's kind of... unusual."

Kern's face goes flat, and for an instant, I see a hint of deadliness. Then, it disappears. "Roland always said this was going to happen eventually, no matter what we did. But we had two reasons for F-prot, and keeping the secret was the less important one. The vipes *have* to be contained. We need to make that argument, and this is going to be our best chance."

He hasn't really answered my question, but I jump on his last statement. "And if we lose in federal, then what? Take it up to the Supreme Court or something?"

"We're not going to need a second shot," says Kern. "You know why?"

I don't give him the satisfaction of guessing. My eyes dart over to some skinny, old guy doing laps in the pool and a teenage lifeguard watching him. No one is within hearing range—the kids yelling in the shallow end take care of that.

Kern answers himself. "This isn't the same world as it was ten years ago. It used to be athletes were on steroids. Pretty soon, they'll be juiced with so much active qi, you'll be able to bounce bullets off the chests of the Ravens' defense.

"Used to be kids were prowling college hangouts with date rape drugs. There's cases now of stimwebbing the girls and giving them orgasms just by touching their wrists."

I've never heard of this shit. "Say what?"

Kern nods, barreling on like it's nothing. "Yeah, try convincing a jury you meant 'no' while questions about *that* are flying. Now, you take all that and put it in front of a judge who is what, seventy-five years old and hates everything about this century from data plans to mandatory electric cars, and you've got yourself a chance. Then, you add in the magic word, the V-word." Kern pauses for effect. "That word is *video*."

I blink.

"They show you the video in L.A., don't they? Sikorsky's death?"

"Is that even evidence? Lorenz didn't do that."

"It's not evidence of shit," Kern corrects. "It's a *story*. A story that has yet to be told, on TV screens or phones. A phenomenon yet to be. Ani Sikorsky is going to be the public face of what these sick fucks do when they are hungry.

"That turned-over SUV is going to be burned into the minds of middle-class America, and then it's going to get replay in *election ads*, hon. This time next year, we're going to affect an *election*."

My stomach clenches. Part of me wants to scream and wipe that look off Kern's face: that animated, fervent look of a true believer. And yet, there's another urge, to be taken in by his enthusiasm, and damn the consequences. I can see why his wife married him, why BRHI put him in a leadership position. He can make people believe things.

"Anyway," he says, all cool again, "you wanted to see me about staying on in D.C. If Darcy's agreeable, so am I."

Focus. Play serious. "Yeah, I don't want to go home. I had a bad breakup and a million other personal things, and now I owe one to that Lorenz clown. You know?"

Kern nods. "Most of the team considers it personal now."

"Trouble is, if I get banged up again, then Breunig and the rest will think I'm the girl who always fails. And I'm going to be sidelined.

So, I need to be useful around here in other ways. I need to redeem myself."

He pauses, reading me. "What jobs do you think are not being done?"

I buy a second to think. "Way to put me on the spot." Cute smile. "I know a fat nothing about your operation, but I've got a security clearance. I say we use it. I mean, whenever I hear about cover-ups on the news, people delete stuff, but they forget to delete the order to delete or something, and that's how they get caught."

Kern looks sly. "We've had to do similar jobs before. If you want, I could supervise you on a cleanup team. The more supervisors you have with recommendations, the easier it is to climb around here."

"I'd like that." Infinity the liar again.

He stands. "Well, time's wasting. I'll give you a call when we need you, and right now, I should get this chlorine off me. Unless there was something else?"

I wonder again if there's anything I'm doing that sets him off. Was I looking at him like he's a meal? I've been getting pangs of hunger that don't feel bad yet, but I've been learning the hard way that they can take me from zero to crazy in a matter of hours.

I seize on the first thought in my head. "What's Roland's real name?"

Kern pauses. "How did that come up?"

"He said only you and Breunig know it. Is that club just for boys or something?"

"It's for people he trusts." I find myself looking at the floor, and Kern touches my hand. "I'm sure he'll find the chance to tell you sometime."

"Yeah," I say. Shit, I said it distantly. Focus. "I'm meeting him today."

"I've got to go plan a video roll-out. You stay cool."

"Yeah," I repeat. I'll see him again. Hopefully, before zero to crazy.

* * *

I shift from foot to foot by the grocery carts outside the Whopper Mart, scoping people out and wondering about things. Roland got a good look at my qi signature, but as soon as I snatch somebody, the change will be as obvious as rainbow clown hair. I *think*. I don't *know*.

From what the F-prots say, vipes typically go one to two weeks between blood meals. The real addicts, the easiest to catch, want it all the time. The smart ones hold back and put predation into their schedules. I intended to be the latter, but this week's events have thrown my plans out onto the lawn and changed the locks.

By my calendar, it's been fourteen days since I fed. Not bad, considering how much I've been through in so little time, but there's no way in hell I'm going to survive a year if all I'm going to get per bite is two lousy weeks.

The pangs have gone from twinges to a full-on grinding weakness as I wait for Roland to show. I thought I could tough it out—the pain this morning was comparable to cramps, so I broke into my ibuprofen—but the pills don't take away much. I'm loitering by the Whopper Mart's door, squinting in the sun that shines plenty bright but doesn't penetrate the chills.

I watch people going into the store alone and consider trying to grab one before meeting with Roland—though perhaps "fantasize" is a more accurate term than "consider." I could make an approach, true, and probably get some poor fool into my car or motel room, but then what? Once I do the deed, I'll need to wash up and probably a change of clothes, and then there's what to do with the poor sap, depending on if the victim is likely to live or... or whatever.

I can't do it, so my game plan is to conceal symptoms until Roland leaves. A little blush helps the pale skin. Hands in my pockets hides the shakes. As for the sunlight, I squint rather than wearing telltale sunglasses. I might have to suck up the fashion faux pas and shoplift a baseball cap.

"Hello."

I startle. Roland is right next to me, and I never saw him coming. It's embarrassing. I'm supposed to have great senses and keen jiujutsu paranoia, and here he is, a trained vipe-swatter a meter away.

"Don't do that."

"All right," he says. He has no need to ask what I mean. I bet if I ever snuck up on him, he'd get just as twitchy. "Do we want a basket or a cart?"

"Cart. Your little safehouse is out of everything."

"And your hotel room?"

"I'm dropping it to crash at the house, if that's cush. Better than charging the company for every night, right?"

"It is, as the kids say, cush."

"Okay, now I'm never using that word again." The next few minutes are relatively painless. I concentrate on breathing and pushing the cart and try not to think of strangulation, of sharp implements, of the warm flesh of his neck. He has a nice animal smell; I focus on identifying his shaving cream. "How old are you, anyway?" I blurt out.

"I read *Shady Side of the Universe* when I was an undergraduate. You probably saw the series when you were what, twelve?"

"My dad hated Ulan and everything about qi. I think it scared him." The memory is not a welcome distraction but a necessary one. "I snuck over to a friend's house for it, though. I can still remember Ulan demonstrating with magnets or something, and I was like, 'where's all the flying kung fu and the shooting qi bolts out of your hands?'"

"Sorry," says Roland, "I can hurt people with straight lines of yin qi, but they're short. Bolts will have to wait. Flight... even worse."

"It's not possible?"

Roland smiles and does an Ulan impression, making his speech slow and breathy. "Just as William Gilbert, measuring a lodestone's field in the year 1600, could not predict the creation of computer disks, we cannot predict the consequences of measuring a biophysical field. Qi has changed me, and in my lifetime, it will change the world."

"You sound less Ulan and more Scarlett O'Hara." I pile toothpaste and other toiletries into the cart. "I gather that's in the book."

"It's the part with the magnets," he says.

I attempt to remain unruffled. "And now we know why I can't shoot qi beams."

"Anyone can do it. Passive qi is just life doing its thing. Making it active takes time and discipline."

"Says you with an M.D. and nano-wire in your body. How long did that take to implant?"

"About a year and another year to learn how to use. But you could do the same."

"If I had discipline, I wouldn't be shopping for food while hungry."

"You said you had a first-degree black belt in Brazilian jiujutsu," he says. "They don't give those out for participation."

"That's different." It is. "That's therapy. And if it were all just will and strategy, it'd be one thing, but turning them into math, it's moon language to me."

"It's mostly memorization, then eyeballing how hard to push. And everyone fails at it to some degree. Come on, you wanted clothes."

We browse quietly on the second level, where I pick out a do-rag to keep my hair and sweat out of my eyes. Then, it's back to the first floor to pick up food, which I get without comment from Roland. That's a minor triumph—a balance between the starvation diet of a vipe living on liquid and the high-calorie intake of vipes who eat anything they want when freed from nutritional constraint. Brown rice, eggs. Normal staples. If a weakness shows up, it's in my thirst—I pick up soymilk and plenty of a crossbred citrus GMO juice called Gen-Five.

"So, my fantasy was qi beams," I say. "What's yours?"

"I'm pretty happy doing what I do."

"Secret of adulthood: nobody's happy. Come on."

He makes eye contact, and for a second, it isn't cold. "Teaching," he says. "Jessica always had a leg up on me."

"I heard you run the classes for door entry and hand-to-hand."

"That's all right," he says. "Keeps us in shape. But BRHI in the early days... we weren't afraid to nerd out. Well, depending on the subject matter. I became... unpopular."

"Hah! Too geeky for academia. Love it."

"Quite the opposite. Ulan wanted theory. I wanted application. She tried to curtail my research, so in the spirit of freedom, I packed my bags and found another employer. They liked my tricks, but they made me shave my head."

"Military? Nice."

"Back when China was doing its thing with the Ryukyu Islands, they sent me to Okinawa. They gave me an aptitude test, saw what I could do with a stimweb... it was a lot of me showing very scary men and women where to put the needles."

What the snot does this guy consider scary? "You come out in one piece?"

"I don't like the sound of drones," he says. "Some bad dreams. You?"

"What, like..."

"You had a literal near-death experience. I should know if you're holding up okay." Pause. "As your partner."

"I don't have nightmares." It's a lie, a big one, so I clarify. "About work."

"Really?" he asks, and his eyes are unnaturally green and steady, as though he's genuinely concerned. I think I smell Edge Fresh Scent and Type A positive. He would taste fabulous.

"Mine is all kid stuff," I say, ruthlessly forcing memories back into the lead-lined mental boxes where I keep them locked. "I do have recurring dreams, though." I leap in with enthusiasm, grateful to have another subject. "I know it's all crazy Freudian. Just be quiet and listen. It's that I have a box filled with snakes, but they all want to go exploring. They crawl out, so I have to put the snakes back in the box, but some of them are poisonous, and some of them will eat one another. Consequently, I have to separate them, and it makes my job hard."

"Snakes," he says, with a little smile.

"It's not scary. I love snakes," I say. "I was in this photo shoot once where I wore pythons, and they were super cuddly. But in the dream, there's too many in the box, going in different directions—I told you it was Freudian. Stop giving me that look."

"What look?"

"Like the snakes represent, you know, dicks, or the box—"

"I was thinking vipes. Considering how close you came to being bitten."

"Oh." I feel myself blush and brush a lock of hair over my ear. It's been a long time since I last went red. "This started long before."

We finish with the groceries, making small talk while customers and clerks are within earshot. When we're out rattling the cart across the asphalt, the conversation picks up again.

"I'm surprised more victims don't come forward," he says. "It's one of the deepest human fears, cannibalism. But with vipes, it's different. Did you know the report rate on surviving victims is only about ten percent? No mind control. The victims just... don't seem to want to."

I park the cart by my car, looking at the ground. I'm not sure if it's because of the sun. "Doesn't surprise me."

"They probably think no one will believe them."

"That," I say, "and it probably fucks them up. I mean, most victims aren't strangers. You ever had a friend or a relative turn on you like that?"

"I'd rather not—"

"Okay, bad question, but you get the picture, right? When it's someone you know, it gets in your head, and it takes sorting out." Oh, boy. Uncomfortable silence incoming. I cover. "But listen to me. I'm getting weird when it's probably just what you said. They think no one will believe them." I start loading the bags into the trunk. How did I end up talking about this? Roland seems like he's mulling, which I don't want. Keep going. "You know, they tell us in training that there's supposedly this rush, and it's all sexualized and stuff, but there's something they never mention."

"Which is?"

"Being bitten fucking hurts," I say, slamming the trunk. "Bitten hard enough to draw blood? That's movie-lies, like how people are always having sex and falling off the bed, and they keep going, but when you actually do it, you start saying, 'Ow, Jesus, get off me.'" Roland laughs, so I keep it up. "Or kissing underwater. You're treading water so much your heart is going like this," I hit my hand rapidly against my collarbone, "and all you can think is 'air. Give me air.' The whole sexy bloodsucking thing—I don't buy it."

Roland's smiling. "There are opiates released," he says, like he's admitting something, "triggered by the yin-qi exposure."

"Oh, come on, there are better ways to get high. You can smoke, you can snort, you don't need *stitches* every weekend." That makes us both laugh, and I'm not sure whether to blame him or me for knowing it's all false. "I mean, if I had a boyfriend, and he took a bite of me, I'd be like, 'You're driving me to the ER, and when I get out, you will have tequila and ice cream waiting.'"

He takes the cart off and sends it rolling back into the rack, and the moment is gone, replaced by less giddy thoughts.

"I think this is where we take separate cars," he says. "I trust you'll be okay alone?"

"Yeah," I say, but his brow crinkles, and once again, I guess he might have some kind of qi function or whatever going on, detecting if I'm lying. I want to come clean. Semi-clean.

"Maybe he did scare me a little," I admit. "I mean, I don't know how long I was out or how long I had left. If you'd gotten there a minute later..." I drift off and realize just how real it was. "Listen to me, getting all choke."

"Do you want to leave the containment team?" His voice is formal, but I can smell the slight tang of fresh sweat, a new flavor. I thought Morgan was crazy when I heard he'd checked himself into police protection, but the more I think about it, the more I realize it could be a strength. I'd never have survived my old traumas alone—sometimes you need to go to the cops, to the crisis centers, to your friends. And if you can trust them, if you can stick with it, like Morgan did, you can be groundbreaking news. But not me. I run.

Not today, though.

"No," I let myself say. "I had a talk with Kern already."

"Was there yelling?"

"No, none. I want to do some sanitization. Just... cleaning a lab."

Roland has on his Wait A Minute Face. "I should say, I don't know how you feel about germs, but for many people, a hot lab is more frightening than Lorenz."

"Not for me," I say firmly.

He looks at me, then away, fine-boned hands folding onto his elbows. He folds them weird—he leaves the hands resting lightly on top, ready for action, rather than tucked away under his biceps like a normal person. "Then, you two can bond while I handle our vipe."

I feel as if the words shrink me. Could I possibly have thought it would *help* Lorenz if I take my eyes off this man?

"We've got plans?"

"He's under police protection. Our usual methods won't work. Breunig and the squad are running down his location now. The news may have misinformation. Cops do that sometimes."

"When is this?" I ask. It might arouse suspicion, but I better risk it.

"End of next week, if not later."

Uh, what? "You want to delay?"

"Lorenz is hiding in the spotlight," Roland says, and his eyes are cold, green flakes. "I want him to discover all the problems being a celebrity entails."

Confusing images of paparazzi go through my head. A thought: "You want to dox him?"

"No. The Sikorsky tape is being released to the networks. If they air it, the question on everyone's mind will be, is Lorenz dangerous? He has made sure the whole world will be watching, but he has an addiction. What I intend to do is wait."

I like the sound of none of this, especially the high note in my voice, raised in reflexive protest. "The news said they're giving him blood."

"Cow's blood," says Roland. "They're draining hamburger

packages into a cup and reheating it. Is that what vipes live on?"

I twitch my tongue, realizing the cold calculation. I've always seen Morgan as more competent than me or at least thought I bought him a lot of time. I can hunt tonight, put an end to the thirst. Lorenz just surrounded himself with cops.

"No," I admit. "He's going to have to feed."

20 - RANATH

August 24th

The security wand sweeping over me makes me feel neither nervous nor secure. I've been through so many security checks, the motions are like the opening moves of chess. Sure, they have consequence, but grand masters can do them so fast nothing matters until the midgame begins. The wand chirps at my belt buckle, but I remove it and, in a moment, am cleared. I retrieve my tablet from the clipper cop who has bolted a sleeve onto it, chip plugged into its slot like a mosquito feeding. The little computer is part of my disguise, as much as the two plastic-coated badges around my neck. The sleeve and the forms I sign are the price I pay to get close.

They're doing their best to weed out biomancers, with a double prong of metal detectors and their own team's detection functions laid over the entrance. The functions pick up the copper that the metal detectors don't. Without a web, biomancers have very short ranges indeed.

The guards' submachine guns aren't for the biomancers. They keep away criminals faint of heart.

They won't find a stimweb on me today. The one I usually wear over the skin is gone, but my amplifying bioelectric tracks still lie hidden beneath the surface. They aren't looking for those, nor would they be good at finding them, all nano-thin niobium wire and non-ferrous materials.

I don't carry metal needles, either, but my jacket has four tacks in it, made of a Swiss ceramic and thirty percent glass fiber. To find anything unusual, the security officers would have to resort to a strip search, not an ideal method when there are some sixty-odd media people and twice that many tourists waiting. I don't get so much as a second pat-down.

I leave my phone behind in a plastic bag labeled with a name—not mine, of course. The press credential badge is the easiest part of the act. I maintain a few contacts with a hobbyist crowd whose pastime is ensuring that such credentials are made available to the masses—a phone call was all that was necessary to register myself as Gary Rosberg, a blogger based in New York. When the staffer assigned to seating arrangements did not say I was already on the list, I knew Mr. Rosberg was not attending. An hour and a forgebox later, and I had a visitor's badge for the day and a seat far to the left, on the red benches reserved for low-grossing media.

The cameras scattered about the room are an entire ecosystem. No two are alike. They're on hands, on shoulders, gimbal arms from a gyro-mount or planted on tripods. No drones, probably because the fans make too much noise. There are also precious few directed lights: the overheads are sufficient for modern autocorrection to take up the slack.

It's not hard to tell who has a premium news channel or a local affiliate. The talking heads on television are fashion plates in person, and they clog the view from the rear.

They've set up amid the benches, no doubt due to some fire safety rule regarding blocking the aisles. Their cameras among the old wood and the monitor screens off to the side of the bench make it feel as if the 1890s have been invaded by some alien technological race.

Behind the judge's bench stands an American flag, a Virginian flag and, on the wall, the state seal. A woman with a spear, a helmet, and an unbound breast is trampling a man beneath her, with Latin words meaning *thus ever to tyrants*. John Wilkes Booth said that phrase when he pulled the trigger. Aidan Lawrence echoed those words when he detonated a vest filled with fishing weights and Semtex in the Supreme Court. And yet here the words stay, suggesting bloodshed is not only part of legal proceedings but somehow can give them a blessing.

"All rise," says the bailiff, and the judge enters to take his seat. His appearance is startling. I ran the judge's name through a search engine and found it among a list of people scheduled for mandatory retirement, having received two extensions already. But modern medicine has been good to Bayat. He moves as if he were twenty years younger, his hair is still in place, and his beard, though white, is neat and short. He would be at home named to a Cabinet post somewhere or drinking Chablis on a yacht after a day of SCUBA diving. Actors would want to age like this man.

"Good morning. Please be seated. Now calling for the record the case of *Morgan Lorenz v. the Benjamin Rush Health Initiative.*" He reads off a docket number. "And if counsel would identify themselves for the record."

"Geoffrey Cho on behalf of the plaintiff," announces a dapper, black-suited, shaved-head attorney that I peg as younger than me. I can't see Lorenz. Instead, the room waits quietly as his defense attorney brings forth a small, pyramid-shaped device. "It is my honor to introduce Morgan Lorenz, who for security reasons will be attending virtually."

The gadget whirs and begins the chiming of something booting up. In a moment, an image appears in the air, a luminous ghost rendered layer by layer. Morgan Lorenz's virtual stand-in smiles and sits, clearing his throat as the projector's sensors record the room and play it back to the undisclosed location where the vipe is being held.

Fancy degrees notwithstanding, I'm an idiot. Virtual presence has been allowed in court for years, and Lorenz has motive. I have an app that might let me piggyback and trace the signal to its source, but I need my phone, which is back in security.

The three dark-suited BRHI lawyers announce their names with bloodless formality. The only name I catch is Eloise Campion. Kern had said she would be doing cross-examinations. I turn to the woman sitting next to me, who is busily fixing her lightfield camera. "You don't have anything I could use to look up Cho, do you?" I whisper.

She smiles. "I don't need a machine for that. What do you want?"

"Why Lorenz hired his firm. Isn't Lorenz a lawyer?"

"It's not his specialty, so he's not representing himself." She clicks the camera's cover back into place. I tune back in for the opening statements. I missed what Cho had to say. Campion is up.

"The Health Initiative was aware of the existence of this disease for some time before it was made public," she says. "To follow up on the motion to dismiss for lack of standing, we will be presenting the testimony of experts in qi-related DNA change. They will prove that the resulting damage means that Morgan Lorenz cannot be considered human under the terms of *Cagersheim v. Simmons*. We will also be presenting testimony as to the transmission rates of the disease and possible public health scenarios—" Bayat shifts in his seat, and the lawyer immediately wraps up. "Thank you."

She sits down. I tap my elbow with my finger, right where a tack would go. Bereft of qi functions, I'll have to read the BRHI team cold. They appear confident, calm—they know the real work comes later. Cho, on the other hand, seems in his element but a little hasty.

"*Interesante*," says the woman next to me, recording everything. She'll choose what the camera focuses on later.

"What is?" I ask. I know a few words in Spanish.

"We're going to get the longest pre-trial motion hearing ever," she says.

"That doesn't mean a lot to me."

"It's that whole not-human line of hooey. They're going to present evidence and expert witnesses to see if Lorenz will even get to evidentiary hearings." Based on my blank look, the woman prompts me. "You know, the part of a trial called *the trial?*"

I frown. "Is that tactic likely to be effective?"

"Unless Lorenz has the long green, yeah. Cho charges hourly, like everyone. Can you imagine the pricks who'd run out the clock on this?"

My thoughts flash to Infinity. She'll be in the lab tonight, the one where so much of this began. Not just VIHPS, but my work, my goals, the wiring built into my tissues and the energy that makes me *me*.

Infinity doesn't look very much like Emma Horiyama. I once worked with Emma in those labs, even lived with her briefly before she told me that my research into qi was scaring her. I replied that if *this* scared her, she'd better leave because I was going to change the world, one way or another. Infinity is taller than Emma, harder, all angles and sharp remarks.

And brave.

"Your Honor," says Cho, "motion to compel: the defendant has never fully acquiesced to our requests to access their laboratory in Reston, claiming at least three distinct lines of argument. First, they said it was not safe, then they cited trade secrets, now they are claiming routine data destruction wiped their records...."

One of the BRHI lawyers closes his body language, and I'm glad that Kern hasn't hesitated before acting. He and Infinity had better be in the ABEL lab tonight and have it evidence-free by morning, or who knows what they'll find?

As Cho goes on, and Campion's team claims something or other, I glance at the virtual Lorenz. He has said nothing audible. He is a wan, pale ghost of the man who had made last week's announcement. I stare. No matter how remote he seems, he's as predictable as any animal.

Bayat cracks the gavel. I tune back in again. "What is this, early lunch?"

"They need to verify records," says the helpful photojournalist. She aims her camera at herself, and I realize it's time to shut up and go.

I stand and slip my way through the crowd, scanning faces, guessing flow. Lorenz's legal team takes a moment to pack up their papers and device, and I delay by looking as if I'm tying my shoe. When I come up again, Cho has joined the foot traffic. I make a path, and when Cho reaches the doors, I take the opportunity to hold one and usher the lawyer out with the other hand. I can't make skin contact, not yet.

I keep my eyes down, watching feet, matching pace. I have to look harmless for another thirty seconds, to get clear. There wasn't a watch-mage visible on the way in, but that just means he's good at his job. There will be a detection net up, waiting to be tripped by the first function. I'm betting it is only indoors.

Cho's assistant is handing him back his phone by the metal detectors now, and I know I don't have time to snag my own. I have to get the sleeve off my tablet, now before Cho gets on the move again and into a vehicle. The damn attachments cost a few bucks, so they have proximity alarms on them like bookstore novels. I try to urge along the guard popping the plastic bolts, but I hold off making trouble because that is a fast way to nowhere. Nowhere is failure.

I look over the guard's shoulder just as Cho vanishes out the door.

I pour on the speed as much as I can in the crowd and emerge into the sun only to find Cho has, mercifully, not gotten far. He's on the marble steps of the court, surrounded by genuine media that sticks to him in an ever-larger clump as more of them come out the door. It's good for immobilizing him and also for producing an impenetrable wall of bodies.

Cho talks. I don't listen. I need a story, an excuse, as simple as brushing a nonexistent bug off him or a clumsy faux stumble because I am a tangle-footed camera hound, and gosh, I didn't mean to make skin contact to fire the function—

The function. I hastily feel for the tacks in my pocket and put one in my ear while Cho talks. Then, one up the sleeve I wear loose so I can reach my own elbow and one on the top of my head.

"That's all for today. No more questions, thank you—"

Cho is moving, and I need one more tack. I insert it into the side of my wrist once, twice, three times, drawing little dots of blood as I get it wrong, and I start the locator function, attempting to balance power without the calming pulse of a dialed-up web.

"Mr. Cho? Mr. Cho, hi—" I begin and feel the tack sink in correctly. "Gary Rosberg, 'The Incisive Amateurs.' We're a little blog from up the coast—"

"I'm sorry. I told everybody that's all for today," Cho repeats.

"This is also personal," I find myself saying, and I can tell by the expression that I've bought a half-second as Lorenz's counsel reconsiders. Cho's associates, all in suits, are also staring at me, and I'm trying not to think about one of them being a bodyguard. "I wanted to thank you for representing the infected," I blurt. "I used to know one."

"Really? Would I know the name?"

Ulan, I don't say. "You might, but that's not important. It just means a lot to me that she might be compensated for her suffering. I... I don't even know where she is now. She's essentially on the run."

"I'm sorry to hear that," Cho says, and I know what he'll say in the next breath. "But I have to go, so if you want an interview, you can call the office—"

"I only wanted to shake your hand. You're defending real people, you know." My fingers meet Cho's, and they clasp.

"I know," says Cho.

"Tell me, how are you feeding him?"

Cho blinks. "We have volunteers. If there's nothing else—"

"Forget it," I say. Cho looks at me strangely as the pulse-points fire.

Bang.

Cho and his attendants leave in a group. I permit myself a small smile. There is work to be done, and it could still prove to be grueling, but it is not something to be feared.

The middle game has begun.

21 - INFINITY

August 24th

You know what sucks? Vipe senses and the smell of bleach. The Advanced Biophysics Experimental Laboratory is full of it. Worse, science is officially a thing I don't know my way around. All I remember from school is wearing a lot of protective gear and doing agonizingly methodical measurements. I asked to be excused for religious reasons, and when they gave me a form to say which religion, I wrote down "spontaneity." Then, I tried to prove my faith.

The security booth in front of the lab is empty. Kern goes to shut the cameras down after showing me to the first decontamination chamber (*first?*) and telling me to wash. I take off my clothes, stand under a decon shower that feels like fizzy, whipped cream against my skin and carefully follow all the icon-heavy instructions on the wall. I'm taping down the legs and sleeves of the disposable paper scrubs when Kern knocks.

"Did this project have a name?" I ask when I'm ready.

"Skia," he says. "Means 'shade,' as in yin qi being the shady side of a mountain. Should have been 'Pandora' if you ask me, but hey, you can't always be eerily prophetic."

I don't get whatever reference he just made and climb awkwardly into the heavy, plastic hazmat suit. I've never worn one before. I twitch a bit when Kern uncoils a yellow air hose from the wall and plugs it into my armpit.

My helmet unfogs instantly from the rush of air, and the suit inflates, a hard, swollen shell around me. My hearing is suddenly consumed by the electric whir of the fan's motor, covering even the sound of my own breath. In one orange, rubber glove, I hold the burn bag, strangely out of place in the sterile environment.

Kern waves his keychip at the second door to let us both in.

"How do we kill the stuff?" I ask. Kern doesn't answer, so I repeat the question, yelling to be heard over the roar of air.

He adjusts the volume on the radio to be heard. "Used to be, we didn't even know." He hefts a box of decontaminant and breaks open the seals. It's bluish goo. "This is new. Don't get any on you. It makes Drano look like water."

I grab my share, letting the negative air pressure of the level 5 lab suck me inside. My infection improves my sense of balance, but sometimes it's creepy. It's like my body does things on its own or does them with only a tiny push from me.

I stop at the large, stainless steel sink, where Kern leaves the goo. He walks into an enormous freezer at the far side of the room, and around then, I realize how ridiculous this is. I need to get a sample we can match to Lorenz's infection. But what the hell do I know about bio-evidence? All I know about viruses is that it isn't good to get one, and a fat lot of help that's been. I mean, I've seen some late night forensic shows, so maybe I could check where the sink eventually spills out. But Kern obviously thinks the goo will destroy any chance at DNA typing; otherwise, he wouldn't use it. I need something else and fast.

"What should I do?" I yell.

"Start with the tissue samples. We got them, but we need to wash the guck."

Kern motions to another walk-in freezer. I cross the room, looking at the signs that this lab had once been an office like any other. Someone printed out an online comic, a vampire trying to shave without being able to see himself in the mirror. It's taped up on a cabinet over an electron microscope and a pad full of jotted notations that I don't understand. It's math, it's physics, a secret language I never learned. That means I am far from welcome here.

My breath comes short and shallow. This is the room where a creature was born that now lives by the millions inside of me. I can't kill it. I can't run from it or even confess my fear of it. This room has one purpose now and that is to study and destroy me the moment I utter a word of the truth.

My steps slow as I near the freezer. The air hose blows too loud for me to hear anything behind me. I look back frequently: traitor's looks.

If he could see me now. At moments like this, there is only one person I ever mean by "he." I've practiced cover-ups since I was nine and the traitor's game since I was fourteen. *Born and bred in the betrayal patch, motherfucker.*

Indecision hits me. Can I actually get away with sabotaging this? I thought somehow I'd turn this against BRHI, perhaps switch a label somewhere, but Kern is taking charge. Now, he's removing refrigerated sample jars by the armload and setting them by the sink.

I open the freezer door.

Inside, on the plastic shelving, is visible blood. Nothing tasty—congealed, unappetizing residue. Like a package of ground chuck, some plastic bag of some*one* left this calling card behind. But the bags themselves are gone.

Tissue samples. This is what becomes of the bodies I last saw in a hot van.

"Double bag the drips, stick them in the biohaz boxes, then autoclave them. We'll drop everything by the path-incinerator on the way out." Kern says the words way too easily. I think maybe "path" is for "pathogen" and don't know what an autoclave is.

To avoid looking nervous, I shove trays into the super-Ziploc disposal bags, carefully reading and trying to remember the names on the labels—*Alta, Delano, Kaplan, Ulan, Kern*—the last the only indication they are the names of scientists, not victims.

A few have notations, handwritten scrawls that are stone-cold psycho. "Subject torpidity reached in thirty-two days without blood," says one. I can only imagine the terror of the woman, captured live, probably still clueless to her condition. She'd be imprisoned, slowly starving to unconsciousness and then, much later, death. Another note is simpler: "Reaction to fire consistent with computer model." I gingerly touch the petri dish with black specks. Is that charred skin from a vector who was cremated? Or burned alive?

"When you're done with that, we'll need all the computers bricked." Kern opens vial after vial into the sink, coated in blue chemicals, and my stomach churns as I try to figure out if there is any evidence I can salvage before it's all gone.

I toss the last of the tissue samples into boxes, packed up like picnic coolers for the incinerator. Holding my hands under the decon nozzle, I wash them in a stream of bleach, then approach the four computers on the far wall.

"That I can do," I say. "Let me at it."

"We've already done the F-prot office computers," Kern says as he works. "But no one's been in here since Lorenz's announcement."

I flick a button, logging into the network with the password Kern gave me—which I memorize just in case, but it'll probably be changed within the hour. I find myself opening the files for project Skia. I read quickly, trying to look like I'm deleting.

I need to distract him. "Is this where it happened? With Ulan and all that?"

"I was right over there by the diamond slicer."

"What was she doing? I mean, how did it...."

"She had a petri dish with a cross-section of mouse brain in it. It was brimming with EBL, and she was bombarding it with yin qi. Should have killed anything, if you ask me." Kern has stopped moving. "Then... I guess she was tired or inattentive because she reached for the dish, and there was this pop like a gunshot, and the dish was plastic fragments everywhere, and some got through the suit into her hand."

I cover my right hand with my left. "And you didn't quarantine her?"

"Our specialist biomancer fried her. Like I said, no virus should've survived that. And we hit her with the decon shower. We cleaned the wound, and I drove her over to Helix Health for a gamma globulin test. Turns out dosing EBL-4 in pure yin is like trying to squash an anthill by pouring sugar on it. You know what the only clue was?"

I stop staring at him. The screen has what I want. "What?"

"I asked if she was feeling okay, and she said, 'Just a little hungry.'" Kern's voice comes out slow and falters a little. "So, I took her to get waffles. Problem solved, right?"

"I'm sorry." I listen to the air blower in my suit as the silence stretches on. I take control. "Looks like you've got a wipeout program right here. Check back in ten." He turns away. Score. He's too distracted to question the plan. It helps to think of Kern as an enemy, but I'm hard enough that I don't need help.

I call up each machine on the network and copy the overwriting software onto each. I fire it off on all but one and start to sift. Then, I hit the proverbial wall. I don't have the training to wade through the "levels of antibody binding to the soluble antigens," and the "carboxylic acid added to the phenoxybenzyl moiety." I need something that Lorenz's lawyer can recite in a minute and mean, "BRHI invented this thing, hid its existence by killing everyone who caught it, and goddamn it, at some point, they've got to *pay*."

In just five and a half minutes, Kern comes my way. Quickly, I hit SEND, hoping I can get at least a page or two of incriminating documents. I hit the touch-screen, covering the transmission with a window showing the progress on the other computers.

"Don't waste time deleting," he says. "Just write over the drive."

"Way ahead of you," I say. "See?"

"You do this a lot?"

Fake smile. "I like privacy. You want to wipe the last one?"

With a few key strokes and a plastic-covered thumb against the screen, he does. It leaves a print, the grease of some hot agent, probably.

I bite my tongue. Even with the air blowing inside my suit, I'm sweating. I wonder if this is how the victims of serial killers feel in their last moments. Kern busies himself on the other side of the room, totally unconcerned about whatever specters are floating in my head.

I can do this. I've lied about worse. But the truth always comes out, doesn't it? Not at first, but today I'm pretty far past first.

I blank the last machine. I have no idea if the computer transmitted anything useful. I still need a good skewer to wound BRHI.

"Get the rest of those vials. I'll go over the equipment."

I need an idea and, the way my heart is beating, also a horse tranquilizer. I walk to the sink. Kern is going over the counters with a goo-covered sponge. I pour vials down the sink, following each with a glob of blue, then check behind me.

Kern is spraying bleach from a hand-pumped spritzer onto the microscopes and centrifuges. I have a chance.

As I pour out the contents of the next flask, I splash a bit of one sample on the center of my left glove. When Kern turns back, I clench my hand, and the bloody spot vanishes.

After that, it's easy. Kern finishes the counters and pulls out a sink trap. He coats both sides with blue. He's thorough but not suspicious. I go for the documents, stuffing notebooks and memos into the burn bag. I make it back to the level 2 area and look at my glove, hoping that handling the papers hasn't brushed away the trace of European Bat Lyssavirus.

With my blower unhooked now, I can hear Kern at the incinerator. I snatch the dry-erase marker from the sign-in board and draw it across my palm, the plastic cap scraping just a little out. I drop the marker and cap silently into my pile of discarded clothes. Soon, those will go on, and the cap will go into my pocket.

My eyes water when I take off the suit, and it isn't just from the chemical stench. I keep a tight hand over my pocket as we visit the pathological incinerator at the back of the building. In go the burn bags. As the flames flare around them, I repeat the research team's names in my head. If there is one thing I can do, it is memorizing.

Alta, Delano, Kaplan, Ulan, Kern.

It will have to be enough.

22 - MORGAN

September 1st

I stare at my Lemon Coke and my cigarettes, wondering if they're both defective. I turn the package of Menthols over in my hands, trying to remember if I've seen anything about the company lowering the nicotine level or something. It's the last indignity I need.

I've gotten used to the police around me, a feat that has taken nearly all the patience, diplomacy, and milk of human kindness I have left. My initial night in their custody was a mess that rivaled waiting in an understaffed emergency room. First, there was a receptionist, then a sergeant, then desk workers, all saying to stay with them. Just as it had seemed I was getting somewhere, the shift change was up, and I had to re-explain everything to the next cop who came on duty. Gunmen entered my house and killed my friends and my dogs. Yes, I am employed. No, there were actually two houses. No, I do not have medical documentation of my condition on me, but I can bench-press a motorcycle if you like.

That last did not go over well. I am cordial but not popular with the police at the station. They don't look forward to bodyguarding famous targets who have already been through one assassination attempt. Some didn't believe me, but when one of them put a book down loudly, I jumped. Word got around: I was no fake.

My victories have been limited. I spent the last few nights in a holding cell usually reserved for suspects awaiting their arraignments. I preferred it to any hotel with a flimsy wooden door, but I was up all night worrying about its lack of an escape route. There's an officer specifically devoted to me out in the bullpen, a young type who tells the TV crews that Mister Lorenz is not available for interviews.

Still, the reporters camp out in the waiting room. They clog the station bathroom and drink the vending machine dry. All this just for one shot of me walking out with a cashable expression on my face.

Sour look, jubilant smile, anything that can be fed into the first half of a sentence about me meeting my court date. I loved disappointing them with the virtual appearance. Let them wallow in vampire hype and then eat footage of lawyers, carrying a box.

It didn't take long for Net-savvy people to find my police station. My mail, both e- and paper, is a hodgepodge. I've got friends, even now, who send me links to op-ed pieces, logged chatterbot conversations, and headline collections. I have letters from lawyers trying to outcompete Cho. I got a voice message from a man with liver cancer asking me to infect him so he won't have to take so many drugs. Then, there's the nun who told me Jesus could burn the virus out of me if I walked in the sun, sandwiched between two requests from agents offering a generous price for the print, motion picture, and electronic game rights to my life story.

I guess the story might sell. It has tragedy hitting me at a young age. It has a self-made man narrative if you hype up me clawing my way into law school. But this pseudo-fame isn't about me. It's about some myth of sexy undead superheroes that's been in people's heads long before I came on the scene. Cashing in on that seems worse than dirty. It seems irrelevant. If I can afford to be morally superior, don't I have an obligation to do so?

I put the cigarettes away, turning to my other reading material: the bio-safe Coke bottle. After a second, I throw it out. The caffeine has done nothing to stop my withdrawal headache. There's no recommended serving size for a vampire and worse, I have no idea what I need to eat. I drank so much bagged blood yesterday, it made me sick. When I tried fast food afterward, the fried chicken came up, along with the genetically modified potato cakes. I sat by the toilet, muttering to God, asking what I needed to drink or snort or smoke to take the edge off. Nothing will work, but I can't stop hoping.

This morning was no better. I spent it with six pounds of raw hamburger, draining the runoff into a cup. Thin. Salty. Useless.

"Morgan," says Luis, a uniform who has pulled the late shift. "We gotta go."

"What's happening?"

"Your transfer got approved. Come on, man, get your stuff."
Here, "stuff" means my jacket, puffed out in all pockets with carb-
ridden snack foods. I snatch it from a locker outside the cells and
throw it on. I make a phone call as I walk.

"Geoff, I need a donor and not here at the station. Guys, where
are we going?"

"We'll be taking a cruiser," Luis says. "Out the back. I'll get the
fire door."

"I need to know the location," I insist to Luis.

Cho's voice comes over the phone. "No can do."

Right on the heels of that, Luis says "Sorry, you can't tell anyone."

I stop. Cho needs answering first. "What? You said we had a
donor."

"We had five, but I put the waivers in front of them, and they
backed out." Luis gestures frantically, and I absently follow him, mind
on the phone.

"So do it without a waiver, just *now*. Cow blood doesn't work—"

"Morgan, I can't do this. There's a little voice in my head saying
forget it, and it's *right*. I can't advise that you open yourself up to the
exact same kind of wrongful infection suit that we're spearheading
here. These will be newly infected people who will think you have
money. You will get nailed just like we are nailing the Health
Initiative—"

My ear bounces away from the phone, and I dig the earbuds out
of my jacket. I ignore Cho while I head for the emergency exit. Luis
shuts off the alarm and unlocks the door. The lot behind the station
is wide, well-lit, and clogged with cars. No media in sight.

"Where are we going?" I ask.

"Can't tell you. We're just handing you off," says Luis. "FBI takes
it from there."

I hesitate, noticing for a moment that I've been led outside,
where there are no other cops. Has Luis been bought? Does he want
me to himself so I can be dropped off at hatemonger central? Just as I
get worried, another cop comes through the fire door: Pierce, the one
who escorts me on smoke breaks.

"You key in the map?" he asks Luis.

"It's nothing. We get to 395," is the answer. "Lorenz, come on."

I hook my earbuds in. Cho has hung up.

I follow them toward a cruiser, wincing at my stomach that is now imitating a clenched fist. I steady myself on a car, trying to breathe deeply. I breathe, but that's all.

"You okay?" asks Luis. "You look messed up."

"Medical condition," I say, "and an idiot friend." No one responds. I open the back door to the cruiser. At least it has tinted windows so the media won't ID me. Luis gets in on the other side, and Pierce is up front. I appreciate that Luis is in back so I don't feel locked in alone like a perp. I don't touch my seat belt, steadying myself by hand as the car rolls out. The scents come at me sharply: pine air freshener, vinyl seats, recirculated air.

"It's about an hour's drive," Luis says. "No problem."

"Easy for you to say."

"Did you have blood this morning? I know you were sick."

"I had cow blood. I need a donor," I say between gritted teeth. I fumble out a Menthol, tap it furiously against my hand and roll down the window. "I can't believe this. The only things I haven't tried for the pain are alcohol and heroin."

"Man, if you could survive on alcohol," Pierce laughs, "I know ten guys who would love to get bitten."

Don't scream. Don't scream. He doesn't know. I can't feel the nicotine from the cigarette anymore. Have I expelled it that fast?

"Maybe you got the flu," Luis says. "Lot of people in the station."

"You coulda picked it up from the burger," says Pierce. "Food poisoning or something."

I say nothing, making an effort to shut out their voices. I drop the cigarette out the window and close my eyes. My heartbeat is loud, and my head pounds with it. It brings anger and dread because I know what will happen next. It has happened before, in a friend's house, to someone with my name who looks exactly like me. But I didn't move my body. It moved itself.

I grab Luis's arm and bite into his wrist.

The fact that I'm sitting on Luis's right saves my life. The contact high is weak, and Luis doesn't go slack. Instead, he first struggles to pull me off, then awkwardly reaches for the pistol on his right side with his left hand. I feel it coming and shove up against him, trapping his hand in the tangle of arms. Pierce is yelling something from the front seat, but I don't care what.

The car swerves and hits something, probably the median strip, because then it lurches the other way across four lanes of traffic and off the road. I'm latched on to Luis's arms to avoid being thrown off him, but with the contact high gone, the officer starts to struggle with a purpose.

I have no skill, but I have a lot of strength. I dig my fingers into the bite wound as I grip Luis's arm harder and, with my other hand, seize him by the throat. Luis's left hand goes for the gun, but his angle is poor, and it falls uselessly from his hand. He puts the hand on my arm but can't pry off my clenched fist. The fist has his windpipe in it.

"Nine nine nine! Nine nine nine!" Pierce yells into the radio. "Shoulder of 395, get over here!" He's halfway turned in his seat and is undoing his seat belt. I can't reach him through the partition. If Pierce gets out and draws his gun, I don't stand a chance. Virus or not, I'll be a fish in a steel barrel.

I scramble to open the right rear door as Pierce goes out the front. He tumbles onto the asphalt and stays low. I have only one chance before Pierce comes around the back and empties the pistol into me. I slam into the car as hard as I can and shove like a football lineman.

The cruiser is driven sideways and strikes Pierce in the legs and body like a giant's club. I stumble and go down on all threes, but the damage is done. Pierce, too, is off his feet, knocked into traffic. There is a screech of brakes and an unmistakable thump.

My head clears, and I stare at the dent I just made in the car's frame. My shoulder is stinging, like it's one enormous bruise, but Pierce is done. He must be done, right?

Numbly, I circle around the car to see the mess. The driver of the car is still in shock, probably rethinking his entire life as he stares over the steering wheel. From what I know of personal injury, two things tend to happen when a car strikes a body. The body can go up onto the hood, or it can go down, under the wheels. Pierce, in his stumbling, went down.

I stare at Pierce's gun, now three meters from his hand. I look back to the driver, who sees something in his rearview mirror and turns back behind him. I follow the man's gaze.

One of the cars stopped in the near-lane pileup is a news van. Did they follow the cruiser from the police station parking lot? Or are they just lucky? I can see a man and a woman get onto the asphalt. The camera operator fires up the bright spotlight on the top of her machine.

The light spills over the bashed-in cop car. It spills over the driver who has stopped in shock, and it spills over me. I shield my eyes.

I probably could do something to save myself, perhaps seize the camera and hurl it to the ground. But none of this is happening. Look at the man at the steering wheel. He doesn't know what to do any more than I do. So, I just think. I stand by the still-running cars, and I touch my mouth. My fingers come away wet. The hands I raise to hold back the light do nothing but cast shadows across my face. The image of myself as a blood-spattered horror is now burned into the circuits of the video camera, captured and as immortal as anything ever really is.

23 - TRANSCRIPT

"The Blood Will Tell," *E Pluribus Magazine*
Released online and at newsstands on September 3rd
Morgan Lorenz's attack on two police officers
suggests VIHPS is a vampire virus even worse than feared

"I'M SUPPOSED TO BE THE LUCKY WIFE?" NINA
RODOLFO ASKS, and there are no tears, no quaver in her voice. We
are standing by her husband's bedside at the George Washington
University hospital, three days after the attack in which Morgan
Lorenz allegedly choked him unconscious and drank his blood. To
Nina, there is nothing alleged about it—her husband, Luis Rodolfo,
has undergone two transfusions. Now doctors fear that the lack of
oxygen to his brain while he waited for medical assistance may have
caused permanent damage. The only mitigating news is that it could
have been worse. Rodolfo's partner, Pierce Hauptmann, expired four
hours ago from the same attack. Hauptmann's family declined to be
interviewed for this article.

If it was a terrible week for the Rodolfos and the Hauptmanns, it
wasn't an easy one for the vampires, either. In Detroit this Tuesday,
police shot hit-and-run driver Neville Gleason over twenty times
before he finally succumbed to his wounds. The autopsy indicated
Gleason's tissues were suffused with a previously unknown, qi-
saturated lyssavirus, identical to the one volunteered for testing data
by Morgan Lorenz.

It did not take long for news of the vampire killing to be replaced
by the story of those the vampire had killed—Gleason had human
body parts cut up with a hacksaw at his Sanilac home, believed to be
the answer to over a dozen missing persons cases.

Across the country, police and the FBI have been examining
homicide files from the last ten years to see if vampirism might have
played a part. "This has sent us back to the books," said Dan Bremer, a

twenty-three-year veteran of homicide investigations in New York City.

But nowhere is the paranoia about VIHPS greater than the nation's capital. It is here that the face of vampirism first loomed large, and now those faces have grown younger: Rodora Redding, 15 and Aiko Tsunano, 16, infected two girls and eleven boys in their classes at the Sidwell Friends School, in what police informally call "the Trust Fund Clan." (See related article, p. 33, "The Monsters Next Door.") The D.C. police are instituting a curfew for those under eighteen. To help enforce it, they are calling upon off-duty and early-retired officers and pressing them back to work. Nor are they alone: National Guard units have been posted at the Mall and area airports. "The last thing we want," says one Sergeant Oliver Baker, "is one of these guys on an airplane with some political agenda. We don't know the full extent of their strength and have no intention of it being tested on a cockpit door."

Though such a move may have made the public feel more alarmed, not less, Wednesday's report by Surgeon General Cilana finally provided the panacea we were looking for. Framing VIHPS as a threat to public health rather than a malefic organization of boogeymen, she requested that anyone who had suffered a human bite or had saliva-to-blood contact within the last month to report to a hospital.

There, they would donate samples and be assigned case workers. Within hours, hospitals from Florida to Boston were packed with complainants informing on their friends and neighbors.

Which brings us back to the question we really want answers to: what made Morgan Lorenz need blood so badly that he was willing to attack two armed police officers? The incident did not occur from lack of planning. Lorenz, under medical advice, was consuming cow's blood and more traditional food throughout his stay in police custody.

At the time of the attack, he was being transported into FBI protection, where he was to be given more spacious quarters and a twenty-four-hour guard—everything an infamous vampire could want as he awaits his date with justice.

Motives to wish harm on Hauptmann or Rodolfo are equally elusive. Nelson Goetz, 40, was the uniform on shift before both men; he responded to Hauptmann's distress call when their car rode up onto the curb and was the first officer on the scene. "We're still investigating why this broke down the way it did," he says. "Lorenz got along with our officers. He didn't have a temper. He understood he wasn't safe anywhere else."

The answer seems to be in the blood, the stuff smeared all over the back of the Aero and the pavement. Symon Wagner and camerawoman Lana Miter of Channel 4 news recorded the now-viral footage of Morgan Lorenz, bloodstained and furious, yelling at them before fleeing the scene. His confused look seemed to say, it's the active qi. It defies all reasonable precautions; it is the master, and he is its slave. Like the man-eating plant in the old play *Little Shop of Horrors*, what Lorenz needs must be fresh, and it must be human.

Nina Rodolfo doesn't want to discuss her husband's chances of coming down with the virus. The bite nearly severed tendons in his wrist, and the saliva-to-blood contact is almost assured. She will take care of him as he heals and then wait for his attacker's day in court, whether he turns up as the plaintiff or gets dragged in as a defendant. She hopes when the decision comes, Luis will watch it with her, but more, she hopes he will not fall into the same legal category as Neville Gleason and Morgan Lorenz. We share a quiet moment together, and I try to leave the room before the doctor returns because her grief is, in its own way, infectious.

24 - INFINITY

September 4th

On top of everything else, my dreams have started to fuck with me.

I don't like using the word "nightmare." Before jiujutsu, I had nightmares. In the ones I have now, I fight back. So, my problem's usually with my conscious mind, when I toss and turn and stay up at all hours. Tonight, I'm completely out.

It begins with me locked in my room, memorizing verses—I'm around fourteen. I'm in sackcloth, a robe my father had to special order off the Internet. My classmates always taunted me for looking like a beekeeper, but I was just grateful it covered the bruises.

Aaron is there, which makes zero sense since I was out of this house long before I ever met him, but there we are, Old Testament study buddies, and he's asking me for verses.

"Proverbs 3:12."

"The Lord reproves him who he loves."

"Psalms 52:17."

Psalms are always tough. I manage. "The sacrifice acceptable to God is a broken spirit; a broken and contrite heart, O God, you will not despise."

He rolls up his sleeve, smiling, presenting me with my reward. I descend on his arm and bite into it, feeling it burst and dribble into my mouth, more like a fruit than a vein. He caresses the back of my head, and I go to work, licking and sucking. But he runs dry, and I have to bite further to get at anything good. This, too, doesn't make a lot of sense, but it's a dream, and logic is only a distant heckler in a box seat somewhere. I'm seeing, hearing, tasting the show firsthand.

Aaron loves it. He's gasping and running his free hand all over me and slips it beneath the robe to loosen my pants.

The room shakes. A fist—you know whose—is hammering at the door. Again, that's not true to reality because Andrew DeStard built his daughter's door to lock from the outside. I was a prisoner, and he could enter whenever he wanted.

"Fini!" comes the yell. The dream gets that right. Always my middle name. He never acknowledges my first.

I scramble, throwing a blanket over Aaron. I button up my pants. Then, I search for a gun, a knife, anything. But there's nothing, so I crouch, hands hooked into claws, ready to wrestle and fight. I have confidence, but, of course, the door never opens. The slamming sound grows, until I'm convinced that whatever is on the other side is three meters tall and has the strength of a bear. He's here. He's hunting me.

I twitch. Real body, not the dream. My mind unfogs and I wake, disoriented. I'm not in a bed but on the floor of a laundromat, listening to a washing machine frantically throwing its load against its walls. My phone says it turned into Friday about half an hour ago. I stand up and open the washer. I fish out jeans and towels wadded up into a morass.

The bloodstains on the towels came out better than I expected. Lady Macbeth can suck it. Of course, the lady is right if you get down to the forensic level, with those sprays and lights and swabs that can detect damn near anything, but what I need is something that doesn't make a horny twenty-year-old panic when he sees the cloth laid across the back seat of my car.

I clench my jaw, a little habit I have when I mentally kick myself. The horny twenty-year-old in question was left near a hospital, virus swimming through his veins, and I'm still not sure how I feel about that. I don't want a repeat of the trucker because that guilt still jabs me from time to time. But the other way, I'm just sentimental and stupid. I should have worn a ski mask. I should have pulled my gun. The boy can identify me. If he's infected—and really, when aren't they? —he'll perpetuate the chain unless Roland and the crew manage to track him down.

I could do it myself. I have the boy's wallet with his driver's license. If I need to tie off that end, I can find him. Finding the conviction to do so, that's a question for later.

I restart the washing machine, wondering if Roland is feeling smug that his watch-and-wait strategy proved right. Morgan has gone from crusading vigilante superhero to throw-the-remote-at-the-wallscreen blunderfool. My phone browser history is filled with text about his idiot-minded, impulsive, fucking *stupid* attack on two cops. He's no longer salvation; he's a weight around my neck. *This* is the nightmare. You can't spin second-degree murder, not even if you're—

The thought stops me. I have one very valuable marker cap, a file of dubious import, and a handful of names. What I don't have is Morgan's forwarding address. But someone else is in his corner. I saw that somewhere.

I pull out my phone and call up the name of Geoffrey Cho. A few more, and I find an address and phone number. The question is whether I should dial it.

I gamble. If I were Cho, I'd have cut Morgan loose in a second. He's business. Not a brother in arms, certainly not family. You don't tie yourself to a sinking ship and hope your deep breath will buoy it up.

But I'm not Cho. I have to forget my instincts and get a read on him based on something solid. I stay online searching his case history, and a different picture emerges. Morgan's a solid lawyer, but he grabbed Cho for a reason. The man hunts corporations. He got payouts that would be sickening in scope if the targets hadn't been chemical companies or, in one case, a private military firm.

That last makes me page-up and -down a few times. Cho has gone after the big boys, and there was at least one death threat. He followed through anyway. No wonder Morgan wanted him on his side. The F-prots are BRHI's little private army, but we're supposed to be surgical. We can't stand and bang against a militia or a country. Cho's resume has a win in that column.

The washing machine shuts off with a buzz, and I'm back to Earth. Morgan has fallen off his savior pedestal. And this Cho guy could be a horse rapist for all I know, but he sounds like a litigious badass, and right now, it is Cho or no one.

No one, of course, means Dr. Roland Cawdor.

I ruminate as I throw the laundry into the dryer. Why did he have to complicate an otherwise normal betrayer-betrayee relationship? I could have lived without him... just like I could have stayed in school and cured cancer. That's not all, though. Having someone to sit with me, hold the gauze to my throat and, frankly, worry about me, is something I've been missing.

He mentioned bad dreams, too. Has he lost someone? I remember him standing guard at Yarborough's room. Surely, that doesn't come from nowhere.

It's funny, in that way that isn't funny at all—Roland is professional without being cop-like, a criminal without being crude. I want to question him, all pretense abandoned. Which makes my next move sting a little.

I scroll down on my phone to a mail program I don't use often since it's old and hidden in a nest of folders. I finger it open and log in—password 2KINGSJEZEBEL. There's a single new message that isn't spam, from "ABELSec5," the Health Initiative's Advanced Biophysics Experimental Lab. I open the file. It's filled with data—modern computers can dump an ocean of work in an instant—but it's only slightly more comprehensible this time around.

I attack the corporate-speak with the determination of the smart but uneducated. A half hour later, I zero in on an e-mail referring to a memo I can't find, in which senior management orders that the employees cooperate in a cost-benefit analysis regarding consequences to BRHI's stock price and image should "nondisclosures be violated." That's calculations, the value the Health Initiative assigned to the lives of the infected. Farther down in the text, there's an excuse that education would not significantly drop the case numbers: the likelihood of transmitting the bug remains high regardless of the vector's knowledge of infection. They conclude that they should not disclose to the public; it is not to their advantage.

I scrape my teeth together, furious because it isn't a surprise at all. I could have said something to Darcy. When I signed NDAs, I should have read them. When I brought in the vipes, I could have made a stink about their treatment.

I could have called the cops any night for years. I was a stooge, contributing "tissue samples" because I wasn't brave enough.

Well, I have a tissue sample now. I need a printer.

*   *   *

They say that high-powered negotiators choose their ground like generals choose battlefields, which I only recall once I'm at my destination. I kick myself for going as low-class as possible. But that's what I want, isn't it? Meeting at some hotel restaurant says, "I'm friendly." Meeting here in a parking structure, just a titch after sunrise, says, "I don't even trust you to sit down." Cho is supposed to be on my side, but there's that old reflexive fear again, some blend of being spooked from the dream and traitor's guilt because I'm about to screw some very dangerous people. Screw over, that is.

"I'm Geoff. Are you the young lady who called me on the phone?"

"Yes, hi," comes out of my mouth, instinct turning me into Little Miss Afraid of Rejection. It usually works until Up Yours Cycle Girl comes out. "I have some stuff—evidence, I guess you'd say—that might be able to help Morgan." I wiggle the box I'm holding.

"Let's make one thing clear," he says. "I'm sorry, I didn't catch your name."

Here's Cycle Girl. "I didn't give it."

"Right..." His tone shifts. "What I want you to know is that I don't do miracles. There are rules of introducing evidence at various points throughout the trial—"

"I totally don't care about that," I say. "Sorry to be blunt, but I knew this going in. I am not going up on a witness stand, and I am not expecting you to pull off a massive win through slick maneuvering. I am just throwing the truth at you, and you can decide whether it comes out in a courtroom or leaks to a reporter or whatever. I'm dead. I'm poison. You, on the other hand, know how to be effective when it comes to words and public image and un-criminal shit. Do we understand each other?"

Cho purses his lips. While he pauses, I scan the parking lot just in case. No one else. No figures idling in cars, no pedestrians to overhear. I can drop bombs.

"Miss, you're not my client, so if you're about to tell me you did something illegal, I'm ethically bound not to lie when the police ask questions." He pauses for effect. "Do we understand each other?"

The specter of jail is disturbing—if kept to a restricted diet, I'd end up like Morgan—but Cho doesn't need to know that. "Sweetie, prison has food and showers. The people I'm pissing off have body parts in their freezers." I lift a plastic bag out of the box. "I brought a printout from BRHI's hot labs. That should be good reading. And this is a marker cap with a biological agent on it that you can compare to the strain that infected Morgan."

"When you say 'agent...'"

"Relax, it's in a Ziploc. Just don't open it." That doesn't seem to reassure him. "But the thing you probably want most, it's a list of names. These are people working at BRHI who know about the vipes and the cover-up." I pull out the list. At the bottom, I included the bare bones of what I know about the Forced Protection Program, including its stated goals. I didn't list the F-prots' names. I owe them that much.

"Very interesting," he says, "but I need to know why you're doing this."

"No, you really don't."

"Are you a vipe?" Cho asks, and after I hesitate, I know that he knows. I went hard in the face and stiff in the body.

"What does that matter? Don't they deserve a chance?"

"Look, I love inside info as much as the next lawyer, but if I don't get a good read of you on this, I don't move forward," he says, tense and striving to take control. "You know how many people have come to me trying to help the cause or to get help from me? I have to keep them off with cattle prods."

"I went to a damn *biohazard lab* to get you this."

"Sounds like a brave decision, which, with all due respect, may not have been the most intelligent or persuasive one."

He's not supposed to say that. He's supposed to be my reward for being clever and compromising my soul with serious deceit. I shut my eyes for a moment, then look down at my hands. The cut across my knuckles has healed. I saw a scar for a few days, and then it, too, disappeared. I'm more resilient now, and part of me hates that.

"Fine," I say frostily. "I thought a class-action suit would need every scrap of info, but you can lose all you want. I'll see if someone else is interested. Media, maybe."

I start to walk away, knowing there isn't a chance he'll let me go. He wants his name on television. Two steps away, and I already get a "Wait." I don't stop, still acting, but still angry, too. He takes a few steps after me.

"If you want to make a difference, leave the materials with me."

I keep my face neutral. Then, as if I have to think about it, I hold out the box. As he reaches for it, I snatch it away.

"Last condition," I say. "If you know where Morgan is, you tell me."

"You'll know when I know," he says, and I give him the goods.

25 - RANATH

September 5th

I wait on the stoop of the safehouse, glancing at the tiny windows in the oatmeal-colored door and wondering if calling ahead and making plans means anything to Infinity. She has a veneer of seriousness that makes me think she can be relied upon, but every so often, she tries to chase down some idea in her head like a kitten after a flashlight beam.

I briefly met with Kern at the office before coming over. Kern complimented my success in humbling Lorenz, but we both know BRHI can still plow headlong into a court defeat if management is determined to steer the plane. We commiserated for an hour or so, and as I left, Kern had armed me with a tidbit of information Infinity might enjoy.

The door opens. I have no idea where Infinity was for the previous knocks since she appears neither sopping wet nor rumpled and sleepy. She might have been getting dressed, for she apparently has found a miniskirt and faux-silk top in whatever baggage she brought from Los Angeles. She's applied a little rouge and lipstick the color of venous blood. In my opinion, she doesn't need to—her unbound hair, black and lustrous, is enough to catch anyone's eye.

"Hey, stranger," she says. "Come on in."

I follow her inside, giving the visual once-over. There's a week's worth of coffee filters, Thai take-out cartons, and discarded clothes, shoved back against the far wall in what looks like a particularly messy twelve-year-old's idea of cleaning up. I shut the door.

"All set for company, I see."

"I heard somewhere we were going out," she smiles. "And you are well on your way to being in the doghouse."

Not today. "I can make up for that. I have good news."

"I could use some."

"I'm here to give you money."

"Well, as long as it isn't for anything tawdry."

I bite back a comment about wishing. "Kern has fought a small, territorial war with our Los Angeles branch, and your first direct deposit under our management arrives today," I say. "There's hazard pay included. Kern says you are welcome to stay as long as the F-prot mission remains a priority."

"And how long is that?"

"Oh, Tuesday at least." I get a smile from that, though my own fades. "Being serious, you may not want to spend it all in one place. It is possible the F-prots will soon be seen as irrelevant, and then we're all out on the street."

Infinity stares at me. I know the look. If she had a drink, she'd spit it. "Irrelevant?"

"With the disease vector made public, private companies like us are likely to be prosecuted for going after vipes. The police will be expected to contain the situation."

"Yeah, 'cause those cops did a great job stopping Lorenz," she mutters.

"I didn't say I wouldn't fight for it. But from the point of view of legal counsel or upper management, we have liability written all over us."

Infinity lets out a breath and sits down on the couch. "First you kiss me, then you kick me," she says. "You got any more surprises up your sleeve tonight?"

The setup is too good to resist. "Well, I was planning on making stir-fry."

She looks thoughtful, and I know I've scored a point, but she won't drop her defenses quite so easily. I try again. Smile on. "Did you have other plans?"

"There's a club nearby called Anlace," she says guilelessly, looking up at me. I can see the brown roots of her eyelashes. "You don't seem like a dance guy."

"I have been known to dance," I say, "just not very well."

She looks me over. "Ballroom? Swing? No, wait, you're totally country line."

"My house is in Manassas," I say firmly, "not Tennessee."

Infinity smiles, like she's winning by gleaning info out of me. "It's weird, I always thought Virginia was the South, but you don't have the accent."

"And I thought Californians only knew the parts of the Bible that appear on TV every holiday season."

"Don't worry," she says. "Cults are plenty Californian. My next question—you got a favorite kind of alcohol?"

"I don't drink."

"Well, crap, what else is there to do in this town—go to the zoo?" I look thoughtful, but she kills that idea. "How about we pretend we're buzzed already and dump our life stories on each other? No, wait, that's lame. But I do want to hear how you get your hair that color."

I make myself shrug. "Yin qi can do interesting things to hair melanin."

"I once had a white skunk stripe in my hair," she volunteers. "People said I looked witchy."

"Why'd you stop?"

"My dad hit me for it," she says. "He was into that."

"For your hair?"

"For a lot of things, but that was back when the Earth was cooling and the dinosaurs roamed. Now that you know that about me, I want to hear something about you. I'm betting you did not put a skunk stripe in your hair."

I pause. I'm used to acting normal, not being normal. My go-to social instinct is to lie and fake stories like the intel officers trained me to do. But lies are for targets, and Infinity is less like a target and more like a hummingbird. Topics and words and polite social laughter dart and flit around me without bothering to land.

"What else can you guess?" I ask, buying time.

"That when I mentioned that thing with my dad, you wrote me off," she says matter-of-factly. She's good. Or at least practiced.

"I did, a little," I admit. "I don't have a lot of experience in that department."

"Points for honesty." She shrugs, and I relax slightly. The judgmental vibe coming from her is disappointing, but I'm not going to shy away now.

"Are there points for stir-fry?"

"It sounds better than the food at Anlace, which I only know through search engines. So long as I don't have to blindfold myself to see your secret lair, I'm in."

"I could give you a ride."

"I'm not comfortable with that."

I pause for just a second, wondering what kind of messes she's had to extract herself from. I've practically performed surgery on her. Is this a different kind of trust? "Can I ask why?"

"In case you turn out to be like everybody else."

I'm not. And I like proving it. "Driving directions, then."

"Right," she says. "See how easy that was?"

26 - INFINITY

September 5th

I try to formally break up with Aaron over a headset while driving into the dark and tree-covered parts of Manassas. It doesn't go as badly as I feared, which means he doesn't have an FBI team waiting for my call, triangulating the signal. Instead, a woman answers the phone. Once I've pried out of "Kristin" that Aaron has vindictively sold most of my stuff, the *fait* is pretty much *accompli*. I screwed up my courage to rip the bandage off the wound, only to find myself too late compared to the people who'd had time to process the drama.

I justify it fine. This infection thing is a sort of free pass where karma is concerned. You're entitled to freak out a little, confuse your boyfriend, flee the state. Owning up to it, and acting like an adult is extra credit, which is good, because that's probably my worst subject.

I've brought a tissue box this time, but I don't use it. As I roll into the driveway and come up the path to ring the bell on Roland's door, my attention is wrapped around a hypothetical conversation in my head. I imagine Kristin and Aaron grilling me. Is there someone else? Not a sexual fling but someone with whom I can think about the future? And my answer at the moment would be to start making static noises, complain about reception, and hang up.

Then, the door opens, and I'm back in my element. Roland is there with the sound and smell of sizzling meat wafting out from the house behind him.

"Oh, no web tonight?" I ask since the backs of his hands are bare.

"I don't like getting food all over it," he says. "Come on in."

The neatness habit seems to extend to the rest of the house. The living room to my right has couches that look as if people sit on them once a month, and I don't smell any pets. Shoes are stacked near the door. I almost take my boots off before noticing his are still on. All the better to make an exit if I have to, I suppose.

"You all alone here?" I know the answer, but hey, small talk.

"Unless my neighbor has a telephoto lens I don't know about, yes," he says. "Take off your coat. Stay awhile."

Belatedly, I open the foyer closet and hang up my jacket. As I near the table, I notice a mostly-full bottle of Irish whiskey.

"I thought you didn't drink," I say.

"That was a present, about seven or eight years old. I was going to re-gift it."

"You know it's the time spent in the barrel before bottling that counts, right?"

Roland adds oil to the stir-fry. It roars back at him. "I won't tell if you won't."

"Were you saving it?"

"Not consciously," he says. "Just did a little house cleaning before you came over. Do you want any?"

"I'll make you a deal," I say. "You tell me why you don't drink, and I'll tell you why I do. Then, we either have some of that whiskey together, or we don't touch the stuff all night."

Roland gives me a look. He knows my game—I wouldn't have challenged him if I didn't think I could win—but he seems amused. "Who's first?"

"You," I say.

"I initially stayed off it because I heard it killed brain cells, but that's really vanity. There isn't measurable loss of function. Then, I stayed away because you never know when you're going to live or die by a mistake. When I was stationed abroad, one of our more alcoholic agents got rolled for his wallet, which was then used to get access to his passwords and get into our system. So, my superiors broke out the polygraphs and interrogated us to see if I'd ever done the same. I was selected as a risk."

By the time he's done, the stir-fry is as well. He serves it up. I don't need prompting to grab a seat. Roland doesn't seem amiable. More lost in thought.

"You got scars?"

155

"Nerve damage in my feet."

"Did they break you?"

"Excuse me?"

"The interrogation. Did they break you?"

Roland looks down. "They break everyone. Otherwise, they don't let you go." He doesn't sit down. Maybe he wants to run. "The worst part is when you tell the truth, and they don't believe it. That's when they hurt you just to be sure, and you... you wonder how stupid you were to salute the same flag they do."

I nod.

"It's also a bit of a scene when you're trying to explain to them that the drones could be targeting the building at any time, and they are obsessed with their dominance game. That's when you have to admit you will do anything, say anything, because you want to live."

Roland pauses, and for once, I question all the alarms he's set off in my brain. Sure, he's dangerous, but hostility is born of fear. A python can bite, but if you're not food or a threat, you can get along fine.

"So, why do you drink?" he says, and I come back to Earth.

"Because life should be celebrated."

"We can do that without alcohol."

I'm prepared. "But at one point in our life, we *couldn't*. When we were young, we didn't have that freedom."

"Sounds as though it's freedom that should be celebrated, not life."

"Sure, but..." I seize on it, and the words tumble out. "I don't know anything about what you were like when you were twelve or fourteen or whatever or if anyone ever made you appreciate how good we've got it now, but I kind of keep those moments in the back of my mind all the time, all right? It's freedom, but not screw-what-you-think-I-have-free-speech freedom. I don't drink to escape. I drink because I know I went through the fire and came out the other side, and I'm glad about it. Does that make sense?"

Roland looks down. Is that twice now? I can mess up even a cool customer like him.

"Because you mentioned a young age," he says gently, "I'm going to assume this has something to do with your father. Is that all right?"

"Yeah," I say. "It has everything to do with him."

Did he break you? It's written on his face. Instead he says, "How bad was it?"

Don't screw this up. Don't screw this up.

"You want the version with the pain or without it?"

He considers for a second. I like that. "Well," he says, "I understand we get points for honesty."

The room gets brighter: my pupils have dilated. There isn't anyone around to make a bet, really, which is unfortunate because I'm completely sure he'll lose his shit when I drop the truth on him. I'm a walking emotional baggage carousel, and Roland is the kind of guy who only brings carry-on.

"There's a part in Leviticus 18 he used to quote," I say, "and it goes like this. Bear with me 'cause it's long."

"Long is fine," he says, and his green eyes seem worried for me, as if things are going to get worse just because of talking about it, and what the hell. Maybe they are. I begin.

"You shall not uncover the nakedness of your son's daughter or of your daughter's daughter, for their nakedness is your own nakedness. You shall not uncover the nakedness of your father's wife's daughter, begotten by your father since she is your sister.

"You shall not uncover the nakedness of your father's sister; she is your father's flesh. You shall not uncover the nakedness of your mother's sister, for she is your mother's flesh. You shall not uncover the nakedness of your father's brother, that is, you shall not approach his wife; she is your aunt. You shall not uncover the nakedness of your daughter-in-law: she is your son's wife; you shall not uncover her nakedness. You shall not uncover the nakedness of your brother's wife; it is your brother's nakedness."

He's staring at me like I've grown a second head. "I'm not sure what that means."

"Did you notice the one that was missing?" He thinks for a moment. I give him a hint. "It's the obvious one."

"Daughters," he says at last. "It leaves out just plain daughters."

"Yeah," I say. It's faint, though. "It, uh... I later learned that there are other parts of the book that say no daughters, but for the longest time..." I shake my head. "You get the picture."

"I'm sorry." It comes out of him automatically. "I don't think I've known anyone before who was... violated, if that's the right word."

"Not to make assumptions about your life," I say, "but you probably have. They just didn't decide to tell you."

He stands up, and for a second, I think I've hit a nerve. But in a moment, he returns to the table and puts a shot glass down in front of each of us. He pours the whiskey.

"Freedom," he says, and we drink. He looks as if he's holding back a cough as it goes down, but overall, he handles it pretty well.

I start in on the stir-fry, and the conversation turns to how he made it. I pour myself a second shot when he starts talking about his parents, whom he stopped speaking to when he changed his name. The third shot brings out the story of my friend Rachel, who gave me a place to stay and helped me press charges when I finally fled from the house.

I hold off on a fourth shot and have a little water instead when he reveals he never had friends that close. By that time, I've decided there's a better-than-even chance I'm going to stay the night and resolve to be open for a fourth shot as soon as I come back from the bathroom.

"Which way?" I ask.

"There's two. One's on this level. One's downstairs."

"I totally want to see this place. Stairs it is," I say.

"There's a railing if you have to use it."

"Watch me, you tease." I go down the stairs with balance to spare. I'm socially stirred but also sharp, coordinated. The bathroom is deliciously cold, and I catch a look at myself in the mirror. I'm not staring at a hot mess anymore. I see a girl, yes, but one re-forged into a woman by my friends, by therapeutic sex, by endless struggles on the mat in jiujutsu. An available, confident survivor.

When I emerge and am about to go upstairs, a smell gets my attention: wood and something musty. I'd never have noticed it before my infection, which makes it curious. The door to the room has a stiff handle, like it's locked, but a little nudge, and it comes open—it's only ninety percent closed. The latch didn't catch right. Opening the door, I'm hit with a wave of heat and humidity, a jungle in comparison to the cool night outside or the cold sink I just touched.

The room is a spotless white. I don't know why the chairs are up off the floor—something to do with cleaning before company came over, I guess. Slowly, I close in on the room's main attraction—the enormous wood and glass terrarium fogged up with water vapor. Its occupant is large enough to need a lot of room. I don't recognize the gray snake inside. It has big, attractive eyes and a mouth line that curves up like a grin. Its head isn't triangular, so it's not a viper. It's lean, probably one of those harmless racers from the southern U.S. It lies very still. Asleep?

I lean down with my face close to the enclosure and am rewarded by the snake flicking a dark tongue out. I examine the latches on the terrarium door and flick them open.

"You're a cute one," I say. "Do you like petting?"

27 · RANATH

I'm busy putting away dishes when something tells me I'd better check on Infinity. I heard the faint sound of a toilet flushing before I drowned it out by running the kitchen sink. But when I'm done, there are no footsteps coming back to me. I dry my hands and look down the stairs—Infinity isn't far from Ena, and even though I locked the door, it never hurts to be careful.

"Hey!" bursts out from downstairs, and instantly, I know what has happened. I fly down the steps to find the door open and the rooms lit by the pale glow of Ena's ultraviolet lamp. Infinity has her by the head and is trying to force back her long, writhing body into the vivarium.

I snatch up a snake stick and use the spring-loaded jaws to firmly push Ena back. Infinity is smart and backs off as I go in, and I slam the door closed. The latch goes on.

"Did she get you?" I bark. "Are you bitten?"

"Yeah, it's fine," Infinity says. "Just a nip. Didn't really hurt—"

"Infinity," I say, staring directly in her eyes, "meet Ena. She is one of the most venomous snakes *on the planet*. Do what I say, when I say. I've got to save your life."

I can see the pale blue of her eyes go thin, swallowed by the black. She looks incredulously at the vivarium. "Why the hell do you have a pet you can't pet?"

"She's not a pet. She's a wild animal in captivity. Show me all the bites."

Infinity extends a hand. "Just once before I grabbed her." One red dot is a clean puncture; the other fang skated along the skin. That's good. Maybe it didn't deliver a full load. "Do you know how to suck the poison out or—"

"You don't want that. I'm going to have to inject you with antivenin. A lot." Nearly everything I need is within reach. I open the freezer and start pulling out fistfuls of tiny bottles. I slide a package of syringes over to her. "Open one of these. No, better make it two."

"How long do I have?"

"Time is tissue." I look over at her. "Brain, nerves, heart. Mostly nerves, but it's not good for any of it."

"You didn't answer the question."

"You have alcohol in your system. It makes things worse."

"How *much* worse?"

"I'm going to try to heal you to slow the damage." Explanations will have to come later. "I need to grab my stimweb."

"What do I do—think calming thoughts?"

"Actually, yes." I dash up the stairs, two at a time and trip near the top. I swear under my breath about alcohol. I soon have the kettle on and am running back down with the web and a handful of tacks. I take off my shirt to wire up and put tacks in my chest, my hands, my scalp.

It isn't long before the kettle boils, and I mix in cool water to put the bottles in a warm bath. Then, I take Infinity by the hand and kneel down with her.

"Stay still."

I grasp her arm with one hand and use the other to adjust the stim. In moments, I am generating yang qi and seeking her meridians to establish the connection.

Liver. Heart. Lung. I can't find them.

Something is out of balance. Yang roils and flows through her with every triphammer heartbeat, and when I grasp it to attempt to strengthen it, it overcomes me. It is powerful and young.

Young? She isn't old, but she doesn't match up with what I know. I see energy like this in twenty-year-old men, and more to the point, I did not feel it back when I healed her neck. It is wrong, like finding fire in a snowbank, but it is far from harming her.

I feel for her abundance of yin-within-yin and find it pulsing at her core. She is using her energies instinctively to block the venom's spread, and she has two separate, distinct signatures: one on the inside, one out. It is exactly the sort of thing that can throw off my locator beacon. Infinity has someone else's aura on, and there is only one way she could have taken it.

"Any good news?" she asks.

I wish. "Well, your chances of dying just went down a great deal."

"Any bad news?" she says, and I know at once that she knows. I size up the situation and find nothing good. If she gets hostile, the chances that I can reach my pistol are low. I'm in close quarters with a vipe who specializes in a grappling martial art. My own martial arts teacher, when posed with complex questions like this, gave me a simple rule to follow: *do not commit until they commit.* So, I don't.

As politely as possible, I say "I'm pretty sure you're aware you're a vipe."

I'm not sure what to expect when I say it. Maybe a denial. Maybe she'll get dangerous. But she does neither. She lets out a breath—not a sigh but a conscious attempt to stay calm as things go from bad to worse.

"Right," she says quietly. "Is that likely to save me?"

Slightly fogged by the drinks, I'm not sure in what sense she means it. I go with the medical opinion. "Well, you've had a blood meal very recently, I'd say within the last forty-eight hours. It makes it harder to lock on to your signal, but your ability to recuperate will be at its peak." Keep clinical. "Do you feel tingling or numbness?"

"I did for a minute there, but it's off and on."

"That's you fighting off the neurotoxin. Had this happened a few days later, it would be a lot worse."

"So, what's the plan?" she asks.

I have none. Am I within my rights to explode in anger? To make her beg, let her suffer for her betrayal or at least for her drunken, suicidal, and downright stupid move? She has done more than lie. When my hands were on her neck, bathed in her blood, a scratch on my skin could have exposed me.

"First," I say, taking a deep breath and forcing a smile, "I give you antivenin."

"I wasn't sure about that," she admits.

"You're my patient," I say gently, and I get up to make more preparations. I put on a rubber glove, take a second syringe and dilute a dose in saline. I must ensure she isn't allergic to the antibodies before I give her anything larger. "Here we go. Test case first."

She holds still as I prep her unbitten hand with an alcohol wipe. Needle stick. In moments, I have the catheter and IV going and take closer note of her wound. I clean it and find the tiny holes clotting over. The wound site hasn't even swelled. Vipe healing at its finest.

"I need to watch for symptoms, but they'll take minutes to appear," I explain. She is not smiling now. "When did it happen?"

"When I was taking my hand away," Infinity says. "At first, I stayed still not to scare him—uh, her—but then I figured she wasn't interested—"

"I mean the infection."

"A few weeks back. Still getting used to it."

The bigger question looms, so I say it. "Have you had to kill?"

"I don't really know," she confesses. "Maybe I did. The first time was sloppy." As she looks down, a strand of hair covers one eye, and I am somewhere else. Lovers, parents, psychiatrists all saying that normal people don't feel *those things*. Normal people see life as sacred. They don't want to be the ones deciding who has the right to live. Normal people need to be petted and cajoled and given orders, so it's a *we* rather than an *I* that pulls the trigger. She shows all the signs I never have.

I am not normal. Infinity knew it, but she came here tonight anyway. She didn't shrink back at any point tonight, and I need to do the same.

"Whoa," she says, bringing her head up after a minute. "Drowsy."

"But no itching?" I ask.

"Not really. Still some tingles. Hot, too."

"Itching would be an allergic reaction. Fatigue is the venom. We'd better fix it." I swap out the syringe load and start putting the antivenin into her in earnest.

"I feel terrible..." she says.

"That's normal."

"I mean, you saving my dumb ass twice now. Morgan, I... I let him escape."

"We'll sort through your guilt in the morning. Right now, roll up your shirt."

She does so. I put the crook of my web arm around her waist. We are ab to ab.

"Oh," she says. "Don't mind the sweat. They say it helps you get rid of toxins."

"If you live, we can go to the spa. I'm just maximizing the contact area."

Infinity grimaces. I adjust the web. The inverse square is practically at zero; I am free to build a reservoir of power. Then, I feel out the roiling energies in Infinity, two auras fighting for their lives, bound together by blood and qi. The blood is now compromised, carrying its lethal load throughout her body. It clenches like a fist around her nerves, her meridians, her brain. I can feel the venom sliding into her on pathways slick with alcohol, see it trying to choke out the light. I coax her liver into absorbing water and whiskey from her system, replaced by saline and antivenin. But the energy I'm creating is unstable. Like a sniper waiting for a shot, I'll need steady nerves, timing, and a little math. I have one of three.

"Infinity," I say, "I'm going to adjust your central nervous system."

"You gonna jam a hypo in my heart?"

I shake my head. "I don't trust my precision right now. I'm drunker than I've been in my life. I need to stick to my strength, and that's affecting minds."

"Uh... how does that help?"

"I want to access the portion of your brain that handles immune response," I say. "If the poison and the alcohol depress that system, you're in trouble."

"Well, stop talking about it, and do it."

"With no precision, it involves me controlling all of your mind for a short time."

She pauses. I start to explain. "That's why I'm asking permission—"

"But you said the poison was going to my brain."

"Well, to be precise, neurotoxic venoms only—"

"I don't want to hear any more. Just get it over with."

I take a calming breath. I pull off my glove, bring up my left palm and cradle her face. Then, I start the function.

It is not telepathy. There are no voices in my head. It is as if I can take her mind in my hand and feel it bound up in dark emotions. There is fear, of course, but buried deeper is a tight core of anger. It is hard not to compare her to Ena, who has fear and hostility to spare whenever she meets with a surprise. But Ena is wild, free with every emotion. Here, I know that Infinity holds her anger down with iron bars, using defense mechanisms that she has developed—

I stop. I am not going to do this.

"Have you got it?" Of course, she asks. She can feel there is no difference.

"I've changed my mind," I say. "The antivenin will be enough."

"Say that again?" She is incredulous enough that I realize my mistake. The anger will not dissipate if I let up. It will only boil over.

I explain the truth. "I made some calculations. You should be okay—"

"Are you going to make some more and find out I'm *not?*"

"The antivenin will be enough," I repeat. "Long-term damage will be avoided, and you're healing like a vipe."

"What's this really about?"

I hesitate. "My judgment is lousy, and I don't want to control you," I say. "You can live without me giving you any additional trauma."

Infinity stares at me.

"Fuck you."

"I'm sorry," I say automatically.

"You think 'cause I got abused, I can't make a mature decision myself?"

"Some people take it well. Others never recover. We're under the influence, and I don't want you to regret anything—"

"I eat regret for breakfast. And if I can ignore *snakebite*, three shots of Jameson's are not going to screw me up. Just don't act like you're noble for doing it."

I realize I am scowling. "It actually—" I catch myself. "Let us just say, I feel it's more polite to let you make up your own mind than to take it over and remove all doubt."

"Well, that's just great," she says. "I'm trying to say I trust you."

"I'm trying to be worthy of it."

For a moment, it seems as if she has no answer. "I want it," she says at last. I can tell that another refusal would be more insulting yet. So, I act.

I create energy inside her head, worming in just as surely as the venom in her veins. I feel my way to her brain's locus coeruleus, and once I have massaged it, she fairly hums and quivers, cortex washed in norepinephrine, ready for orders. The specifics, the science, comes to me more easily when intoxicated; it's cemented in how I think. I dial her heartbeat to a calmer level, play with her lungs for better oxygenation of the blood.

My mission is not to calm her but to rouse the parts falling into a dangerous sleep. When I finally awaken her core, I feel something primal: meridians open wide and burning like a star that vaporizes a comet on impact. Behind that is a black hole that can suck in even that star and crush it with no apparent bother.

It takes time. As soon as it is over, I release her.

"Whoa." Infinity leans onto the floor as soon as she can talk. Automatically, she self-consciously rolls down her shirt.

"How do you feel?" I ask.

"It was like... I don't know, dreaming or anesthesia or something," she says. "I was trying to move, but I knew I didn't really want to."

"You did want to," I say. "I stopped that."

"Man, if it were me," she says, "I would have fiddled around while I was in there and said, 'you're going to agree this was a dumb decision when you wake up.'"

"I'm on your side."

"No one ever is," Infinity tells me. "Not completely."

I have no answer for that. "Are you feeling any more symptoms?"

"No," she says, clearly surprising herself. "I can breathe. I can feel every part of me... the worst thing is this catheter."

I reach for a cotton swab. When I turn back, she has removed the needle already. She puts the back of her fist in her mouth, then takes the swab. "Didn't think you should touch it," she explains. "Blood and needle."

"You should be done," I say. "Antivenin, alcohol, too. You've been, well... purified."

She looks askance, probably at my choice of words. "I've got to leave, you know. I mean, you're one thing, but Kern and Breunig, they don't forgive and forget."

"I didn't know," I say dryly, "that you were given to understatement."

Infinity smiles and reaches out to gingerly hug me, careful not to push on any of the needles sticking out. Before I know how to respond, her lips touch my cheek, putting a warm kiss there and leaving just as quickly.

"See you around, stranger," she says and is gone from the room. I pull out the needles, debating running upstairs, insisting that somehow this could work out, but there are no more words. I put my shirt back on as I hear the door shut. She will be in her car, driving in the only possible direction: away.

I walk to the bathroom, where I remove the web and put the needles down on the cold, empty countertop. I wash my hands, an old habit to be performed after every surgery.

In the mirror, I notice a droplet of red on my cheek. Her wound, her mouth, her kiss. It lies on my unbroken skin. Safe, as far as such things could ever be. I know I should be repulsed but only let the water run, as if by standing still I could keep her here.

28 - INFINITY

September 7th

There isn't enough room in the car. I know this, but I don't have the time to acknowledge that uncomfortable truth when there are about fifty more gunning for me. There is no question I'm worse off now than I was a month ago. The game is up, the uncertainty gone, and assuming Roland is a good corporate narc, I'll have F-prots hunting me from two coasts instead of one. Where do I run to now—some storm cellar in Kansas?

I throw the last items on top of the stuffed back seat—clothes that didn't fit in the laundry bag. Said bag is full because the suitcases are packed with everything I brought from Cali, and this new bag includes pots, pans, and clothes I got once I realized I'd be here for the winter.

I slide into my seat and carefully buckle myself, leaving my jacket open and putting the arm belt behind my body. I want to be able to get at my shoulder holster quickly. Then, I make a last, instinctive check—yes, there are tissues on the passenger seat. Better to bring the whole box than waste it and have to buy a packet.

Hoping the little Atlantis doesn't violate motor vehicle laws, I pull away from the safehouse and into the on-again, off-again world of D.C. traffic. I hate it—the exit ramps sprout on either side of the road, instead of just on the right like a sensible city. I drive manually because that's what you do when you've disconnected your traceable GPS, and I careen across three lanes when necessary to make my turnoff. Forty minutes later, I'm where I need to be.

Morgan Lorenz called me this morning. I think it's legit. Cho knows the number of my new burner phone; Lorenz is still in contact with Cho.

I tried, with my limited skills, to check the call out—it wouldn't surprise me to discover it was a ruse to flush me out of hiding. All I got was that the call was voice-over-Internet from a cybercafé. The voice sounded like him, and it came on a pre-dawn Sunday morning. Unless Roland scrambled the F-prots that very night, the boys in boots will be being briefed only now, not executing some plan with faked audio.

The talk itself was short. Georgetown. M Street. He would meet me.

I find parking about a block from the café. I do a casual walk around the area to play spot-the-cop, and no one seems vigilant enough to rate as a pro. There are couples walking with shopping bags, foursomes laughing at some triviality or other, a homeless man bundled up behind a cardboard sign and a woman trying to hail taxis that are always occupied.

I focus on the taxi-hailing woman the most, as she consistently looks around like a pro might, but by the time I make my second circuit, I see the woman finally get in a rideshare and zoom off into the distance.

Just then, my senses kick in. The sound of shoes on sidewalk. Someone is behind me.

I whirl, nearly on top of the homeless man, all sandy beard and body odor.

"Where's your car?" he asks.

I'm not stunned long. I cross my arms to put a hand on the Glock. "What's it to you?"

"Infinity?" he asks. I realize my mistake. It's Morgan. He's grown a ratty mop of a beard, he's in scum clothes, and he added a cardboard sign so he can disappear completely.

"Shit, sorry. It's nearby. You got everything?"

"I got nothing," he says. "Let's go."

We hurry to the car and get in, albeit with him picking up boxes and bags out of the shotgun seat. I notice his scowl as he stashes them on his lap but figure he doesn't have anything to smile about.

"Where are we going?" I ask.

"Someplace safe."

"Where's that?"

"I was hoping you knew."

I try thinking positive thoughts. When that fails, I start thinking of desperate ploys. "Last time I was in it this bad, I hit up a battered women's shelter. The cops won't expect you there."

"If you want me to dress in drag, I'm going to need better clothes."

I think the shelters might accept a man, but they'd ask questions, which could trip us up. What would our story be? Two domestic abuse victims coincidentally fleeing... what? A bisexual polygamous husband?

"Option two," I say, "we rob a bank."

"No," Lorenz says. He doesn't even look at me.

"I wasn't serious."

"I am," he growls. "I may have to assault people, I may have to infect them, but I sure as hell don't have to rob them."

It seems crazy to me—he's either naïve or somehow hasn't figured out that his accounts would be frozen. "You want to just live on blood?" I ask.

"Want, no. Can, yes."

"And for income—"

He waves the sign at me. HOMELESS, HUNGRY, HONORABLE.

"You've got to be kidding," I say. But there's another part of me that twitches in shame. I remember emptying that trucker's wallet before trash-canning it in Arkansas, and here he is, lasting a week without stealing. This is the Lorenz I watched on video. The crusader I'll never be.

"Are you going through with the trial?" I ask.

"I don't have a choice. And you? You in this for love or money?"

"It's the right thing to do," I say. "And the money's not that good. I've made a pad, but it won't last long. Credit cards create trails. Hey, car?" The dashboard lights up in response to my summons. "Where's the low-rent section of town here?"

"Wait," Morgan says. "That command uses the GPS chip. They could be—"

"—looking for the car to link to the grid, yeah."

"Aren't you going to hit cancel?"

"It'll spin its wheels. I already disconnected it. I have a spare chip in the glove box."

Lorenz opens it up and moves stuff aside. "Where?"

"Possibly the trunk," I think out loud. "Under the luggage."

"Are we at least charged up?" he tries.

"I was going to do that after I met you." At his disbelieving look, I smile. I got him. "You're funny when you're desperate. Check it out— full tank."

Lorenz gives me a dark look. The message gets through. If I'm not reliable enough for this, he'll be gone in a second. "I saved up a little money. Made it all cash." He nods.

"How long have you survived?" he asks.

"The truth? Just a month."

"Oh, boy."

"We're going to need to practice working together," I say. "It's going to be you and me against the world."

Lorenz holds up a forefinger. "Actually, you're wrong there."

29 - RANATH

September 7th

I sit in Kern's office, listening and brooding. I am unused to entering the room with a sense of shame or confusion, and as a result, I remain quiet. I do little to prompt conversation. Kern is, as I suspected, busy.

"I'm saying I have a stack of the things on my desk right now," Kern says loudly into the speaker phone. "I've never heard of the manufacturer. I've never seen the product before. Someone cashed in right quick."

I turn over one of the dark blue boxes heaped on the desk. Red lettering spells out that the Virally Activated Medical Prognosis home test kit is 99.5% accurate and is the same test being used in hospitals. It gives no details of how those numbers were attained or the names of the hospitals privy to this testing. The curvature that turns the "M" into little stylized fangs suggests its target demographic is more concerned with mind-numbing fear than well-cited sources.

"Yeah," says the speaker-phone voice. "There's four or five reliable companies in this field so far. Not selling junk like the old days. Used to be you couldn't spit without hitting someone claiming to have discovered some qi phenomenon or other—"

"I was there," Kern says, tired.

"Okay, so we ran them by our guys. Most of them, they're little needle-stick things with—hold on, let me get this right—hema... hemagglutination assays?"

"Yeah."

"The team said they're nothing surprising. Barring human error, they work. We had some tissue samples on ice. They tested right. Of course, the crew is more worried that they'll produce false positives—"

"Well, the main question I want you to ask over there," Kern interrupts, "is, 'are any of our people in these companies, and are they profiting?' If someone gets it into their heads that we not only released the bug, we're selling ancillary products of any kind—I don't even want to think how bad that looks."

I take Kern's tablet off the desk, type, and slide it over to him: WHO IS THIS?

Kern taps a response: LEGAL.

"Now, I believe you had something to say to Dr. Cawdor. He's here."

"Dr. Cawdor, I'm Eloise Campion. I'm on the response team for Morgan Lorenz's allegations. Dr. Kern says a member of your team may be less than loyal. Is that accurate?"

I point at the phone. "What have you told her?"

"Just damage assessment," says Kern. "She knows Infinity got into the lab. What we need now is for you to recall any situations where you told her anything confidential."

"Why would she need to know that? We're assuming Infinity's with Lorenz now?"

Kern has on that face he makes when delivering terrible news. "It's safest if we assume, yes. Eloise, hope you don't mind if we go dark here for a second. We need to organize ducks."

"Make your row," says the lawyer, and Kern kills the volume. He seems like he is trying to be the adult in the room.

"Let's get one thing clear," Kern says. "I assume from the emergency code in your text she still knows everything from the last three years. You did *not* put the memory cramp on her?"

I don't want to hear any of this. It comes out in my voice. "I did not."

"Should I ask why?"

"Because she wasn't a target at the time."

"Okay, but there was a point where you realized she was a vipe, and then presumably after that point, she departed, and she was still a vipe as she did so, right?"

I drum my fingers. This is not going to go well.

"What are you thinking?"

Lies are for targets. That rule didn't work with Infinity. I opened up, and now a dozen specters of what could go wrong dance in front of me. I could be subpoenaed. My identity change could unravel. The families of the vipes could descend on me in a mob. D.C. does not have the death penalty, but Virginia does. Still, I cling to the mantra. "I'm thinking I fucked us royally, but that is no new revelation."

"Stop right there. You did not fuck us. She did. You get her as soon as possible, and we can close up the can before the worms get out." Kern must have read my face because he adds, "Alive, dead, however you want to do it."

"That's not the wisest course of action—"

"Forget wise. Wise is gone. I want real. We can plan for anything. Just tell me what she's going to do. You know her best."

Focusing on the problem helps calm me, which is no doubt why Kern wants it. I see a few scenarios: Infinity can lie low, she can join Lorenz's case, or she can go to the press.

What comes out of my mouth is, "No."

"I'm sorry. I don't see how that's productive," says Kern.

"You want me to be real," I say. "The reality is, either I shoot her in the head, or I somehow tie her up in some unbreakable Spider-Man restraints, bring her to the drop-off point, and then... what?"

"Roland, I don't actually know the full extent—"

"Yes, you do," I insist. "You're going to argue in court that she's not even human. What do you think's going to happen to her if you succeed? Never mind that bit about all men being equal and endowed with certain inalienable rights. I don't know how you get around that one."

"We've got a case that lays out several precedents," Kern says. He looks natural saying it, as though there is no trouble at all. "I mean, if you want to see a crisis, look at the other side. They're meeting with the Nonhuman Personhood Project—"

"So, it follows that she's a gorilla? Or does she just need to be put down like one?"

"Well, after we registered the DNA with the International Commission of Zoological Nomenclature, it follows that they're not *Homo sapiens*. They're *Cruor*—"

"That's a rubber-stamp process, and you know it—"

"Ranath, for someone who designed our protocols, you are being nutbar-level recalcitrant. What did she do to you? Did you fuck her or something?"

"We just talked."

Kern holds his fingers to the bridge of his nose. "That's worse."

"Look, I am on board with the idea of damage control, but protocol says we bring her in, and then what? She was one of us right up until we found out. She didn't change. We're the ones making this a death sentence. You and me. No one else."

"That is *not* accurate. I recognize emotions are high, so I am *not* being unreasonable. You can wipe her mind from here to eternity. Problem solved."

I hesitate.

"What?" says Kern. "I know you can do it. She'll probably agree it's the best option, for God's sake." I say nothing. "Look, if you need time, I'm sorry, we don't have any. I'm giving you a nonviolent solution. Either take it, or explain what the fuck your problem is."

He does not know. And I will not tell him. "I change identities a lot in this business," I say. "But there are people I refuse to be."

"Well, that's amusingly cryptic," says Kern. "Look. We're not coming to a solution on this, and Campion's still on hold. Take one of these stupid tests down to Eppy, and get yourself screened. I want their report saying you're clear by tomorrow, or else a fantabulous amount of shit is going to hit the fan. And in the meantime, I'm telling the team about her infection because she could try to take them out, and they deserve to know. Do we agree on that, at least?"

I stare at the cardboard box. Kern has maneuvered me into a question where the only possible answer is yes. It may be out of genuine concern, but con men also do that when they want agreement. It prepares the mark to agree to a more important question. But what does he really need my consent for?

"One thing," I say. "Campion, the lawyer. Has she talked about settling out of court?"

Kern looks puzzled, then guarded. "No," he says. "She thinks we can win."

He can't hide it. "Lies are for targets, Marcus."

That hits Kern hard. He tries not to show it, but he pauses too long before coming up with what he needs to say. "There are things I can't tell you unless you are completely committed."

I could make you. A function. A wrist lock. A bullet to the leg. But I have given years of service to BRHI, and if I throw them out in a burst of temper, what do I have left? Not Infinity. No, I am the knight that rides into the valley of Saracens, trusting that my king is not an idiot.

I snatch up a VAMP box. "You deal with Campion," I say, before I walk out the door. "You will get your clean test, and then I want to know exactly what our strategy is."

30 - INFINITY

September 7th

The two people coming up the driveway look as much like vipes as I have ever seen. They are not the vampires of movies or television or games. There are no sunglasses at night, no out-of-period clothing, no accessorizing canes and rings. Seriously, my leather outfit, now quietly tucked away in a closet, is closer to the cross-media stereotype than anything the newcomers have. The telltale sign isn't clothing; it's the glower. Their faces wear a look that says there's no humor left in life, no friendship that withstands their condition. They are together, but they don't look at one another for reassurance. They're lost in some scene in their minds, more important than anything passing before their eyes.

I identify the woman first. Morgan said the names of the vipes were Lyman and Deborah. Deborah stands out only in the way that would appeal to a vipe: she looks weak enough to overpower. She's small and mousy, disappearing into her coat, scarf, and toque. Her eyes never leave the street. Despite the weather, she holds herself as if she'll never get warm again. I don't have to guess how Deborah's time since infection has gone.

Ly doesn't look great either. He's Manson-lite, sporting wind-blown hair and a black, full beard that says personal appearance is his last priority. His blue, quilted coat has stains on it of dubious origin, but none has the telltale brown of old blood. Still, he seems aware of his surroundings, more a predator than the woman in denial next to him. He drove a weathered, silver minivan like he had kids once.

"Who are you?" he says, as they come to the door.

"My name's Infinity. I'm with Morgan," We shake. "Did you find all the exits okay? We're off the grid, and my directions are probably fruity."

"We got lost a little," Ly says. I nod, then glance over to Deborah. The woman is looking at me like I'm plutonium.

"Are you..."

"Yes," I say, and Deborah nearly drops in relief. "Everyone here is one of us. Come on in. Meet the family. Can I take your coat?"

Ly gives Deborah a glance. "Uh... no thanks," he says.

"Rough nights, huh? You'll get them back." They hesitate for a second more, and then, Deborah takes her coat off. Ly follows, and soon we are headed into the apartment like any other normal party guests. I lead them upstairs to the dining room table, which is small but extended out by a card table butted up against it. Normal and folding chairs ring it, filled by Morgan and the two other vipes who arrived just before dawn.

Cass Iver, the first, is a large Anglo who has a biker's blond moustache and the girth of an older man used to being in the saddle. He works at an auto parts store and reminds me of the nameless trucker I preyed on. I can't shake the feeling that there must be legions more like him—men lured in by the code of the road to help vipes claiming car trouble. Whoever infected him had guts or skills— he looks as if he could break a few noses even if he were down four pints.

The second man, Ferrero, hasn't given his last name, or perhaps not his first, having contacted Morgan over the Net, where he answered to the name "Enigma42." He is younger and darker in complexion, somewhere between Italian and Hispanic. Trying to subtly guess which isn't easy since he apparently speaks both languages. He says he was a chemistry teacher, and his infector had been a student.

He has money. Cass has money. For now, we can afford things.

The table in front of them is saturated with food—brisket, vegetable, and pasta dishes Morgan cooked. I demonstrated what I thought were adequate culinary skills until Morgan took over and shooed me out of the small kitchen, claiming there was no room for two. He emerged victorious from a fight with the oven by the time I returned with a bottle of wine.

"Ly and Deborah, this is Cass and Ferrero. Morgan, you've met over the phone."

"Welcome home," Morgan says, rising and shaking their hands. "Don't take this the wrong way, but can I get you anything to drink?"

Ly gives a little chuckle. I can't see Deborah's reaction. But a few moments later, they are seated, drinking from the only glasses the furnished apartment came with. Both are digging in rapidly. "You sure know how to make someone feel human again," Deborah says. "We've been going without food. It's so much money if you don't need it."

Ly addresses Morgan. "Yeah, drinking, vaping, food, we gave up so much we're coming to you like prisoners. What happened to turning into a bat and getting laid whenever you want?"

"I would have liked flying," I say. "Or hypnosis."

Ly points at me. "That's what I'm talking about. My fantasy is not healing bloody noses and being good in gym class."

Cass looks incredulous. "You don't like the strength? I feel like Superman."

"We are a long way from Superman. How much do you lift?"

"I went to a gym to test it out," Cass continues between bites, "and I still don't really know. I tried a bench with free weights, and I stopped at three hundred 'cause my spotter said he'd be no help with anything heavier."

"Pounds?" says Ly.

"Kilos."

"Jesus," Ferrero says. "No wonder gun sales are through the roof."

Ly smirks. "Well, the day you come up with a practical use for that, let me know." Cass's face falls. "Do you just drink blood, or do you need regular protein for that?"

"Nutrition's not enough to make a difference," says Ferrero. "If it was, we'd need mouths like a baleen whale."

"If I could have everyone's attention," Morgan interrupts smoothly, "since we're all together, I'd like to take a moment to address some important issues."

"You're the boss," says Ly. It appears he speaks for the table. Morgan continues.

"If you look at us, you would say that we are gathered here together for a reason. And I know what we all are thinking: we are here because of the virus each of us carries. But I don't subscribe to that belief. I have lost my job, my friends... they even got my dogs.

"A few days ago, when I was covered in blood and hiding beneath a manhole because everybody on the street was staring at me, I thought I had lost my entire life. I injured one man and killed another because of my infection. I told myself I had no control. But that simply is not true.

"The virus can take many things from us. But we say whether that is the end or just another opportunity to fight back. We can rebuild what it takes away. For every friend we have lost, we will make another. For every enemy who says we deserve death, we will live another day to spite them. I look around at each of you, and I know you are the ones in control. You chose to come here, to say that you are still human, and no virus, no corporation, and no court can devalue the person you are.

"A great man once said that he had a dream of a world in which his children were not judged by the color of their skin but the content of their character. That dream even today is not complete, but it did change the world, and this country is a better place for it. My dream is that we see our trials through to the end and only accept a victory that recognizes in us the same life and liberties any human being ought to have."

Ferrero is the first one to applaud, and the rest join in. It is a small sound, weak to the ear, but it is what we have. I stand up, and the others follow suit.

"I guess someone took a public speaking course," Cass jokes.

"I had time to think," Morgan says.

"Can we have a toast?" suggests Ferrero. "To seeing our trial through?"

"To winning," Cass rephrases, and we murmur assent. Glasses ring.

At that moment, I feel better than I have in years. I don't usually fall for pretty words, but this feels different. I saw Morgan at his worst, and never did he hesitate or seem less than certain of his cause. He is genuine, and now, so am I. That must count for something.

"But do we know how to do it?" Deborah asks. The room is quiet for a second, and she adds, "I mean, tell us the details. You can't physically be in the court, right? They'd arrest you."

They all sit down. "We've given that some thought," Morgan says, "and we have a plan."

31 - KERN

September 7th

I put the hardcopy lab results on the safehouse kitchen table. Next to it goes a desktop paper shredder. None of the F-prots move when I drop the news on them. Then, Yarborough, as if it is his job to call everything bullshit, speaks up.

"Is this a backhanded way of telling us we suck?"

I keep on my serious face. "There is no team I would rather have sanitizing the scene, but this turn of events is unfortunate in ways I haven't fully comprehended yet."

Olsen seems angry. "That vipe didn't give her a love tap. He stabbed her in the neck."

"Staged for our benefit," Breunig says. He and I have conferred, and now we present a united front. "He knew she'd live through it because of her infection."

"That sounds like one dubious tactic," says Olsen. Her head is in her hands, and she clenches her lopsided hair. Her eyes are closed, recalling. "Not only that, you're saying Infinity was infected before the raid. That means that all of us, Cawdor included, went through training with her and didn't notice a thing?"

"I said there was a leak," Breunig says. "I just thought it was in management."

I break in. "I spoke with her superior in L.A. He said there were no signs. But she did have a week or so where she was incommunicado. That must have been her transition period."

The medic sits up. "I should have had her get tested after Lorenz's house. Fuck, we should have screened her before we even cleared her for the run."

"She even joked about it," says Yarborough. "'No, no, I didn't get bitten, here. I made soup.' What a cold bitch she must be."

"I need a shower," says al-Ibrahim. "And a blood screen."

"That brings me to the other lab results." I offer the paper, and Yarborough steps up to take it and read. "You may want to sit down."

Comprehension dawns on the F-prot's face. "Okay," he says. "I thought this meeting could not get worse." He hands the paper to Breunig. It does not take long before he wordlessly passes it to Olsen and al-Ibrahim, who looks over Olsen's shoulder.

"Well," says al-Ibrahim. "I guess that explains why he's not here."

"I know it's hard to believe," Breunig says. "He was a pro about exposure."

Yarborough nods. "Dude was ice."

Al-Ibrahim snorts. "He was single. If DeStard wanted to lick you, you'd find a reason."

"I am a long way from being Roland," Yarborough says. "Is there a way we can get confirmation on this before we do... whatever it is you want us to do?"

I maintain eye contact. I have to get this right, or a lot of plans will come to a screeching halt. If Ranath or the rest of them figure out the line I walk, I will not have long to live. "The sample was retested to avoid human error. Getting a second sample from Roland is not in our procedure, for a very good reason. If he were compelled to feed or perceived us as hostile..." I let them think. "I'm sure you know his capabilities better than I do."

Yarborough looks green. "I'm just saying, maybe the guy has earned a trial, too, you know? This kind of thing has to have happened before."

"It happened in the early days of the program," Breunig says.

Al-Ibrahim takes it in stride. "So... what happened to the poor guy? Girl. Whatever."

Breunig is blunt. "They became a vipe, and to gain allies, they started infecting deliberately. Both had to be terminated."

"Do we know that she bit him?" tries al-Ibrahim. "I mean, maybe he'd be willing to hunt her down at least."

Olsen is irritated. "What is up with you assuming her mouth was on him? He was covered in her blood when he healed her. A bad hangnail could have done it."

"However he got it, he got it," I say, trying to take control. "All the wishing in the world won't make that go away. Now, before anyone decides to contact him, I should also point out that though he revealed Infinity's infected status, he did not approve of tying her off as a vector. He thought I might be able to arrange something. It was evident that he was emotionally compromised."

Yarborough leafs through the report. "That really doesn't sound like Roland."

I warm to the lie. I've rehearsed it. "I'm not saying he wasn't himself. He tried to make it sound logical, and to be honest, he said a lot of the same things you four are saying now. Shouldn't we just talk to Infinity? Bring her in? Restrain her? I know that whole process because four years ago, I went through it with Dr. Ulan.

"We tried the reasonable solution, and it made things worse. She fed, she infected, and now we are where we are today. Roland understood that for years, but no matter how understandable his new position is, it is wrong." Yarborough starts to say something, but I cut him off. "I can't speak to his mental state, but he's a smart guy. As soon as he found out Infinity was infected, I'm sure he did the math and guessed that he could be positive in days. You know him best. Is he the sort of F-prot who gives up when he's frightened? Or does he get dangerous? Would he infect? Recruit? Train others?"

The words sink in. I have them.

Yarborough stares at the lab results, as if he can find a loophole in them. I pray that there's nothing wrong in there. I prepared it to fool Olsen; to the grunt, it should be airtight.

Breunig is the first to speak. "Roland had a saying. 'Killing's a lot less dangerous than fighting.'"

"Yeah," al-Ibrahim agrees. "I don't want to fight that guy."

Yarborough hands the hardcopy back to me, and I know he's on board. I put the report in the shredder. The machine whirs, and then there is nothing left to do.

"You won't have to," says Yarborough. "I'll start cooking."

32 - RANATH

September 9th

The safehouse looks well-cleaned: if Infinity fed here, I can't tell. It smells more like lemon-scented sprays than a serial killer's den. I do my due diligence with pistol out, clearing every room, just in case she's hiding. But her possessions aren't here. Her mess isn't here. If that weren't obvious enough, there is a note left on the kitchen counter. It's under a little wooden block of some kind, a paperweight perhaps. The note itself is full of cross-outs, but it's legible:

Roland,

If you're reading this, you came looking for me. I don't think any kind of threat will warn you off, so let me set something straight here.

Lying to you feels like one of the worst things I've ever done, but that doesn't mean I won't do it again. I've seen this pattern before. Because I've got a pretty face, guys convince themselves they're in love and forgive me all kinds of things. That is a mistake.

This little carving is from the first commandment I ever broke. It's a graven image of Baal, god of the Canaanites and the princess Jezebel. When I had no future, and no god listened to my prayers, I made this, to keep a secret from my father. It reminded me that even the most powerful men don't know everything. But I have no secrets to hide anymore, so it's yours.

I appreciate everything you did for me, but I don't deserve it. Let me go. Just because you saved my life doesn't mean you can save me.

Infinity
P.S. I vacuumed and cleaned out the sink traps, so don't bother looking for hairs.

I pick up the lump on the table. It's a cherry-wood tablet, probably ten centimeters long and well-worn. The image is of a man with a scepter over his head and a stalk of grain in his other hand, wearing a sword at his waist. It is cool to the touch, as if it has been washed recently to get rid of any identifying residues.

What strikes me about it is that it obviously has been made with care. I read the letter again and think of her in high school or college, praying to a dead god. And I consider the question of exactly which secrets of my own I wish to keep.

I pocket the idol. If it has been washed, there is little I can do to track her with it. I pace through the living room, periodically squatting low to the ground to see if she has missed any hairs. As I work, I review the letter to discern her state of mind. If she is worried about me as a physical threat, she will be careful in her feeding habits. If she is distraught, she is less likely to clean up after herself. That means victims alive and infected.

And why am I here? Will I really track her?

I go into the bedroom and pause by the nightstand. Am I clinging to procedure to save me from thinking deeply? I decided long ago that what I do is a public service. Police are ineffectual against a threat like VIHPS; I was not—am not.

Every time a vipe eluded me, whenever they struck victims while the team was still chasing financial records, whenever I ran down a false positive, I told myself that I would not quit. I had the pride to say the best vipe hunter in the world was staring out of the mirror back at me, and I would not let that standard slip.

But who among the victims of the infected ever asked for my help? Were I to tell them what I do, there would have been no gratitude, just fear. My work is secret, for with it comes shame.

"Here's the question," I say to myself. "What qualifies as having second thoughts, and what's just thoughts?"

I run my hand over the bed and pillow, feeling and looking for any trace of her. Infinity has long hair, which I know from personal experience sheds at a steady rate. But I find nothing on pillows or sheets. Not far away lies a roll of masking tape, no doubt used in the cleanup effort. I check the trash cans throughout the apartment: all the bags are missing. Her thoroughness is unusual. Simon Walter

Davis would not have written an emotional letter and still remembered to give the pillows and floors a once-over.

I check the broom in the kitchen pantry, another likely spot. Nothing. In my experience, completely getting rid of traces is nearly impossible, and I wonder if she has gone so far as to borrow someone else's cleaning supplies and return them afterward. I examine the vacuum cleaner—amazingly, it too has been picked clean.

She wasn't afraid of me at my house. But now?

I try the bathroom. I fish a finger into the drain and get wadded hair, but the strands are mostly brown, possibly some previous occupant's. Reality being what it is, the safehouse probably sees use as a house, period, whenever BRHI has the need. I crouch low, thinking.

If Infinity had family in the area, she'd have run to them already. With no source of income, she'll likely turn up in police custody or a hospital. I can't imagine her benumbed enough to let the police clap on the handcuffs. She will be shot resisting arrest. Unless I find her first.

And how merciful can I be?

A glint of gold gets my attention as I check behind the toilet. Something lies in the narrow gap between the sink's counter and the wall. I have long enough fingers that I can reach it. It's a closed, brass-colored tube of lipstick. It seems odd that Infinity would forget it, for she certainly can't have packed many after relocating to D.C., but then I remember a conversation about her previous careers. She modeled for a time, and we do not throw away our skills and tools when we move on to new things. We keep them, like weapons, and when she met our team, she no doubt had a few tubes for making an impression. I take the top off gingerly.

It is a plum color, passed over in favor of the red berry I've seen her wear. That does not matter now. The business end of the lipstick is worn down. There will be skin cells there.

I have her.

*　*　*

I let the autopilot take over as I fish in the grocery bag on the passenger seat. I acquire a yogurt, key lime flavor, and break out a spoon from a small package I keep between the seats. I don't like autopilots as a rule, but if I'm going to be burning yin in earnest tonight, I should prepare my gut flora to take the hit.

The setting sun flashes between the trees as the Chevy cruises out of the sprawl and into what passes for rural in the era of never-ending population growth. I tune the radio in briefly to NCR, authorize a microtransaction and play spot-the-tail in the rearview mirror. No cars do anything unexpected; no faces seem familiar. I finish the yogurt and cue up a playlist of classic rock. The best thing about being old is having a decent soundtrack.

When the car pulls into the home stretch, I retake manual control. I can see figures in the cul-de-sac at the end of the road and slow down to navigate. The neighbors have set up a hockey goal. A team's worth of twelve-year-olds are taking shots with tennis balls at a very beleaguered goalie. I click the garage remote and roll down my window as Parvati comes over.

"Roland! Sorry for the delay. Samar wanted to try out for the team, so we're giving him the stress test. Did I remember you playing goalie some year and getting awards?"

I attempt to remember what I've told her. She's been so completely off my radar that I'm honestly not sure. I go with the truth. "No, not on a team. I went to a camp, once, but it was basically to give me something to do for the summer. I got a 'most improved' because I started off so terrible at the beginning of the session."

"Oh," she laughs. "I was telling them you might help when you got home. If you remember anything, he'd love to hear from you."

I have to laugh. "After the day I've had, something normal would be good."

"Trouble with the contractors?"

"We don't use any at the office."

"For some reason, I thought you did."

A thought occurs. "Let me just send the car in," I say, and Parvati steps off.

"Okay, kids, other side of the street! Roland wants to see what you've got!"

I press the Go Home button on the car's dash and grab the remote off the visor. The car is pretty bright. It idles forward slowly until the kids are out of the way and then heads into the garage. I go over to the new goal setup, click the garage remote and gather my audience.

"Everyone bear with me," I say to the kids. "It's been a while since I've done this. The first thing to do is to push, not hit. It gives you more control. Here, I'll need a stick—"

For a few seconds, I have no idea what happens. I am hit in the back, as if one of the kids plowed into me, and I sprawl onto the asphalt. Only after I realize the kids and Parvati have also been knocked down do I register the sound of destruction that pounds my eardrums louder than any gunshot. I prop myself up on stinging forearms and look back at what is left of my house.

The main structure still stands, but the garage is gone. Giant holes gape where the walls were, and the beams of the frame are bowed outwards. The garage door is in the driveway, ringing as debris rains down on it, shingles and wood and smaller things. The Chevy's windows have all blown out, and its roof is now crumpled down. Black smoke billows from it, mixing with the plume of white dust above the house spreading into the trees.

My first coherent thought is that a drone has hit the building with a missile. It doesn't matter what the truth is. The danger is that whatever caused this could do much worse.

"Who's hit?" I yell. "Can everybody run?"

The words sound faint. I need to heal my eardrums. But it's not a total loss and I can read Parvati's lips a little. They're bloody from the pavement.

"God, what is this?"

"Get away from the house," I say. Pain registers in my head and neck. The kids start talking, but it is mostly expletives. "Everybody!" I bark. "Call 911. Get everyone in a vehicle and get out of here."

"What happened?"

"Someone tried to kill me. They could still be here. You have to leave."

That gets them on the move. I scan the skies, but don't see anything like a drone. I shake my limbs—nothing broken. I pull my pistol and advance on the rubble of the garage before realizing six teenagers are getting a good look at me doing so. I don't care. If someone is following up on the hit, I'd better be prepared.

The knocked-off garage door has nails sticking out of it. Mostly bent, some in pieces, some embedded sideways into the aluminum. Then, I get close and see hundreds of holes shredding the roof of the car. The shaped charge and its nail bomb were targeted. The concrete floor of the garage was slammed the hardest—the doors and walls were just gravy.

The door closing was the cue. A day's surveillance would have shown my usual routine: pull into the garage, close it behind me via remote while still in the car. Who has that knowledge? Not Infinity. Not Morgan. This is someone new, or it is Breunig and Yarborough? And Kern, who knows where I live.

The building is on fire, but it isn't an inferno made to look pretty for a movie camera. The worst of it is trying to breathe. It is all dust and smoke, with the chemical crap smell from the garage's cans of paint and WD-40. Had the car or lawn mower not been electric, their fuel would have gone up like fireworks. As it is, most of what I smell is burning upholstery. The trash cans look like a giant punched them. Every tool I ever hung on a peg board is scattered across the lawn, which hasn't started to blaze yet—

Ena.

The interior door to the house is off its doorframe, and it blocks the route inside. I pull my shirt up over my nose and charge into the cloud of dust.

I first shove through the debris with one hand, then give up on the whole pistol idea because if someone is lying in wait, it sure isn't inside. I struggle into the front hallway, stepping on the glass and picture frames all over the place. A moment's thought for the front door—yes, there is a second bomb there in case I opened it—and then,

I'm on the stairs. There, too, are broken frames: my university and medical degrees, my certifications from the Army, lying on the stairs so I have to kick them aside. I need a clean path because the door saying RESPECT is in front of me, and if I screw this up now, I'll be all kinds of dead.

My foot comes down on the snake stick at the base of the stairs. I snatch it up. The basement is dim, and I don't risk flicking on a light in case a third bomb is waiting. The white room's musty smell is refreshing compared to the stench upstairs, and Ena's UV light shows that she is agitated. Her body is pressed up against the glass, trying to climb out the top.

Ena has a trap box in the enclosure. If I can encourage her into it, I can carry her safely. I unlock the cage, open it, and Ena pours out. She slips away from the pincers once, twice. Then, I get her neck and tail. I aim her head at the trap box, but she crawls to its side.

A roar comes from upstairs. The stove is gas. In Okinawa, they taught that you had to shut off the gas line in an earthquake, but I hadn't thought of it.

I have no time. I grip her with the stick and run for the stairs with absolutely no idea what to do next. The guns are in safes, but not all the ammo is. Enough flame could turn this place into Swiss cheese. I want to get the Kriss, but black smoke is everywhere now.

I have to go through it. Crawling with my hands full could make me lose my grip. The smoke and the particles burn my eyes with such pain that there might be an actual ember in them. The heat from the kitchen is so intense, I don't know if I am running next to fire or through it. I blunder into a doorframe and then into the hood of the car. Ena bumps the hood, wriggles, and my left hand gets wet. I don't care about being crapped on. I use the shredded car as a guide and cough my way through the acrid smoke. Only when I can smell the fresh air of the street do I open the least-painful watery eye to figure out what the hell I can do now.

Parvati's van is down the street, all hands aboard. My scalp is hot and painful, but I don't dare let go of Ena. I run across the cul-de-sac to the curb. Tomorrow is Thursday, and the highly responsible Parvati left out her garbage cans.

I kick one over and tug at the locked top with my hand full of shit and snake. The lock comes free, and once it is empty, in goes the back half of Ena. After some slick wriggling, the top is back on and clamped firmly shut.

Finally, I touch whatever the hell is happening on my head. It hurts more, so I shake my hair until the embers have fallen out. With the hand that is only covered in dust, not feces, I dab at my still-closed right eye, trying to get out whatever has lodged in there.

Assess. Then recover.

I start jogging, dragging the garbage can behind me. I need to get away before either the cops, or the F-prots arrive. Their surveillance will still be in place. My phone must be considered compromised, but if I make it to a gas station, I can call a taxi. Then a rental car. Then many other things.

I feel for the pistol. It has four rounds in it. One for Breunig. One for Yarborough. One for Olsen. One for al-Ibrahim. It is not a realistic plan, but it is all I can think of right now.

And as for Kern, my anger alone can destroy him.

33 - RANATH

September 14th

It becomes clear over the next few days that the F-prots don't have much of a plan, either. I guess they don't immediately have a good story cooked up for the cops, and that means none of the cooperation that usually puts pressure on a fugitive. I cross into Maryland to withdraw from a bank and turn the cash into a motel stay. I keep Ena in the locking can in the room with a DO NOT DISTURB sign on the door. I pour energy into the points of my head and neck to speed healing. Then, I get on with the business of finding a potential ally.

Infinity's signature is not easy to latch onto, nor does it stay still. I attempt unsuccessfully to make contact over five days, but her signal eludes me. When I was new to F-prot, I worried myself thin in situations like this. The source of interference is all too obvious. Every feeding is like a middle finger jabbed in my eye. But I conserve my cell samples and bide my time. As she goes without blood, her signal returns. The trick is catching her just before she feeds again.

I have performed enough tracking functions to have a rough feel of the signal's distance. When I first detect it, it moves slowly, then takes a sudden acceleration, typical of a vipe who has gotten into a vehicle. After a few fits, she takes a long, linear path into the city. I get into my rental car, letting the function slip into the back of my mind while I drive over the 14th Street Bridge.

The signal doesn't map to Washington's street grid. Only when I notice its low elevation does the truth dawn—Infinity is riding the Metro.

Time to guess which stop. Perhaps she's going to a demonstration in front of the Capitol. But as I get close, the road ends: First Street is closed off with giant orange barriers and National Guardsmen in black, ballistic silk waving me east.

Once I'm clear of the Capitol, I weave through the semicircles surrounding my next guess: Union Station. In the shadow of stone eagles and flags and fancy, dynamic maglev rails, I park hastily and run in.

I push through the lobby. It's all overpriced shops and weak interior lights. I go for an empty corner and kneel as if to rest, glancing at the crowd. It's thin without the commuter rush. No transit police but enough witnesses to hang me if something has to happen.

I breathe deeply, exhaling for a count of eight to relax into the function. Instead, I think of Infinity, bags packed, car ditched, bound for parts unknown in the northeast corridor.

No. Even if she has an e-ticket, she'll have to wait at the gates like everyone else. I spread out my net. It would be just like Infinity to leave no gap between her arrival and boarding time.

Thap-thap.

I get nothing at first, soured by performance anxiety. My face is clammy. I wipe it, rehearsing what I will say. I have brought her wooden image, to give it back to her. I'm not sure if she'll want it. But as a pretense for not being a complete stalker, it's as good as any.

Then, I feel her by the tracks, tasting a strange mix of emotions in her elements. I would think she'd be full of loneliness and fear, but here she is, impressed, welcoming, companionable. If she's working a prey item, she's preternaturally calm about it. She's also moving: going down.

I run after her, and my stimweb threatens to shake loose and dim the qi function. But I know where the Metro entrance is. I put my hand in my pocket, over the pistol, and run through the crowd, identifying passing people. No one upstairs has Infinity's shape or age. I choose the stairs over the escalator: faster, less crowded.

I hear her laugh as she goes through the turnstile. Someone is with her. I get only a glimpse of a head scarf and sunglasses and freeze. I can jump the turnstile and confront them or blend. A third option: I could get back to the car and follow them overland. No. Damned if I'm going to lose visual contact now. I dash to the ticket machine and feed in bills because I can't dock my phone. It's at the bottom of the Potomac River, where the F-prots can try to find it.

As much as I want to rush after the women, being spotted could provoke Infinity. Besides her considerably dangerous martial art of choice, there aren't metal detectors here, and she wears a firearm. I want to rule out at least one of the two before making a move. I stay on the upper platform, out of sight, until the lights by the tracks begin to flash. As the subway train floats in, I go down the escalator and hook around its opposite side. I wind up some five meters behind her, out of her line of sight as she enters.

The women sit by the window as I rush for the next car back. I move to the interior door and get a good look at her through its glass. I only see the corner of the strange woman's face—she has not removed her sunglasses. Vipe, maybe. But Infinity has her own eyewear off, so it's not a question of light level. Drug use? Eye exam? No. The sunglasses are a wide, old style. She doesn't want to be recognized.

I leave my post as the exits open and glance down the side of the train. Not their stop. Next stop, too. By the time I return, more people are in Infinity's car, and I can't see her at all.

"Coming up, Gallery Place-Chinatown," announces the driver cheerfully. I rack my brains. Did Infinity know any celebrities in her time in Los Angeles? But that makes no sense—who crosses the U.S. by rail rather than air?

I tap the tacks in my skin. This surprise can't shake me. When the next stop comes and goes, I squint through the dirty glass and find Infinity's car is still full. I wonder about the woman's head scarf. I can't imagine Infinity sustaining a friendship with a devout Muslim or, for that matter, a devout pretty-much-anything.

Another stop. They're still laughing. The woman's Western pantsuit is not a good clue, but I strive to place the nationality of the head scarf. My best frames of reference are a Jordanian girl I met briefly at MIT and an Iranian newscaster. I'm pretty sure the two are significantly different. I'll search-engine it later: I can't be distracted now.

The train pulls in to Metro Center. Infinity follows the crowd. I hurriedly exit. Once, she hesitates, looking around, but her gaze sweeps right past me. The women descend yet another escalator, me shadowing them.

Infinity doesn't get on the first train. She holds her companion back. They converse, then turn to the opposite track, where another train is getting ready to depart. Infinity points at the display on the side of the train. Wrong destination. The two women go up an escalator, not the one they came down. This is my opportunity.

I sprint up the stairs by the original escalator. As the two women head up to the Red Line's double tracks, I stand on the far side, immediately across from them. If Infinity is going to reach me, she'll have to dash thirty feet over two maglev rails. I grip the weapon in my pocket.

"Lost?" I call.

They look over, and both freeze. Infinity puts a protective hand in front of her friend and hisses something to her. The woman hurries away, glancing behind herself fearfully.

"I thought you had a car," Infinity says.

I'm not in the mood for small talk. "I thought you were an idol worshipper. You and your friend, do you just stay off the topic of religion or something?"

"We've got lots in common. What happened to your hair?"

"Let me tell you." I jerk my head, and we walk in parallel down the length of the tracks. Hardly anyone is near us—the Red Line has just come and gone. There is a chance of being overheard, but she is a more immediate threat than some curious bystander.

"They tried to eliminate me," I say.

"Right." One utterance. She quashes my hopes, then checks for F-prots.

"Have I ever lied to you before?" I ask.

She shrugs. "It'd be fair play."

"Are you with our friend Mr. L now?"

"What do you care? If you're independent, run for the hills."

"You said you had no secrets left."

"Give me a break. It sounded better than 'peace, out.'"

"If this trial doesn't shake out in your favor, things are going to get worse for you. I want to get your side some information before the fact discovery is complete."

"My girl's our expert." Infinity frowns. "What do you have that she doesn't?"

"You got a pad?"

"Just a phone."

"Pop open the notes."

"I can memorize. What's this about?"

"I bet she doesn't know where the vectors end up when you bring in a live one," I say. "Do you?"

"No."

"Right, we started compartmentalization when some of the field operatives got squeamish. But originally, here in D.C., I was the one bringing them in to a place called Greenbriar Health. Remember the following address." I tell her, and she repeats it back to me.

"This is what, because we're on the same side now?"

"You said no one ever is. I disagree. I'm not on Kern's anymore, that's for sure."

"Doesn't mean I'm giving you anything." The silence stretches painfully long. She is an interesting, resilient, beautiful creature, but I must remember in my affection that she is not me.

Infinity speaks. "Assuming the team doesn't jump me the second I get off my train, I'm supposed to take this back. I give it to the crew, they give it to the lawyers, the cops then raid the place. That's what you're saying you want?"

"What you do is up to you. Just consider. Law is slow, and crime is fast."

The track lights start to blink on her side.

"This wasn't a good idea, you know." Her words speed up. "I don't know how you latched onto my aura or whatever, but I'll have to feed more often, now. I mean, I can't talk to you. Even if I could trust you, Morgan can't afford to. The other vipes, they'd shit a brick oven—"

"If you trust me—" I start.

"I can't. You just forced my hands. You think about those people I have to infect, and ask yourself if seeing me was worth it."

It stings. All my planning, all my skill, and the wrong words crash it all. "I was going to give you your present back," I say. "One of these days you're going to have to tell me which of the commandments was toughest to break."

Infinity stalks away, shaking her head as the oncoming train grows louder. Then, she looks for her companion, then turns back to me. That turn is everything.

"Number five," she calls, "honor thy—" and then, the train shoots in front of her. I can't see anything through the windows until it stops, and both women are obscured. I feel paranoid. Even if Infinity isn't hostile, another vipe, an expert in something, could be highly dangerous.

I should slap myself. The truth just revealed itself too late.

I run across the tracks. It's dangerous, but as long as you jump the third rails, you're fine. I vault onto the stone lip of the far side, hoping they are there. But either they're stuffed in the cars or they've gone to the surface. I kneel on the floor, trying to feel which it is.

Where once there was a vibrant tug on my net, now it feels like trying to catch water. It happened too fast for her to have fed. I'm being blocked. I pull out the tube of lipstick and paint my hand with it, but the skin cells are gone now.

There is nothing to do but hit the cold, reddish hex tile of the station floor. I missed every clue. A stimweb. An expert witness, afraid to show her face and body because she would be recognized. Infinity wasn't the real threat. The vipe who has always gotten away, the one most familiar with my locating methods, she is countering my functions with her own.

I step into the train to leave behind anyone who might have seen me jump the tracks. My head is a jumble of commandments, missed opportunities, and Dr. Jessica Ulan.

September 15th

"State your name for the record."

"Marcus Kern," I say.

Campion, lead lawyer for the Health Initiative, starts our routine. We practiced plenty, and today is the payoff. It's all too easy to get distracted by the packed house, the scurrying media trying to get good camera shots and the stare of Judge Bayat. Instead, I let my gaze settle on Campion's polished features. The sharp arch of her sculpted eyebrows. The gold of her earrings. The crochet-braids of her hair. Her confidence buoys mine.

"Dr. Kern, did you supervise work at the Benjamin Rush Health Initiative's Advanced Biophysics Lab on the date of the outbreak?"

"Yes."

"And have you supervised contact with that department since then?"

"Yes."

"Has your work there given you experience with people infected with Virally Induced Hematophagic Predation Syndrome?"

"Yes, just about every day."

"Did you observe biological changes in the individuals infected with this syndrome?"

"Yes."

"And what were your conclusions in a broad sense?"

"That VIHPS-infected individuals were medically unable to join normal human society."

"What observations led you to conclude that?"

"There are deep physiological changes in them. Bone, muscle, brain—where do you want me to start?"

"How about the brain? How does it change?"

"The brain undergoes a substantive development in the number of synapses between the sensory strips and the rest of the cerebral cortex. This development is unparalleled in normal adult human brain development."

"Can you be any clearer, for those of us who know a synapse is part of the brain but aren't really sure what it does?"

"A chemical synapse is basically a connection between a neuron, that is, an informational processing brain cell and another kind of cell, like a motor cell. We start off with about 10 quadrillion synapses when we're young, and stabilize to 1 to 5 quadrillion when we're older. But normally the number doesn't go up again after that. VIPHS changes that equation."

"What do you think this change to the brain does?"

"Based on our interviews with VIHPS vectors, that is, carriers, we think a few things are going on. The first is that the brain wires itself to respond to its senses differently. The vectors say they can smell and hear better, and our tests seem to back this up. They're more sensitive to light hitting the structures in their eyes."

"You said that's the first thing. What's the second thing?"

"Well, technically what's next is, after some changes occur in the brain, the body releases hormones and a storm of electrical signals. This increases absorption of calcium and compounds that increase bone mineral density. They also show a slight strengthening in skeletal muscle."

"Slight?" The lawyer looks askance. "Dr. Kern, from all accounts, an infected person is strong like a bull."

"Yes, but if you'll look at a vector, you know, a carrier of the disease, he doesn't look like a bodybuilder. His strength comes from different physiological changes."

"And what are those?"

"The increased mineral absorption leads to ossification—bone growth. The bones become slightly more striated. If you look at them with a microscope, you can see they are rougher, which leads to more muscular adhesion points.

"In short, because the muscles have better grips on a reinforced bone, they can generate and withstand greater forces."

I watch the man behind the bench. Judge Bayat has been listening, slightly bored, but now he rises in his chair, puzzled. Campion's eyes go to Bayat as well. There's an opportunity here. If we can establish ourselves as Bayat's guide through the science, half the battle is won.

Campion feeds me. "Dr. Kern, that doesn't sound like something that would make me nonhuman. In fact, that sounds like a pretty good deal."

"The other reason is just as important."

"I don't have to ask, do I? You want to enlighten us."

I flash a smile. "The other reason that they're strong is because they use more primitive parts of the brain."

"Objection," Cho says. "Inflammatory."

Bayat gets involved. "Dr. Kern, avoid pejorative labels. And while you're at it, I think we'd all like to hear how any part of the brain can make someone stronger."

I lay it on. "We did functional MRI scans on vectors and on humans making the same grasping motions with their hands. In the case of the humans, the predominant brain area lit up was in the cerebrum, in the primary motor cortex. Now, you can guess why a motor cortex has that name. It controls movement functions. But more specifically, it controls them *in conscious humans*. And not all functions. Just voluntary activities like walking, turning your head, stuff like that. Your lungs, your heart, your blood flow, your balance, that's part of the cerebellum, down in the brain stem. Now, I don't know how familiar you are with the biophysics of qi—"

"Assume we're not," Param Bayat interrupts.

What? "I thought you presided at trials involving—"

"Mr. Kern, I am telling you, assume we're not. I want to hear your explanation." Bayat looks at me coldly.

Bayat's walking straight into my plan. If he wants the lecture, I have the theatricality to back it up. "I'll start with an example. Have you ever seen a demonstration of iron shirt qigong?"

"Assume no."

"Well, you're in luck. I brought a friend who can demonstrate. For safety reasons, he's not infected. Your Honor, can we—"

Campion overrides me. It's her prerogative to ask permission. "Your Honor, may Dr. Karras approach so we can observe Dr. Kern's expertise in action?"

"What would this entail?"

"Counsel accepts Dr. Karras as a demonstration subject so Dr. Kern can prove his biophysical expertise. May he approach?"

"He may. Just keep it relevant."

Campion turns and gestures to the crowd. A middle-aged man with a slight paunch rises and approaches the bench. I met Karras through Ranath, back when the three of us were young and enthusiastic about all things qi-related. We go into the routine: Karras removes his shirt, causing a lot of confused faces among the reporters and onlookers. This is not on their agenda.

"Is removing his shirt necessary?" asks Geoffrey Cho from across the room.

"We will be going into anatomical details." I say. "I want Dr. Karras's physique clearly visible so there's less doubt about the results. For the record, Dr. Karras does not have what most people call six-pack abs. Most people would say, if you punched him in the stomach, you'd probably expect him to double over and start sucking air. Correct?"

Campion thinks I'm addressing her. "What I'd expect is that he'd get really mad." Laughter from the audience.

"Yes, but the point here is demonstration. I promise he's not going to hurt anyone. Now, if you hit him in the stomach, nobody would think his brain would save him. I mean, if he stands right there, he can think all he wants. His ab muscles are not going to get stronger, correct?"

"Objection," Cho calls. "Witness keeps asking questions, and counsel is answering."

"Sustained. Dr. Kern, stick to explaining."

"All right. The usual answer is no. Maybe if he worked himself up with adrenaline, he'd get a little tougher, but we're not even going to allow Dr. Karras that luxury. I would like to ask Ms. Campion to assist the demonstration. In the interests of showing how the brain can strengthen the muscles, I am going to request that you hit Dr. Karras in the stomach as hard as you can."

The silence is nervous. Campion looks around. "Are you sure you two are friends?"

A low murmur of laughter.

"Counsel..." Bayat says, with a finger gesture that says, *move it along*. We have done our homework well. Bayat presided over a similar demonstration eight years ago. Instead of asking what the hell we're doing with fisticuffs in a courtroom, he looks bored.

"Okay, I'll do it," says Campion. "No harm intended."

"No problem," says Karras, who looks completely unconcerned.

The lawyer takes a breath, balls up her fist and swings.

Karras snorts out a small puff of air as there is a brief *thap*. Campion looks bewildered. Karras's expression doesn't change.

"That it?" I say.

Campion's face hardens. Without a word, she tries again. I know a little about punching, courtesy of Ranath and Karras, and it looks like Campion saw boxing on TV and is attempting to emulate it. She puts her body into this shot, swinging low and hooking into Karras's unprotected stomach. Then, the lawyer steps back, shaking her hand.

"Are you all right?"

"My wrist stings. He's like a rock."

Geoffrey Cho frowns. "She's not doing it right." Sinclair, the bailiff, also looks unimpressed. Bayat's expression is neutral. Maybe I can get away with just a little more.

"I hear the voice of a skeptic. Your Honor, with your permission, I'd like to extend the invitation to Mr. Cho, Mr. Sinclair, or anyone else who would like to try."

"Dr. Kern, this isn't a sideshow. Mr. Sinclair is going to keep order over this courtroom. If Mr. Cho has issues with what is going on, specifically your expertise, I will allow him to rebut. Mr. Cho, explain your earlier comment."

"Well, Dr. Kern hasn't really gone into his explanation yet, but I don't think that punch was very hard."

"Do you think it was faked?"

"I think it was at least an untrained punch, Your Honor, and not necessarily demonstrative of the point Dr. Kern is trying to make. This whole thing supposes that he's using qi, not muscle. But Dr. Karras doesn't have a stimweb, he's not being hit all that hard, and the main point, really, is that Dr. Kern, Dr. Karras, and Ms. Campion obviously all know one another. This demonstration has been rehearsed."

"Dr. Kern, do you have anything to say in response?"

"These are all excellent points, Your Honor. There is a mountain of propaganda and misinformation about the nature of qi. For centuries, people who have reached Dr. Karras's level of martial training have exploited it and claimed all sorts of things. They've said they're the sons of gods or enlightened, and most of all, they've said, 'I'll only teach this to you if you give me a lot of money.'" The audience laughs. "Seriously, I would like to extend my invitation again to Mr. Cho. If he thinks he can show us a proper hit, it would only help."

"Your Honor?"

"Mr. Cho, I do not want to get into an extended discussion of your technique versus Ms. Campion's, so with the caveat that you absolutely do not get carried away, you may participate in Dr. Kern's demonstration if it will help your case."

"Well, I'm not sure it will, Your Honor, but it will certainly resolve whether this is a fraudulent display or not."

The audience murmurs. Karras smiles at me. I give it back.

Cho approaches, and I notice he's slightly taller and larger than Karras. I try to assess Cho's musculature, but the suit hides it.

Cho gives Karras a head nod, an abbreviated bow. "You ready?"

"Anything you've got," says Karras.

Instantly, I know from Cho's eyes that something is wrong. Cho drops one foot back, balls his fists and lunges, driving a karate-style kick into Karras's stomach.

Karras shifts slightly and exhales, and Cho stumbles backward, knocked off balance by a sudden reverse of momentum. The whole thing is over in about a second. The crowd murmur is like sweet honey.

"Mr. Cho," snaps Bayat, "I allowed this demonstration as a matter of verification. I did not allow it as a venue for venting testosterone. You are extremely fortunate that your burst of temper will not get you disbarred. Are you able to continue?" Cho is leaning on a table.

"Yeah," he says, too distracted to add the honorific.

"On the matter of fraudulence, then, have you... reached a conclusion?" The spectators laugh. "While I'm glad we're putting on an entertaining show, Dr. Kern did promise us an explanation of how this is accomplished. Sit down, counsel. Dr. Kern?"

My turn. "All right, now if we simply look at the size of the muscles—" I try to slow down. Public speaking is about cadence and clarity. "—you would think Dr. Karras would be on the ground. Mr. Cho was using his thigh muscle for that kick. It's the biggest muscle in the body, but it worked against Mr. Cho. This is because Dr. Karras is not using simply his stomach muscles.

"The muscles of his ankle, his calf, his thigh, and his hip all squeeze in ascending order. Like an egg that is so much stronger top to bottom instead of side to side, this path of muscles through his body provides a straight line of force down to the ground. Along that path, he's pushing back. When that fist hits him, he's quite literally hitting back with his stomach and stopping that fist. It's just not visible. That's why it's called an internal martial art. You can't see it. You can feel it, you can see its effects, but for centuries, it was a mystery.

"Even the people doing it passed on the knowledge of how to do it without knowing how it worked. There was a pattern for how to learn it, and they taught that.

"If you went into the right martial arts class, they would tell you to relax, to visualize and to have 'no mind.' That's important. I can tell you, squeeze that bottom muscle, then the middle, then the top," I say, drawing a line up Karras's leg. "But if the signal from Dr. Karras's brain is just a tiny bit off, he might tighten them top, bottom, middle. And he'd get knocked flat like anyone else. It has to be in order and in under a quarter of a second." I snap my fingers. "That's how fast a punch or kick is from the moment the other guy starts it. If he *thinks* wrong, his foundation falls apart."

I pick up my glass of water from the witness stand and drink for a moment. It's tepid, but I need it. Cho sits at his desk pretending to be interested in flicking a pen back and forth. I'm making an enemy today, but Cho is the opposition. He was going to be one anyway.

"So, what's he doing? He's literally not thinking. He's still got brain activity on an fMRI scan but not in the same areas you and I do. He has shifted control of his posture and his muscle contractions away from conscious control and into the subconscious. His cerebrum shuts up, and the cerebellum does all the work. The body gets only one smooth signal, no hesitation. People call that clarity all sorts of things because suddenly gaining an altered state of consciousness feels like a mystical experience. They say you're enlightened, or the loa are riding you, or in China, they thought they felt qi... internal energy.

"Normally, fiddling around with traditional teachings, it'll take you five to ten years to learn Dr. Karras's trick. With a stimweb, it's closer to five to ten months. As for VIHPS... it's five days. Our fMRI scans indicate that one hundred percent of the time, vipes' bodily movements are under direct control by the cerebellum. Every single adult VIHPS-positive individual free of brain damage can do what Dr. Karras has just demonstrated. You can struggle and hit them, and it won't do a damn thing."

A susurrus goes through the crowd, as people shift in their seats and whisper in ears. My eye's on Bayat. The old man is calm, a rock in the rain. He showed little expression on his face during the visceral theater, but evenly matched cases tend to go the way that the crowd twists in the gut. I've scored, even if Bayat is too good to show it.

"Bone ossification, muscle attachment points, subconscious cerebellar control. That's what makes a VIHPS individual able to overpower a normal human being ninety-nine percent of the time. Does that adequately explain the biophysics for you?"

"It does," Bayat says.

"Objection," Cho raises. "Inflammatory."

I blink. "Explaining biophysics is inflammatory?"

"Overpowering a human is not a traditional measure of strength. Inflammatory."

Bayat is unimpressed. "Ms. Campion, was that statistic submitted to opposing counsel?"

"It is among the documents we sent, Your Honor."

"Ms. Campion," says Cho, "You sent over twenty-two thousand pages of discovery. My staff and I have not yet been able to review every page. I would like to reserve the ability to make the objection at a later point after we have reviewed the material further."

Bayat steps in. "You've had one month to review all discovery, and we aren't even in evidentiary yet. You have until tomorrow to argue this objection. Ms. Campion, continue."

Campion is all business again. "Dr. Kern, do these changes make a VIHPS-positive individual more dangerous to society at large?"

"Undoubtedly."

"More dangerous, to the level that they cannot be exposed to society?"

"Yes, but not by itself. I mean, we still have guns in this country, and we figure most law-abiding people can be trusted with them. But vector brains also change in a secondary way that is certainly the tipping point."

"And what is that?"

"They're addicts of human blood," I say. "You don't give an addict a gun."

35 - KERN

September 16th

The questions on standing drag on into a second day, when Cho approaches.

"Dr. Kern," Cho says, with all the polish of new silverware. My eyes are on my sleeve, as a glitch of mayonnaise has migrated there from my lunch. I look up and get a flash of Cho's eyes and his smile. I only know one other man who smiles after getting knocked on his ass, and he is someone worth fearing.

"Have you ever met the plaintiff, Mr. Morgan Lorenz?" Cho asks.

"I have not."

"But you feel comfortable judging him unfit to be in our society."

"I do."

"You don't consider this prejudicial in any way? Understand, please, I am not accusing you of prejudice. I would simply ask if this is a scientific conclusion."

"It is based on our observations, which have stringent controls."

"And this is because you view every VIHPS-infected individual as a danger to our society, no exceptions?"

"Yes."

"So, even if an infected person were in a wheelchair, you would call them dangerous?"

I try a little righteous irritation. "Actually, I would, and I'll explain why. Even in that case, the vector would still need to feed. Obviously, he or she could not overpower victims easily, but if he convinced someone to voluntarily submit to the feeding process, he could still pass on the disease. Then, you have another infected individual, who *can* chase down prey, can spread their own infection, et cetera. Everyone here needs to understand; this is a merciless plague."

"But what occurs if the donor of the blood already has the disease? Do they get worse?"

"They can usually survive the process."

"I see," says Cho. "And there's no new infection."

I realize I'd better say something. "It is not, however, possible for a community of vectors to feed solely off one another, if that's where you're going."

"Not possible or not possible given our current level of understanding?"

"Not possible."

"Well, I'm sure you believe that to be the case. Are there other studies?"

"Not that I know of. And if you have some secret papers by some source other than the Initiative, by all means bring them up, and we'll subject them to peer review."

Cho turns as he paces. "So, the only studies on this disease are from the Benjamin Rush Health Initiative, and you are comfortable basing your expert testimony solely on these studies. Is that correct?"

"It follows evidence as we best understand it. That is as close as human beings get to an objective truth."

"But science changes all the time, does it not?"

Oh, please. Is this ace really going to go down the only-a-theory road of so many politicians? "Science stays the same. New studies give us new information."

Cho covers. "I'm talking about the overall view. Theories do get disproven."

"Certain theories sometimes get disproven, especially if their methods were shoddy. We obviously don't believe ours were."

"How long would you say you have been studying how qi affects the brain?"

"Formally?" Crap. What was the last anniversary? "I became a doctor about nine years ago, but I tried to learn everything I could about the webs as soon as I heard about them. So, what do we call that—thirteen years?"

"And did you work with anyone more senior than you, someone who knows more about the subject?"

"I did at first."

"Who was that person?"

"I had the privilege of working directly with Dr. Ulan."

"The founder of qi studies. Do you know when she began?"

"About twenty, twenty-five years back. You can read that in her book."

"So, this entire field of studying qi is only twenty-five years old. When was the first known case of VIHPS again?"

"The first known case, also Dr. Ulan, happened four years ago."

"Is that a long time in the history of scientific advancements?"

I can think of a few fields to compare it to, but trying to spin it is futile. "No, it's not."

"Therefore, it's entirely possible that we may learn much more about VIHPS-infected people's biology in the future. Is that correct?"

"It's possible, but certain basic facts aren't going to change. They're still going to be addicted to human blood, for example."

"I see. Are you familiar with the drug methadone?"

"Yes."

"Could you explain for us how it is used to treat heroin addicts?"

"I'm not an addiction specialist."

"You're a doctor, are you not?"

I'm pissed enough to answer. "Methadone's given as a substitute for heroin, usually a daily injection."

"That's interesting. You're saying addiction can be alleviated. Is it not possible for science to come up with a similar substitute for human blood?"

"We don't think so."

"Can you explain why?"

"It's far more about turning passive qi to active than it is about whatever nutritive value human blood has. We've tried cow blood, chimpanzee blood, cadaver blood, refrigerated blood plasma without anticoagulants—"

"If I can interrupt, you say it's more about qi."

"Yes. They need a living human as prey."

"Are drugs known to affect the qi of the user?"

"Many, though largely negatively. Alcohol and heroin, for instance—"

"What about beta blockers and zinc supplements? Don't they have a positive effect on the generation of qi?"

Bayat's watching. Can't scowl. "I know they have no effect on slaking a vector's thirst."

"But it is possible for drugs to affect the brain and alter qi generation?"

"Yes."

"And it is possible to create drugs that treat addictions?"

"Yes, but I don't believe where you're going with this is remotely plausible. Maybe in fifty years, we'll have nanomachines repairing their brains—"

"Yes or no—"

"—and you can buy a six-pack of them at liquor stores—"

"Objection, Your Honor. Goes beyond scope of the question asked."

"—but neuroscientists, hematologists, they can't solve it. People are being murdered for their blood *today*."

"Dr. Kern, rest assured that everyone in this room knows what the stakes are," Bayat says, and I know I'm losing.

Cho takes over once more. "So, in this time of crisis, you have trust in your fellow scientists at the Benjamin Rush Health Initiative."

Trick question? Can't be. "Yes."

"And there is great consensus in these doctors' professional opinion, then, that a VIHPS-infected individual's brain is fundamentally different than a normal brain, and there is no substitute for the effect that qi has on that brain."

"Yes."

"And the structural differences in the brain, do they affect more than the strength that was demonstrated earlier?"

"Yes, they shape up to be the brains of addicts."

"So... they will lack certain attributes." Cho fiddles with papers from his desk. "Would you say they lack... reason, due to this brain change?"

"If something got in between them and a fix of human blood... yes. They become obsessed. Reason does not help."

"How about... judgment?"

"Absolutely."

"Self-control?"

"Yes."

"Willpower?"

"These seem like synonyms."

"Mr. Cho, is this going somewhere?" asks Bayat.

"It is, Your Honor. Dr. Kern, you hold that your basic theories will not change substantially over time. I have here an excerpt from a textbook on neurology that makes statements similar to yours. Have you heard of Dr. Robert Bean?"

The name scratches at me, but I can't remember why. I think of biomedical engineer friends of mine at Hopkins, UVA, Harvard. Nothing. "I haven't."

"I'll read a portion of his work. It says: 'The frontal region of the Negro skull has been repeatedly shown to be much smaller than that of the Caucasian. Considering this fact, the conclusion is reached that the Negro has a smaller proportion of the faculties pertaining to the frontal lobe than the Caucasian. The Negro, then, lacks reason, judgment... self-control, willpower...' Shall I go on?"

"That's quite enough, Mr. Cho," says Bayat.

"What textbook is that?" I say.

"Dr. Robert Bennett Bean's *The Races of Man*, circa 1935. Times have changed since that view of the brain was presented. Wouldn't you agree, Dr. Kern?"

This little shit doesn't get to paint me like this. But shouting that my boss and ex are both black will sound desperate. "If your doctor were alive today, and he isn't, I doubt he'd get past peer review."

"He did, Dr. Kern. Dr. Bean attended the Johns Hopkins University, as you did, and went on to teach at the University of Virginia, using *The Races of Man* as a textbook. Do you consider your work infallible, Dr. Kern?"

"Of course not."

"Do you not think your team might have made a mistake as Dr. Bean did?"

"No." I look at the audience as if they'd help. Where's their love now?

"Why not?"

"Because I know the people involved, I've seen their work, and I've watched people I know succumb to this disease."

"You mean Dr. Ulan."

"Among others."

"When were you first aware Dr. Ulan had contracted the virus?"

"I suspected it from the moment she had the accident."

"And what symptoms did you first notice?"

He wants the hit list? Fine. "Paranoia. Agitation. Sensitivity to sunlight."

"To sunlight or all light?"

Caught. "To... bright light."

"Tell us about how the paranoia first manifested."

"Dr. Ulan was irritable and hostile when we suggested she might be infected."

"Hostile? Did she become physically violent?"

I prepared for this. "Yes. I cut my finger slicing a bagel. She attempted to feed on me, and I only got away with the help of the staff restraining her."

"Really," says Cho, and I'm about to smack him. Isn't this an asked-and-answered thing?

"Yes." I can't read Cho's expression. He's up to something. "If you ask the staff, they'll tell you the same thing. She wanted to drink my blood. It took three or four of us to stop her, and she spent the night in restraints. It wasn't long after that she broke out of the room and attempted to feed on an orderly. By the end of the first week, we ran out of Haldol—that's a sedative—and we put her in Forced Protection."

Cho isn't irritated or even thinking on his feet. He's trying to contain a smirk as he looks out over the audience. I follow his gaze and see only a mixed bag of middle-aged reporters, half telegenic and half print/screeners. I keep to rehearsed lines.

"Her stay in Forced Protection lasted for a few weeks. Then, she escaped."

"And how did that happen?"

"She infected one of the staff during a sexual liaison. He was able to undo her restraints and the doors, and then it was a short trip to the parking lot."

Again, Cho seems unfazed, and it hits me. This should have been me solidifying my lead, and instead I've jumped on a petard and started hoisting. I've been batting away Cho's questions one by one, heedless of the throughline. It's all about my personal experience, and the experience is the lie. But Cho couldn't know that unless he has a rival source waiting in the wings.

I look once more at the audience, searching for graying hair, for sunglasses. There, a woman three rows back, her ears and hair hidden under a head scarf. The woman I haven't seen in years, an expert even more qualified than me.

The Lorenz team has their mouthpiece, and her teeth are going to be sharp.

36 - JESSICA

September 17th

Honestly, Kern and I are alike in many ways, but I will wait until the heat death of the universe before saying that in public. He, of course, swore in on the Bible, assuredly to win points rather than out of genuine belief. I take an affirmation instead. If I have a soul to mark with dishonesty, I'll make myself suffer for it long before any deity gets the chance.

"You get up there like Galileo," Morgan told me. "You tell them what reality is." I didn't have the heart to tell him that Galileo caved at his trial multiple times before the famous bit of defiance. I'm not going to do a damn thing like Galileo. I'm going to do it like Ulan.

Cho approaches me, all white teeth and moussed hair. He looks a little like my younger brother, twenty years and a mountain of paranoia ago. I haven't seen him in person since the infection. But the questions are familiar, rehearsed, comforting.

"Dr. Ulan, where was your last place of official employment?"

"It was at the BRHI Advanced Biophysics Experimental Laboratory."

"And how did your employment there officially end?"

"I became infected with a level 5 biohazardous material, a yin-qi-saturated version of European Bat Lyssavirus-4. I stopped going to work there because it was contagious."

"Contagious how?"

"Saliva-to-blood and blood-to-blood. It cannot be airborne."

"And how did your infection occur?"

"I was saturating a petri dish with yin qi. The energy broke it, and the virus got in the cut in my hand."

"Were you violating safety protocol at the time?"

"No. A level 4 lab is built to contain viruses like Ebola or simian hemorrhagic fever. A level 5 lab adds qi sterilization procedures. It was, at that time, considered as stringent as we could possibly be. Nonetheless, our precautions proved inadequate since my infection got through."

"This virus is the originator of Virally Induced Hematophagic Predation Syndrome, correct?"

"It is."

"You have this so-called predation syndrome now, as we speak."

"Yes."

"Am I in any danger?"

"No."

"Dr. Ulan, we have heard from Dr. Kern. He said, based on his work with you and other infected persons, he judges VIHPS-infected vectors such as yourself as a different species. He says you are medically unable to join society. What is your opinion of this?"

I scrutinize the crowd. Marcus is too busy or too chicken to be here. I pick a camera to speak to. He'll watch this, all right. "I have carried this disease for four years now. In that time, I haven't resorted to violence once."

"But Morgan Lorenz has. Dr. Kern says every single infected individual, including you, resorts to violence to feed. And the vipes we have seen on the news have all consumed human blood from overpowered victims."

"If they didn't, they wouldn't be on the news very much. I wasn't."

"And as for Dr. Kern, who keeps records?"

"I challenge his findings, I doubt his story, and in both instances, I would know. Feeding can and must be done without violence." I'm in control now, so I can keep the pain out of my voice. I began with consenting adults, but they didn't stay consenting. They were hit from all sides with vomiting and burning muscles, and if that didn't change their mind, the first time they bit their wife did. So, I practiced The Talk and The Move. As the names stretched on forever, so did my road from D.C. to Annapolis to Wilmington to Philly to Brighton Beach.

Those who were loyal, I taught. Those who were not only saw tire tracks where I once lived. Morgan's gang is struggling with consent, but the nuances of that argument are not for public consumption.

Cho continues. "Are you worried that you might resort to violence in the future?"

"There's temptation, of course, but you can't live your life without that."

"Temptation to feed?"

"Temptation to violence of any kind. I get cut off in traffic, too."

There is an amused murmur from the media in the benches. Unprofessional, but that's real life for you.

Cho paces slowly as he talks, alternating facing me and Bayat. "So, you can drive a car without hurting anyone, you can feed without hurting anyone, and you can apparently sit in court and hold a lengthy conversation without hurting anyone. Do you feel this proves Dr. Kern's statements incorrect?"

"I do."

"He alleged you attacked him once. Could you walk us through that?"

"There's not much of a chronology of events there. What he says didn't happen."

"Did he cut himself after you were infected?"

"If he did, I don't recall it."

"Did you at any point attempt to drink his blood?"

"No."

"Was there anything between you that could've been misinterpreted as a physical attack?"

"No."

"So, your position is, he's lying."

"Yes."

"No further questions, Your Honor."

"Counsel, your witness," comes Bayat's voice. Reflexively, I look for a friendly face in the crowd, but the vipes have all stayed behind. We voted, and I was the tiebreaker. Going on the stand is how I can make things right again, and if there is any kind of physical danger, we've already lost.

Campion takes the floor. She approaches but doesn't cross the last meter or two. "Dr. Ulan, you said you were infected four years ago. Is that correct?"

"Yes."

"And what jobs have you held down since that time?"

"I write from home for medical journals under a pseudonym."

"Why do you use a pseudonym?"

"Because Dr. Kern and BRHI have been determined to find me, restrain me, and confine me based on my infected status."

"I see. Well, it certainly is brave of you to come into court today."

This woman has never had to identify a body at the morgue. She hasn't huddled in a subway, certain the person she thinks is following her is a hitman. She hasn't slept by the side of the road in a car in the Pennsylvania winter, praying she won't freeze to death, because home is not safe. I put those years into my voice.

"I'm glad you noticed."

"Have you held down a job that brings you in face-to-face contact with other people?"

"No, I have not."

"How successful would you say this career is?"

"Not very."

"Could you elaborate? Did you file any taxes?"

"I did. I fell below the poverty line, so I actually got a refund."

"Not only do you pay less in taxes, your contribution to society is directly diminished by your infection. You're living off other people's income and tax breaks where once you were a pioneer in an advanced medical field. Is that what you're saying?"

"I wouldn't say it's any worse than being a housewife," I point out. "Or, for that matter, a recluse such as Henry David Thoreau."

"Dr. Ulan, you did not choose this lifestyle, did you?"

"No, I did not. It is, however, significantly less predatory than Marcus describes."

"But it was not your choice. You are less able to join society because of your infection."

Is that all you have? Lawyers are supposed to lay verbal traps, and this one barely scratched my ankle. But I know better than to yell what follows. Ice is better than fire. "I'm unable to join because your corporation wants my head."

"Then, let's talk about this corporation and why it wants you. How many people did you infect during your last few months at BRHI?"

"Three."

"And who were they?"

"The first was Adam Corus. He worked in the security department."

"Is this the staff member Dr. Kern said you had a sexual relationship with?"

"I didn't. I did, however, infect him, so Marcus can assume what he likes."

"Who were the others?"

"The others were Tyler Schwartz and Sarai Saleh, also known as Eva."

"If I'm not mistaken, all those individuals are dead now. Is that right, Dr. Ulan?"

I'm fine. I buried that grief years ago. "Yes."

"And did these individuals resort to violence to feed their hunger?"

"Yes."

"Doesn't that make you partially responsible for the assaults on their victims?"

"No. They had the same choice I did, the same choice anyone has. I chose persuasion. They chose something else. I'm not them, and I'm not Morgan Lorenz, either." It is not kind to, on national television, slap the man who reached out to me, but I must draw the distinction. If we win, Morgan will forgive me anything.

"Dr. Ulan, when you say 'chose something else,' you are aware that many vipes choose first-degree, second-degree murder, correct?"

"Yes."

"And they don't need to eat, either. They can live entirely on drinking blood."

"That is possible, but most patients prefer to eat normally."

"Yes, I understand Morgan Lorenz was being fed during his captivity, but he ended up drinking blood anyway. Were you aware of that fact?"

"Had Morgan come to me when he was first infected, things might have been different."

"We are not here for speculation, Dr. Ulan. Yes or no."

"Yes."

"Dr. Ulan, how many people have you infected with this disease over the course of the last four years?"

"I don't know."

"Do you feed on one person a week? Two?"

"It varies."

"Give us a number, please."

"One is usually sufficient."

"There are fifty-two weeks in a year, are there not?"

"Yes."

"So, at one a week, that's fifty-two a year, and over the four years you have been infected, does that not total more than two hundred people exposed to your virus?"

"Not all people exposed to the virus contract it."

"Do you know its exact transmission rate?"

Do I look like I have an epidemiology lab up my ass? "No."

"But you know the first three people you bit or sucked or whatever got it. Now, Dr. Kern mentioned their investigations into whether or not those who contract the virus may be predisposed to it based on the level of hostile qi in their brain tissue—"

"Objection," says Cho. "Counsel is not asking questions. She's lecturing the witness."

Campion shoots him a glare. "Your Honor, the witness is straying from answering questions. I ask for some leeway as I provide context to questions."

"Dr. Ulan, please answer the questions asked, and Ms. Campion, a few more questions than context. Continue."

"If you dispute Dr. Kern's research, Dr. Ulan, tell me: have you conducted experiments on your virus in a controlled setting since your infection?"

The room pauses.

"Yes, I have. I can produce my results for evidence."

There is an approving murmur from the crowd. I don't share their enthusiasm. I thought Campion dropped this line of attack, and lawyers don't ask questions to which they don't know the answer.

"Have your papers undergone peer review?" Campion says.

"Not yet, no."

"I see. Dr. Ulan, if your research passes peer review and is approved, don't you stand to greatly benefit?"

"In what regard?"

"You would be able to seek restitution from BRHI, for starters."

"I'm not participating in this lawsuit except as an expert witness. It would be a conflict of interest." I'm grateful for Morgan's idea now. We just dodged a shot.

"That's admirable, but you'd probably be employed full-time again, right?"

"Having my inalienable constitutional rights restored to me is not an ulterior motive," I say. "It's called getting back to normal."

Campion's face falls, but she takes a glance at one of her team, who signals by grabbing one wrist. She recovers. "Dr. Ulan, do criminals have their rights taken away from them when they are imprisoned for their crimes?"

"No, they have their freedoms legally restricted."

"Then, if you were a judge, and Morgan Lorenz or—who did you say? Sarai Saleh—or any of the other violent people we have heard about were in your courtroom, would you not see fit to put them in jail?"

"I find the situation more complex than that."

"Yes or no, Dr. Ulan."

"Yes, but it is not all I would do."

"That still sounds like a yes to me."

"I would seek to treat them, which BRHI does not do."

"Most other people infected with your predation syndrome are not the same as you, are they, Dr. Ulan?"

"Objection. Speculation," says Cho.

Bayat calls it. "Sustained."

"I'll rephrase. In your personal experience, what percentage of infected use violence to feed?"

Faces flash in my head. Adam, videoconferencing with a bloody mouth and tears streaming from his eyes. Najva, who had starved herself rather than be made impure by drinking blood until I practically force-fed her. Brion, the bondage dom who expected a safe word that never came because our mutual victim had passed out.

My gaze settles on the cameras. Morgan is watching. My mother will be watching. Can I boldly proclaim *none?* It is what the moment needs, a counterbalance to Kern. But I am Ulan, and lies do not counterbalance lies. Only the truth does that. I have basis for shame, yes, but I also have basis for pride. In the end, I look Campion squarely in the eyes.

"I can't give a number," I say. "I don't always ask."

Campion shakes her head ever so slightly. "Thanks for your time. No further questions."

I let out a breath. I've survived, but the perception of my expertise has surely crashed and is bleeding out. Campion didn't even berate me for my inconsistency, which is pretty insulting.

I return to Cho's table to pick up my sunglasses and scarf. It would feel good to slink away, to meet up with the vipes and complain late into the night. But the cameras are still on me, and if I so much as shed a tear, it will be ink and pixels within the day. How many infected people will lose hope if they see that?

I gather the scarf but don't put it on. My scarf is my shield. No sense donning it on television and giving the mobs accurate info about my clothing habits. The sunglasses, yes.

"Can't stand the good times, huh?" Cho says. "You did pretty well."

"I don't need a spin room," I reply, making for the exit. The sounds of BRHI's lawyers reach my ears, but they are far away. I want to believe they can't hurt me now, but I have seen their company's reach before, and it is far, far too long.

37 - RANATH

September 17th

My surprise is like any magic trick—its effect is dramatic, but it is simple, almost pedestrian, if you are the one doing it. I'm outside, near one of the courthouse's square columns, where a fresh turpentine smell remains from the day's recent graffiti removal. I listen for the press surrounding Ulan as she exits. When I spot her sunglasses, I follow. I maintain my qi function to remain unobtrusive, but I hardly need it. When cameras flash and questions fly, everyone is focused on navigating the crowd, not searching it.

Jessica stays calm. "I'm not answering questions now," she says. Then, louder, "No questions, but here, I'll give you an image."

She removes her sunglasses and stands under the statue of Justice. This particular one has scales in each hand. The flashes go crazy, and no small number of journalists back away to fit both her and the statue in the shot. Now that they're repositioned, she has room to leave

Jessica heads down the pathway to the street parking, and I hurry behind her. Her car chirps as she unlocks it, and I crank up the qi function's power as I slip into the rear seat. Ulan belts herself, starts the car, and I let the function drop.

"Hello, Jessica."

She jumps and sees me in the rearview mirror. She spins around. "Ranath?"

"Roland, now," I say. "Usually."

"What's the gun for?" I drew it slipping into the car. It's at low ready—aimed down casually at the floor.

"Dealing with stupidity," I say. "Fortunately, I don't think you qualify."

She pauses, obviously thinking about it, and comes to the same conclusion I did. In the time it'd take to extract herself from her seat to try anything, she'd be full of holes.

"You want to ask questions or something?"

"Correct."

"About Morgan?"

"I thought about it," I say. "It would seem logical, my grilling you on his whereabouts, since you are obviously flocking to his little movement, but then, I thought, I don't need to know that unless I'm going to come calling."

"I thought you'd be chasing him."

"I gave Infinity a gift last time we met," I say. "I don't know any clearer signal that I'm no longer hunting vipes."

"Yeah, I wonder why I keep getting that false impression," she retorts.

"I need insight about Kern," I say.

Jessica blinks, blindsided. "I've been gone for years," she says. "Anything I would know would pale in comparison—"

"—to my mountain of inside information. No. It's not like that at all, and I need to know why."

I lean forward slightly. "Jess—Forced Protection tried to kill me. He tried to pretty it up. He tried to protect me in a fashion. But I was going to ask him questions, and he threw me out and told the wolves to start biting. Something about his motivation does not add up."

"Well," she says after a moment, "don't leave me hanging."

"This entire suit could have been settled out of court," I explain. "It would have been cheaper by far. It would limit the damages to those currently infected at the time of the suit. And I'm sure the option was put on the table, and I'm sure Kern was among those people who said no. We will not go gently. We will beat you down. But I don't understand the calculation. Do you?"

Jess takes a moment to digest the new thought. "When I met Kern, he was always a little starry-eyed. He talked a lot about potential, big prizes."

"Idealism? That doesn't seem like Kern."

"He could be clinging. This is all he's got left."

"No, he'd cut loose if necessary. His divorce taught him that much."

"Do you know if he started looking elsewhere for a job?"

"We've had conversations. It would've come up, and I would have known."

"Okay, so he thinks he can gain more this way. I don't know, Ranath. I came to say my piece and get out. What Kern thinks doesn't keep me up at night."

I have sympathy, but I don't let it show on my face. "I don't believe you. I remember a Jessica Ulan who said to her students that we must train, above all, our minds. That we should not let them rest easy because we have so little competition in our field, but we must perfect ourselves to be able to teach others what we know. 'We are the bandwidth,' you said, 'between the mysteries of the universe and future generations, whose numbers speed toward the infinite.' So, if you are trying to convince me that while Kern was preparing his deposition, you were napping on a couch somewhere, unaware of what he might say that could take away your right to exist, I would like to ask where Dr. Ulan is and what you've done with her."

I was hoping to break through, but she's just frustrated. "Ranath, I've been practicing getting my part right. I haven't had time to think about him. We rehearsed some questions, but that was for that lawyer. Kern's the one you need to interrogate."

It sounds like truth, which is not what I want to hear. I'm silent.

"Are you angry?" asks Ulan. "Does this mean I'm dead?"

"I don't like hurting people out of anger," I say.

"Really? Just how many of my infected friends have you killed?"

I don't owe her an answer. A week ago, I'd have self-righteously explained how my kills are quite cold-blooded. Now, that sounds terrible. I stay clinical. "If I'm going to admit to anything, I'm not going to do it in your car."

She gives a throaty laugh. "They sure trained the life out of you, didn't they? Here I am with a question that requires a thimbleful of trust, and you're off in psycho-land thinking my car's bugged. That's it, isn't it?"

"You just posed for a photo op that's going to be seen by a hundred million people," I say. "I'm not in the mood to be naïve."

Ulan looks at me in the mirror, the dark, wrinkled flesh under her eyes making her look tired. "You ever talk to any of them beforehand?"

"Talk to whom?"

"The vipes. Is it just something you do because you don't know any better or—"

"I have met many vipes. I have talked to many vipes. I have seen their degeneration in the hospitals, and I know what I have done. And before you get all righteous, I think it's safe to say I've had a few experiences you wouldn't have predicted."

"Really," she says. "She talks about you, you know."

"Unsurprising."

Ulan smiles. "Well, that's cute. You know exactly whom I'm referring to."

"The number of vipes we mutually know now stands at three or four, including you. I have one last question, and then you're free to slink."

Ulan gives a little snort. "If that's what the price is—"

"The building in Glenn Dale. Why haven't you been there yet?"

"How do you know we haven't?"

"You'd have talked about it by now, believe me."

"Infinity hasn't brought it up to the others yet. She's afraid to explain how she knows you. Seriously, I've known you a lot longer, and I can't afford to trust you. Just saying you're helping isn't good enough."

"What would convince you?"

"Hand me your gun."

My eyes narrow.

"Okay, then," she says. "We understand each other. Can I go?"

I haven't gotten what I want, but that's not her fault. I might have one last card to play. I open the car door. "Before you do that, I would like to attempt to do you another favor."

That makes her indignant. After a little fumbling, she exits the car as well. I hold up a hand, and she keeps her distance. Without taking my eyes off her, I feel around in the rear wheel wells. The gun stays in my pocket, in my other hand.

"What are you doing?" she asks.

"My former colleagues are predictable." My fingers find a bump, and I pry it free. If it had been my car they were after, Yarborough might have mixed up his usual hiding spot. For Ulan, he has no need—what's the likelihood she'd search for something like this?

I present the little plastic-and-electronic disk to her. It has little grime on it—it's been placed recently. Jessica holds it in her hand and stares at it like she's been given a human tongue.

"Is this what I think it is?"

"The price of going public. The F-prots want to follow you home," I say. "And there, they would find vipes."

It falls from her hands, and I think at first, she's recoiling from it, but when it bounces on the asphalt, Ulan crushes it with her heel. The little bug shatters. She grinds her shoe against the electronic wafers that emerge, her expression that of a mother tiger that has scented man. She looks around, as if whoever planted it might still be loitering.

I rub it in by mistake. "If you want to live in psycho-land, there's always room for more."

"I don't want to hear it," she says dangerously. "You've made your point."

"I didn't fake it, if you're thinking that," I try. "If you went to your car at lunch, they probably put eyes on you then and planted it."

"I don't want explanations. I want you to get the smug look off your face. At this point, I wouldn't put anything past you."

"I guess we won't talk again," I say, but I can't just leave without trying, one last time. "I'm sorry, Jess. I didn't come to disturb you."

"I know," she mutters. "You're just too good at it."

**From Syndicated Linkstorm Talkcast "It Burns," with Roger Burns
September 17th, 9:00 p.m.**

BURNS: Good evening from the United States of Transylvania. Let's get to business because what's going on in this country is beyond the pale. I'm speaking, of course, of the testimony today in the court case of *Lorenz v. BRHI*, in which we learned some important facts. On this show, facts matter because they're how you present reality. It's the other sides, the dinoparties and the heartbrained left, that distort and lie to scare and control people. Our linkstorm is how you fight against that. People come up to me saying, "Roge, Roge, you gotta speak out about the undead. You gotta warn people," and I must correct them. These people, vampires, they're not actually dead. They're different from what you see in the movies and TV.

See, I make that correction because the reality is even worse.

You know the drill by now: every time I say a keyphrase, a link will flash in the stream. Let's go.

"VIHPS is a disease," say the heartbrainers. No. The flu is a disease. This is a plague, and like the plague, it's not going to stop until there are millions of dead in the gutters of America and all across the world. Why? Math. These vampire people, we don't know how many of them there really are. It could be hundreds. It could be tens of thousands. "So what?" you say. There's 400 million Americans. That's a drop in the bucket. No, it's not.

It's not because every single one of them is driven to communicate their disease at least once a week or so. This isn't a disease that can be isolated. It will be spread deliberately, and it <u>won't kill its host</u>. That means the original vampire, and every single person they bite, are all going to keep infecting and infecting, until everyone on Earth has the disease, and then they'll have to turn on each other. Or—and this is the rosy scenario—the vampires choose to <u>kill their victims instead</u>. One a week per vampire. That is the rate they need to feed. Those are <u>the facts Lorenz's expert witness brought out today</u>.

So, what do you call that if you're a normal human being? You call it a war. This is a war on blood. We didn't start it, but we'll finish it, and that is the mentality the judge must have, for the good of the species. Because if they give the other side even an ounce of credibility, they are idiots. I can knock down the arguments against it one by one or all together. Okay, I'm taking your calls. What vampire-coddling firehose of stupid have you heard from your Solar Citizen friends? Hello, caller one, what's your name?

LILAH: Lilah.

BURNS: Lilah, you are on like a light switch. Tell me how the stupid burns.

LILAH: Hi, Roge, I saw a bumper sticker saying, "if corporations are people, why aren't vampires?" What do you have to say to that?

BURNS: Well, first you're getting your political philosophy from <u>something you see in traffic</u>.

LILAH: Oh, God, not me. That's not my car.

BURNS: Okay, but let's address it, though. A corporation is a legal entity. That's the law of the land. But more to the point, a corporation is responsible to someone: its shareholders. Human beings consciously chose to create the corporation or invest in the corporation to advance their own interests. A vampire has none of that. The only master a vampire serves is its thirst for human blood. Normal hunger, normal thirst, self-preservation, all basic human drives take a back seat, all right?

But here's what the apologists don't get. There's a key philosophical point here. Crimes are voluntary actions. If you make the choice to shoot someone in the head, premeditated murder, you just threw away your right to freedom or life... whichever, based on what penalty you get and what state you're in. That's why educated people like in the Freedom Forever Party say that the death penalty isn't murder; it's justice. It's the killer's own choices that get him convicted and snuffed. It's acknowledging that free will and responsibility exist.

We're going to go to another caller now. You are on the air. Tell me how the stupid burns.

BRAD: Brad here. I want to address the one I hear all the time. My mom keeps telling me that BRHI's claim is ridiculous. She's like, "A disease doesn't change people. You can't lock someone up without violating their civil rights." I don't know about that—

BURNS: Glad you brought it up, Brad. "It's absurd." I've been hearing it all week. "Taking away someone's civil rights because they have a disease is absurd." Bull pucky. This isn't the flu we're talking about here, or even pre-vaccine Ebola, and believe me, if it were Ebola, we'd quarantine them. Nothing absurd about that. This virus, it alters human DNA into a biological killing machine. And we take away people's rights to liberty and the pursuit of happiness all the freaking time. It's called jail. You're taking murderers, which is what these vampires are, and stripping the right to walk free from them.

BRAD: I said that, and she's like, "innocent until proven guilty. That's how we do things."

BURNS: That's wrong. It's a fair point, but it's wrong. For starters, I have trouble believing some guy addicted to human blood isn't going to have some of it on his hands, but let's say that <u>mythical beast</u> exists. Take the lib-brat claim, "If you can't pin a murder on them, if they just infect, and it's all consensual, you can't lock them up."

BRAD: Exactly. Suppose they said there's no legal whatsitcalled, prior case. Precedent.

BURNS: You tell them there is. It's called <u>Kelly v. Seven Star Health and Hospice</u>. Twenty years back, this woman, <u>Moira Kelly</u>, was infected with HIV and syphilis. You would think after she'd gotten one of them she'd be more careful, <u>but she wasn't</u>. She was a sex addict—seriously, she was clinically <u>diagnosed</u>—and they <u>locked her up in a mental ward</u>. She <u>sued</u>, saying she couldn't be confined indefinitely. And in the trial, the hospital said very simply, if they let her out, there was no doubt in their minds—none—that she'd infect people. She was a <u>danger to herself and others</u>, just like these vampires. And the court ruled in favor of the hospital. So, no precedent? Bovine fertilizer.

BRAD: Thanks, man. I'm out.

BURNS: Next caller, tell me your name and how the stupid burns.

UMBERTO: Yes, I am Umberto, and I'm wondering why no one has called this virus God-related yet.

BURNS: What, you mean like a punishment wrought by God?

UMBERTO: Yes. If you look at the advantages a vampire has, there are many. There is strength, there is resistance to wounding and disease. But if you look at all the other viruses we know throughout history, none is so advantageous so fast.

BURNS: I hear what you're saying, but how does that jibe with punishment?

UMBERTO: It's like in movies, where there are superheroes made by mutation. That would never happen. Mutation is tiny little things like eye color or allergies, almost never beneficial. But this virus, it is so magical, you cannot help but see the hand of God in it.

BURNS: Yeah, I've wondered that myself. I mean, the atheists have lost all credibility ever since qi hit the big time. You just can't explain these miracles we're starting to see every day. And now, of course, it stands to reason that if you're going to get good stuff like qi infusions to slow bleeding, you're also going to get the bad. I mean all the bad: black magic, agents of the Adversary running around, end times and all that.

UMBERTO: Keep your eyes open, my friend. And remember, it is no crime to demonize one who is an actual demon.

BURNS: Guess we're back to bumper stickers. Next caller, you're on the air.

JANIS: Yeah, Roger, my name's Janis, and I've been listening to your show, and you serve up the biggest dose of stupid on the air.

BURNS: Gee, never heard that one before. Get to your point, please.

JANIS: You've been inciting bloodshed for a week now. You can't just yell into the megaphone of talkcasts and say, "we're at war with the infected." What about that case in North Carolina? Ten people grabbed a fifty-two-year-old man and lynched him.

BURNS: Miss, I was not one of those people.

JANIS: They lynched him! And you helped, didn't you?

BURNS: No, I did not.

JANIS: You put it in their mind. You legitimized it.

BURNS: If you're going to confuse someone <u>talking about an action</u> with the people <u>doing that action</u>, you have no concept of responsibility.

JANIS: Are you going to denounce what they did?

BURNS: I don't know the facts of the case.

JANIS: You're not even going to come out against lynching?

BURNS: I am saying, if he were attempting to assault them or <u>drink their blood</u>, then it's entirely possible it was an act of <u>self-defense</u>.

JANIS: It was a mob of ten people!

BURNS: There were ten people because he could've dead-lifted nine of them.

JANIS: You're not denouncing it at all. You're encouraging it.

BURNS: I am saying we have a justice system so we don't <u>rush to conclusions</u>.

JANIS: That man was a father, a husband. And if Lorenz loses, it's going to be open season. You will see mobs in every state, in every city.

BURNS: We can hope. Good night, Janis.

39 - MORGAN

September 18th

I'm trying to be gentlemanly, but when I run my tongue over Infinity's ankle, it's hard to stay impersonal. She's in the bathtub without a drop of water to be seen, dressed down to a T-shirt and underwear so as not to stain any good clothes. Her muscles are taut as she braces herself. I lap at her cut. She clacks her teeth together, and really, I'll just stop there. It doesn't help that her blood is sharpening my brain until I feel invincible.

She's feeling it, too. She puts away the single-edged razor blade in the soap dish so she can hold on. I keep my tongue moving until the handle turns on the bathroom door. Jessica pokes her face in. "You're wanted downstairs."

I hesitate, then put Infinity's ankle down. I stand up from where I've been sitting on the toilet's lid. Jessica shuts the door again, and Infinity laughs.

"Chaperones," she says. "Get me a bandage, would you?" I treat the cut in short order, and she stands up.

She almost doesn't make it. I catch her as she stumbles.

"You okay?" I blurt automatically. The last time I cut her—

But her grip is strong. "After five bites? What do you think?"

"I think if you're not, we've got to find another method and to hell with what Jessica says." With the mouth-to-blood contact broken, I'm coming back to normalcy, but I still feel like I should rule the dinosaurs. My perfect illusion lasts two seconds. Jess opens the door again.

"In New York, we have a coordination test. If you fail, we lower the number of drinkers by one." As Infinity puts her pants and shirt back on, I run the shower to wash away the bloodstains. Jessica goes into schoolmarm mode.

"Stand on one leg, arms out. Touch your nose," she orders. Infinity gamely does it. "Alternate hands. How do you feel?"

"Like a cow leaving the milking machine, except horny. Did I pass?"

"You've still got Deborah to go," Jessica says, considering. "She can last another three or four days. Feed her then. But I'd say you pass for now unless you have reservations."

Infinity makes a face. "If I can turn one infection into feeding six, I'm a goddamn goddess."

"Then, it's settled," I say. "You hunt, you drink, you come back and feed the whole family. Cass said no witnesses saw you leave with that boy, right?"

"We ran the checklist," she confirms. "Hey, weren't you wanted downstairs?"

Good point, but it's hard to be bothered when I'm this baked. I go down the steps. "All right, where's the fire?" The other vipes are in the living room, but instead of being all smiles having gotten their blood tonight, they look grim, Ly most of all.

"You three having fun?" he asks.

I take it in stride. "I could parachute from space, and my day wouldn't get better."

To my surprise, Ly and Cass share an even darker look. It's the look of a vipe who's killed to feed and is now considering it a problem-solving tool. "Then, maybe you want to bring us into the inner circle, too?"

I have no idea what he's talking about. My brain is still on the women upstairs and maybe some sexual jealousy thing. But that makes no sense. It must be something else.

"It's this secrecy," Deborah clarifies. "We had to find out from Jessica that you and Infinity have new information."

Oh. That's nothing. I smooth it over. "It's just a lead she found, a tip from a contact."

"Someone tipped the F-prots off to us?" says Cass, and I see the problem. Of course, they'd be terrified if I held that back. Time to fix it.

"Wait, that's not what it's about at all. If it were, all of us would be on the highway right now. No. She means she heard that there is a BRHI vipe-holding facility in the D.C. area. We were considering checking it out. I just hadn't made the announcement yet."

"Like this is their prison for vipes?" asks Ly.

"Prison, hospital, morgue," supplies Infinity, at my elbow and sounding like she's fighting through the fog. "When I worked in F-prot, the ones we took alive were secured and dropped off at a facility like this one."

"So, there's a chance we could find more of us?" says Cass. "I wanna do that."

"Is that a good thing?" asks Deborah. "I mean, more mouths to feed—"

This is turning into chaos. I have to step in. "Hold up. We need some context here. You all know I used to associate with other vipes, right?" Nods. "I think most of them were killed, but if any were taken alive, it sounds as though this would be where they're being held. When Infinity and Jess came to me, I said I can't make this decision. We only go in with eyes open and if all of us are on board."

"Time out," says Ferrero. "If this place is strong enough to hold vipes, I'm not thrilled at the idea of walking inside it."

"Hey, he's talking about a rescue operation," says Cass, as if that's why he wakes up in the morning.

"I'm sure the second roach to walk into a Roach Motel is doing it to save his buddy, but that doesn't help him much," Ferrero grouses. "Going in based on a rumor, that seems sketchy to me."

"I know the source, and he doesn't have motivation to lie to us," says Jessica.

"What about whoever fed *him* the information?"

Ly steps in, raising his hands calmingly. "Okay, so we know it's a risk, but we also know it isn't safe for Jessica to testify anymore. I say we have to start thinking about solutions that aren't just legal."

"Yeah..." Ferrero hedges. "I'm not big on crime."

"No one is." Maybe it's the blood, but I feel that I could be talked into it tonight, and for that reason, I'd better articulate everything.

"Seriously, for years my biggest fear was that I'd do something unethical by accident and get disbarred. And if you go online tonight, you can find jokes going around middle school playgrounds about whether in a blindfolded test I prefer the taste of Coke, Pepsi, or cops." The teacher glances downward. I've hit home. I continue. "Now we're stuck with a choice that isn't a real choice—we can infect or kill. But taking the lesser evil isn't where our responsibility ends. We owe those victims, and we owe all *their* victims. And what we can do is try to end this situation as fast as humanly possible."

"This is way out of our league," Ferrero counters. "What's our plan? Break in, cut through some bars with a hacksaw and try not to get shot?"

"We've got a few guns," Cass points out.

I'm about to object, but Ferrero is faster. "Jesus Christ, that doesn't make it better! Here's a thought. We bring cameras. Upload whatever goes on in there. Give them an image problem they can't bury under a mountain of money."

Cass is testosterone-driven but not stupid. "Okay, that sounds worthwhile, but if we're assaulting a building full of enemies, I say we shouldn't throw away any advantage. Show of hands. Who's done it? Who's broken in somewhere?" He raises his hand. "Infinity?"

I look at her. Her arms are crossed, and she's staring off into space, but she notices me. "Yeah, I've done that," she says absently. "Morgan?"

"I've had it happen to me," I say evenly, "and I lived through it." Cass's enthusiasm dims.

"This is a task worth doing," Jessica says, "but if I'm going to remain our public face, I need to excuse myself."

"Fair," says Cass. "Deborah... are you with us?"

"As long as I'm not put in a position where I hurt anyone," she says.

Ly frowns. "You do know we're vampires, right?"

"I told you the first time I ever bit someone, I threw it up after. You're not going to make me into someone... someone who..."

Cass and Ly have no idea how to be gentle. I step in. "We understand."

Ly turns to Ferrero. "You don't have a childhood dream of running for president or something, right?"

Ferrero doesn't look amused. "I want a vote."

"Looks like it's me and Cass so far for yes," says Ly. "Infinity?"

Their hero for tonight frowns. "The last time I was in court, the truth came out, and people did the right thing. I think we should wait until the trial is over." I knew I liked her.

Deborah speaks up. "I'm only in if we have no other choice. Right now, we do."

"That leaves you," Ferrero says to me. I think back to the heroes of my adolescence, the Kings and Ghandis and the Warren court, and wonder if they ever had to make decisions stoned on blood.

"I say no."

"You were just saying you might have friends in there!" says Ly.

"*Might.* Wishing won't make it so. It's a natural instinct to say we've got to take action. But we can't ignore what the consequences could be. If some headline reads 'Morgan Lorenz and Gang of Vipes Gun Down Security Guards,' kiss everything goodbye. Jess has ten friends in New York that she's spent months training how to feed peacefully. You want to explain to all of them why they've got to dodge vigilantes?"

Ly rolls his eyes. "Like it can get any worse?"

Ferrero frowns. "Read any history book ever."

"History books also say you gotta fight back against your enemy," says Cass.

Ferrero is incredulous. "And how's that going to go? You gonna kill ten of them? Fifty? That's going to get the result you want? No. Courts don't work that way. And if you think politics works that way, ask the Democrats and Republicans why half their people are now in the Solar Citizens and Freedom Forever parties. When you fire the gun, you lose."

"Half left, yeah. Half stayed," says Ly. " Finish the vote."

I call it. "All in favor of breaking into this prison-hospital-holding-cell place?" Cass and Ly put their hands up. Ferrero shakes his head a little. Deborah looks down. Jess snorts as though she finds the lack of support entertaining.

"All opposed?" Ferrero, Deborah, and Jess raise their arms. Infinity holds her arms crossed, her brow furrowed.

"You abstaining or something?" I ask.

"Remembering," she says. "I want to keep our options open. These people are brutal. Honestly, I think we all want them thrown in the wood chipper, but taking millions of dollars from them sounds more civilized. Let's do that." She raises her hand.

I raise mine. "Okay. Now, I don't want any resentment because of this. Everybody's got opinions. We can agree to disagree. Our focus right now is winning the battle of Alexandria."

Cass gives me a nod, and I know things are going to be all right. I shoot a glance at Infinity. She showed some presence of mind tonight. I feel better just having her in the room, but now she isn't making eye contact. Loss of blood? More likely guilt from her feeding. I don't bring it up. This is no time to single out anyone. We will see this through together.

Closing Arguments in *Lorenz v. the Benjamin Rush Health Initiative*
September 28th

THE COURT: Ladies and gentlemen, good morning. We are ready to proceed with closing arguments of counsel in this case. Under court procedure, each side may have different attorneys argue different parts of the closing. Mr. Cho, you're going to present Mr. Lorenz's case?
MR. CHO: I am, Your Honor, may it please the court.
THE COURT: Yes.
MR. CHO: Your Honor, we have heard a lot about viruses and definitions of the human species and what we should legally throw out over the past few weeks. But the elements of the suit are fairly straightforward. Did what happened to Morgan Lorenz and so many other human beings qualify as medical negligence? Was there willful, wanton conduct? Does this count as wrongful infection?

Well, you ask, what's an infection? It's the presence of a bacteria or virus not normally found in a human body. EBL-4 is that infection. And what's wrongful? In law, something is 'wrongful' if it works loss or harm to anyone. We have learned beyond reasonable doubt that good people have lost everything to this disease. Dr. Jessica Ulan went from being a respected scientist to living under an assumed name. Luis Rodolfo and Ani Sikorski lost their lives. And as for Morgan Lorenz... he is not on trial here.

We have a phrase in law for what we saw these past few weeks. *Res ipsa loquitur.* It means 'the facts speak for themselves.' We have been dragged through an extremely extended motion to dismiss for lack of standing for an unbelievable premise: that a virus can cause you to stop being human. Even though the Health Initiative has leveled a claim that Morgan Lorenz is not fit to join human society, that claim is not about Morgan Lorenz. It is about every single human being who tests positive for EBL-4.

A moment's thought shows what a terrifying precedent this could set. Can anyone with a dangerous virus be labeled nonhuman? A person with HIV? Smallpox? Of course not. The fact that qi was involved in its creation gives it no special status. These people are humans.

BRHI made this argument because they have no leg to stand on. BRHI could have told this court, 'no, you must have gotten the disease somewhere else. Here are all our records for comparison.' But they didn't. And when we demanded to see those records, their lab in Reston was sanitized before our arrival. But one sample was still viable. And the RNA in that virus is identical to the virus in Morgan Lorenz's body. So... was cleaning that lab the act of an innocent party? Or was it the act of a corporation that does not want to pay the damages that are due to their negligence? Remember, they continued to study this virus for four years since the outbreak without reporting its presence. If that is not willful, wanton conduct, what is?

Recall *res ipsa loquitur*. The facts speak for themselves.

Do new viruses brimming with active qi occur naturally? No, they do not. They were entirely unknown to science until twenty-five years ago. And four years ago, the pioneer of the field made a breakthrough that created an entirely new form of life. When this virus escaped their inadequately protected lab, she was working for the exact same company whose representatives are sitting over there. You heard from the pioneer in question, and she knows what they let loose because it is in her bloodstream to this day. *Res ipsa loquitur*. The facts speak for themselves.

So, will we say this infection is not wrongful? That it endangered no one? That there was no negligence in dealing with a level 5 biohazard that has now infected what must be hundreds of people? No. We have heard the facts. The Benjamin Rush Health Initiative are guilty beyond a reasonable doubt. All else is a distraction, made of aspersions and fear. Thank you.

THE COURT: Thank you, Mr. Cho. Has the defense chosen who will present?

MS. CAMPION: We have, Your Honor. I am presenting it start to finish.

THE COURT: Very good, Counselor. You may proceed.

MS. CAMPION: Your Honor, I would like to thank Mr. Cho for presenting some very lofty rhetoric about the responsibility you have, to safeguard individuals infected by a very terrible virus. It is natural to have sympathy for Mr. Lorenz or for Dr. Ulan. We all want to help others. But blaming the men and women working in the Health Initiative's ABEL lab is not a legally sound strategy.

Counselor Cho would have you believe that BRHI is responsible for the spread of the VIHPS virus. But every corporation consists of individuals. And the individual most responsible for Jessica Ulan biting three of her fellow employees is none other than Jessica Ulan. She told us to our face that she has a choice when she feeds. If she can control herself enough not to use violence, why did she not refrain from drinking the blood of her co-workers? Either she could manage it and violated safety protocol herself... in which case Morgan Lorenz should be suing *her*... or her cravings for blood are too much to resist.

We spent so much time on a motion to dismiss because those cravings matter. Dr. Ulan admitted she must feed every week to survive. Assuming she only feeds when absolutely necessary, then she has spread the virus to over two hundred people. Assuming conservatively, if just eighty percent of them survived, in one year those victims would infect some seventeen hundred people. In another year, her victims and their victims would infect over seventy thousand people. The year after that, it's almost three million.

What percentage of them will resort to violence, even murder, to feed? Do you consider it the correct course of action to award that many murderers a large sum of money? I know what my answer is, and it is hell, no. My answer is that Morgan Lorenz and all those infected with VIHPS should be confined to hospitals where there are medical professionals and security and restraints if necessary.

The counsel for the plaintiff said many things in his closing statement, but there are other important points he does not contest.

He does not contest that the plaintiff can live solely by drinking human blood. Nor does he contest that the plaintiff killed two police officers to drink that blood. He does not contest that the police officers' struggles were useless because the plaintiff cannot be harmed by normal punches or kicks. He does not contest that the plaintiff cannot even be present for this trial because he is in hiding. These are not in dispute because they are facts, and as we heard, facts speak for themselves.

I do not ask that you harden your heart or restrain your noble impulses to deliver justice. That is what we are here for. But our sense of justice can't be limited to those who have testified in the past few days or who filed suit in order to get paid. It must include all the people who were not here today because an actual, honest-to-God *vampire* chose to drain them of blood and end their lives. Unless you take action now, the numbers of those people crying out for justice from their graves will grow and grow. That's the math. Thank you.

THE COURT: Thank you, Ms. Campion.

41 - INFINITY

September 30th

I slam the passenger-side door and zip a seat belt across myself. "Drive," I say, glancing up and down the street and at the rowhouse I just left. The rain that was my enemy three hours ago is my ally now. It's dusky and gray out, and no one wants to look up, let alone be a witness.

Deborah hits the ignition button next to the dismantled self-driver. "Run the checklist."

Right. The checklist. I squeeze my eyes shut. "Just a minute."

"You're baked, aren't you?"

"Put the frosting on top," I grin.

Deborah is humorless. "Prints," she says, kick-starting my memory.

I can do this. "He opened the door. I got him soon after. My fingertips were coated, and I didn't touch a thing."

"Did he live alone?"

"He said he did. It should be a while before anyone finds him." I know it isn't necessarily true, but I'm feeling too good to worry about details. That's why Deborah is here.

"Still," Deborah says and puts the car in drive. I pout, then check myself in the side-view mirror.

I expect my face to be a red smear, but somewhere through my pleasant haze, I remember I cleaned up while inside. I've forgotten my victim's name already and want to keep it that way.

This one was kind and platonic and barely made a noise once I got him. It was like a reward for playing the game right, and now I'm ready for the hot tub we don't have.

Deborah keeps prodding. Witnesses at the gym? Cameras? Were we seen leaving together? Everything comes up clean. On the interstate, my phone chimes. My fight-or-flight kicks in, and I answer immediately.

"Morgan, how'd it go?"

"Uh, Fini, it's... it's a little mixed."

"What'd he say?" asks Deborah.

I speak to the phone. "Out with it, or you don't get none."

"Well..." he says, and I imagine a million awful things, "they convicted on wrongful infection and awarded damages."

"They did it!" I scream at Deborah, who lets loose a cry of her own. "Did they just make us fucking rich? What's the award thing worth?"

"Hold on for a minute," Morgan says. "The Health Initiative's appealing. They petitioned for cert with—" his voice goes indistinct.

"What's that do? You're breaking up. Morgan?"

Bang. The car lurches. The red emergency lights flare up on the dashboard, and everything goes *eep eep eep* like the car is backing up. Deborah freezes. I drop the phone and seize the wheel immediately as the car's hazards flick on and off. We're slowing down.

"What the fuck are you doing?" yells Deborah. A car whizzes by us on the right and another on the left. *Eep eep eep* blares the noise.

"Brake!" I yell. Deborah steps. The car lurches again. "Merge right!"

"How do I do that? Let go!" But I don't let go. I glance back, see an opening and jerk the wheel. We roll onto the shoulder of the highway.

Deborah puts it in park, and the *eep*ing stops. She loses her seat belt.

"No!" I shout. "Don't go out. Stay down!" I undo my own belt and open the glove compartment, where my pistol is waiting.

"Were you followed?" Deborah's terrified. I grab the phone, hand it to her.

"Tell Morgan someone just shot at us. I'm going out there."

"What if they're waiting?" Deborah says but holds the phone up to her ear. "Uh, Morgan, we're by the side of the road. The car got hit or shot—"

"Open the rear door to give me cover."

Deborah nods. Morgan's talking, but neither of us is paying attention. Deborah wriggles awkwardly into the back seat and unlocks the rear door. She shoves it open, and I pop my own door. I'm out, flattened, looking underneath the metal and plastic. But no car has stopped by the side of the road behind us.

"D? What's the dashboard say?"

"Where are they?"

"There is no 'they' yet. Hit the analyzer on the dashboard."

"It says right front tire."

I turn around, waiting for someone to smack me or shoot me, but instead I only see a torn-up tire, ruptured and riding on the rim. A tiny, metal head sticks out of the black rubber.

"Deborah..." I say, "if I ever make a decision with a gun again when I'm high, fucking slap me. It's a nail. Tell Morgan we ran over a nail." I pause as Deborah relays the message. "And ask him what's up with the court."

Deborah hands the phone back after multiple reassurances that Morgan doesn't need to rescue us. I holster the pistol and shield the phone from the spatting rain.

"Okay, false alarm. I'm stupid. Let me just establish that and get back to you spilling the beans on this other incredibly important thing. Why do you sound like your wife just left you?"

He rolls with it. "We ended up on the express list of cases approved for review. There's a rumor that Fennel took an interest."

"Who's Fennel?"

"Chief Justice Fennel? SCOTUS?"

What? "Is that Esperanto? You gotta remember my brain is on toast here."

"The Supreme Court took an interest in our case. After the first Monday in October, Cho's gonna be doing an oral argument for us."

"We're going to the Supreme Court?" I shout. "That's fucking galactic! You were all moping, and we're going to be a part of history?"

"Fini," Morgan says sternly, "they don't usually get involved at this stage. Unless they think it's constitutionally relevant—"

The rain is getting harder. I slip back into the car. "Oh yeah, that's your class action talking right there!" I slam the door so it's easier to hear.

"No, if they had no problem with the ruling, they wouldn't have stepped in." In response to my silence, he says, "Listen very carefully. There is a high probability they got involved because of the constitutional question of BRHI's claim. If we'd just won, it'd be a footnote. This much attention means they want us for a precedent. Either to say we definitively have standing... or definitively not."

"Uh," I'm too bleary. "Break this down for me at the house when I'm sober." I hang up.

"What'd he say?" Deborah still looks alarmed.

"Uh, you know those agreements you click on before you install an app?"

"Yeah?"

"He sounded something like that, and it's about to fuck us. Don't call for assistance. I'll change the tire." The next few minutes are very mundane, except for the part where I forget you are supposed to step on the tire iron for leverage. I casually twist the lug nuts off the wheel.

Before I put away the deflated tire, Deborah speaks up. "Here, can I get a picture of us on our adventure?"

Really? "Maybe don't make posts that say, 'this is me with my vipe girlfriend?'"

"I don't post," she says. "Not since. I just keep them for myself." I nod. Deborah shoots us with her phone. Grinning at the camera fits tonight's craziness.

"What do you think? Top five?" I ask.

"Top hundred," Deborah says, "but I have about ten thousand, so that's pretty good. Just going to caption it, 'my hero,' and we'll be done."

"That's me, Miss Minimum Technical Know-How."

Deborah looks puzzled. "Also, you just saved us."

"Not really."

"Well, you *would* have." She captions the shot.

My smile disappears. "Seriously, do not use the h-word on me."

"I thought—"

"I am *not* someone to look up to, okay?"

"Oh, come on. All of us kinda think—"

"Deborah, stop your thought there. When someone tells you they're not a hero, you listen to them. Otherwise you are setting yourself up *bad*."

"Of course, yeah," Deborah says, backpedaling. "But if I can ask, uh—why aren't you?"

I rub my face. My catalogue of misdeeds is getting longer all the time, but the one that grabs me—no. I have to prioritize. Morgan still doesn't know that I've drawn vipe blood as well as human. Neither does Deborah. I want to be far away in a cozy retirement home before they find out that wrinkle. But I need to talk.

"I know a hero," I say. "I had this friend, Rachel. She found out my father was... well, I don't have time to go into it now, but he was worse than any of us. She thought that by sleeping over at my place she could defend me, and when it turned out she couldn't... well, shit, she pressed charges and aired the entire thing out."

"Oh, God," Deborah says. "That *is* brave—"

"No, I'm getting to the brave part. My dad had this cult of people around him, and they hated the hell out of both of us, and they broke her windows, and even when her parents and the lawyer were saying we should settle, she said no, he needs to be in jail, and we fucking won. He did time, and after he got out, he went back in for narcotics 'cause he picked up a habit. He's still in L.A. County State, and her, she's like this IT expert for the Navy making anti-missile coilguns and shit, keeping us all safe. *She's* a hero," I finish. "Me, I'm a survivor. Not the same thing."

Deborah doesn't buy it. "But you're still here," she says. "That took something, didn't it?"

"I guess," I say. "I don't want to get in people's faces about it, though. There's lots of things I should be ashamed of—"

"Oh, hon, you can't think of it that way—"

"No, not *that*. Lord, I mean like the time I fucked someone who wasn't my boyfriend, even if he cheated first. That, I had control over."

"Oh," says Deborah, "all right, I think I see."

"So, there really isn't much I can cop to that qualifies as guts," I say. "Pulling out a gun, even that's 'cause I'm scared." Deborah seems to think about it, clearly dragged out of her comfort zone. I don't expect any more from her. She's a civilian if there ever was one—

"Wait, that's not true," Deborah says. "Real cowards, they don't admit to things. You do. You're not scared of what I think. That's something, isn't it?"

I allow it. "Okay, so I'm better at it when you're around." That gives Deborah some cheer to hold on to, and I like it—anything is better than going down the road of confession.

"How about I do it, too?" Deborah asks.

"Do what?"

"Be brave, dummy. If you ever need help," Deborah says, "I promise, if you need me to do something big, that I'll do it with a smile on my face, okay? Anything you want. But you have to promise to be at least as courageous as me."

I almost laugh at the idea, but then my face freezes. I have everything now, don't I? I can wrestle and fight and shoot, and here is this naïve nobody offering to sacrifice for me, to me, like I'm some pagan deity. On some level, it's wrong, having this power, but I can't feel bad. Doesn't loyalty fire everyone's heart?

"Okay. I'll remember that." I fish out a tissue to wipe the black smudges from my fingers. "Now, come on. Let's get home. We still won today. Everybody's gonna want a celebratory bite."

42 - RANATH

October 3rd

The Arlington County police department is hardly the most imposing building I've ever seen, but I still pause for a moment before going in. I give a last look at the car. Ena is my moral support. She's in the locking trash can in the back seat because the hotel started asking questions. It's cool tonight but not cold enough to be a danger to her. After I'm done here, we will find another place to live.

I rub my hands against my itching new clothes and wish for the hundredth time I had a partner to practice on. I did the next best thing this morning, spouting an improvised story to a motel clerk who looked bored enough to talk. He hmmed and uh-huh-ed through it. He didn't spot flaws, but he was a poor substitute for any interrogation a police officer might drop on me.

Let's do this. I push into the police department and find the front desk. It's busy, being a Saturday night, but well-staffed. The wait is short.

"I had my wallet stolen," I say. "I was wondering if by some miracle anyone turned it in."

"What's your name?" says the bulked-out female officer working the desk.

Simon Walter Davis, I don't say. It's tempting, to be sure, but any F-prot searching for such things would be familiar with BRHI records and would raise a red flag. I want to get out of trouble, not into it.

"Percival Nathan Cross."

"When did you lose it?"

"It was stolen, I'm pretty sure. Yesterday."

"Keith, do we have any wallets since yesterday?"

"No," comes a voice.

"Sorry. Just a second. I'll get you the form. You'll want to report it. Got a pen?"

"Yes, actually."

She wanders off and returns with papers. "Fill this out. Someone will be with you soon."

I settle down and detail the nature of the problem. It's not long before the door opens. An officer who looks like an old catcher's mitt calls me back into the bullpen. We sit by his desk.

"Mr. Cross, I'm Officer Watson. Why don't you tell me what happened?"

"I was at a restaurant in the hotel I'm staying at–"

"You're from out of town?"

"Yes."

"Where are you from?"

"Massachusetts."

"Boston? Springfield? Where?"

"Boston," I say. It's far enough away that flying makes sense, not so far that it'd be a problem driving. "Anyway, I was in the hotel restaurant, and I've got my wallet out, and we're fiddling with the stupid prepaid card I've got–"

"A credit card?"

"It's like a credit card, but you put money on it and take it off. It's a whatsitcalled, here, I'll show you." I pull out an Urbanbank card. "This is the sole survivor of my wallet right here. You pay Urbanbank to put cash on it, and then you just use it like a debit card. I give myself a few hundred bucks a month, and if I hit the limit, then I stop shopping. That's how I stay out of credit card debt."

"Smart idea." The cop examines the card, noting the name on it as Percival Cross. I filled out the application form under that name three days ago.

"Well, it was until I bent the fucking–excuse me. Until I bent it. See how it's bent just a little from being in my wallet? The strip wouldn't scan, and while I was fiddling with the card and the checkout girl, I put my wallet down on the counter. It was there thirty seconds, and it was gone. Driver's license, credit cards, discount cards, library–I don't even remember all the cards I had in there. Gone."

"How'd you pay for dinner?"

"It was lunch." Details matter. "But whatever, I was afraid I was gonna be washing their dishes, but I made a stink about how I just got my wallet stolen in their restaurant, and they were free to throw me out. They were nice enough to waive it for me instead of adding it to the bill." I pause. "Do you mind if I curse?"

"Go ahead."

It seems like the officer is taking a more protective attitude, buying my story. Now, I just can't slip up. "Thanks, I had old-fashioned parents, and you being police, it didn't seem right."

"Well, in my experience, you're in for a rough time," Watson says. "First, you're going to have to cancel your credit cards and get them re-issued, and a bent cash card isn't going to help you with that. Now, while your hotel bill's probably covered, I assume you're going to want a plane flight home."

I fake being stunned. "I didn't even think of that. They won't let me on without photo ID."

"However," Watson says, "if you give me all the details, we'll see what we can do for you. I can give you a police report you can use that explains that your driver's license and other ID documents were stolen. Now, you weren't traveling with a passport, correct?"

"No, I actually don't have one."

"Do you have a birth certificate or something you can use to get a new driver's license when you get home?"

Home. Home has the fire safe that contains my identity documents, but I can't go back there. The place will have been picked over by investigators, and the F-prots will have set surveillance in case I return. I've often fantasized about recovering my research from that safe, but I cannot slip into sentimentality. What matters now is whether or not my image has gone out to this very station as a person of interest who needs to be questioned.

"I think my parents still have that."

"What did you use the first time you got a driver's license?"

I'm ready. "A Social Security card. How do I get one? Same thing?"

"Okay, why don't you give me your name and Social Security number, and we'll get started on this report?" Watson calls up a document on his computer.

"Percival Nathan Cross, and the number is 015-511-0251." I've looked up the state prefixes for the old system, just in case the lie has to check out.

"Birthplace?"

"Cambridge, Massachusetts." I take the details from what I know of MIT.

"Home address."

"1428 Elm Street, apartment 3, Boston, MA 02139." Pure bullshit, but I can update this one at any time with a simple change of address form.

"How long have you lived there?"

I didn't plan for that one, but I take it in stride. "About three years."

"Do you know the date?"

"I know the month."

"We'll say it's the first, then." Score. I have the officer fudging for me.

"Home phone?"

"I don't have a landline." I give the number of the prepaid phone I grabbed recently.

"Birthdate." I give my own. Some things are sentimental.

"Marital status."

"Single."

"And you don't know who might have your wallet and information now."

"Not a clue." The officer ignores a large section.

"All right, Mr. Cross," he says and makes a final few clicks. The printer on a nearby desk rattles its internal appendages and announces, "Printing Job One." A few seconds later, and Watson slides a warm sheet in front of me.

"I'm going to need your signature."

I sign. "What happens now?"

"You make copies of this form. You'll want to get it notarized because some credit card companies ask for that."

"Don't notaries ask for photo ID?"

"With this form, you should be okay. Now, you show it to the DMV in your hometown, and they hook you up with a brand-new driver's license. And last, we come to the boxes."

This isn't in the plan. "I'm sorry?"

"The boxes down at the bottom to make my life easier and your life harder," Watson says. He takes the sheet out of my hand and points to the checkboxes at the bottom, reading.

"Box one, 'Are you willing to provide help in prosecuting anyone who would have this information now and is using it in an illegal manner?'"

"I sure would," I say. "I guess I fly in if there's a court date or something, right?"

"Yes. Still want it?"

"Do it," I say.

"And box number two, 'Do you authorize law enforcement officials to release this information if it helps investigate or prosecute the person illegally using your info?'"

"Completely. Identity thieves deserve what they get."

"Then, we're done," Watson says, and I feel my shoulders fall in relief. It's all in character, but it's as real as it gets. "You just make those copies I mentioned—"

"Thanks for all your help, officer," I say, making sure to give him eye contact and a sincere handshake. "Unless there's anything else I need—"

"It's not Easy Street from here, you know," the officer says. "If someone else is using your credit cards and your cash card runs out, you can get in trouble quick."

I pretend to consider. "Most of the bills I handle online—"

"You'll want to change your passwords. Someone with the cards can sometimes reverse-engineer to get at the good stuff."

I nod. "Point."

"You got a friend you can stay with if things get bad?"

Friends? Ones that aren't separated by decades? "I think so... never put it to the test."

"Whose name comes to mind?"

I have no idea. I see Kern's face in my mind, but that is as unreachable as the moon, as is the whole F-prot team and Ulan, whom I think of for good measure. There are my parents, my senior officers, all a world away, and last, of course, comes Infinity. I linger on her, but all that comes out of my mouth is, "I only know one. Her name's Ena."

"Emma?"

"Ena. Japanese word. Totally different." I insist a little too hard. "What's she do?"

"She's unemployed."

"Is she married?"

"No, not yet."

"Better ask her roommates, too, if she's got any."

"I'll do that." I start making up a last name for her, to be ready for Watson's next question. But there is no next question. We finish the paperwork, and within fifteen minutes, I am out in the parking lot.

I find myself instinctually looking for my old car and find the rental. It's only a number, like the stock I must sell, like the bank accounts I must drain. I planned for this, as much as one can. I disappear better than anyone I know, and that has always been a source of pride.

Ena is the one thing that will follow me into my new life. Snakes are not social animals: she lacks the parts of the brain necessary for love or sympathy. She can live out her days never seeing another of her kind and never suffer for it. I have always found that interesting, but interesting and ideal now seem like two very separate things.

43 - INFINITY

October 18th

I watch the heap of salt disappear into the swirling water of Ferrero's solution and wonder when the magic starts. I've seen my share of sleight-of-hand, but I know Ferrero doesn't have access to any magician's props, so he'd better dazzle me. It's been a long time since I had my sense of wonder stimulated.

I touch my hand where I was bitten. Maybe not a long time but long enough.

Fererro's got some patter going. "Good, as you can see, we have our eye of newt and our powdered hemlock, a little touch of table salt, and if I may have the lighter... thank you." He takes the cheap, transparent disposable from my hand. "Now, who among us has money to burn?"

"Wrong crowd," says Ly. Morgan's with Deborah in the kitchen, and Cass and Jessica are out on some errand Morgan hasn't described.

"If I may borrow a bill? A hundred, perhaps. A twenty, a five, a one..."

"I've got four quarters," Ly counters.

"David Copperfield never had to put up with this," Ferrero says, pulling out his own wallet. "Here, an ordinary one. See for yourself. It has not been tampered with in any way."

"Turkey's on in two minutes," yells Morgan from the other room.

"Are we starting without Jess and Cass?" I fire back.

"They're off the highway now. Where are the tongs? We need to get the corn out."

The tongs are in Ferrero's hand, but I want to see them in action before they get taken away. I check out the dollar bill and give it back. He holds it in the metal's grip.

"Now, before your eyes, I dip it in the magic solution—"

"Which is apparently the alcohol we used to kill your lice," comments Ly.

"And we give it the spark of Prometheus's mighty fire, and... voila." Ferrero says. Flames leap to the dollar bill and engulf it, turning the cash into a raging torch.

"Like the bush when God spoke through it, it burns, but it is not consumed," Ferrero announces, shaking the bill. The flames die out almost instantly, and there's the bill, untouched.

I nod. "Not bad, God. Can you top it, Ly?"

"I'm double-jointed. That count?" I frown at him. "What? A buck is nothing anymore. Would've been cooler with a hundred."

"None on me," Ferrero says. "Everything went toward dinner tonight."

"You should have asked. I got some from a bite—" I reach.

"Morgan's rule. No blood money for tonight."

I hadn't heard that, but I have no chance to follow up. The door opens.

"Jess, where you been?" I call.

"Secret mission," the doctor says. "Has Morgan made the announcement yet?"

"We were waiting on you," Morgan says, and in moments, everyone is arranged around the table, with a gigantic roast bird and actual wine glasses. Plastic, though.

"This beats the hell out of ramen," says Ly. "You gonna tell us what the occasion is yet?"

"Avoiding the Halloween rush," jokes Cass.

Morgan stands up straight. "As I'm sure you've noticed, what we have here is a traditional Thanksgiving feast minus, of course, the actual date of Thanksgiving. I decided to do this because I wanted us to have a day of our own, for a new tradition.

"Cass and Jessica spent the night camping out near the Court, trying to get any possible information. As you probably suspected, the justices went home Friday night, but their clerks and such spent the weekend working. After a little trickery, our champions found out that our case will be in the decisions that come out tomorrow."

Suddenly, Ferrero and Deborah start to clap. The others join in the applause. I follow suit, but I'm confused. Is this just for Cass and

Jessica? No. It's because we have come far, and that itself deserves recognition.

The room grows quiet. Morgan continues.

"I suggest that, once every fall, we gather like this. We put aside the differences that have come up... because they will... and we celebrate the fact that we made it another year. Tomorrow, our lives may get significantly better or otherwise. There are no guarantees. But if we make it to next year, we should remember those who fell along the way. I mean, of course, the people we feed on, who, God willing, will recover from our visits but also those of us who could not stay or even died for us. And I'd like to inaugurate this decision with a toast."

We raise our plastic glasses.

"To those who would be with us and cannot be."

I say nothing as the drinks tap together. The list in my head counts backward: Roland, Owen, Aaron. It flashes on the people I left bleeding at truck stops and health clubs, to my gang of F-prots in L.A., to my father in well-deserved prison. Some simple words and some thrift-store goblets are making me realize one thing links damn near all the names.

"You're supposed to drink it," Cass stage-whispers over at me. Embarrassed, I try the wine. I'm going to need it.

* * *

It's later, nearly one, when I catch Morgan out in the rowhouse's little enclosed backyard. The other vipes have migrated up- and downstairs, and I immediately know something's off. I slide the glass door aside and join him at the porch railing.

"Buck fifty for your thoughts," I say cheerily.

"What happened to a penny?"

"I tip."

"I'm debating," he says. "I came out with Deborah when she wanted a smoke, and she slipped me a cigarette before going."

"I thought you quit."

"Was clean eight years. Then, I was in custody. I miss it. Not the smell or the flavor. Just the talking it starts. 'Course, I like not being addicted to something, too."

I snort. "What's that like?"

"Right." He pauses, distant. "Anyway, I was just thinking that every political movement starts with your friends. Then, I had a little insight. Your friends always try to talk you out of things that don't make you happy. Even when it's important to you."

I pull out Ferrero's lighter and put it on the railing between us. "I skip that part and go straight to being an enabler." He doesn't take the lighter. Mirroring his somberness, I ask, "Why are you really out here?"

Morgan exhales a plume of frozen breath, stark in the porchlight. "I was making up my mind. The oral arguments are done, the decision is now... and Cho thinks it's all over. No more hiding for any of you." I nod. Morgan and Cho rehearsed endlessly for the tiny half hour Cho got in front of the justices. "That made me think we'll get a good decision, and I want to turn myself in. Not contest the murder charges. If you want, you can try all night to make me see reason."

I do.

I start with the most obvious argument. If he goes to jail, he can't feed. I go into all the shit I've done to feed him, then the prisoners he'll face, the years of his life he'll waste. Morgan stays with me, never angry or indignant, explaining it all away. Ulan told him that without blood, he'll go into a kind of hibernation, so he thinks he'll do the time in his sleep. It'll be easy to isolate him, and he doesn't fear revenge from law enforcement.

Finally, I blurt, "But we wouldn't know what to do without you. I mean, can you imagine me with this pack of misfits?"

"I actually can," he says. "Between you and Jessica, I think you'd do pretty well."

"Pretty well isn't good enough!" I shout, more forcefully than I intend. "You're great, Morgan. You're one of those people who make it look easy, when the rest of us are living lives of complete fuckupitude. Why is it I'm the one with the gun, and I always think of us as you protecting me? At the toast, I was cataloguing all the people I've run away from. My boyfriend, my prey, my F-prots. I'm injustice incarnate, Morgan. I can't be with anyone longer than a few months before I turn traitor and move on to some other meal."

Morgan takes it in stride. "You've never run from me."

I hesitate. *I shot your friend,* I don't say. *I owe you.* But once again, I'm not brave enough to speak it aloud. It'll make a mess that won't convince him to stay. "So, you run from me, is that how it works? We need you."

"This is your brood, too," he reminds me. "When I met you, I was the one in the hole. I can make a speech and work a room, but you're the one who's essential to the pack's survival. And what I have to do, it will work. What's the number one thing people say about me in the outside world? Murderer. Cop killer. And they label us all like that. But if there's one thing this country loves, it's a comeback. They want to see sinners get redeemed. It makes them feel safe. And when they feel safe, it's better for all of you."

I fume but don't explode. What he's saying makes sense. I've seen enough celebrities walk out of court or rehab to recognize that there's a script involved. They apologize, they talk about their struggle with addiction, they tell kids not to do what they did. Always, they gloss over the fact that they ignored such advice from the previous gamut of celebrities. Yet the masses stay glued, and whoever is interviewing them praises them for their forthrightness.

But I can't compare Morgan to the limousine litter. They cut every deal they can to avoid jail time, and that, I guess, is where Morgan's motives lie. He wants to preserve the scraps of nobility that the professional scoundrels throw away.

"Is this just about guilt?" I ask. "I mean, if anyone's a sinner in our crew, it's me. I'm doing the biting."

"You've had to kill, haven't you?" Morgan says quietly.

"No. Maybe... I don't know." Again, the parade of victims. "I've taken more."

"I can take the pressure off. One less mouth."

"That's not going to make anything better if Cass and Ly shoot up an ambulance to piss off BRHI."

"Jessica has a moral compass just as good as mine."

"A compass doesn't work if you never look at it. You're the only one of us they respect."

"Lean on Ly, appeal to Cass's hero complex, and you can do this. You know you can. They're your family now."

I stop, unable to say anything. I've spent a long time running from anyone related to me, but there were moments, clear and happy, in the early days with my mother. I choose to believe Morgan means those.

"Here's the deal," I say, unsure of what'll come out of my mouth next. "Take it before everyone. The whole group will be affected by this. They should have a say."

"You like democracy, eh?"

"What do I know? I can't imagine those guys in 1776 had this shit in mind."

"Sure, they did. They left us a system because they wanted people to shape this country. They didn't want to shape it for us."

That's comforting. But not enough. "I haven't changed your mind, have I?"

He softens. "I'm going to miss you."

"Yes, well," I say, adjusting a strand of my hair that fell across my face, "there's a lot of that going around."

I give him a little kiss. Because that's what you do when you say goodbye.

44 - INFINITY

October 19th

I've tried, for many years, not to be a details person. I'm good at them—I've got a head full of verses that can rival Homer if you want me to gab, but it's a buzz-kill. The world of parties and clubs and modeling gigs are all about keeping it hot, not measuring how much carbon you burn. It took the F-prot program to re-engage my brain, and even there, I still went by instinct. When I focus on details, I'm reminded of home, and I end up twitching in hate.

This morning, I'm miserable. I got no sleep the night before. I closed my eyes for what felt like five minutes, and then came the godawful 3:30 alarm. I start cleaning because the dirty plates from last night mean there's no free counter space to turn leftovers into breakfast. In between runs to the trash cans outside, I massage my arms. They itch with the thin cuts of razors I used to feed the pack. I'm exhausted, but I'm also wired, feeling young and tough and ready.

We get out of the house after a few hours, cramming into Ly's van. Ferrero manages to spill his coffee in the front seat the first time Ly comes to a stop. The aroma stinks up the place; I stopped liking the stuff when I got my vipe nose. Deborah keeps the window cracked, letting in the cold air of empty pre-dawn streets.

We get to the Court soon enough, park and step out into the chill. A crow caws from atop a traffic light wire. We set out in sunglasses, coats, and hoodies.

As we reach the marble steps, my radar comes up with threats. Not a handful. Hundreds. The National Mall has been overwhelmed by a massive throng, separated out by police barriers holding back two disproportionate masses. I've never seen so many tents.

The smaller group are a mixed bag. Some are young people in the black leather and lace of vampire fans. Others have gray in their hair or beards to complete a hippie look that's probably older than the chief justice. Many have homemade signs, the largest being a red-white-and-blue banner held at chest level by six protestors, saying, "INALIENABLE" MEANS INALIENABLE, with copious underlining. The other scattered slogans are on posterboard; one saying MY COLD IS A VIRUS, TOO lies next to a pile propped against a tent. I see one BITE ME, JESS, but for a moment I'm not sure which way they mean it.

Then, I realize that the hostile protestors are all on the other side of the steps. My heart freezes because a woman with a megaphone has spotted us, and she starts barking orders. The numbers are at least ten times that of our defenders and a hundred times as many as the cops. The crowd raises two dummies suspended by nooses. Their faces are rubber likenesses of Morgan and Jessica. Fat wooden stakes have been driven through their chests. Everywhere I look, I see rage—only some of them can see us. The others don't care who they scream at. Their signs say things like WE ARE ALL SIKORSKI and I'LL GIVE YOU BLOOD with a picture of a pistol next to it. Some of them shout at the cops, who have pulled away a few individuals with pitchforks— actual pitchforks and what look like juggling torches—and are trying to process them without having to pepper-spray everyone in sight.

"Uh," I say, "anyone else see this crowd?"

"Yeah," says Morgan. "Looks like a big one, only smaller."

"How early did they get up?" I ask, more in wonder than curiosity.

Cass shakes his head. "This is normal. It's not personal."

I point at the effigies, but Cass waves it off. "Don't let it shake you. There's people who've waited their whole lives to hear there's real monsters they can shoot."

I look over at the vipe supporters again. "I'm going to go over there and network," I say. "Maybe find willing donors for a change."

"Don't," warns Jessica, with a dangerous edge to her voice. In response to my confused face, she clarifies. "We all want that, but one bad feed, and they'll be back at your door, madder than hell."

I want to argue, but as I turn to Morgan, I see he isn't paying attention. He's staring up at the top of the stairs by the locked double entrance doors, where the media clusters. A pretty-boy talking head with a camera pilot and makeup artist behind him is interviewing a young, black woman holding a wide-eyed girl, probably two years old, on her hip. The girl is warmly wrapped and sucking on a soother. The woman was dressed up in formal Sunday best, but her eyes hold no joy. They are the eyes of a survivor. The pit of my stomach churns, not from hunger.

"Morgan, last chance," I urge. "We can go. We can hear about it over a screen."

Morgan says nothing, enraptured.

I nudge Deborah. "Okay, who's the mom?"

"Luis Rodolfo's wife."

Morgan calls out "Nina?" and cameras of all kinds start to orient on him, from drones to glasses to shoulder-mounted ones like old bazookas. The show is on.

"Are you who I think you are?" Ms. Rodolfo asks.

Morgan pockets his sunglasses. "There's nothing I can say that will make things right. And this is a bad place to say anything private, but I just wanted you to know I came here today to turn myself in." Nina looks disgusted or perhaps so skeptical it's the same thing.

"Why would you do that?" she says.

"You can't get justice and give none back," he replies. By now, the camera drones are circling, trying to get both of them in a shot. The vipes stand in front of the locked doors, fanning out. We draw a look or two, but next to the real story, we might as well be wearing camouflage.

I watch the cameras, mostly multi-lensed, rotor-driven ones that look like they have jumping spider eyes in four directions. Would Darcy see me? Kern, Aaron? Then, I realize, the hell with it—I should show Morgan has a community now. All it'll take to give that impression is three vipes standing behind their spokesman, so I'm in, sure as sin. The pretty-boy interviewer addresses himself to Morgan. I don't recognize him—his microphone has a bird logo on it, and I rarely stop on his station during my channel flipping.

"I'm standing here with Morgan Lorenz at the Supreme Court building just before it opens. Mr. Lorenz, in all probability, the last our viewers heard of you was when you became a fugitive from the law. Did the manhunt for you affect your decision in any way?"

I watch Morgan, nervous over a dozen things that could go wrong. The cops are a breath away and could easily descend on us. The wisdom of holding a press conference first and turning himself in second was never clear to me, but if he did it the other way around, he probably wouldn't get a statement out at all.

Morgan looks cool and even-handed at the camera. "No, and I want to say this without demeaning the police at all. I don't think they were close to discovering my location. I didn't go out in public, so their presence did have an effect, but this day is about me coming in of my own free will."

"Do you believe that the justices will rule in your favor? That they'll say you are medically able to stand on your own and join society?"

"I don't presume to know the mind of the Court, but I believe we've made a strong case, and the truth is on our side. I think we'll do okay."

"I notice you've brought some people with you—"

"Yes, we have Dr. Ulan, as well as some friends."

"Are all these people positive for VIHPS?"

"We're a support group. You guys want to say hi? No, they're shy. I'm the only camera hog." I watch his charm work, broadcasting a clear signal of a regular person doing the right thing, and in that moment, I envy him.

"Here, don't bother my friends. I'll give you the visual you want," Morgan says and gestures for us to back up. He poses underneath the west façade of the Court and raises a hand like he's a rock star. For a second, I think he's gone drunk with fame; then, I realize he's pointing at the words etched in marble over the entrance, reading EQUAL JUSTICE UNDER LAW. Cameras click and chime.

There are more questions, which Morgan answers swimmingly. I exchange glances with Jessica. My self-defense instincts tell me to get the hell away from the hateful crowd, and I'm all too aware that they have a clean line of sight straight to Morgan's head. But no shots ring out. Instead, the crowds swell as everyone presses forward, and chanting starts. Morgan has to speak up to be heard. I see Jessica scowl before I realize what the crowd says:

Not an inch
Not a drop
They kill moms and
They kill cops

For a moment, I think Morgan will yell something back, but he comes out with a big smile at journalists and enemies alike. He doesn't say a word, but I believe he has the right answer to all this.

The doors crack open. The Court's police filter out, identifiable by the badges and patches over their body armor. The media start entering the doors. Then, my heart skips a beat when the police lock eyes with the vipes. One of them points. They approach in a group of five, and Morgan puts a restraining hand on me.

"Mr. Lorenz," says one of the officers, "this way."

* * *

The justices file in. They walk like they're old and tired, but as they look out into the audience, I see them harden. My brain screams danger, but that's guilt-driven paranoia. Chief Justice Fennel has spotted Morgan, and she's not afraid in the least. That's reassuring. It also fits with what Morgan said about her. She's still got shrapnel in her hip from a twenty-year-old bomb blast. I wonder what that's like: sitting on steel wherever you go.

"We will now deliver the opinions of this court in the case of *Lorenz v. The Benjamin Rush Health Initiative*," announces Fennel. "Justice Trousdale will present the bench opinion. The slip is being distributed, and Web is uploading. Kindly keep the noise to a minimum." Interns walk the aisles with stacks of paper.

Dread begins to squeeze me. Morgan's take on Trousdale was that he's one of those Freedom Forever Party ideologues who'd ban sunshine if he got a chance. Would he be reading the majority opinion if he weren't on its side? I doubt it.

"It is this court's prerogative to address the petitioner's claims first and the respondent's second. But first, I would like to address the fact that the petitioner has not shown his face in either court, though he was quite able, for all the days of trial and oral argument. Now he is here. Let me just say that your absence was noted, Mr. Lorenz, and it did not benefit your case.

"On the first charge, of wrongful infection, the burden of proof lies with the petitioner to demonstrate that the respondent knew the dangers of the VIHPS virus and yet infected him or allowed him to be infected. It is the opinion of this court that this was not adequately proven. Mr. Lorenz was infected by a Ms. Marie Kovar. This is an undisputed fact. Ms. Kovar was not an employee of the institute, nor did she represent their goals, nor was she told to infect Mr. Lorenz by a member of the institute. On this count, we conclude that Kovar was the prime contributor to Mr. Lorenz's infection, which she did of her own free will. The burden of guilt rests on the conscious actions of she who transferred the virus and understood its communicability."

I set my teeth. Blaming the victims. I should have expected that.

"On the second charge, of willful and wanton misconduct, the criterion that must be met is to prove that the respondent did or failed to do something that a reasonably prudent doctor or other health care professional would or would not do under similar circumstances.

"It is the opinion of the majority that the Initiative went to great lengths to attempt to contain the outbreak of the VIHPS virus. Reasonable precautions were taken given the science of the time, which was woefully ignorant about the ability of the virus to survive. There was no conduct of a heedless nature. Indeed, if Dr. Ulan is to be taken at her word, their attempts to find and contain the infected were overzealous."

I bite my lip. Is that it? BRHI's entire F-prot program, the targeted abductions, the slumping body when I pulled the trigger to save Yarborough... for all that, they use one word?

"With the petitioner's claims resolved, the court now turns to the constitutionally important question introduced by the respondent's motion to dismiss on lack of standing. The question is this: whether individuals infected with the VIHPS virus in its advanced stages can have all the rights and privileges due every legal citizen of our country, or whether they must be curtailed in some fashion for the common good."

That part sounds better. He's recognizing inherent rights. Ones that can't be taken away?

"In review of this matter, this court found no direct precedent and deliberated to resolve three questions.

"First, is it within the bounds of a doctor or public health authority to classify a living creature as human or not human and grant or restrict the freedoms and essential rights thereof? Second, are the criteria they use to make this classification reasonable, just, and fair, or should they be altered to bring them in accordance with the law? Last, do VIHPS-positive individuals present such a clear and imminent danger that this decision must be made for all infected or only those who have demonstrated a predilection toward violence and other unsociable behavior?

"The answer to the first dilemma, regarding defining humanity, can be found with ample precedent within case law. *Roe v. Wade* ultimately supported medical professionals drawing a line between constitutionally protected humans and that which is other. The line in that case was drawn across time: a collection of human cells, whatever its DNA says, is not designated human nor granted the protections of the law until approximately twenty-eight weeks, when a fetus able to survive outside the womb is considered protected. This is not the only precedent set by this landmark case; its opinion considered that the doctor may also make a judgment in order to preserve the life and health of the mother.

"The case recognized that an essential freedom protected by our Constitution is bodily autonomy: freedom from being forced to support another organism that is a danger to one's life and person.

"However, this court finds that once personhood is recognized by society, there are no circumstances under which it should be removed save death. To do otherwise is to invite catastrophe.

"Imagine an infection that removed your right to vote, to own property, to marry or reproduce, to be paid a wage or even emigrate from the very nation that does not recognize you as human."

I shoot Morgan a look. He's stone-faced, and I want him to smile. Even if we lost on wrongful infection, this is a win, isn't it? Instead, Morgan glances elsewhere. I follow his gaze to Cho. The lawyer looks as grim as if he just found a lump under his skin.

"The second dilemma, the question of criteria, is significantly hampered by the absence of good record-keeping on behalf of the Initiative. This has led Mr. Lorenz's expert witness, among others, to conjecture that this was a deliberate practice, to cover up wrongdoing in a program that went as far as terminating captive infected."

Trousdale's voice drones on while I wonder what happened. Ulan made allegations, but those couldn't be turned against her, could they? Capturing or killing infected is a sign of criminal activity, not extreme heroics. I tune back in as Trousdale continues to rattle.

"The Health Initiative has been assumed to be innocent until proven guilty in this regard, and they have made many strides in establishing their criteria by what few standards exist for scientific rigor in the largely unexplored field of qi biology. Dr. Ulan granted us the only other perspective, which brings us to the third consideration.

"Though Dr. Ulan and others like her may take precautions not to commit violence upon any person, the changes in an infected person's brain are significant, comparable with the physical alterations brought on by addiction to narcotics. Even granted that she may have lived a paragon's life following her infection, she still exposed more than two hundred people to her virus. The analogy of the grafted gun may suffice to illustrate the dangers inherent in VIHPS.

"Suppose for a moment that Dr. Ulan owned a pistol grafted to her hand and was an upright and law-abiding citizen. While the temptation to use the weapon in daily life might be strong, she could simply choose never to do so. She would fire it only at firing ranges or in defense of her life and thus not menace society at large no matter her threatening potential. Now, imagine if this loaded pistol replicates itself and could somehow force its owner to graft the replicas at the rate of one per week to anyone, even individuals who never wanted to or prepared to own a firearm. These replicas would then do the same to their owners and reward them with a narcotic high when they did so. Through no fault of her own, Dr. Ulan would find that she has made the world a much more dangerous place, as would her infected victims and their victims *ad infinitum*. We cannot allow Dr. Ulan's example to be followed in any capacity whatsoever because it is not sustainable. To paraphrase the book of Timothy, the law is not made for a righteous man. The law is made for the good of the bulk of humanity, and they, when infected with VIHPS, are as a rule unprepared for their condition and as medically unable to join society as Mr. Lorenz himself."

The quote has me snarling. First, they cite Roe and now the Bible. This is custom-made to gouge out my guts. Then, I feel a strong grip on my hand. It's Jessica. I squeeze back in solidarity.

"This court recognizes that the medical facts call for urgency in their application. It may be the place of a court to adjudicate the restriction or restoration of the rights of an infected individual, but it is practically untenable.

"While the court ruling is being made, the virus will run its course, and more infections or violence will result. To stop the spread of this contagious and perilous infection, a doctor must be granted the power to diagnose those with late-stage qi-positive EBL-4 and restrict their freedoms as he sees fit without judicial review. It is to this end that the court pronounces its judgment. The ruling counts five votes for the respondent and four for the petitioner."

My brain stutters. "Did they just say BRHI can operate as it always has?"

"No," says Jessica. "Now, they have legal cover."

I hear boos and realize their source. Cass, Ferrero, and Ly are standing and trying to get the masses to join in, but the norms aren't doing it. The gavel bangs.

"Mr. Lorenz, your friends will be ejected until they can respect the decorum of this court," announces Chief Justice Fennel, and Cho immediately gestures for Ferrero and Ly to be silent. Morgan rises, too, but the downhill slide has started. The bailiff approaches, followed by uniformed officers who come out of nowhere. I focus on them. I can read eyes: something bad is going to go down.

Cass snaps at the bailiff. "What are you here for?"

"Sir, come with me please," is the answer, and I know how this will end. The woofing will end in a shoving match, and that ends with guns. I'm on my feet in an instant: this is something I can solve. Draping my hands over Cass, I pull him gently off-balance into me.

"Walk me out, love," I say. "We don't need any more of their shit." Cass stumbles, into me and then onto his feet, disoriented by my cooperative tone. Ly and the others look to Morgan.

"Come on, we're leaving," he says, and in that moment, I think of how fucked up it all is, how nice we have to play here in the face of BRHI's crimes. And worse, I'm doing their work for them, hauling an angry friend away. I focus on half-carrying, half-dragging Cass. He's making noises about how lucky the bailiff is and how this isn't over yet and whatever smack comes to mind. Then, I reach the outside hallway, staring at a dozen-plus blue uniforms and nobody else.

The phalanx of Supreme Court Police stands ready, and it takes me a second to process what they're doing. Their pistols are out of their holsters, but they are all pointed down at the floor, the sight of the ready but inoffensive weapons sending exactly the message they want.

"Morgan Lorenz," says one of the cops, all crew cut and chest radio, "it's my duty to inform you that you're now under arrest. The rest of your friends are free to go."

Divide and conquer. Without the last sentence, the cop would be committing suicide.

"Morgan," says Ly, "don't tell me this is what you want."

"I needed a day in court," Morgan says. "It's over. I told you what I had to do."

"Infinity," Ly tries as Morgan presents his hands. The police apply cuffs. "We can't let them do this."

My instincts scream at me as I watch Morgan disappear into a crowd of ballistic vests. It doesn't matter that I've said goodbye. I'm barely here, remembering strangers saying my mother died and fathers and verses and promises broken. I'm a child again, suffering humiliation because I know the alternative is worse. I want to say something cynical, something that can reframe this as a test we can tolerate, but nothing comes.

I grab Ly in one hand and Cass in the other. Running is exactly what we need now. My yank breaks them from any resistance they were going to put up and starts the vipe retreat. We leave the battle behind us, with Morgan gone and the rest of the troops following me, as if I have some idea when or how we can rally again.

We push through a crowd of journalists waving printed opinions at cameras and hired paralegals translating the language like it's any other day. We emerge to the cold, bright world outside, to the awful sound of the wrong side cheering.

45 · MORGAN

Unknown date

The smell is the worst. The stench of the gas eats at my sinuses and the back of my mouth. I don't know what the gas is, just that it's used like chloroform is in the movies. I guess it's the stuff to sedate people before surgery—the kind where they tell you not to eat for twenty-four hours beforehand so you won't puke while you're under. Because there's been puking.

My cell is about three and a half meters to a side but twice that in height. The roomy space above is not for aesthetics. It's so I can't reach the black plastic bubble in the center of the ceiling that conceals a camera. I tried jumping from the cushion. It's all I have since a bedframe could be broken and used as a weapon. For the same reason, my toilet is a hole in the floor.

I rub the inside of my elbow. The closing of my wounds is my only way of telling time. I have no clock, no phone, no wristwatch. My last blood drawing was more than an hour ago—the tiny scab has completely vanished, leaving the skin whole.

I don't know where I am. The police took me away in a van that was all steel and stronger stuff, and I spent an unremarkable night in jail before they switched it up on me. They asked to administer a sedative, and I, rather foolishly, agreed when it was clear they weren't really giving me a choice.

They had an officer present to talk with me until I lay down to rest. That was the last sign I saw of real law enforcement.

The door bears the marks of my fists and feet. Strong as I am, I still can't kick through metal, and I sprained something in my foot in the attempt. After tiring myself out on it, I discovered it didn't muffle sound completely. Or maybe it did, before I made it less-than-airtight.

I can't hear much, but there is definitely a murmur: someone talking close to the door for extended periods. I guess there is monitoring equipment there. I lie down on my cushion and pretend to sleep. There's nothing distracting to think about, so my mind runs over the most ominous parts.

They fed me shortly after imprisoning me. I woke up with a girl in my room. Lean and young, maybe below eighteen, and all red hair and freckles. I peppered her with questions and got only a frown in response. I guess she'd been ordered not to speak. She presented her arm like a serving tray. When I finished the bite, the fans whirred, bringing in gas, and it was all over. Then, weeks later judging by my healed foot, the same girl. Not even scars to mark where I'd been. That's when I knew she was a vipe like me. She only answered one question, ever.

"Whose turn is it when you run out of blood?" I asked.

"Yours," she said.

That was it. They are not interrogating me. They only want to puncture me, suck out their samples and discard the skin like those little juice bags that kids bring in their lunch boxes.

Maybe I could theoretically fight back against whatever vipe will try to feast on me, but if they cut off my supply, I'll get weaker and weaker.

I am going to die here. Part of me thinks I deserve it. Were I to prosecute myself, Luis Rodolfo and Pierce Hauptmann would be enough to put me in a cell like this. But when I look at the freckled girl, it's different. Seeing another person subjected to my fate magnifies it.

The whirring fan starts. The air turns into a cold mist. It's the gas. I keep my face wedged into my pillow, breathing shallowly, using the cotton as a filter. I feel lightheaded, but either my plan is working, or I'm starting to build up some immunity. I can clearly hear the door open a few minutes later. They think I'm unconscious, and who can blame them? I can't count how many there are by sound alone, but I can tell the room is filling up.

"Cart in three, ready?" asks a faint voice through a radio. "One, two... lift." I hold still as they reach around me and heave, turning me over so I rest face up on a crashcart. Then, when someone touches my arm, I can't resist. I open my eyes.

I'm surrounded by the orange and black of hazard suits and darkened face shields. One of them has me by the arm and holds an empty syringe. Without thinking, I grab that wrist hard.

"What are you doing?" I find myself saying. I can't get hateful words out of my mouth, not on instinct.

The doctor I grabbed recoils but can't fight my grip. "Get him off me!" I hear, and the others are galvanized out of their shock.

"You don't need me!" I yell. "This isn't science! This is punishment!" Instantly, I regret shouting because I get a lungful of gas, and I feel my brain loosen its hold. But as more hands grab me, it takes little effort to cause more chaos. I draw my hand back across my body, and the syringe doctor comes with it, knocking into the ones on the opposite side. Everyone grabs me.

Trying to roll off the gurney, I lurch. My body feels like a barbell tumbling to the floor. There are more shouts, but they are distant, confined inside the helmets. I land on all fours.

"Come on!" I yell, struggling to get to my feet. Hands seize me, but I push back. "It's punishment! Say it! Punish me!"

Another lungful of gas ensures I have no balance, but I'm leaning on them now. I only have long enough to think that some of these jokers might not be doctors when the electroshocker hits my gut.

My body jerks as abs and chest all become a tight ball. It doesn't hurt so much as it makes me unable to move. My back muscles lock, and my hand on the crashcart rail clamps down. I try to heave the cart into my assailant, but it only rattles as my arm fails to respond. The man with the shocker fires again. I'm hit in the opposite shoulder, but my back is already as tight as it goes. I stumble. I can't even crawl. My limbs are useless, and my head hits cold tile: pain at last.

"C minus," I get out. "You didn't say it."

I lie face down, barely able to gasp for air. My diaphragm tightened, too. The tile sucks the heat from my body as the breaths full of gas finally get to me. My will dims. I don't want to kill these people. I don't care who they are. All I know is that they will hurt me beyond belief if it will get them an iota closer to breaking down the science of the virus. What I don't understand is why.

46 - INFINITY

November 14th

Ferrero's little Chevy Quasar has lousy visibility compared to Cass's truck, but like so many things now, there isn't much I can do about it. I'm craning my neck and getting blinded by headlights while I'm trying to get on the highway. Meanwhile, Ferrero's in the back seat trying to change his shirt in a way that keeps all the stains on the towels.

"How you doing back there?" I ask, guessing the distance to the bend in the road behind us. It's the only thing keeping our license plate from being spotted by witnesses.

"I don't know. Two people might have seen me leave," he says, and I accelerate, stomping too hard on the pedal as I process what he said.

"Wait, someone saw you? Mask or no mask?"

"No mask when I was with the donor, mask when I had the blood on me. That's when they freaked. We can't keep using the things. They scream 'crime in progress.'"

My thoughts are stuck in recirculate mode. I'm supposed to be the expert at this. What I get instead of a plan is a car blasting on its horn because my merge sucks.

"Do we go back?" Ferrero asks.

"And do what? Ice a witness? Stop digging the hole." I brake, switch lanes, and a motorcycle nearly gets smacked as it zips by. I hold my foot down, catching up to speed.

"Are you trying to kill us?"

"Yeah, because the number one killer of vipes is rear-end collisions," I snap. "Look, we just won't hunt there again."

"Amen to that," Ferrero says, distantly. The truth lies unspoken between us. There are a lot of places we can't go back to. Underscoring the point, I nearly take the turnoff for the place we

277

lived during the trial. After Morgan was taken away, Jessica laid out in no uncertain terms how easy it would be to make him give up the location of our townhouse. Within twenty-four hours, we had a deposit down on another two-bedroom and vacated the old one.

It's just for now, I remind myself. I'm still repeating that mantra when the rowhouse swings into view twenty minutes later. A taste of evaded responsibility is as addictive as anything else on my lips these days.

We pull up, and I do a quick visual check of the car—it doesn't have any suspicious stains once Ferrero has pulled the clothes and towels out. Looking around, I attempt to place any vehicles that haven't been there before but soon give up. There are too many; I'd have to bust out the notepad in my phone. I catch up to Ferrero, who is knocking at the door.

Deborah opens it. I point my fingers at her like a gun. "You should be packing if you're opening the door," I say.

She defends herself. "I could see it was you. Besides, if it was a cop, I'd be busted."

"If they ask, tell them you're scared of vipes," I say. "Now, we do this. Laundry and feeding. Where's Jessica? She's first."

"She's on the phone."

"With?"

"I dunno. New York."

I let out a breath. We all have our vices, and Jessica's is staying in touch with her old friends. "Okay, Cass, you're up."

Cass gets up from the couch where he and Ly were watching the news. He grabs a razor blade from a box of disposables on a folding table. As he goes to get his fix, I think I see a flash of coldness in his eyes. I'm going to say something about keeping the razors out of sight but decide it's not worth it. If I looked in a mirror tonight, I might get the same chill.

"Right," says Cass, "Ferrero, I got one rule for this. Want to hear it?"

"A rule?"

"Yeah, it's real simple. Just bloodsucking. I don't kiss afterwards."

His tone leaves no uncertain ground.

"Got it," says the smaller man.

"Good, let's knock this out, then." The two of them go upstairs, while I take off my coat. I sit down by Ly. He's cleaned up his beard but kept most of it, creating a look somewhere between a country-western star and the Devil. I eye his bowl of blueberries. As I said, vices.

He seems lost in the screen, but I'd better check in. "How're the berries?"

"Squishy."

"How's the news?"

"Worse." He shows me his aging tablet, smeared with fingerprints and dust, and brings up a screen. "A *Wall Street Journal* poll says twenty-nine percent of Americans say anyone who tests positive should be executed. Forty-eight percent say locked up."

"Better than fifty-one."

"Margin of error is four points. Where did you hunt tonight?"

"Uh..." I was at the wheel, but Fer gave all the directions. "College Park, why?"

He shows me the story. "They found our guy from last week. Police say they have some leads on a quote, 'gang of vipes familiar to us.' And vigilantes, those Vipe-Free America guys, killed a vipe in Anacostia. How'd our teacher man do?"

I hesitate.

"Oh, Christ," says Ly. "You had to think about it."

"It's nothing much," I say quickly. "He thinks he might have been spotted before he could get his shirt changed. The mask was on."

"Fucking great—"

"We're not going back there. And we're switching vehicles for next time."

"We can't keep this up," Deborah interrupts, leaning on the doorway to the kitchen. "He loses his nerve, his lure sucks, now he's forgetting to check for witnesses. It's not just a learning curve. He's not *good* at it."

"Are you volunteering?" I say, sick of the conversation already.

"Ly and Cass could," says Deborah.

"If you'd like to contribute," I say, "please go upstairs and help with the towels." Deborah rolls her eyes. As she disappears, I feel as if I just reprimanded my teenage daughter.

"It needs to be you, Infinity," Ly says. "You're the best at it."

"You just like the taste," I growl, defensive. Maybe calling him on it will send the message. The truth is I don't like him lapping at me. Morgan held them in line with ideals. All I have is the threat of choking them out—a poor way to enforce discipline.

Ly shrugs with his face. "What can I say? I'm human."

"Five out of nine assholes agree," I mutter.

"Any progress on finding Morgan?"

God, not now. "I was driving. You got anything, mister I-have-a-tablet-in-my-hand?" I can see by his face that he doesn't.

"Infinity!" Deborah calls, rushing down the stairs. "Trouble!"

The look in Deborah's eyes is enough. I take the stairs two at a time, blasting past Deborah to the upstairs bedroom. Inside, laid out on the floor like a quilt, are different colors of towels. Crumpled in heaps are Ferrero's sweater and shirt—Cass still wears his. He's lying on the prostrate smaller man, pinning him.

"Fer!" Ly strides over and grabs Cass by the hair, pulling his head back. It's then I see how much blood is on his face, on the towels, all over Ferrero's upper body. Cass's gray-blue eyes are all swallowed up by deep black pupils.

"Hey—" He flails, and I step in. This will get worse.

"Stop it, or I hurt you," growls Ly.

"What is that for?" Cass barks. "He likes it."

"Off." I break Ly's grip and address Cass. "You're taking too much. Let him go." He doesn't move, and for a second, I think we're going to have to mess him up. Maybe it's the threat that makes him back down. Maybe it's just shame.

"I was going to leave enough for you."

"Doesn't look that way from here. Lord, he must be down a *liter*."

"It's not that much—"

"Fer?" I hold the bleeding man, putting a hand on his neck to stanch the flow. "Wake up, Fer." I look back at the door. Deborah is watching. I can't just start in on him now—

I stop myself. I'm thirsty, and it's getting hard to concentrate.

"Fer, wake up," I say, hoping that if he talks, he'll look less tasty.

His eyelids flutter. "Fini?" He moves his head, then realizes how much pain his neck is in and tries to cup it in his hand. He gets my hand instead.

"Try to sit up. You're losing a lot of blood." He does. "I don't believe you two. Did you think for one moment where the rest of us would get *ours* from?"

Cass looks bothered. "He can heal—"

"No, he can't!" I snap. "Have you been listening when Jess talks? He's only fifty-five kilos. That's about four point five liters of blood. You take one. The rest of us take three hundred milliliters each. That leaves him at two point three. You want to see how well he heals with half his blood volume gone? I'll give you a hint. It's called torpid. Then, we get to figure out who goes out next time because he's dead to us."

Cass looks confused. "Wait... you didn't say how much he had before."

I'm about to bark out something nasty, but he isn't wrong. I haven't said it before. I had assumed that I'd know what to do, and they'd learn by osmosis. I didn't drill them on F-prot math because I thought everyone knew what I knew. Or that they'd listened to Jess. But really, who pays attention to the schoolmarm other than Memorizing Girl?

Okay. Damage control. "You may be right. I'm not going to say I did, but you need to know how much we can take. We all do. We have to be professionals about this until—"

Until he gets back, I don't say. I collect myself. "Cass, please dry off and get downstairs."

"I'll watch him," Ly says.

"No," I say. "We don't need the two of you having words. You and Deborah are up to feed. I'm going to watch *you*, and then I'm going to go out to get something for me and Jess."

"I'm sorry," says Cass on the way out. "I didn't know."

"Go."

As Deborah comes in, and I hold on to my bleeding friend, it occurs to me that I'm going to have to launder my clothes again before going out, and I won't get to sleep until fuck-it-thirty.

I say to you, stay away from these men and let them alone, for if this plan or action is of men, it will be overthrown. The line comes to mind too easily, like a song lyric ringing in my head. It is my punishment, like my father had intended it to be.

"Are you all right?" Deborah asks. "What are you thinking?"

"Man makes plans," I say, "and God laughs."

47 - KERN

November 19th

I close my eyes as the makeup assistant powders me down. I calm my breathing. Jess taught me how, a million years ago before she sold videos on the technique. I figure if I can beat a hostile audience like the F-prots, this should be apple pie. It isn't. My hands stay sweaty no matter how often I paw out a tissue from the packet in my sport coat.

"Five minutes," someone calls, a production assistant or some other person in charge of getting the word out. My only frame of reference for all the people I see scurrying around is old sitcoms about the crews of TV shows.

"You done?" I ask, and when the man nods, I get out my phone and tap my way through menus to call Diana.

A coiffed young woman in a business suit answers. "Waterford and Price," she announces, then sees my face. "How much time is left?" We rehearsed carefully, and she knows her role without asking. Today requires it.

"Five minutes. Get your attack dog on the line now."

"Roger," she says, and a new window opens, patching in another line. A ringing phone icon tells me what I need to know.

A hand on my shoulder brings me back to the room. "You're not gonna be on that thing on camera, are you?" It's Edison Field.

"I'm just assembling the troops."

"Nerves?"

"Nah. It'll all be over by the end of the day."

"It'll be the beginning," the veep corrects, and I nod. Our long-term strategy goes far beyond this little show. Field steps off to confer with a project lead, so I focus on the phone, which shows the grinning face of a South Asian girl in a pinstriped pantsuit. Truth be told, she's probably in her thirties, but anyone with a smile is a kid the way I count it.

"All right, you in position?" There is no reaction. "Can you hear me?" She stares at the screen intently. A window opens, and text comes through.

Can't hear on NYSE floor, it reads.

I nod and put my thumb up. The kid mirrors it. I kill the volume and take out my glasses. I hardly use them since I got my eyes fixed, but they have a port, and that's what I want right now. I flick the glasses' power stud and a display on the lenses flares up. The glasses join my phone's network. When I put them on, the numbers are small but clear: BRHI stock is trading at $59.93 per share.

I join the photo op team headed for the stage. It has a podium and a blue curtain and nova-bright lights shining down in stagecraft tradition. As I squint through the lights, I can see how many press showed up. Our PR team deserves diamonds.

"I feel like we should have a presidential emblem behind us," says the project lead, who told me to call him Matt. I'm still fuzzy on his last name since he's been acting lead for about twenty hours, and our usual lead is sending me pictures of her brand-new infant. I take his photo with the glasses to look him up on the staff Web page and flash a grin at him.

"This is no time to be thinking small."

Field, the warhorse, takes the podium. "Good afternoon," he says, and the recording devices chime like a pond full of mating robotic frogs. "Thank you all for coming. It gives me great pleasure to announce that our company has made public health progress that bears notice. I'd like to introduce you now to Dr. Matt Nolan, our project lead who will make some introductory remarks, and then we will open it up to questions and answers."

Nolan steps forward. "Thank you," he says, a little too loudly into the microphone. "For the last year, I've had the privilege of working with a talented group, an army, really, of people who have been at it night and day. We are proud to say that we are beginning clinical trials on a vaccine for qi-positive European Bat Lyssavirus-4, the organism that causes VIHPS."

The reporters don't say much: they read the press statement already. The number on my glasses is still a flat 59.93. I wonder. This early, will anyone care? Or will they demand results?

Nolan continues. "The first phase of the trial will involve approximately fifteen hundred subjects from groups at high risk for VIHPS. They will be given a series of six injections as well as a stim treatment to counteract the unique attributes of EBL-4. At the end of the trial period, their VIHPS incidence rates will be compared to those of a control group. I will now take your questions. Yes."

A bearded cowboy of a reporter, minus the hat, lowers his hand. "When do you expect the first phase of the trial to end?"

"In order to observe a statistically significant number of exposures, we estimate wrapping up Phase I by May. Yes?"

A grandfatherly-looking black man is next. "When you say high-risk groups for getting the virus, could you give us some examples?"

"I believe Dr. Kern could answer that most succinctly. Dr. Kern?"

Nolan moves out of the way, and it's showtime. I'm about to respond when the number in my glasses goes down. 59.75.

Focus on the face in front of you, I tell myself. *The investors probably haven't heard yet. We might not even be live.*

"Through our sampling, we've found many different factors that contribute to being exposed to the virus. I should be clear: when I say high-risk groups, I'm not talking about genetics or immune system reactions after infection. I mean when vectors have decided to take a blood meal from the subject.

"For example, we've found that in Los Angeles, we had our data strongly correlate with the swinging community. Not because sex communicates VIHPS—it doesn't—but because there were three or four promiscuous vipes in the area, and they infected in places they knew, which included some specialty bars in West Hollywood. In D.C., it's gymnasiums. So, when we say we're starting the vaccine, it'll be three studies of high-risk groups in New York, L.A., and D.C., given to volunteers willing to risk exposure." I pause for breath.

59.9, my glasses read.

Trying not to pause, I add, "Does that answer your question?"

"It does."

The hands go up again, and I point at a young brunette in a solar skirtsuit. Somewhere vaguely, I consider that Nolan may want the microphone. Too late.

"You said—Mr. Field said—that the Initiative is using a qi-positive treatment as part of the regimen. Given the rarity of qi-positive doctors, what steps are you taking to prevent them from getting swamped when this goes out to the general public?"

"Our first effort is to come up with a treatment that works, and due to the tenacious active qi in this virus, we felt fighting fire with fire was mandatory. As for distribution, our door is always open to new applicants. It is our sincere hope that stimweb users will want to learn the techniques perfected here and spread them to other users. We're not going to hoard that secret and say, 'oh, you only get it if you're rich.' We want that aspect to be public knowledge, until there are enough stimweb users out there to halt this pandemic. Next, please."

When I look back into the corner of my glasses, there is writing. I strain to read it, and when I see the number—62.54—I realize what it says.

They just heard.

"Dr. Kern," someone calls, and I point at a hand in the crowd, "do you have anything planned to help those already infected by the virus?"

"Thank you," I say, thinking fast, "that's an excellent question." The number in my glasses is up to 66.15. "Our current approach to combating the VIHPS pandemic is to focus on the vaccine for a number of reasons. EBL-4 is a very robust virus. Attempting to counteract it before it gets a hold on a target immune system is, we believe, a much easier task than trying to do so after the fact." The number hits 70, and I struggle to remain on-topic. "However, our plan is to look out for the unfortunates who have become victim to this virus as well."

74.80.

This is it. They've probably got the TV on. They're watching me. Now, sell the savior act.

"Our goal is to immunize everyone who wants to be immunized through this vaccine so that the choice of a vipe can change. Imagine if, instead of biting into an unprotected human, the vipe bit into someone who couldn't get infected."

78.90. A flashbulb goes off. Thanks, clown.

"The amount of blood lost in a feeding situation can be very small, less than what you'd lose donating at the Red Cross. If that were all that happened—no violence, no infection—the disease wouldn't be the problem that it is today. If we can get enough people immunized, the vipes can live with their disease. They can find a pool of willing donors, and over time, the number of new cases will simply die out."

81. By the time I read the number after the decimal, it changes.

"Does that answer your question?" I finish. The reporter nods and sits. I'm done. I smile at Field, who grins back. Field retakes the podium, and I rub my hands together to dry them. If the veep notices that I have a display up, he doesn't seem to care.

The price hits 270 that day before I sell a quarter of what I own. For the first time in my life, I'm a millionaire.

November 28th

I pull into the National Harbor lot in the cold hours between midnight and dawn. My skin prickles as I see the multicolored lights of two black-and-whites. The sight confirms that I have, at least, been disturbed for a reason. That's no comfort. Every time I've visited a sidewalk lit up in red and blue, people volunteer all kinds of reasons.

I find parking on the street—the lot's structure is strung with police tape, no doubt to the frustration of whatever poor saps still have their vehicles inside. Crowdsource cars pick fares from the people who decided to come back in the morning. I spot al-Ibrahim among the civilians.

"What have they found?" I say by way of greeting.

"The one on the gurney had a close encounter." Al-Ibrahim jerks his head at a small man resting on a collapsible crashcart. He's probably destined for an ambulance ride but not in terrible condition, or they'd have wheeled him off already.

"You run any photos by him?"

"Didn't need to. He's one of ours."

I reconsider, looking again at the man by the ambulance. Now that Ebe mentions it, I've seen him before—and a few of the faces in the crowd nearest him.

Yarborough got the F-prots a gig not long ago, consulting and training for a sizeable pack of concerned citizens. I didn't know where they'd gotten the funds, and it was never in my interest to ask. That concerned me less than the false confidence of these amateurs. It's a tide that I can never hold back no matter how many warnings I give. Its results are predictable, the human cost all too avoidable. But it's rent.

"So, he went fishing, got a shark?"

"He said he spotted a woman, mid-twenties, black leather jacket over workout clothes. Overheard her conversation. She sat at a man's table, complete stranger, and started to hit him up to come home with her. Twenty minutes later, they walk to her car."

I fold my arms. "He's sure she wasn't a prostitute?"

"Our hero phones his friend for backup, tries to delay her. She's wise to it. She gets in her car, he calls her a vipe, gets in front of her vehicle, draws his nine. She hits him with the car. Driving. Not, you know—"

"I know. You were right to call me."

"I figured your kids were in bed by now."

"Fucking Dracula is in bed by now," I say, more observation than complaint. As I look over my teammate, it's clear there's something more. "You're grinning. What do you know?"

"Do the words 'Chevy Quasar' mean anything to you?"

He's got my full attention. "He got eyes on the car? Guaranteed?"

"Eyes, face, shoulder—"

"No jokes, Ebe. Is this reliable?"

"He says he drives one, too. He'd know it anywhere. Dark red. Didn't get a license plate."

I don't care. My brain kicks in like I've vaped nicotine, but if I know anything, it can't be as good as it sounds. Infinity is a professional. After an incident like this, she'll try to switch vehicles. Then again, she can't do that forever. Cars, even rentals, cost money and create paper. We already figured out she used a pickup truck and then changed it up to some kind of sedan. The question is, can she get another? Or are the cops going to pull her license plate number from a security camera and end up with her home address?

"This is good stuff."

"Yeah... still wish it was some other vipe, you know?"

I give the police a glance. They're no longer threatening or even an inconvenience. They're like dim-witted little cousins, parroting their parents' rules no matter how asinine. Vipes can fill a golf course with victims before the police cuff a single one, let alone try them or convict. That's almost as bad as denying justice outright.

"You know?"

"No," I say, snapping out of reverie. "Ebe, you can't think like that."

"Don't worry. I can still do the thing. I'm just saying I might go home to my crying pillow afterward."

"I don't doubt you, Ebe. If I didn't think you were a pro, you would have been off the team years ago. But you can't say stuff like that to everyone."

Ebe shrugs. "Roland's gone. F-prot's gone. From here, it looks like it's just you and me. Unless..." he looks thoughtful.

I assess. There isn't much point in hiding. "I was going to announce the good news to the whole team. You know about the stock price, right?"

"I got a call from Olsen, yeah. I told her not to break a mirror high-fiving herself."

"Right, well, it means a lot of powerful people are wealthy again. That means in addition to any options we own, we might get contract work. Only without a contract."

Ebe gets it. "Oh," he says. "Quiet stuff."

"I can't say who, and I can't say what, especially here."

"Yeah, yeah, of course—"

"Just know that we might have to impress someone real soon."

"If I see the bitch," al-Ibrahim says, "I won't pause for meaningful conversation." I nod. Ebe is usually as good as his word. Still, I prod him.

"Where are your thoughts, Ebe?"

"Just looking at that guy and thinking about that car. I'm wondering if she's out there laughing at us."

Maybe it's the nature of the job, but I don't see her laughing.

49 - INFINITY

November 28th

I return home after midnight, eyes puffy from some overworked tear ducts. I fucked it up. Like an idiot, I went out without backup because like an idiot, I'd been arguing with cranky vipes because like an idiot, I let them vote on who went out on hunting night and when. I feel like that video game series with the big, sticky ball except I'm picking up testaments to my own criminal incompetence.

The door behind me slams as I close it just a little too forcefully. I doubt it will wake anyone. We're all night critters now, even once-a-morning-person Ulan. I stuff my coat into the foyer closet and try to get past the living room without greeting anyone.

It doesn't work.

"Hey there," Ferrero says, looking up from the wallscreen. Its glow lights the living room: bright with a shot of cracking sea ice, then dim when showing barren coral reefs.

"Hey. Where is everyone?"

"Ulan's in the basement, Cass is out getting a part for the truck, Ly's upstairs, and Deborah's trying to sleep. How was hunting?"

I could mention the vigilante, the clusterfuck, how messed up I am. But that takes time and hassle. Of all the vipes to alienate, I'm least afraid of Ferrero. "I didn't get anything," I admit.

"Well, even the best batters only hit .400." He turns back to his programming.

"Thanks for understanding," I say.

"Any time."

I leave him there, wondering about his taste in television. Science news doesn't captivate me. I find people more interesting. Ferrero is starved for ways to keep his brain sharp. He once told me that he missed his kids—not that he has biological ones. The ones in his classroom forced him to stay one step ahead of them. Watching him in front of that hopeless wallscreen will choke me up if I stay too long; that's how shaken I am.

I find my room dark and empty and only bring the lights partway up. I've just kicked off my boots when my instincts tell me to suddenly look behind me.

Ly leans over me, and I nearly clock him. "Fini," he says, upbeat. "Been waiting for you."

"Bad news," I say, not meeting his eyes. "I got interrupted."

"I'll help you tomorrow night, then," he says. "But now, I just want a little."

I look at him square on, and even in the dim light, I can see he's jonesing. Under the beard, his cheeks are sunken, his eyes glassy. He's propped against the doorframe like a drunk, though I don't smell any alcohol.

"A little becomes a lot," I say.

"Oh, wait, no." He straightens up. "I know what you're thinking. I know better than Cass. When you explain, I listen."

I don't take my eyes off him. I try to figure out if I can get rid of him faster by agreeing or by trying to slam the door.

"Come on," he tries. "We don't need to tell anyone."

I bite my lip. It would be nice not to lose so much at once. Ever since the Cass incident, I've gotten leery about having so many mouths on me. If I get lightheaded, I can lie down after, and it's probably best to keep Ly on my side. I'm tired of political decisions like that, but oh, well.

"It'll feel good," Ly says. "You look like you need a treat."

"All right," I say, "one nick. Stick to capillaries."

"That's my girl." He gets out a fresh towel from the hall closet. He pulls a few bandages out of the box by the side of the bed and a single-edged razor blade from its paper sleeve. Then, he hesitates.

"You have a bad night?"

"Long story."

"I miss Morgan, too," he says. "I like a noble gesture as much as the next guy, but there's a thing called common sense."

I give him a skeptical eye. "And you have that?"

"Hey, I just point out flaws when I see them. I ain't saying I'm any better." He gives a smile. "If you measure me and him up, he's got the nobility and the vision, and I've got an extensive knowledge of bass guitar."

I snort almost imperceptibly. Aaron had been lead guitar.

"Sucks, right?" he says. "Had to leave it behind, had to ditch my friends and my lady. Man, I wish I had just my shitty Gibson one time. I would rock your world with it." I smile. "There we go," he says. "And I didn't even have to bring out my Chuck Berry imitation."

I recall the name from Aaron's music history jabberings. "How do *you* imitate Chuck Berry?" I ask.

"Give me sixty seconds," he says and heads out the door. I sit on the bed and in moments hear him coming back up the stairs. He enters, stupid grin and all.

"You done warming up?" I ask.

"Ready to go," Ly announces, fiddling with the door handle for a second and then holding out two fists like I'm supposed to guess which one holds a quarter. "On three, Chuck Berry. One..." he says, taking up an air-guitar-playing stance.

"Two." He opens one hand. In it is a blueberry.

"Three." He chucks it at me.

I facepalm after the berry bounces off my shirt. "How much real food have you been eating?" I say, trying to maintain dignity.

"I like to feel normal," Ly says. "Cheaper than cigarettes."

"Oh, great," I say, looking down at my shirt. "A stain."

"It's water," he says. "I washed it because after the joke, I usually eat it." I pick the berry out of my lap and hand it to him.

"Well, you got me wet, where many have tried and few succeeded." It's funny to watch his brain stop for a second.

"Man, why do you talk like that?"

"Like what?"

"You're just... sometimes you talk about sex the way guys do. Like you're not afraid of it or what people think."

My mind flashes to my long and storied history, and I toss it all out. Tonight is not the night I want a heart-to-heart. "It's what I do instead of therapy. Half of it, anyway. Were you going to bite me or something?"

"Yeah," he says, brightening. "You said capillaries. Let's do the shoulder."

"Fine." I remove my shirt. He does likewise, and I look askance.

"Stains," he says. He fluffs out the towel and spreads it on the floor. We kneel on it together. It's hard not to look at his musculature, to smell his sweat. He attempts to brush my hair aside, and I hold it back.

"One tick," I say. "I'll braid it." While I do so, I give him a nervous smile. He's looking at a lot of pale white flesh, and it doesn't take a vipe's senses to guess that he's thinking about dropping the razor entirely and just using his teeth. But he holds himself back. Then, I'm done.

"I'm starting here," he says and presses his left hand to my shoulder. They're big hands, warm as they touch me, and grasp firmly. I swallow and move his razor blade to a spot just above my collarbone.

He presses, and the blade sinks in. Adrenaline shoots through me, and he clamps down as I flinch. It's a tiny and clean cut, nothing like Morgan's inexpert knife slice so long ago. In a second, everything around it turns warm and wet as Ly's mouth envelops it.

As his tongue makes contact, the pain dulls. I hadn't even known I was carrying tension in my shoulders, but they relax under his touch. His hands wrap around my arms, and I close my eyes. We've done this before, and I know his routine. After a little lapping, he'll withdraw, give me a smile and apply the towel.

But he isn't doing that now. He strokes my wound with the tip of his tongue, slides it around in spirals and rubs it against my muscle. As he touches it, the qi flowers, sending electric tingles from my shoulder outwards. I stop wondering when he kisses my neck.

"Ly," I say, "that's enough."

He pulls his head back. "Feeling lightheaded?" He's smiling.

"No, but—" I close my eyes as his tongue returns, a second injection of morphine. For a few seconds, all I can do is blink, reminding myself that this has to stop. His hands move from my arms to caress my back, and I'm relieved to notice that he isn't gripping me quite so strongly.

Then, his fingers unhook my bra.

"Hey," I snap. "What's that?"

"Therapy," he says into my neck.

My hands get between us, holding him back. "No. Not okay—mmh." His response is to stick his tongue into me again, letting delicious waves tighten up my diaphragm and keep me gasping for air. His hands slither under the bra, uprooting it as they travel forward. I let it fall away and seize his wrists. I have to push him off *now*, before I lose all ability to concentrate.

"Ly, *stop*."

"No, you stay nice," he says, squirming higher and spreading my arms forcefully. "I've waited too long for this." He's strong, and for all my height and virus and training, I still end up on my back as his weight shoves me down onto the towel. He bites down on my trapezius, holding me in place while my writhing hands make him struggle. His pelvis rubs against mine as he wedges himself between my legs. I can feel him against my thigh, hard and questing. Nothing between us but denim.

That's when all pretense fades away. This isn't about blood, and it isn't about me. He's using the bite to remove resistance, just like a knife or pistol would. He wants to erase my struggling because I don't matter to him. I stop hearing his voice. I hear my mother's, my boyfriend's, my sensei's. Ly is not a friend. He is a trigger, and the gunshot goes off in my brain.

Never.

I shove my head against his to force him off the wound and retaliate—I clamp my legs on his torso in a jiujutsu guard and bite down on his shoulder. He shouts something—what, I don't care, but it breaks his mood with pain. He slaps me across the face, and my fist pops out. I have vipe strength but poor positioning, so all I give him is a bloody nose. For a second, we stare at each other, knowing it's a fight now. I can think clearly again. What I think is that I will punish everything he does.

His hands go for my pants. Big mistake. My arms are free. I seize his hair and drag him back down so he doesn't have enough space to punch. He's going to want to because the nails of my other hand are tearing at his face: he twists, and I don't get the eyes, so he's just red with fury.

Ly grabs at my throat but just gets the base. Another mistake. He's squeezing it like in the movies and expects me to get weak. His face is in mine, bristly and dangerous in the eyes, unkempt enough to look like that damn no-razor-shall-touch-his-head style that my father—

Never.

I weave an arm between his, leverage him off my throat and hike my legs up high as we struggle. Ly tries to stand, but I'm still grabbing his right arm. He recognizes too late that I'm trying something.

I hold onto his wrist and cinch my legs around his upper arm. He's strong, so strong that he lifts me up until only my shoulders are on the floor, but that won't matter soon. I hyperextend his arm and straighten my body out, using my hips as a fulcrum.

His arm goes past a hundred and eighty degrees, and there is no scream. It refuses to break. He drops me on my head against the carpeted floor, but I've fought through pain before. My feet are close to his head, so I lash him with a kick that leaves him staggering. I drag him down to the floor, and we tangle limbs up again.

I hold on as he squirms and makes guttural noises, and then someone hammers on the door. Ferrero's shouting, and some part of me clicks the picture into place. The bastard locked it.

"Get in here!" I yell.

With a crack and a bang, the door flies open. I let go, scrambling for the towel to cover myself as Ferrero bursts into the room. I snatch up my bra as I get to my feet, and the teacher gets between us. He turns on Ly.

"What the hell are you—she trusts you!"

I keep my eyes in their direction as I fasten my bra again. Ferrero shoves Ly. It's a mistake, but my thoughts are too slow to warn him. Ly puts his head down and runs square into Ferrero, driving like a football player. I stumble to the bed and out of the pair's way. Ly has size and rage; Ferrero has neither. He goes under as the bigger man bowls him over, bloody face notwithstanding.

That's when I stop caring if he hurt me: when he hurts my friend.

Ly's back is to me, and they're on the floor. I cover him, my weight shoving him down onto Ferrero where he can't do much damage. I wind my feet around the psychotic vipe's left arm. He turtles up, trying to protect his limb from all threes, but that's no obstacle. I grab his far arm with my own, diving over him to peel him off Ferrero and roll us both face up. It's called the crucifix, and other than a painful collision with furniture, it works fine.

Ly's immobilized but writhing, all blood and beard and rage. Before I think about it, I grab his head and pull it toward me. I can choke him. Talk to him. Warn him to stop.

Never.

The neck cranks. The neck breaks.

I feel him go limp. Then, Ferrero is on top of both of us, punching Ly over and over out of sheer anger. I lie there, watching the punishment, calling out Ferrero's name, but the schoolteacher is having none of it, pounding meat uselessly.

"Ferrero. Ferrero. Ferrero."

At last he stops. "His neck," I say. "I... I got him."

"Good," snaps the man. "And you all get out of here!" he yells at the gathering crowd in the doorway. "This is between us!" It doesn't make much sense if thought about, but thinking is the last thing any of us are doing. Jessica and Deborah back up a step, but no more.

I pry myself out from under the blood and the hair and lay a hand on Ferrero. "It's okay," I tell him, telling myself just as much. "It's okay. It's okay."

Jessica enters the room, taking control. "Which one of you is hurt the worst?"

"I don't know," I say. "He was feeding on me, and it all went to shit." I finally tighten my loosened pants and get a shirt, too. Something feels wet as it slips on, though I can't say if it's my blood or his.

"Hold still." Jessica puts a hand on my forehead, faith-healer style, and adjusts her stimweb. "Near-concussion, needs a blood meal," she announces, moving on to Ferrero. "Minor cuts, probable bruises."

"You know what he tried to do," Ferrero says. "He's a dog, a goddamn rabid dog."

Ulan looks over the prone body. "Fractured capsule in the arm. Fractured third cervical vertebrae. Spinal cord injury. Pulse weakening. No breathing."

I see Deborah's hand go over her mouth. "Did she... do it?" Deborah says, a whisper.

"He's beyond my qi functions," Ulan says matter-of-factly. "As for artificial respiration, we'd have to do it until they got him on a ventilator."

"So... she did?"

"I don't know what I did," I say, trying to get my bearings. Deborah keeps staring at the gouges in his face.

She fumbles. "Couldn't you have—I don't know—" I know what she's thinking. I am, too. I didn't know my strength. Or didn't care.

"I tried," I say. "I hit him, I arm-barred him, everything. I'm sorry."

"For what it's worth, I believe you," Ulan says.

Deborah doesn't give up. "You said he's... can't we help somehow? Give him blood?"

"There's something we could do to ease the pain," Ulan says neutrally, "but it carries with it certain baggage."

"What?" asks Deborah.

"His qi is still infusing his tissues for the moment," Ulan says. It takes Deborah a second before she gets it.

"Shut up," says Deborah. "Just shut up right now. He's still one of us."

"Infinity didn't feed," Jessica growls. "None of us has." I've never heard her voice so cold. "She's not capable of donating right now. If you'd like a minute to mourn, go ahead, but he's got eight minutes to brain-death, and then he's no more use than a dining room table."

"You—!" Deborah yells. "You can't say things like that. You're the one who's never killed anyone!" She looks around, panicked, realizing her audience. Me, covered in blood. Ferrero, the angry victim. Ulan.

"Infinity, tell her—" she tries. "Cass is going to be back."

"I'm not waiting for him," Ferrero barks. "That fucker nearly killed me. He doesn't get an opinion. He'd take it all anyway. And this guy! This one, he nearly killed me just now!"

"This isn't about hate." Jessica insists. "He's in pain, and we can erase it. He's dead already, and us? We need to survive."

"Infinity," Deborah pleads. "You're the leader. Aren't you?"

I stare at her, denials all over my mind. *Accident. Temporary insanity. Capital punishment.* None of them will fly. I want to rant the truth. *I just look slutty and get you blood. Ferrero's smarter. Jessica's got the experience, and if I hadn't enraged him—*No. I'm not going to think like that. I say the first thing that comes to mind.

"He committed a crime, Deborah. I didn't want to hurt him, but we can't go to the cops. We can't go to our parents. If you want to leave, go ahead. I know I want to, but I have to stay or else it will get worse."

"He was supposed to be our friend." Deborah looks at Ly's eyes staring up at the ceiling. If they blink, I'm going to lose my nerve right here.

"That's exactly what I thought," I say, and I find my voice unsteady. To cover, I try to take over. "Look at me," I say, walking between Deborah and Ly. "Look at me, honey. He didn't care about me. When Fer tried to stop him, he didn't care about Fer. And he wouldn't have cared about you.

"Now, I need to ask you something. Blood. How many more days can you last?"

"Shut up," she says, but it's weak, and she's crying.

"Tell me. How many?"

"Two."

"All right, so you can walk out of here with your head held high. You can leave us behind, and then in two days, you've got the same choice you always have. And you're going to have to do it, or you'll just pass out and never wake up. Are you going to pass out on me? Are you going to just die?"

"I want to."

299

"Yes or no?"

Deborah holds her breath. Then, "No."

"Then, you're going to need blood. Now, I want you to look at Ly. You know how it feels when we drink. He's hurting, and you can take away his suffering."

"I didn't—"

"Drink," I say. "You're the only one who can help him." It feels disgusting. I don't know if Ly's fate is better or worse this way, but it's what Deborah needs to hear.

"It's going to have to be all together," says Ulan. "We've talked too long. By the time one of us is done, the qi will have dissipated."

I give her a look that says, *thanks for twisting the knife, bitch,* and find the razor on the floor. I cut Ly's wrist, handing the arm to Ferrero. Then, another on the other wrist. Then, I hand the razor off to Ulan, who rolls up Ly's pant leg and chooses a vein on the ankle.

Deborah hesitates, and I know exactly what's in her mind. *If you ever ask me to do something...* she said, but there is no point in bringing that up. Then, Deborah makes her bite, and a cold certainty goes through me. This is not a home anymore. It's just where the vipes live.

As Deborah drinks, I leave the room, stomach growling and all. I'm never going to touch Ly again. Cass and Ferrero can drive the body out to some deserted place and bury it. There is no time for tears, from this or from anything before. I have a rescue to plan.

50 - RANATH

December 1st

There's something you should know about the phrase "fighting fair." It's a contradiction. Any contest with stakes high enough to warrant violence is a contest worth stacking the deck in your favor. It doesn't matter if it involves padded gloves, police batons, or guns—the very definition of skill is defeating the opponent without being touched in return. As I enter the Supreme Court building, this is foremost on my mind. I've lost a lot, but I can always lose more. Adversaries are not tests of character—they are obstacles that lead to jail time, broken jaws, bullets in the head.

I carry no gun. The quiet pistol, in a metal detector, could trigger a pat-down. They might find all the parts, or they might not, but my goal today is nonviolent, and carrying it for defense is a far worse choice than trying another method altogether.

My real opponent is Morris Hirsch, whom I only know through careful casing. I sent my burner phone's agent program to hunt down social media posts from people who work at the Court. From there, I dropped innocent-sounding queries until I got Hirsch's name and found out two things. He likes to talk, and he is bloody deadly.

Hirsch doesn't publish papers like the BRHI academics—I found him contributing to a newsgroup for security personnel who want to know what qi-pos training can do for them. Hirsch had answers. He worked the campuses of Georgetown and AMU, where the kids came up with qi tricks to get them laid or high, and the Chesapeake Detention Facility, where his functions were what kept him from getting stabbed.

Reading between the lines, I now assume Hirsch has developed a function that alerts him to ill intents. This isn't hard to divine. He's lived as a human hostility detector and paid the price.

Hirsch burned out until he scored the job at the SCOTUS. Other than saying he loved the change, he's grown quieter online. References to work are vaguer, guarded. Paranoid, sure, but cogent.

From the security queue, I can see Hirsch's sidearm on his hip, the tacks in his ears. He wears hair long on one side, with many braids knotted like Inca quipu. I suspect the knots are the digits of functions, high-powered because they are worked into his body. Hirsch has so many that he could probably choke down an arsenic sandwich with no effect or at least slap a gun out of the way as it is being drawn. He'll spot function bombs, sustained illusions, and who knows what else.

I am armed with my brain and a cardboard box.

My method of entry is not based on influencing minds or the fact that I have been training in qi functions for five or ten years longer than Hirsch—indeed, it might be a disadvantage that the security mage is younger and probably hungrier than I am. My entry method is based on two principles of human behavior.

First, when in doubt, humans are messy.

Second, when in doubt, humans are lazy.

They will be checking for stimweb tacks at the door; therefore, I wear none. The F-prots might have sent them an image based on my appearance, so I had a hairdresser chop my half-burned locks. Then, I dyed my hair red, including the short beard I've grown out. I found button-down pinstripes at a thrift store that can blend in any century. Once I finished a loitering pass, just in case I attracted attention, I cut the beard down to a goatee and re-dyed head and facial hair black. And last, there's the box. It's not much of an ace—just cardboard stuffed with folders and printouts of mind-numbing crap I pulled off the Net. But at fifteen to nine, there's a crowd of staffers heading in to work, and I join them looking purposeful.

The guards by the detectors wave me through when they see my badge, stolen and copied from a staffer who made the mistake of eating lunch outside the day before. They run the box through the X-ray but don't give it a second look. Humans are lazy.

To get past Hirsch, I apply my most pleasant face. When I smile,

I can, for a time, forget that everyone here would be a deadly enemy if they knew my thoughts. I focus on treating them like potential friends. I must mean it sincerely—without believing it, it will not work. The point is not to act normal, but to *be* normal, and when I am, Hirsch has nothing on me.

I'm in.

I follow a thirtyish man dressed like an up-and-comer, probably a paralegal. The public halls go by quickly, and we soon approach a door with a card reader. I adjust my grip on the box.

"Let me get that for you," says the man. Humans are messy.

I head down the hall to a room that looks like it might be a records office and see immediately that it has moved into the modern age. I'm used to hospitals, slow as dirt when it comes to going a hundred percent paperless. Behind the main desk here are workstations of air-projection monitors, servers-on-chips, and other toys that will make my box look out of place. I set it by the door. Time to improvise.

"Excuse me," I say to a plump, graying pro whose desk plate reads CELIA BYRNE. "Hi, Aidan Brown. I've been told someone needs to contact an expert witness from about three months back. Do we still have the subpoena records for a doctor—" I fumble for a piece of paper and bring it out, "Ulun? Ulan? Jessica Ulan."

"Who's this for?"

"Justice Standish's office. They said a law firm, uh... Sanders and Crowell, they're called. I think they want to hire her to appear."

"Sorry," she says. "It's not our policy to give out her contact information."

"Just hers?"

"Yeah, she's had death threats."

"But the record exists, right?"

"Excuse me?"

"I mean, if I'm going back to Standish, and he says he wants this info, I need to be able to tell him he can get it if he really wants it, right?"

"Well if Standish wants it or his office, you should be able to access it from there."

"Oh, all right. Which database is it in?"

"Recordsoft."

"Sorry to be such a pain, but I don't want to have to call you up as soon as I get upstairs and find out he's a complete computer illiterate. What directory?"

She clicks on the screen and turns the monitor to show me. "Contact, Witness, Expert, Federal, Virginia, Eastern District, BRHI v. Lorenz."

"Great. Thanks." I smile at my new friend. "Celia."

"No problem," she says, and I walk down the hall carrying my box, just another employee. In ten seconds, I spot another mark.

"Excuse me, which way to IT?" I ask.

"You mean IS?" the man responds.

"God, is it that obvious that I'm new?" I mutter. "All right, IS."

"You're gonna go down this hall, take a left, and follow the left wall around the corner. There's an elevator. Go down three. Take a right. It's the big pit." He pauses. "Do they seriously want paper? They give me shit for keeping printouts around."

"Between you and me, I'm getting hazed." Crinkled face. "Cleaning out my manager's files. It's like taking out garbage, except I have to write down everything I throw out and everything I keep."

"Well, good luck." The man continues down the hall.

I turn and immediately regret it. Had I kept my eyes on the floor, I would have been fine, but I have a habit of meeting people's gazes, and in this case, I lock them directly with Hirsch, who is coming down the hall, looking purposeful.

I can't get by with looking down again—it telegraphs guilt—so instantly, I raise my eyebrows in a welcome. Hirsch mirrors it. I'm about to get away with passing him by when he takes the same turn I do.

"Delivery?" he asks.

I laugh it off. "I wish. Gotta sort this stuff."

"I've had paperwork that bad," Hirsch says.

I haven't considered the minor details of Hirsch's life, but I choose quickly. I could avoid engaging, but it seems more natural to care. "If you've got a secret to making it go faster, I will owe you big time." I leave the verbal door open. Hirsch walks through it.

"When I'm losing focus, I pretend the papers are love letters, and I've got to read them very carefully because there's no one in the world more important to me than the person who wrote the paper. Then, I pick up the next one and do it again."

I stop thinking about anything except if the method will actually work. I'm at the elevator now, and Hirsch is either tracking me, or else he is also going down. *In for a penny,* I decide. "I don't think I've ever gotten a love letter."

"Never?"

"Scout's honor," I say. The phrase helps win trust among people who were never Scouts. "I've gotten texts, but that's not the same thing."

The elevator door dings. I enter and hit a button, always keeping my mind light. Hirsch is almost close enough to touch.

What would happen if—

Out of the corner of my eye, I find Hirsch staring at me.

But then it is over, and Hirsch is casual again. "If you've never gotten any, I suggest you start sending some."

My thoughts are on an idol and a note. What could I write? *I do not think you deserve to be at the mercy of our mutual enemy, as the law suggests?*

"I'm better at conversation," I say.

Hirsch notes the chime of the elevator. I get out.

"Whatever grabs her, I guess," Hirsch says. "Just never pass up a chance, I say. They're like butterflies. Hold 'em too hard, and you squash 'em. Hold 'em too loose, and they fly away."

"Right," I say absently. The doors close, parting us. I try my best not to breathe an audible sigh of relief. Even a thrill of victory still encased in my head might set off Hirsch's radar. And, of course, worrying that I did so might be yet another trigger. I'm fighting blind.

It can't be helped. I can only trust that the private lives of a building full of people give me some kind of cover by creating static.

I strive to focus as I reach the door marked INFORMATION SERVICES and leave the box in the hall. The desks here are all over the place, cramming in as many data jockeys as possible. Shelves of moving bins, spare peripherals, and gutted wafers separate the techs.

Forget it all. You just came from upstairs. Bright and cheerful.

"Hi," I say to the one nearest the door. "Who does data recovery?"

"Novak." A finger points the way.

"What can I do for you?" asks the tech. He looks as though he hasn't gotten out of his chair since he turned forty a decade back.

"I'm hunting down a bug," I say. "My Recordsoft is missing its files. All the files in two directories are gone, and I don't know if they've been erased or my machine just hangs when trying to load them or if I just can't update—"

"All right, let's look," says Novak. "I can log out. We'll log in as you—"

"We can do that in a minute, but first, while I'm here, can we see if the files exist independently of me?"

"Sure," he says, opening Recordsoft on his computer and entering his password. I can't read it, but that's not what I want.

"Find me your mystery file," Novak says, turning the touch-screen my way. Now, I produce what the woman upstairs said—Contact, Witness, Original Jurisdiction, BRHI versus Lorenz. Nailed it.

"Huh," I say. "Looks like it's all here. The files even open." I double-touch a name, and up comes SUMMONS REFERENCE:

> Dr. Jessica A. Ulan
> 441 Whitewood St.
> Brooklyn, NY 11220

This is marked OBSOLETE. Below it:

> Dr. Jessica A. Ulan
> 2241 Hanover Ct.
> Gaithersburg, MD 20882
> 301-202-1606

"That's not showing up on your machine?" Novak asks.

I keep playing my part. As long as I'm within these walls, I stay in character, or I'm toast. "No, when I click, I get a little hourglass icon, and nothing happens."

"Try hitting refresh. If that fails, rerun the nightly updater. And if that doesn't work, ping me, and I can remote desktop you."

"This is gonna be one embarrassing morning if refreshing solves my problems," I say. "But thanks. I'll contact you if I can't get it done."

I walk out of the IS pit to my box in the hall. I give a casual glance for cameras and passersby, staying calm. The mnemonic in my head is everything. I get out a pen and write Ulan's home address on the back of a manila folder in my box of formerly useless paper.

I carry the box out of the clerks' wing, past the metal detector, out of the qi pulses and into the bright, winter air. No one challenges me.

I don't write a letter that night. I only get to the second paragraph before deleting the entire thing.

51 - INFINITY

December 3rd

After five and a half days of detective work, I have concluded that television lies a lot. Growing up in L.A., I usually assumed that crime shows didn't tell the whole truth, but only now do I realize how much gets glossed over between scenes. Trying to find Morgan vacillates between having zero leads and having a hundred, and there's no way to tell if we're right on top of him or just burning our retinas and phone minutes.

We ruled out the local jails and prisons back when he first disappeared from custody. That left the possibility that he was killed, but I won't believe that until I see a body. Now that we are reattacking the problem in earnest, we started with the basics—we went through the online phone books calling every BRHI-affiliated hospital, health center, and laboratory from here to Cape Town. Jessica, who's more calculating than she looks, came up with a story for us to tell. The caller said their husband or wife was infected, and they needed to be confined and treated. This usually got us passed around to several departments, but we ended the calls as soon as BRHI staff started talking about where to send police for the pickup.

About the time I dumped my third phone, Ferrero came through. He got the only real victory that kept us going: confirmation of that Web site-less place called Greenbriar Health, just as Roland had said.

It wasn't much, but my job was to turn it into gold. As the calls progressed, we claimed to be nearly every doctor on the list. The live human we could reach was cold and answered no questions: quite a giveaway. Finally, after all of us tried our best lines on the ice-princess receptionist, Ferrero came up with a brute force method. Each of us took a section of numbers from 0001 to 9999 and attacked the automated stuff. When it asked for an extension, we punched it in, one after another.

Whenever someone answered with their name or department, we simply hung up, wrote it down and added it to a growing list. What we dug up were names of doctors and lists of daily drug regimens that provoked furrowed eyebrows from Jessica.

We pulled furniture away from one wall and projected our results on it using a phone. I smeared interesting notes like the security desk with highlights, producing a colorful spiderweb. At the center of this sits a sheet that Deborah produced, a series of extensions with question marks next to them. That part's enemy contact. Every single one of these, from 1670 to 1688, had been answered with a calm, neutral "Hello." Like the person answering had been trained.

I stand in front of those numbers now, staring and wondering. Then, the non-sound of feet shuffling on carpet is behind me, and I whip around. It's Jessica with a laundry basket.

"Want to help fold?"

"I'm busy," I say.

"Talk to me. It makes ideas evolve."

"I want into this place," I say. "I want to know everything about it, and all the plans I can think of are very, very stupid."

Jessica's concerned. "You want to put a gun to someone's head?"

"It sounds less rational when you say it." I hadn't planned on being that transparent, but it feels good that Jessica knows where I'm coming from.

"Well, you haven't fed in forever," she says. "You're half a meat pie away from going Sweeney Todd."

"I'm all right."

"I didn't say you weren't." Always the diplomat. "But think out loud. Don't listen to the lizard brain."

I sort the load of darks and colors, noticing a hole in the armpit of a Hellroarer concert shirt I've had for years. Refusing to admit defeat, I put it aside for sewing. Then, I come upon one of Jessica's hijabs.

"You know, if this were a movie," I say, "this headscarf would trigger a breakthrough. I'd play with it like it's a blindfold, and then we cut to getting inside dressed as guards with a blindfolded prisoner or something."

Jessica doesn't look amused. "It's not a magic wand, I'll say that. Covering up saved me a lot of trouble as a vipe, but of course, it brought its share of harassment."

I fold one of the black ones, watching her to see how she does it. "I never got why women wore them here. At home in the old country, sure, but when you have the choice?"

"It's the opposite," Jessica says. "When the government says you must, you hate them. When it's your choice, it's freeing. The woman I got them from said covering up made her feel like she wasn't just a body. She was to be respected for her mind. And that made her feel safe."

"I have a gun and jiujutsu for that," I say.

"So... you're fear-free?"

I feel a sting of shame but don't want to give Jess any satisfaction. "Feeding time is a little scarier than it used to be."

"As long as you don't fall down the stairs and break your neck, you have nothing to fear from me. I was just taking advantage of a terrible situation."

"That's even creepier."

"I'd rather not fight. You adapted well. I'd be wracked with guilt, but I thought your explanation was quite effective."

I scowl. "Chalk it up to being experienced. I'm not giving it again."

"You may have to. Being a leader means—"

"I don't want to hear it. We are getting in this place, we are getting Morgan back, and he can do whatever he wants after that because I'm out. I'm *done*." Taking a breath, I calm myself. Jessica looks colder.

"I wouldn't tell others about this."

"Oh?"

"They look to you for direction. If even you can cut and run, they will do the same at the first opportunity."

"But you won't?"

Jessica straightens in her chair, and I can tell I hit a nerve. "The world is a better place with Morgan in it. Vipes would do well if they had him at the head of a genuine movement. I just want to see you succeed."

I glare at her. "You can be a real bitch, you know that?"

Jessica's face falls. She says nothing for a second, so I fill the void. "Morgan's in prison. Probably worse than prison. From what we can tell, he's in BRHI's back fucking parlor, and you're thinking about his value as the leader of a movement. They could be putting oven cleaner in his eyes like they do with animal testing. They could have him dead and dissected on a table, and you want him back to see us *succeed?*"

As soon as the words are out of my mouth, I'm sure I've gone too far. A dozen different apologies war in my head. The last thing I should be doing is cursing the woman who is our best insight into how the enemy works and the only one of us who seems to care if I starve to death.

"I'm sorry," Jessica says at last. It's not something I often hear from someone of my mother's generation. It feels like throating the alpha wolf, mixed with that creepy forgiveness that priests give me.

"So am I. I didn't... well, honestly, I meant to snap, but not that much. Just... choose your words more carefully, I guess."

"I blocked out what he could be going through. I... I've been only partially here, you know. Let me throw away my phone for a minute and tell you I'm on your side."

"Seriously?" I consider. "Even if my plan involves pulling a trigger? Would you bail?"

"I said I'm with you. Cross my heart."

I feel the deep relief usually reserved for skydivers. "Then, what's your take on the others?" I say. "They tell you things they don't tell me."

"Deborah spent a half hour today looking into a mirror. I doubt she likes what she sees. Cass will follow you. He wants to atone for not being here when... well, he wants to do violence. Ferrero feels protective toward you and trusts your judgment. And me... I've found your hospitality... considerate."

"Then D's the one to worry about," I say. "Either we cut her off, or we trust her with something important. She has to identify herself as one of us, or it's poison."

"Now that sounds more like a leader."

I snort. "I thought it was just how you manage bad friends."

"Did you have something specific in mind for her?"

"We should play to our strengths," I say, "and Deborah's might actually come in handy."

December 8th

With little else I can do, I tap my thumbnail against my teeth in a staccato rhythm. Edison Field is one of the few people in the world who can make me wait, and of course, behind his office door, he is either reveling in it or as clueless as a pirate with two eyepatches. I'm forced to stare at the receptionist and the trade papers and the sunset that is making me squint. I have news, too confidential for phone or e-mail, and it's put me in my own personal purgatory while God decides what his schedule looks like for the early evening.

I check my watch. I left my car parked far from the curb, and sure as taxes, I'm going to get a ticket for it. I hadn't cared when I ran inside expecting to burst into Field's office, but it's prickled at me for the last half hour, the easily fixable mistake I dare not fix. I told Pieter that I'm here because it's urgent and security-related, but that somehow isn't the secret password or whatever the hell Field wants.

On a suspicion, I get to my feet and conspicuously walk around looking at the art on the walls and the industry awards BRHI has claimed. When I get behind Pieter and see him splitting his attention between a phone call and a social networking Web site, I lose it. The future of my company is not going to be dictated to me by a twenty-four-year-old.

"I'm going to wait in his office," I say and start down the hall.

Pieter's eyes fly open, and he pulls off his headset to give chase. "Dr. Kern, you can't. He's meeting with investors."

"I see," I say, coming to a halt, "and would you like to tell me which companies those investors represent?"

"What?"

"Play along with me for a minute. You have his schedule, correct?"

"Yes, it's uh—he's meeting with Fenghuang Holdings."

"And what would be the worst-case scenario were I to disrupt this meeting?"

"I don't see what you're—"

"Just say it."

"Well, we could lose them as an investor. They put in stupid amounts of capital."

"Do you have an idea of their net worth? You must have some idea. You run all the paperwork down to Legal."

"Uh, no, I mean, I know how much they've invested per annum..."

"And how much did they give us last year?"

Pieter actually makes eye contact. "About six hundred and forty million dollars."

"Pieter," I say quietly, "I mean this with all seriousness. I cannot tell you the subject of my visit, but this particular business could make Fenghuang look like a piggy bank. Now, have you ever known me to do impulsive, misguided things?"

He doesn't answer, looking down again.

I catch his damn chin. "Hey—look at me. Have I ever lied to you?"

"No," he says, alarmed.

"Then, you know I'm telling the truth, so what's making you uncomfortable? Is it just the confrontation?"

"I'm just worried that I'm not doing my job," he says, "if I let you back there."

"You are doing your job. But I have to do mine. This is just a judgment call that I had to make. Think of it like an emergency. If your plane is on fire, and you can't open the exit, don't get in the way when someone else can. Does that make sense?"

"It does," he says.

"Now, I believe you have a phone call to get back to."

"Right," Pieter quickly runs off.

I walk. I crack my knuckles, open Field's door, and push my way in. Field is on a video call. I get a brief glimpse of a smiling woman decked out in a skirtsuit and hear a few words of Cantonese before I grab the remote on the table and pause the call.

"What the hell is that about?" says Field. "That's Hong Kong you just shut off."

I slam the door behind me. "We might lose ENDGAME," I say.

Field's scowl disappears. In its place is a measured furrow of the brow, which is probably the closest thing the old man has to showing abject terror.

"And on what are you basing this assumption?"

"Greenbriar Health has been getting scoped," I say darkly. "I can show you a graph, or I can bombard you with a mountain of the suspicious shit that has been going on at that place. Which do you want?"

"Tell me what's been going on."

"It starts with phone calls. People trying to get information out of the employees."

"Password scams?"

"No, and that's the suspicious thing about them," I explain. "They aren't aiming for bank account information or credit cards. They're people posing as doctors, asking questions about vipes in storage, trying to get personnel lists for the security staff. But when asked for credentials, they get vague or hang up."

"And you think these are part of some nefarious plan?"

I can see his doubt. I back it up. "I'd say it was just a prank or a cyber mob. But the security staff sent out a memo saying to report all incidents of strangers asking for pertinent info. Guess how many responses they got?"

"Tell me."

"Thirty-six." Field keeps a poker face, but I have him.

"That's some evidence," says Field, "but what makes you think this isn't some crew looking to get into the drug closet?"

"If that's all they wanted, there's easier ways. One inside man, and it's done. These people are searching, they've got medical expertise, and letting them anywhere near ENDGAME is—well, I don't exaggerate when I say we could all be out of business."

Field's eyes have drifted off to the left, and there's a short silence as he thinks. "What happened to that Cawdor creep who jumped ship? Did you tie him off?"

"He has disappeared and has caused no damage that we know of."

"Did he know about ENDGAME?"

"Never."

Field visibly relaxes. "How long would it take you to move the operation?"

"The equipment would take a few days, but if we just want to get the cutting edge and the records out of there, we're talking hours, two or three."

"Find me a good destination for them, and do it," orders Field. "And call in every marker you've got with security from other facilities. First, you burn the evidence, and second, if someone so much as breaks a window, I want them shot."

"For that," I say, "I know just the people."

53 - BREUNIG

December 8th

I have them assembled by the afternoon, and it only takes that long because Yarborough's stupid phone managed to turn itself to vibrate, and he's wearing it in a fanny pack where he never feels it. Kern waits to brief them until he arrives—I insisted either we're doing this together or not at all. It ate at Kern, I could tell, but I'm damned if I'm not going to establish some boundaries. This man dismantled our livelihood. If he wants the machine back in action, he's going to show some respect.

Kern met me halfway. He got Greenbriar's police liaison on the phone to smooth the path for the rest of the team. I scheduled the meeting and got Kern pitching to the troops.

"What I want is in two steps," Kern announces. "The first is an extraction."

"Who's the target?" asks Olsen.

"Just me with portable cargo. Breadbox size or so. I go in, I get it, I get out."

"It's not that simple, or we wouldn't be here," says Yarborough.

"I'm expecting trouble. How much, I don't know."

Christ. "Estimate." I forgot just how maddening Kern can be when expecting miracles in a decidedly non-miraculous profession.

"It's likely the vipes in the area know Greenbriar has something they want. They might be there as soon as tonight." Off the team's eye-rolls, I step in.

"Come on, people, intel goofs are a fact of life. The faster we can assess, the faster we can get in and out before they do."

Yarborough doesn't let it go. "About the vipes. I didn't hear a number."

Kern looks unsure. "We know it's a team. Four or five minimum."

317

"Maximum?"

"That depends on how many new ones they've created."

"Okay, then. Timeline."

Kern pauses only briefly. "Since June."

We all freeze. No one else wants to say the words. I know what they're afraid of: Infinity's betrayal and Roland's loss might be fatal wounds. Fighting back is a good antidote to fear, but fighting a superior enemy is a fast way to die. It takes determination, weapons, and, most importantly, intelligence. So, I speak.

"Okay, Dr. Kern, that's what we in the business call a Foxtrot Lima."

"Excuse me?"

"Fuck Load," al-Ibrahim supplies. "Do you know how many that could be?"

"There haven't been any reports that have the vipes working in large groups, but I'm aware it could be dangerous. That's why we need to get in and out q—"

Yarborough isn't listening to him. "We're gonna need full kit and ordnance. We're going to have to be cleared by security to wear the suits. We'll need to brief all their employees—"

"If we get there on the day shift," Kern tries, "there will be more staff to support you in case there's an incident—"

Olsen talks over him. "That's more chances for friendly fire. Unless we are crystal clear about our presence, and we are on their radio channels to coordinate, assume someone dies."

Kern looks ruffled. "If there's an incident."

"The whole point of this is to plan for incidents," Olsen snaps.

I agree with her, but the conversation needs to go back toward friendly territory. "Okay, what I'm hearing is a list. We need a meeting with their security. We need to brief every single one of the staff who will be on-site tonight—"

"—they're still going to have to be alert for vipes—"

"—right. I'll cue most-wanted-vipe photos for a presentation—"

"—We'll need to ask them if anything's gone missing: key cards, codes—"

"—Do we have a hard number on headcount tonight?"

"Hey!" It's Kern. Their eyes go back to him. "There's also the matter of the second step," he says. "The extraction's purpose is to deny the vipes access to my cargo, but it is conceivable that they could also be breaking in to create video for propaganda purposes. Consequently, during the extraction, I would like a sanitization."

"*During* the extraction?" Yarborough says incredulously.

"Yeah, hold up. Why not have the on-site staff do it?" asks Olsen.

"Because the staff at Greenbriar are currently compartmentalized to avoid strategic leaks," Kern says. "As are independent contractors such as yourself. It's nothing new. Think of how rarely you talk to the L.A. teams, New York teams, the Haiti team..."

"We have a Haiti team?" asks al-Ibrahim.

"Whoa, using lack of communication with L.A., that's not something that supports your argument," adds Olsen. "If we'd coordinated ourselves with L.A. better, we might have gotten clued in about DeStard."

"Dr. Kern," I say, "I think it's important to say why we're reluctant. We get that compartmentalization is necessary, but when it puts the team at risk—splitting us up in the face of what could be a *frighteningly* superior force—then we have to check out that decision. And compartmentalization sounds very close to 'you have no need to know, so shut up, and do your jobs.' Do you see where we're coming from?"

"That makes perfect sense," says Kern, in a tone that still seems unfriendly. "However, you have a combination of clearance and skills that make you uniquely suited for sanitization. To my knowledge, the vipes will not be targeting me specifically. I see myself with an escort of one to two of you while the rest do the cleanup. Now, if I recall from your service records, some of you are skilled in incendiary drone piloting?"

Yarborough looks lost. That skill is the last thing he'd ever expected to come up again.

"What about it?" Yar asks.

"I mean, you know how to use bots and plasma torches, right?"

"Yeah, that's just garbage pit duty. I pulled that all the time—"

"Exactly. You direct the team, I get in quick and out quick, and if the vipes try anything, we bring down the hammer from team and security staff both. Capiche?"

Yarborough looks to me. "What do you think?"

I look at them. They want to do it, I'm sure—they hate being idle, and fear is a surmountable obstacle. If one of them goes all in, the others will follow in solidarity. But the situation Kern presents is an unforgiving reality. "The last time we went in hastily, we had two casualties. If it weren't for Roland, we would have lost one. We do not have Roland now."

"The one turned out to be our leak," points out al-Ibrahim.

"That's not the point," I say. "Getting slugged by a vipe is a serious injury with Roland and death without him."

"No, but this time, if we have no leak, they won't know what hit them," al-Ibrahim insists. "Last time, Yar was against it, and he was right. We didn't have surprise. We didn't have a plan. This time we do. We'll be in a hospital, so medical's covered."

Olsen says, "We should add 'briefing the trauma team' to the agenda."

I frown. "We can, but we must realize if that happens, our planning has already failed. Our strategy should separate vipes from each other so large numbers can be isolated and killed."

"It's the Corus job but a little bigger," says al-Ibrahim. "We just make sure hospital layout is on the agenda during our exercise with the security team." Most of us have seen the outside of Greenbriar, but our duty ends when we deliver vipes or vipe bodies to the double doors. Security and medical personnel always take it from there. We barely sign the vipes in.

"Yar?" I say. "You're the one who paid the price last time. If this sounds sour to you or false confidence, you let us know."

Yarborough snorts. "You ain't a champion without some rematches." I look to the others.

"You're gonna need me," says Olsen.

"Gonna be there," says al-Ibrahim.

"Giving some," says Yarborough.

"Good, then we're moving forward," I say. "Though, there is the matter of compensation. I've got a freelance contract written up. But if we know for certain there will be vipe contact, not just us hunting them but them coming after the building, armed and dangerous, we're going to need a significant amount of hazard pay."

"It so happens the Institute has recently increased its liquid holdings," says Kern. "I understand the technical term is a Foxtrot Lima."

54 - RANATH

December 8th

I pull up to the rowhouse well after the twilight is gone from the sky. I know it's a spectacularly bad idea. Not only is it night, but I have no hot van, no backup to distract police or onlookers. There are multiple vipes in there, and a four-shot pistol is simply not enough in case of a confrontation. But going back to my old house to grab the Kriss out of the fire safe is predictable and, therefore, likely to trigger some trap set by Breunig. Guessing the trap is a fool's game. They missed once. They will be careful a second time.

I'm not suited up, either; the heavy armor is at The Block—impossible to get. I have just a trench coat to keep me warm and a vest to keep me whole. I usually call the pistol my last resort and my stimweb the primary weapon. Today, my only real weapon is my mouth.

I scan the area for the hundredth time. Sitting behind the wheel of my car is the best spot to avoid attention, but it grates on my martial instincts to be sandwiched in with no place to move. Satisfied that no one is around, I dial up my stimweb for concealment and go over my fingertips and palms a final time with rubber cement. Ballistic cloth or gutting gloves are better, but they both block access to stimweb tacks, and I'm not relinquishing that advantage.

When the glue dries, I fiddle with the pistol in my right coat pocket and open the door. It will be a swift approach; I am parked half a block from Ulan's place. At least, it had better be Ulan's. The address I got from the Court was vacated, and I had to cramp the landlord to find this one.

My car buzzes.

I crouch, startled, then realize I have my burner phone in the cup holder. It rattles four times before I'm satisfied that no one's seen me, and I reenter the car to see who it is. It's one of my decoy accounts requesting voice-over-email. I set up mail on the burner but never shut this off in the default settings. Who would call me?

The answer is Parvati Kamath, my neighbor. I answer.

"Yes?" I say.

"Roland? I guess you're alive."

"I can't talk," I say.

"So why did you answer?"

I permit myself a smile. Parvati has mom-level perception. "Because I can't ever see you again, and I wanted to say goodbye."

"The police were here. They want to question you. I said I didn't have any idea who could have done it."

"You are a treasure."

"Roland... who *are* you?"

"That's a very fair question," I say, "but I'm afraid nobody will like the answer."

"Fix that."

"In progress," I say seriously. "Take care."

The call cuts out. She is the last vestige, the last person besides a bill collector who would notice that I am gone. With my new identity, I am no one and nothing.

I exit the car. I orient myself on Ulan's rowhouse porchlight and steal toward it, not too fast, not too slow.

The garage is sized for two, but its door has no windows, making it impossible to tell how many people are home. Cars line the street but are not stacked in the driveway, an encouraging sign. Were the place packed, I would have to lurk outside in the hopes of encountering the vipes singly, a bad state of affairs.

I ring the doorbell. Nothing.

I move out of street view, taking cover in between the houses. They have fences, which could mean dogs, but none are outside, not in this cold. I duck to look at a ground-level basement window, but everything is dark. I leave the window and approach the rear of the house.

Here, the lights are on inside. I creep onto the back porch, noting the stabbed-out cigarette butts on the rail. Whoever it was—Infinity and Ulan don't smoke—never bothered to get an ashtray and had something against grinding the butts under a shoe like every other smoker on the planet. A possibility: vipes often have no income. A nicotine addict will still pay for cigarettes, but ashtrays are optional.

I can see no one through the window, but that means little. I need to find out whether anyone is home and whether the house has an alarm. I take the simplest way to do both, by turning down my qi function and knocking on the back door.

The door is a cheap, solid plank of wood and has no peephole, yet still I instinctively move to its side to wait for a response. Some vipes answer doors by shooting through them.

No answer comes. I hear only the distant whir of a motorcycle driving by. I knock once more, wait and decide to risk the alarm. Concentrating and adjusting his function back up, I draw the burner phone and fire its lock-picking app. It goes to work on the smartlock, leaving only the most generic of access records behind.

I draw the pistol, and its laser sight flares on, a tiny, bluish-green dot. Targets recognize red dots from countless movies. A half-second of confusion could save my life.

I gently push the door open. At any moment, I'm expecting Infinity's Glock to ring out, but I see and hear no one. There are two approaches to clearing a house solo. One is to assume the shit's going down and make contact before the confusion wears off. The second is to creep in, eyes and ears ready, hoping to get tipped off by sound as to how many people are in the house.

I take the second approach, if for no other reason that unfamiliar houses have tripping dangers. I move in a crouch, trying to stay high enough that the fringes of my coat don't catch under my shoes. There's a reason no one wears overcoats in a SWAT team, but here I am.

Seeing stairs both up and down from this central level, I choose down. There tend to be more rooms upstairs, more angles to cover, and gun safes are often in basements. Better to cut off anyone inside now.

I open the nearest door a few steps down and see the garage. There's her car. Maybe she's home. Maybe she's not.

I enter a small, messy basement with a cheap futon-bed spread out for sleeping. That means space is at a premium upstairs—probably at least two bedrooms holding vipes.

The stairs disappear under my feet. I reach the upper landings and hold the pistol loosely. The laser sight's pressure sensor shuts it off. No sense letting everyone upstairs know where I'm aiming as I come around the corner.

First room clear. Second room clear. Third room is a fucking closet. Last room is a bathroom. I am ready to punch a hole in the drywall. My one potential ally in this world, the one I walked into the lion's den just to find, is simply gone again. Did I alert her somehow?

Coming back here is a poor plan. I quickly search the bathroom and strip black hairs off the hairbrush. I might still have a chance if I can find enough—

I stop, thinking. I hurry downstairs to the living room. There, aimed at the wall, is a TV projector, still running with a soft orange light indicating sleep mode. I touch it, and it wakes, flashing a password prompt.

MORGANLORENZ, I try. Nothing, of course. Infinity will have gone for a strong one.

It spits out its hint: *Royal whore.*

An insult? I try FENNEL. Nothing.

But this is Infinity. And she's told me of a princess, hasn't she? I go online and soon have a hypothesis. There are letters and numbers, but I know half of them, and when the cracking app comes up with the second half, I nod. The words are seared into Infinity's heart, the rebel who rejected Yahweh: 2KINGSJEZEBEL.

The TV projector wakes up and shows me a mess, the web of a funnel spider that craps out pixelated windows. Notepad programs label the photos and video, and spreadsheets of numbers fill the toolbar. At one end of many tabs is an oversize map labeled LOT 561 GREENBRIAR HEALTH, and on it are lettered thumbtacks in dozens of colors. They are placed by the doors, desks, halls—security positions.

I page through it, stopping on a spreadsheet of just a few chilling numbers.

6:00—acquisition

7:00—shift change

8:15—insertion

8:20—exfiltration truck in position

8:30—contact with Lorenz, distraction

8:45—max departure time

I check my watch, sure that I've already missed it. I can wait here and hope to catch them unawares as they return, but I don't know if any of them will make it back. If Infinity is leading this charge, it will probably be as disorganized as her sock drawer. Vipes and criminal masterminds have little in common. That leaves one option.

I turn the lights off as I exit the house. It will save electricity, and before this night is over, they will know I'm after them anyway.

55 - INFINITY

December 8th

Between you and me, I don't think we're even going to get in the door, but here goes.

We followed two previous vehicles from Greenbriar Health but lost them as traffic thickened with witnesses. When they turned onto the highways, we let them go. This time, when we spot prey, the opportunity is there. Our unaware target is a scraped-up, black Umsung Shear, a low-end sedan. Probably owned by some intern or custodian looking forward to the end of the day when he pulls out of the lot. Deborah, at the wheel, follows the car as close as she dares as it makes its exit and rolls down the length of Central Avenue.

The Shear stops at a red light, and no other cars are nearby. Our truck's rear window is open, and Deborah shouts "Go!" to us in the back. Cass and I yank down ski masks and hit the pavement running. I'm at the driver's side door in an instant and have the muzzle of my pistol wedged against the glass.

The driver goes all in on the escape and stomps on the accelerator, but Cass has already got a grip far under the rear bumper and knows car makes like I know Scripture. The tires on the rear-wheel-drive Shear spin uselessly as he lifts it off the ground. I don't appreciate defiance, so I shatter the window with an elbow and flick the lock so I can rip open the door.

"On the ground!"

The driver reaches for his seat belt, and I nearly blow him away, but I channel my rage into helping him to the asphalt. The car crashes to the ground next to us as Cass lets it go.

"Wallet and phone," I say, before seeing the target has his access card on a retractable reel clipped to his belt. I strip it from him. As he's wondering what the hell that's for, Cass grabs his arms and forces them behind his back where I can cuff him with a plastic zip-strip.

"We're good. Trunk him."

Cass grabs him by the neck and frog-marches him to the trunk of his car. I get into the driver's seat and pop it, and thirty seconds later, I'm driving down a side street, followed by the truck. We leave the car there and are headed back to Greenbriar before five minutes are up.

The Greenbriar campus has nothing green, and the closest thing it has to briars are a dusting of broken glass by the side of the curb, courtesy of car accidents long past. East D.C. is an industrial park just a letter away from southeast D.C., which my personal safety app has filled with red X's. As such, the facility isn't so much a rural fortress as an urban one, all heavy doors, windows wired for alarms, and their own armed security constantly putting eyes-on.

When I scouted this place, I pronounced judgment on the storm of failure that was going to happen if we resorted to gunplay to get in. A half-dozen guards stood at the main entrance.

I thought at first they were all private security, but I IDed one as a liaison from D.C.'s finest—if any survived long enough to bark into a radio, they'd be getting backup. Cass related an anecdote about the time he had seen the D.C. police surround a house with five bank robber suspects inside, known to be armed. Sixty cops had shown up for the task, and the gang had surrendered without a fight. The size of our team, incidentally, is five.

My plan is to get in and out, no shooting required, before anyone finds the ditched Shear or the driver. He'll probably guess that his mugging has a purpose.

The truck pulls in to the parking garage. Ferrero and Cass stay in the cab while Jessica, Deborah, and I do one final check, trying to keep our hearts out of our throats. If we don't look and act unconcerned, our mission will be over in seconds. Deborah and I wear hospital scrubs under coats. Brunette wigs and colored contacts keep Jessica from looking like she did on the news and hopefully throw off any APB out for me.

Jessica holds the purloined access card. She leads the walk past the cops and into the lobby of the main building, talking the whole time.

"So, this week we're getting it all done," she prattles, "registry, florist, invitations."

"Did you find anything good?" I drift toward the front desk to sign in, but Ulan smoothly takes my arm with a look that says, *if they don't ask, you don't do it.* She directs us to the security gateway. Showtime.

"Telephones here, ladies, and devices in the scanner," says the guard brandishing a bin. Another mans the chemo/X-ray device. It's a good thing we found the place was phone-free before we tried the assault. It's no surprise that employees taking pictures is taboo, but how they manage to hold back that tide is beyond me. Everything has a camera attached these days.

Jessica goes first, putting a laptop bag into the scanner; our headsets are in the bag, but being paired with the computer, they arouse far less suspicion than if we were wearing them. Her phone goes into the plastic bin.

Jess trucks on. "Well, we can't do the invitations until we nail down a location, so we looked at hotels. But every hotel was too much like going to another medical conference. Now, we're thinking someplace more natural."

"So like, what? A botanical garden or something?" Trying to stay distracted and calm, I find myself wondering where Ulan's husband went. She mentioned she was married once, but no other details have escaped.

I put a phone into the bin as well. It's not mine, of course—our dummies were acquired from a pawn shop just for the occasion, wiped down as much as possible and dropped in with gloved fingers. They are bricks, never to be seen again.

After Jess, I step through the metal and plastic of the scanner, raise my arms and let the machine do its work.

"Smile for the recognizer," says the chemo guard, and I do my best DMV expression for the camera. We know it looks at images that match face, clothing, and hairstyle throughout the world, not just their private database.

Some bright security manager thought IDing strangers was a priority and weighted results by location and number of searches. That's why we took photos of ourselves in these clothes, whipped up social media profiles to match, and set bots to do a few million searches so the first image that pops up will say I'm Jill from Obstetrics, looking exactly like I do here.

Now, it's Deborah's turn. Time for the op. I snap my fingers and grab the bricked phone. "Crap—one second. I need to tell Aaron I'm in late." I meet the guard's skeptical eyes.

"If you want this back, you've got to go out and in again," the guard says.

"Seriously?" I say.

"Hon, don't make trouble—" warns Deborah.

"I'm just wondering. It's not like I have much of a line to hold up—"

"I'm sorry, ma'am. It's our procedure—"

"I mean, I know her, and she doesn't mind waiting a second—"

"Just do it," says Deborah.

"Right, right," I say and walk around the line to get my phone back as Ulan accepts a ticket for her device. Jessica tries to divert the guard with the bin, but the guard keeps her eyes on me whenever possible. Deborah pulls her phone out when it's her turn and promptly drops it.

"Oh—" she squeaks, coming back up brightly. She deposits it and is through the detector by the time I come around to retrieve my own. I take out the brick and pretend to dial.

"Aaron," I say into it, "it's me. I'm working late tonight, out until at least eleven. Don't wait up." A touch later, I frown at Ulan. "All that, and he's not even home."

"Step inside," says the guard, tired of me. I assume the position in the detector's chamber again and go through.

I accept my ticket and peel off my gloves and coat, gathering them up in a natural motion that includes me scooping up a black fanny pack lying on the floor. A pack that slid past the detector by small, overlooked Deborah when she bent over.

"Wait," says the guard. She's dealing with Jess at the recognizer. "I can't get a match." Of course she can't. Jess's makeup includes dashes of glitter, a popular kind I know that looks like a tasteful fairy princess and scatters the near-infrared spectrum that security cameras love. You can't scan a face made out of a disco ball.

"So what do we do?" asks Jess innocently.

"Photo ID," the guard says, and Jess hands over her fake. This is the test. If the wig and the sparkles don't futz the guard's brain, or if she places Jess as the vipe on TV, this is going to go south real quick.

She hands the ID back. Not even a smile.

Jess is back in the game. "So we chose this mansion, like a castle. A virgish little place. You ever been upstate?" We walk on.

"I used to go," says Deborah. "Back when I was young and rich."

We use the stolen keycard, and a door soon clunks behind us. We're in a hallway, free and clear. Or, more honestly, we are the exact opposite.

"I thought we were lunch meat," mutters Jessica.

"Camera," says Deborah, and I spot a black hemisphere on the ceiling. "Do you think anyone caught the handoff?"

I walk on. My fingers zip open the fanny pack under my wadded coat. I feel two things inside—Deborah's actual phone and the grip of my pistol, sealed in plastic to hide residue from the chem-sniffer.

"I hope not," I say, "but I've been wrong before."

This is a room like any other room, I tell myself, and I don't believe it for a moment.

The most obvious feature, the one with the wow factor, is the plasma drone, a three-meter-tall monstrosity somewhere between a forklift and Frankenstein. It has gripping hands and blast shields for dealing with its own kind of specialized workplace. Despite what its name suggests, it doesn't have a torch attached to its wrist like most models of its ilk—it doesn't need one. In the wall, a meter away, is the business end of a closed and locking plasma furnace, capable of heat in the thousands of degrees. It can reduce metal to slag and anything less than that to fine particulates. Since breathing in superheated garbage fumes makes for poor life expectancy, the drone is here to do all the close-up work and save the operator some back pain in the bargain.

The garbage is not normal, either, but the team seems to be taking it all right.

"Guess they had to end up somewhere," says al-Ibrahim. He's looking at the rows of drawers along the wall and the slabs in the center of the cavernous chamber, each of which is piled high with the overflow—mummified shapes that are mercifully faceless yet still unmistakably identifiable. He fingers a bag in curiosity. It's some kind of biodegradable gauze-like material built to hold in liquids, but the most important thing it does is keep in the smell. This close to the furnace, they get ripe.

"The goal is to incinerate them all by five a.m.," I say. "That will provide us a few hours' window before the cleaning staff is cleared to come in. Every one of these has to go in the plasma furnace and be unidentifiable ash. That means bones, it means teeth, it means their fillings. Is that understood?"

"Yeah..." says al-Ibrahim, peering at a sheet-wound body but being very careful not to touch it no matter how much he wants to. "I could see how this visual here could be, uh, misinterpreted."

"All I say is, I'm glad someone's doing this shit," says Yarborough. "It's a war out there."

"Just how long did you go collecting these guys?" asks Olsen.

"We needed a statistically significant sample," I answer.

"For what population?"

I hesitate at her familiar tone. But Olsen is their med tech, not a grunt. "Well, the United States, for starters," I say. "With a number that large—"

"Fifteen hundred vipes or so?" Olsen says. "I knew we delivered a lot—"

Yarborough snorts. "No way. We did five hundred tops, and here—if you open all the drawers, you get maybe a quarter that. You'd have to have other teams—"

"All right, compare notes after class," barks Breunig. "Yar, you know drone piloting best. You're on first shift. Olsen will be with you. Ebe and I are going to get Dr. Kern upstairs and out of here. We will return to check your work." He touches his headset to unmute it. "Central, this is Black One. We are on the move."

I don't hear the reply but assume from Breunig's hand motion that everything is received and understood. It is time to get what we came for.

*   *   *

I ram my key home, and we burst into the room. The first thing to hit me is the smell. Better than the burn room, but it's still too many mouse feces and too few cedar chips. There's some rule or other about what substrate to use in laboratory conditions, and whatever litter it is, it doesn't have cedar's masking aroma. I flick on the utility light as opposed to the UVs that simulate sunlight, and the sounds of scrabbling double.

Breunig enters the room, weapon out, while al-Ibrahim keeps checking the hall. Nothing here requires firepower. The walls of the room are hidden behind racks of clear plastic bins, each with a cross-shaped divider down the center to keep four mice isolated for their protection. Each is labeled in arcane script, but I've seen the box I want before. It doesn't take long to find it and pull it off its shelf.

The four mice inside twitch their noses and take a few steps. They are small, black rodents like any of a hundred others. I stare at them for a second, as if I could somehow see some trait that belies their value. But their deviations can only be viewed under microscopes, in blood spectroscopy, in immunosorbent assays. Even then, not a single biologist in a roomful would see what I see in them.

Right now, what I notice most is that their water bottles are low.

"That's the cargo?" asks Breunig.

"That's all," I confirm. "Disappointed?"

"I didn't know if you needed a big sample size or something," the F-prot says.

I shake my head. These four are the cutting edge. All else can be replicated. "I'm going to fill up their bottles. Then, we're out of here."

"Copy that." Breunig glances at Ebe, who gives him a hand signal. I don't know what it means. I guess everything is clear.

I move to the sink. I assumed the mice were well-cared for, but even at a place as important as Greenbriar, discipline can slip. Whatever security-cleared wage monkey we hired to maintain the room must have cut corners. No one would want to spend more time in here than they had to. I pop the top on the plastic bin. The mice squirm, and as I see one climbing to the top of its water bottle, I abruptly realize that brushing it away is not the wisest move. The one rule of animal handling I remember is simple: if it has a mouth, it can bite. I'm not afraid of pain. Saliva is something else.

I shake the mouse into its cube and find a glove dispenser in a cabinet above the sink. As I roll them on, I see the rear end of one agile little bastard humped over the side of the bin. I grab for it a second too late and hear the non-sound of the tiny body hitting the floor.

Instantly, I slam the lid on to prevent the others from doing the same. Lab animals are fragile as a rule, sickly and easily stressed. They could die on me—

It's over in a second or two. I have the mouse—a female—back where she belongs. I swap in the water bottles and seal the bin, which I reinforce with strapping tape.

As I work and the F-prots do nothing but guard me, I feel a particular pride in the menial nature of it all. No one below me knows the importance of this mission. No one above me would stoop to do it. I can secure an asset, as surely as if I were a secret agent on assignment. Not a Hollywood superspy but one of those poor saps in World War II behind enemy lines with nothing but binoculars and a radio. There's merit in such work, if the stakes are high enough.

I finish by putting a cardboard transport sleeve around the bin to keep the animals calm. "Ready to move," I announce.

Breunig immediately goes to work. "Red One, this is Black One and White One doing exfil. We have cargo and are starting the motor." Al-Ibrahim presses a button.

Then, nothing happens. Neither F-prot moves. I start to, and Breunig puts an armored hand on my chest to keep me back.

"What's wrong?" I ask.

"Shh," is all I get. I can't see much of Breunig's expression under the riot-helmet getup. What I can see are the eyes. Those are staring as if he's getting some very bad news.

Then, as urgently as the moment came, it was over.

"All right, new plan. White One, you're going to floor one to meet two from Briar Team. You will then track the intruders. If you do not have advantage, do *not* confront."

My pulse quickens at the word *intruders*. They are here for me. There is no way for them to know, and yet somehow, they know all the same. I watch al-Ibrahim dash off and turn to Breunig.

"What's going on?"

"Two personnel went silent. Both biomancers."

"What happens to us?"

Breunig mutes his mike. "Our plan is intelligence, then avoidance," he says. "Once Briar Team gets a handle on how many of them there are, we make a break for it. Until then, sit tight."

I let out the breath I didn't realize I'd been holding. They have it in hand. These are men and women who've dealt with vipes hundreds of times. Every time, they had survived, and those opposed... well, we saw their ranks a few floors below.

I almost convince myself by the time the lockdown alarm splits the air.

57 - INFINITY

Finding the door is guesswork. For all our scoping of the site, for all the phone tag and planning, we still must wander the halls practically looking for signs saying, PRISONERS HERE. I figure Morgan's in the basement, behind concrete walls. Deborah rattles off facts about the D.C. water table and how Greenbriar won't have dug too low. Jessica recommends the center of the building, like the keep in an old-fashioned castle. We try everything—ten minutes here, ten minutes there, walking the knife-edge of panic. In the end, it turns out I'm right.

My nose tips me off. There's a whiff of lemon in the air, like the faint scent I used to get from the drop-off guys in L.A. I remember because I once asked if it was aftershave or something, and the technician had laughed.

"Gas," I say.

Deborah stops pushing the gurney we acquired. She tries not to scream. "What kind?"

"The kind they use to knock out vipes. Starts with an S."

"Sevoflurane," says Jessica. "The stronger the smell, the closer we are."

"Let's just hope it's not too strong," Deborah says. She's right. This is the last place on Earth we want to be unconscious. But the dosage to keep down an unfed, near-comatose vipe would be too low for the likes of us. Right?

I try a metal door, reasoning Morgan will be in the most reinforced place. It pushes open invitingly, and only after the three of us are through do I spin on my heels and dive for it as its weight slams it shut. My hand is caught by its edge, and it's like a hammer on my fingers. Deborah and Jessica look at me strangely.

"One-way door," I explain. "We had them in L.A. You need a zone card to open it from the inside."

"Stay on the outside while we test it," Jessica says. "We'll see if ours works."

I step back through the door and shake out the pain in my hand, feeling it warm up and start healing before any bruise forms. I can hear the thumps of Jessica trying to get out a few times. I open it once more.

"Okay, someone needs to hold it," I say. "Deborah, you're up. I need Jess in case Morgan needs a doctor."

"Got it." Deborah then reconsiders. "I could wedge my coat in there—"

"Don't leave it alone," I say. "If anyone finds it, we'll need you to talk your way out of—"

I'm cut off by a deep, grating blast, which is murder on sensitive vipe hearing. We've left the door open too long, so the alarm is blaring.

"Jess, with me." I dash down the corridor, and Ulan wheels the gurney. There's nothing to do but find our goal as fast as possible. I run until the doors look promising. I rip a few open, getting offices and quiet rooms complete with restraints tables that could hold down God.

Then, just when I'm ready to give up hope, I see a door that must be it. It looks like it belongs on a submarine, all steel or titanium or whatever badass alloy they've rigged up special. It has a wheel rather than a handle. I claw at it until it opens.

The room is a cell, all right, a lot worse than the ones I've seen when bailing my adolescent idiot friends out of county lockup. There's a funk and stink from a human who hasn't been bathed in weeks. There's a showerhead but no white porcelain toilet: just a hole in the floor with two slightly raised places to put feet while squatting. The only comfort in the room is a pallet, and on that, under some kind of paper-thin hospital blanket, is an unkempt man with a month or more of beard. I've seen him like this before.

"Morgan?" I say, and his eyes open.

Jessica wastes no time. She has her headset on and fires it up.

"Bravo, distraction is go."

My sharp ears pick up an affirmative from Ferrero. Then, Jess is at Morgan's side, helping him stand. I nearly tackle him with a hug.

He hugs back, and it is the most reassuring thing in the world. No. I *want* it to be the most reassuring thing. He isn't going to know what to do. He won't lead us out of here, and he never had the answers to stop the power and the tyranny of the bastards who threw him in here. He can't even stop smelling like shit.

When we let go at last, I take Morgan on my arm and help him through some shaky steps forward. Then, I let Jess hold him up because I should be—

—watching the doorway.

Standing there is a hard-shell suit of armor, all black and matte except for the shine on the face shield. The M12 carbine it holds is trained on my chest, and behind this figure are two more, in the light blue dress shirts of police officers, sandwiched under dark ballistic vests.

The suit of armor flips up its visor, never altering the barrel of the gun a millimeter. I see eyes I don't quite recognize, but the voice cements who it is.

"Infinity," says al-Ibrahim, "down on your knees before I shoot you all."

When I jump out of the truck, I ain't even human. You gotta think that way if you're going to win. The Marines taught me that before they threw me out for some bullshit drug charge. Point is, you visualize yourself as whatever it takes. A machine, a hunting animal, a superhero. Me, I've got warrior tricks from a half-dozen different civilizations. I've got bandages around my stomach like a yakuza, tourniquets around my arms like a Moro. Knives and guns are oiled and slung; the hair's held back by a bandanna. I wanted to wear the Stars and Stripes, but it's in the wash, and I'm going to die clean, so tonight it's the tiger of Shotokan karate. The supplies in the bag over my left shoulder clink and rattle as I hop down. Ferrero, the only witness to my dramatic exit, ain't impressed.

"Remember, take no risks," he says, quoting Infinity's planning sessions.

Infinity doesn't know everything and Ferrero, even less. "That's for them. This is for me," I reply, and I slam the door. Ferrero rolls down the window and calls after me.

"Cass! They got vehicle barriers. I'm not bailing you out!"

He doesn't sound mad at me anymore. I turn. "If you could, would you?" I say.

Ferrero seems to stare through me. "What..." he starts. Then, "...yeah."

That's when I know I need to say something. Because I'm never getting another chance. All I can come up with is, "Don't ever change."

I check the extended magazine in my Haribon one last time. It's an ugly pistol-like weapon that holds thirty rounds and could graduate to being a full submachine gun if it grew a little switch. I stalk out of the parking garage with it in my hand, giving the camera at the entrance a sullen glare. I feel droplets on my face and hair as the wind picks up and nod to myself. If I'm going out today, I want Thor and Zeus to take notice.

The thing you have to understand is, since Infinity pulled me off Ferrero, I've had this shame hanging over me. When you hurt a man like that, you can say sorry a billion times. It won't be enough. So, I'm going to beat that shame down, with bullets and fire and guns, because tonight is the night where everyone knows how much they actually need me.

Ferrero thinks it's a fantasy. Maybe. But if I've learned anything about crime, it's that it's dangerous to get between a man and his fantasy.

The main doors to the hospital are glass. The six cops are now just three, visible at the security line and the information desk in the lobby beyond. The missing cops are no doubt going after Infinity. I'll change that.

I rip open the door with my free hand. Suddenly, the faint alarm I've heard from outside is a deafening blare, and it puts me on edge right when I need it. I see motion and terrified eyes from behind the bag scanner and react automatically. The Haribon lets loose its deafening pops, and a woman's head falls out of sight. I turn on the information desk and see three more faces—the first a receptionist, the other two cops, looking up from a monitor.

I sight in on a head just as the cops get their pistols free. My gun is a steady hammer, bone-jarring and authoritative. Again, I can't see bullet holes or blood before the first man falls, but he collapses plenty fast. The second one gets off a shot, but I never stop moving or firing, and it goes wild. I come around the desk, still firing, and the man's pistol clatters to the ground as he doubles over, clutching his arm. When I get around the desk, the first officer is clearly out. The second one is curled up, like rounds got through his vest, or maybe the impacts just beat him up.

I turn to the receptionist. I'm about to pull the trigger on her, but she looks like she would be saying Hail Marys if she hadn't forgotten the words. She's crawled under the desk. There's no point in finishing her. The alarm has already been sounded, and it isn't as though she'll be the witness who puts me away. If someone wants that, one look at the security cameras will do.

"You got a PA in this place?" I shout over the alarm.

"What?"

"Do you have a public address system?"

She nods and then crawls slowly out from under the desk. She presses a button on the phone and offers me the receiver.

"Here."

I grab it. "This is a message to all you fucking cops," I say. "You want to fight someone, fight me. I'm the one killing your boys here at the front desk." I aim at the second prone guard's head and hold the phone receiver right next to the gun.

"Wait," says the receptionist, but I don't.

59 - INFINITY

In between pulses of the ear-shattering alarm, I gauge the distance between me and Ebe. To grab him, I'll have to clear a good three meters before he fires the weapon filling his hands. Then, there's the gurney. Can I knock it into him before he squeezes the trigger? No, too slow. It's off to the side, and the doorframe will block anything but a straight shot. If there's any road out of this one, it's through my brain and my mouth.

"So," I say, "this is a step up from being the wheel man."

"*On your goddamn knees!*" al-Ibrahim snaps.

"Okay, okay, we're not troublemakers here," I say. I have the pistol in my pocket. If I can reach it, maybe I can fire through my coat, but how can I get all three of them? It can't discourage me. Being captured here is death and worse. I kneel, hands on my head.

"Docs study you so much," Ebe says. "All they need to know is two words. *Can die.*"

I'm not offended. I'll take talking instead of firing. If I can get my hands on Ebe's gun and keep him between me and the other two—

It's not going to happen. As Ebe comes into the room, he snaps his face shield down. The two badges behind him start to fan out. Just as I feel relief that they aren't all aiming at me, one cop changes, recognizing me as the threat. But I can't let them take me, take Morgan, take Jess—

Then, the cop in the back does something strange. He crumples to his knees and plants his face on the floor. I watch his gun bounce for a half-second before realizing that the more important thing to see is the figure behind the cop moving to the next one up the line. It falls on him with an open hand to the back of his neck, not like a karate chop but a firm grab, and then the second cop stumbles, too.

The boneless body drapes itself across Ebe's calf, and the F-prot whirls at the sensation. He sees the culprit, but just as he brings the gun around, the newcomer holds it at bay and stabs a tiny pistol under Ebe's chin.

With a sudden crack, Ebe's helmet jerks. No bullet hole emerges from the top—it's tough enough to catch the round and to let it ricochet around in his skull. Ebe falls, and his killer falls with him. I clear out of the way on instinct, and only as he hits the tile do I take in the full view.

It's Roland. I know his coat and his miniature gun even before he strips off his ski mask. He looks as if he did it to gasp for air because he's weak and supporting himself on all threes.

I have a million questions, foremost, how the hell he got in here looking like he's about to rob a bank, but I remember he has some kind of spell to help with that. Never mind the most pressing thing: he looks like he's about to gush out a gallon of blood. I immediately go to him.

"Holy shit, are you all right?"

"No, but I sincerely hope you are. Grab the other two. They're not dead."

I shoot a glance at Jessica, who is still supporting Morgan. It's up to me. I steal a look outside and, satisfied that no one is coming, throw both cops onto Morgan's cushion. I strip them of their weapons and buckle the restraints over them. It'll be tough to stand and move.

Jessica puts Morgan down and dials up her stimweb. "Here," she says, taking Roland's hand. "I can help." He looks at her as though she's offering a dead fish, but he takes it anyway.

"So," Jessica says conversationally as I work, "I guess I misjudged your loyalties."

"If I were judging people for mistakes," answers Roland, "I'd start with myself for not bringing a tank battalion."

"How'd you get in?"

"Lured out their biomancers. They're in a Dumpster. I have a key card, a function, and a wicked hea... oof." He stops leaning on his hand. There's color in his cheeks again.

"Now for Morgan, or we're never getting out of here." She puts a hand on the vipe and takes a long, cleansing breath as she begins to work. "And Roland, I'd appreciate your being up-front about what this rescue is going to cost us."

"Jess," I warn, annoyed.

"My price," Roland says, "is a five-minute conversation, starting sometime when we're not in the middle of a felony."

I'm about to say "done," but I hesitate, wondering what it is that Roland knows. His eyes are on me, not Jessica or Morgan, and that says volumes. If he's here for me, that means—

Cass's voice comes over the PA system. "This is a message to all you fucking cops," it says, and I know it's a bad idea as soon as the words hit my ears. "You want to fight someone, fight me. I'm the one killing your boys at the front desk."

The gunfire echoes through the entire hospital, and I find myself watching Roland's face. Does a part of him die inside when he knows a vipe has killed, and he can't stop it?

When he speaks, it's business. "Tell me he isn't part of your plan."

"We're going to slip out in the chaos."

"The chaos of a lockdown?"

I don't need negativity. "I'm taking Ebe's armor. Unless you object?"

"I'd prefer we take his house, but this will do." The moment in which I might have said a soft word to him disappears. Disappointment hits me, but focused and angry is just how I need him.

"We need to get to Deborah," I say. "She was at a one-way door."

"Agreed. Jessica, get Morgan on the gurney. We'll cover ahead and behind."

A raspy voice startles me, and my mind pieces together the statement after it's done. It's Morgan, saying, "Can this guy get us out?"

I have fears, which I promptly slap aside. I need to encase myself in Ebe's armor and hope the ballistic pants don't fall down while I'm running.

"Yes, get on the bed already," I order. "Jess—mask."

"Looking normal is our best bet," Jess warns.

"Can't do it in mixed company." I thumb over at Roland, who is obviously not here to play doctor. The paralyzed men have uniforms but not a helmet like Ebe. I pick up the F-prot's rifle, and it beeps at me, a light turning red.

"Biometric safety," Roland says. "F-prot special. It only works for him."

"It's for show," I say and substitute my pistol for Ebe's in the holster. "Come on, we've been here way too long."

We half-run, half-shuffle down the halls. I attempt to balance watching the rear with keeping up with the long-legged Roland. Jessica hustles as best as she can, pushing Morgan along until mercifully we reach the one-way door. It's still open—Ebe came from another direction.

Realizing I'm now a friendly-fire incident waiting to happen, I click on my headset. "Deborah!" I shout, forgetting to use the call sign. "We've got him."

"Who the hell is this?" asks Deborah, directing herself to Roland.

"Inside man," says the hitmage, in the same tone as *eat it*. "Time to go."

Deborah looks for confirmation from me, and I nod. "Nice to give me some warning," she grouses, and then we are on the move. The door, allowed to shut for the first time in minutes, clunks solidly, and the alarm shuts off.

"Finally," says Jessica.

"Your distraction seems to have worked," says Roland, "but it won't last."

"You got a plan?" challenges Deborah. "'Cause if I saw you dragging Morgan out, I'd check credentials, uniform or not."

"We need to get to the ground floor to get out. There's cameras in the elevators. Now, they might all be going for the front desk, but we must assume they aren't. First, we send a team up in the stairwell to scout and draw any fire. Then, a team with Morgan goes up in the elevator. We both make a beeline for... do you have a vehicle?"

"Yeah," I say into the headset. "Ferrero, get ready. We don't know where we're coming out, but we're going for the first floor. Do you copy?"

"Just tell me when to pull up."

"Not yet." I glance to Roland's cold eyes. "I'm with you in the stairwell, right?" He nods.

"Jess is going to need someone to cover her," says Deborah.

I hold out my pistol. Deborah looks at it in fear.

"Can you do this?" I ask.

Deborah slides her camera phone into her pocket and gingerly takes the pistol. "I guess now is a bad time to say I hate guns—"

"I hate funerals," I say. "Take it."

"Avoid whomever you can," orders Roland, "and play innocent. Use the pistol when you have surprise. Give us a full minute to get their attention. Then, go."

My whole team hears the gunfire over the PA. I try to contact al-Ibrahim, but the ominous silence lets me draw the obvious conclusion.

"Black One, this is Red One. Request permission to move to front desk."

I speak up quickly. "Negative. Hold position."

"Saying again. Red One is offering medical assistance to downed teammates," insists Olsen.

I hesitate. The last I heard of Ebe, he hadn't even been going for the front desk. Had he gotten that far out of position? "Black and Red, I say again, hold position until Briar Team has eyes on front desk. Identity of wounded unconfirmed." I switch channels to hear what the Greenbriar forces are doing. "Briar Team, this is—"

"—holy fucking shit. We have fire. There's fire on the floor—"

I hear gunfire. Another voice. "Officer down. Officer down—"

"—he's got suppressing fire—"

"—get us crashcarts. We need them on the first floor—"

"Do *not* try to rescue wounded. Repeat, do *not* try. He can see you—"

"—where the hell are those armored guys?"

I want to stand there stunned, but I trained myself out of that long ago. "Briar Team, this is Black One. I am en route to front desk."

"What did you say?" asks Kern incredulously.

"I am en route to the front desk," I go cold. The more I take control, the calmer I get. "Me, not you. You are going to maintain a safe distance."

"Well, seeing as you're my only escort, I'm sure as hell not staying here."

"I understand that," I say carefully. "So, I think we'd better review something real fast."

I show Kern a hand signal. "This means stop." Another. "This is find cover. Somewhere other than directly behind me. This last one is retreat."

"Look, all that is undoubtedly useful," says Kern, "but—"

I don't give him a chance. "We do not abandon each other. Not for love, not for money. I will get you out of here, but that means I need to coordinate both our teams, or else they will get overrun. Do you understand?"

"Yes," says Kern.

"Yes, what?"

"Yes, I understand." He's irritable.

"What's this?" I order, bringing my hand up.

"Stop."

I signal again. "Retreat," says Kern.

"Now, we're talking." I trigger my channel switch. "Briar Team is engaging and needs direction. Black One is assisting. Cargo will maintain dispersement, and then Black One exfiltrates in a controlled manner."

"We're going to support Briar Team?" asks Yarborough.

"No. Black Three and Red One stay in position. You are mission-critical right where you are. Moving out." I head off before they chatter about how tactically unsound this can get. There are vipes who could be coming at us from any direction.

What I need are the extra eyes of the security forces. If we continue on in a panicked mess, and there are many vipes, we will be divided and conquered. And I must assume many vipes, or we're all dead.

I cover the halls and stairwell with my M12 as well as I can until we reach the ground floor. I hesitate at the sprinklers. To go through the stairwell door is to enter a rain of water, and I can smell why—there's smoke here, billowing and stinging to the eyes.

"Briar Team, can we get Plant Operations to shut down the sprinklers?" I don't need visibility problems and weapon misfires at a time like this.

"Negative, there is fire on the floor," comes an insistent voice. They aren't talking about gunfire. The vipe sons of bitches are arsonists, too.

The hell with it. I signal for Kern to stop, cover my carbine with my body and run into the spray. Down a hallway, I spot Greenbriar security. Four of them, huddled against the wall, soldiers in a trench afraid of going over the top. I reach them in seconds. They've found a comfortable puddle in between the water sprays. Even through my armor, I feel heat coming from around a graceful bend in the hallway. It's not a genuine corner. Corners have concealment.

"Are you the only cavalry?" grunts an officer.

"Situation," I say.

"They're dug in behind the front desk, lots of ammo and firebombs. There's three of ours down on the floor between us and them. Can you give us covering fire?"

Great. I'm kitted out in full-body armor, true, but ballistic cloth doesn't make me Superman. A stray round to the head or the knee, a high-powered rifle round at a seam—these things are the marks of mistakes, not a well-executed plan.

"What's that desk made of?"

"Polycarbonates and flak sheets," says one. "We're supposed to be the ones behind it."

"Jesus," I spit. "Okay, I'm going around to get a look, then coming right back. Stay behind cover. Fire to secure my retreat." They nod.

I stick the M12 out as far as I dare and pull the trigger for a short burst, feeling it lurch. I yank on the trigger twice more, hurry out and see what's there. Glass glistens across the tile, lit by pools of fire beneath choking smoke. The fire hasn't spread to the walls—on the cold tile, nothing burns but its own fuel—but the downed officers are in that inferno and beyond hope. I keep sidestepping, keep shooting, then dive back as the officers shelter me with their pistols. My foot skids on glass and water, and I count myself lucky—

Glass shatters, and released flame roars. This firebomb hits farther than the others, only a few feet away. The sprinklers' drops do nothing to the gasoline fire but send it spiking upward.

I look back to see if Kern followed, but he hasn't. Good. He should be nowhere near this.

"Did you see them?" asks the man next to me. "Did you see the vipes?"

"No," I say. "I don't need to. Here's our plan."

61 - INFINITY

I pound up the stairs ahead of Roland. He's not at a hundred percent, but I'm not bringing that up. I flatten against the first-floor exit, trying to locate the distant gunfire by sound.

"You hear anything?" Roland says. I hold a finger to my lips.

"Shoes coming closer. And I smell smoke."

I quietly step back and ready the carbine like a club. I don't want to kill, but if they come through that door with a gun, what I want will matter as much as a spit gob in the Pacific. The sound of the shoes pounds on my heart, and when at last they recede, I draw in a long, slow breath to celebrate the moment. I draw open the door gingerly, hoping not to be noticed.

For my virtue, I get a face shield full of water and nostrils full of smoke.

Instinctively, I back up, and Roland takes my place, attempting to cover both ends of the hallway while getting wetted down. He, too, retreats and lets the door clunk shut.

"We need another exit," he says. "One without guards."

I seize on an idea. "Second-floor windows."

"Yes." We run up another flight and out into the hallway. The stench of smoke is bad here. It can't be helped. Morgan might handle a slog up two flights of stairs and a jump down—anything more is in question.

We break for a corridor that goes north-south instead of east-west, hoping we'll hit windows sooner. I find the hall ends in a drab stretch of drywall, and I turn my wrath on an office door. It has a little touch-screen to punch in a code, but I kick right where the door lock bolts it to the frame. My boot and bones hold, and the door splinters and caves.

Inside, there's an office with a window big enough to get through. I dump the rifle and grab the swivel chair in one motion. I smack the window. The glass busts, but the chair twists in my hands. I drop it.

The window is shattered, yet it holds. The shards stick in place, adhered to each other.

"What the fuck?"

"Security laminate," says Roland, urgently looking it up and down. "They didn't want vipes getting out."

"Can you get through it?"

"We don't want to," he says. "Look." He points at a small, white plastic circle in the window. "Alarm. They'll converge here soon."

"This just gets better and better." I snatch up the useless rifle and reach for my headset. "Alpha, we need to regroup." I get no sound. I fiddle with it. "Alpha? Bravo? Come in."

"Did your mike get wet?" Roland says, pointing. I take off the helmet. The face shield has sluiced the water down to where the adjuster clips to my collar.

"Fuck. Go." We turn and run back through the stench, clearing the hall just as the sprinklers come on for this level as well. Roland is coughing and panting by the time we make it to the stairwell. I wish for a windshield wiper on the helmet and look him over.

"You going to be okay?"

"I have to be."

I take point. We hammer down the stairs. We burst into the first basement hallway, looking for Ulan, Deborah, and Morgan.

No one is there.

"Oh, peachy..." I say. We can't get out. We can't fight. We can't even stay together.

"They gave us a minute," Roland says. "It's been two and a half."

I have a sinking feeling. "Don't elevators stop on the floor with the fire?" I try to remember. I always thought I'd have to use that factoid to save my own life, not someone else's.

"Jess would know. She might have looked for another way up."

"We need to find her—"

"We need an *exit*," he insists.

"Yeah," I say. I know I can't give up, even when I'm beaten, but leading is pointless. Running I understand. "Let's go."

62 - CASS

I let the receptionist go. I'm here to fight hardasses. You don't get an honor guard to Valhalla because you blow away some kid on her internship. When they sacrifice enemies on your pyre like the Greeks did for Achilles, it's warriors or maybe a princess or two to deny the enemy a chance at an alliance. I'm not getting a public funeral, but I might content myself with twenty-four hours of coverage on national news somewhere.

I've raided the bodies for a vest and weapons and ammo. I'm waiting. Haribon in one hand, a cop's SIG-Sauer in the other. The last Molotov cocktail is out of the bag and near my lighter on the desk. It was getting wet from the sprinklers, but the gauze stuck into the neck of the bottle is so soaked in gas that it'll light when the time comes. I can smell the stink of everything: bitter smoke, sweat from my lip, and blood on the floor. The raining water is trouble—besides the distracting spray on my head, it's hard to hear above the splashing. And the hall is cloaked in smoke and fire, so watching for motion is difficult. What the guards haven't figured out is that they've got hard-soled shoes on, so I can hear them fine.

It's that SWAT-armored fucker in his rubber-soled boots who I'm wary of. I lobbed that last cocktail far down the hall in the hopes of splashing him. It didn't. It's a good thing I'm only playing for a stalemate.

Footsteps. I hunker down behind the desk and aim at the faux-corner of the lobby where I know they'll be coming, only to hear the steps come to an abrupt halt.

No uniforms come around the corner. They're just out of sight. It's not good. I've got basic training, range time, and paintball games to draw on for experiences. They probably have the same, plus actual gunfights.

Suddenly, another alarm whoops, different from the one Infinity's team set off.

I nearly fire off a shot in anticipation. They're masking their approach or maybe their retreat. My eyes narrow the world down to tunnel vision, ready for anything to come around that one brick curve.

What I see is a hand.

It flashes out there for half a second, and I pull the trigger. The Haribon bucks, but there's no way of telling if the bullet hit its target. The hand disappears, and only after it's gone do I realize it waved at me. I'm being toyed with, and I fell for it.

I set my teeth and aim at the brick curve where the hand disappeared. The angle sucks, but I spang a few rounds off the brick because hey, it doesn't hurt to try.

I'm never going to think that again. Just as I hold off firing to inspect my work, a bang sounds. My body jerks, suddenly filled with a deep, numbing tunnel that shoots cold through my left shoulder. My feet falter.

Emergency exit alarm. He circled around.

The armored figure—what Infinity calls an F-prot—he's flanked by two cops and coming through the main doors, letting another round fly. A supersonic bee whizzes by my ear. Aiming for the head—the sure way to kill a vipe.

That's when they hit the marbles.

The F-prot in the front skids in a hamstring-tearing stretch, nearly taking down the cop behind him. I'm stupid but not so dumb I leave a sector entirely unguarded. I'm already giving back plenty, the Haribon making a deafening series of rips in the air. I'm fast and cool, sighting in on the faces of the cops, yanking the trigger and moving on to the next. When the helmeted head jerks back, and the F-prot's feet go out from under him for a second time, I duck back down.

Holy hell. I got them.

There could be more. There can always be more. I take a glance over the lip of the desk and see the F-prot rolling to his knees, clambering. I aim and fire at the body, but the gun refuses to respond. I look at it—not jammed, just out of ammo. I fire with the SIG, but I can't tell if I hit.

I drop both guns on the security desk and duck down, grabbing the string of firecrackers. They have one function—to be a decoy for the ammo I don't have. I hurl it over at the pools of burning gas, and in seconds, it sounds like the 101st Airborne have shown up to party. Who wants to be out in the open when that kind of firepower is roaring? Happy New Year, fuckers.

I now have time to fumble for the lighter and bottle of gas. If bullets can't bring down the F-prot, fire can. The fuse lights cleanly, and I stand up just enough to throw.

I shouldn't have. The F-prot is limping, sure, but he's firing, and I feel my vest take two solid punches to the torso. The bottle falls from my hand, and I see the armored man get past the door in retreat, gun down. Something is very wrong. The vest hasn't stopped the bullets. My shoulder blade is all pain, all the time. I'm in worse trouble than I feel. They can keep firing on me from two sides now.

"Infinity?" I say, touching a finger to my ear, but the ear bud fell out. I see it on the floor. Next to it is the burning wick of the Molotov, chewing its way up and inside, ready to ignite full-tilt. My right arm's full of gun, so I nab it with the left and heave it over the desk. Getting an enemy with it is too much to hope for, but at least it isn't going to explode on me.

Rounds tear at the desk, and I hear glass shatter. A wave of heat washes over the edge. Incredibly, the security desk holds, though I'm sure the wood paneling on its outside is all splinters and shreds. My body is burning as if wasps stung me, the pain increasing with the swelling. But when the bullets stop, I'm somehow still alive and able to move.

Did they hit my heart? No time to reflect. I can't feel my left hand now— maybe my shoulder or arm got hit again. I grope for the SIG and decide not to get up over the top of the desk—I've been there before, and they'll be waiting to put one in my skull. Instead, I roll around and pop out near the floor, putting the sights on the two officers stacked up around the brick corner. I fire at the lowest one first and then focus only on trying to put a round in the second, pop-pop-pop, like whacking moles at a carnival.

I hide again. I have to cover the door, but I'm not sure I can stand. My chest burns to keep my neck and head up.

Two more. Two more, and I can heal this shit. Lying down, I don't feel so faint. The pain is inconsistent and optional. My heart is still pumping, my lungs still heaving. If they don't hit a load-bearing vertebra, I might be able to take them—

The SIG is out of ammo. Its slide is stuck back.

On the desk. My other hand's useless, but I can clamber for the guards' magazines. I stashed them in what-used-to-be-easy-reach minutes ago. I sit up closer to the interior of the desk just as the guards blind-fire. I see a lot of blood on the floor, but it's not like it's spraying out of me, and really, it could be anyone's. I wedge the magazine between my feet, eject the old one and slam the gun home. With a flick, I rack a round into the chamber.

I hear running feet among all the bangs. A shape blocks some of the lights, and I fire at it on instinct. The barrage at the desk was covering fire, and if I can't get out of this—

My vision swims, and all I hear is shooting. My hand falls away— the firing isn't me. My neck hurts as I force it back into position, trying to resist the invulnerable giant looming over me. The F-prot's gun thunders again and again. I'm under the desk, tucked in securely and seeing everything through some kind of golden filter, dark around the edges as if I'm being dragged through a tunnel. I try to get my gun hand to obey, but it's empty. I'm touching my head instead. The hand is wet, and where my fingers touch isn't smooth anymore. As the F-prot pushes me down with his foot, I don't feel angry at him. I'll rest here a while, and then I'll move on.

Two cops come up behind the armored F-prot, looking me over. "The rest should be easier," says the helmeted figure. "Find them. And get some medical personnel with crashcarts."

"Is this one dead?" says one of the cops.

"You can answer that," says the F-prot, and the cop aims. He looks as if he's wanted to do this his whole life, and now somebody told him he could.

There's a crack from the end of the world, a light and—

63 - MORGAN

I rest my hands on the elevator's walls, inhaling as much as I can. My head is clearing for the first time in months, and the canned air of the elevator is a gift to my nose. Jess holds her hand under my jaw, and I can feel my balance improving. My nausea leaves.

"Don't try to walk," says Jessica.

"I just need a minute."

"No, I mean, appear as my patient."

I obediently get back on the gurney. She releases the door-close button, and we are hit by a wave of heat and fumes and sprinkling water. Mercifully, it's not all fire and we still have oxygen. Jess closes it again, and all that remains is excess water on the floor.

A metallic click from behind unsettles me. Deborah has Infinity's black pistol in her hands. I haven't really noticed that it might go off until now.

"Do you know how to use that thing?" I ask.

"Fini showed me once, but I'm not good or anything."

"Put it away," Jessica says. "We've got to be camouflaged."

The weapon disappears into Deborah's jacket, along with her mask and headset. "Are we sure we want to go out—"

Loud bangs make us all freeze, and at first, I think she's shot herself putting the pistol away. But the noise is from down the hall—a firefight.

"What's that?"

"Suicide by cop, I think," Deborah says, looking as if she's dreaded this before.

"Okay, not this floor," Jessica orders, stabbing at buttons. "And not where we came from 'cause they'll be headed for their wounded there." The doors work, and the cable lowers us down two. "We'll cut across this level and find another way up."

They wheel me out of the elevator. And just like that, a voice makes us freeze.

"Central, I've got three, B2 elevator."

I turn, and my vision swims. Even so, I pick out the bulky cop behind us. He has a hand on his gun, body language authoritative but not hostile. I want to cling to him—he isn't private security. Maybe he's been kept in the dark by BRHI and is sworn to protect anyone, even vipes?

"Excuse me, sir, madam, you can't leave," says the cop. "Are you a patient here?"

I feel a cold fist clench in my gut. I want to yell the truth. I'm a prisoner, not a damn patient. But Jessica jumps in.

"Yes, I'm taking care of him. We just saw a crazy woman with a gun on B1."

"Well, I apologize, but this floor isn't safe either. The best thing you can do is to come with me, and I can lock you in a room. Our backup will be here in a few minutes."

"Backup?" It's Deborah, who sounds more concerned than she should be. I have a bad feeling she just gave the game away.

"We're just trying to exit the building in an orderly fashion," Jessica tries. "Isn't there like a side exit or something we could—"

"Ma'am, this hallway is not safe right now. Walk in front of me, please."

"We're not doing that. We're in fear for our goddamn lives," Jessica tries to step past him. The cop catches her sleeve, and then everything happens very fast.

Jessica tries to push the cop off her, but his hand jerks on her coat, and they spin a little. Immediately, the cop's eyes go wide—he's seen the stimweb.

Jessica shoves, and if the cop didn't know she was a vipe before, he knows it now. He's hurled back at least three meters, losing his footing as he lands and ends up on his rump as he collides with the wall. Deborah goes for her gun just as the cop does and points it.

"Don't move," she yells, "This is—" That's all she gets out before the cop shoots Jess.

He doesn't even see Deborah. The cop fires again and again, all adrenaline and ammunition. Jessica stumbles backward, each bullet hole taking away her balance, making her sway like a marionette held in palsied hands. I stare as Jess stumbles to her knees, expecting someone, anyone, to stop it. Only then do I realize it's up to me and Deborah. Somewhere around bullet ten or eleven, she pulls the trigger. At a range of maybe three meters, she misses.

I don't even know all the details of what happens next. My feet are on the floor, and in no time at all, I've cleared the distance and swing the seventy-kilo gurney so hard it catches air. The cop and gurney cave in a gigantic hole in the wall, showing broken sheetrock and wooden beams.

I reach down, seize the cop by the vest and lift him out of the mess. He might be holding his pistol still; he might not. I hurl him to the floor headfirst and see the gun slide away. Still furious, I kick the limp body. I feel no better.

I rush over to Deborah, who is hunched over Jessica. I try to sit Jess up, finding her body loose, like water flowing between my fingers. But it's not water soaking my hands. When she coughs, shocking-bright crimson paints her lips.

"Can you stand?" I ask.

She shakes her head, a tiny movement. "Spine."

I can't think of the next thing to say. My mind is filled with everywhere she's been hit, the massive trauma she's taken that could kill the unkillable.

"Call Infinity," I tell Deborah. "Get help."

Deborah has her headset out of her jacket. "Infinity?" she calls into it. "Infinity, Jess is hurt bad. Come in." There's an awful moment of silence. "Oh, God, she's not—"

"We need help. We're going to find her." I turn back to Jessica, trying to guess what I can do to stop the bleeding. She has more wounds than we have hands.

"Carrie," she says, or at least that's what I think she says. It takes me a second to figure out it's *carry*. I lift her, feeling a little unsteady but not from her weight. I can do this. I have to.

"We'll get you out of here," I tell her as we begin walking. Deborah jogs ahead, playing scout, looking furtively at every open doorway. "You just heal up. You're my favorite vampire."

"Liar."

"Well, either way, you're going to make it, all right?" Deborah waves us on, and I run.

"We're not," she hisses out, like she's trying to talk without using her lungs.

"What?"

"Not vampires. They live forever."

"Don't talk like that."

She gives me a sideways glance as her head rolls back. "Doesn't matter."

"I'm serious, Jess," I say. "When all of us are dead, kids are going to be learning your name in school."

"Shit," she says.

"I'm not kidding. Didn't you watch the whole trial?"

"No."

"Those bastards tried to register a scientific name for us. We're *Cruorimbibo ulan*."

"Ulan?" she says and gives a little smile before she dies.

64 - INFINITY

I jump back around a corner, signaling to Roland with my hands.
No goddamn way. I saw four guards together, wearing crisp, white
uniforms instead of the light blue ones of the guards at the entrance.
They're carrying long guns of some kind—probably shotguns.

"Stop!" yells a voice from down the hall. Great. That's what I get
for poking my head out. Roland doesn't need prompting. We both
take off, down every twist of the corridors we can find. We see an exit
sign, but it leads to stairs instead of an actual door out. I go down,
only because it's faster than going up. We burst out and mercifully
don't land in anyone's sights.

"Wait," Roland says, after we take another three turns. "Look. No
cameras."

He's right. For whatever reason, this stretch of real estate isn't
monitored, at least not by anything I can see. It's a good place to lose
pursuit.

"Disappear," I say. He finds steel-plated double doors that open
with a button.

"Uh, are you sure—" I say, taking in the warning labels. There's a
trefoil of biohazardous waste and something about protective
garments. "It says level 5 here..."

"That's you," he says, and I slip inside before anyone sees. As the
doors click shut behind us, I feel marginally safer. We're in a dim
room, a shadowy antechamber lit by a pale glow of monitors and a
window up ahead. Instrument panels are arranged below the window,
warm but not inviting. Confused, I creep forward. I shoot a glance at
Roland—he says nothing, but it's clear he doesn't know what this place
is, either.

Something thuds up ahead. Slow and regular, the heartbeat of a
mammoth.

I look through the window. This isn't a lab like the ABEL facility.
We're in a booth looking straight out across an enormous chamber,

like a mead-hall for Vikings or something. The tables studding the floor are covered in white body bags, lit by muted overhead lights and a bright flare like magnesium coming from the end of the room. As I watch, a monstrous shadow blots out the flare. It hurls something into the light and clangs shut enormous doors. A roaring sound drowns out the noises of an armored F-prot by the side of the room, who pulls out a drawer with another body bag.

The monstrous thing heads our way, but it doesn't appear to have seen us. I've heard of man-shaped drones and industrial robots, but the last time I saw one was on a school field trip. I glance over at Roland. He's watching the three-meter metal monster.

"You going to be okay?" I whisper. "I know you're afraid."

"I'm not afraid of drones. I'm afraid of death," he says. "It's too tough to punch, too dead to use qi, and it's bulletproof."

I hear something and point up. The driver's above us. I clutch my useless carbine. Roland puts a restraining hand on it. We're still being hunted. Holding still could save our lives.

The drone thumps along on boxlike feet over to the drawer that the F-prot opened. I'm not sure who it is since it's still helmeted, but Breunig wouldn't be on the menial tasks. Ebe is out.

Whoever it is skips back as the drone reaches down with its grabbing digits and hefts the body into the air. The F-prot moves again, nervously, as the drone returns to the furnace on the far wall. It grasps the locking mechanism and gracefully releases it.

"They're burning them," Roland whispers.

I can't look away. "They're burning *us*."

A body, a faceless mannequin, goes into the light, and then there's a slam of metal.

"How can they *do* this?" I say, trying to keep it to a hiss. "We *know* them."

"It's easier than you think." I look at him. He doesn't say, but I know what he's thinking.

"We're different," I say.

"You, maybe."

"We're different *now*."

Roland seems distant. Then, he points. "That's Olsen. Her rifle's on the table. I'll go. Can you get up this ladder quietly?"

I look at it and nod. I sling the carbine on my back. Roland pulls out the little silenced pistol and dials up his stimweb. I'm about to ask him if he has enough juice to do it, but then something makes me turn away from him and focus on the task at hand. That's a yes.

I move out carefully and crouch low, hoping the tables and the distance help keep me inconspicuous. Olsen, at the far end of the hall, is busy keeping an eye on the drone so she doesn't get squished. I can hardly blame her. I wait for Roland to get close before starting my ascent—if they hear me or spot me, this will all go south immediately.

Now that Roland is half a room away, it's easier to look at him—he's stealing closer and closer to Olsen, ready to pounce—and it hits me. If I can see him, so can the man in the booth. Roland's concealment has less power than he realizes.

The drone whirs and turns. It clicks on a klieg light. Olsen, alerted, sprints for her rifle.

I have no choice. I scramble up the ladder, being as silent as possible, watching in terror as Roland beats Olsen to the gun. They tussle, and Roland fires right in her helmet, but then a second pop sounds, and I realized the F-prot has shot back with a sidearm. There's a blur of hands, a yell of pain and thumps from the goddamn drone as it closes in on him.

I hurl myself into the booth. Yarborough is at the controls, his helmet off so he can see better, and he looks at me in momentary fear before he reaches for his carbine, on the chair next to him. We grab it at the same time, and I tear it out of his grasp. He goes for his pistol and eats the butt of his rifle as I slam it into his head. He and his chair go over backward.

I kneel on his arm, pinning it as I bean him in the skull again with the rifle. I'm about to keep going when I realize Yarborough's eyes have rolled back into his head. Instinct tells me to hold off.

I pry his pistol from him, get the backup pistol off his ankle, and look for Roland.

He has Olsen in a headlock, as if she tried to dive for his legs and was stopped. Roland has collapsed on her, maybe trying for a guillotine choke, refusing to let go because the floor is full of dropped guns. The drone is thumping down at both of them, a metric ton of metal with no one at the wheel.

I snatch at the control stick on the instrument and jerk it aside. The monster turns. One foot strikes a slab, and it trips, yawing forward and landing with a screech of steel on steel. It quests about with its limbs and rises to its feet in some kind of automatic response. I let go of the stick in surprise. The drone stops utterly.

I have no idea how to drive it, so I focus on shoving Yarborough out of the booth. His limp body falls to the floor, and I hurry down after it, holding back the slung weapons as I run to Roland.

I can smell everything now that I'm close. Rotting flesh in the biobags. Burning hair from the furnace. Blood from Roland. He lies on the last F-prot, fallen and ashen, as though he's taken a bullet to the heart. I roll Olsen over first and see her faceplate shattered. The face beneath is nothing but blood and bruises—in desperation, Roland hit her with pure yin qi. He's lying back, too, but I'm grateful to see him blink. He's alive. For how long, I don't know.

65 · RANATH

By the time Infinity reaches me, I'm trying to get my hand underneath my coat and vest. The shot missed the trauma plate and pierced the area near my floating ribs on the left side.

"How bad is it? Did the vest stop it?" she asks.

"PDW," I say, shorthand for a modern gun designed to defeat body armor. "I'm bleeding. Don't know if it's through-and-through. I hope it is."

"Kind of a funny wish," she says, helping me to my feet.

My back burns, and I suppress the urge to sit down again. "Bullets drag clothing into the wound," I explain. "I can't heal completely with leather in me."

She examines my back. "I don't see anything."

I claw at the snaps of my coat, then dig at the Velcro holding on the ballistic vest. I slough both off and hike up my shirt. Warm blood runs down my kidney area. When I touch my lower back, everything feels numb until I touch something hard. Shocking pain makes me wince.

Infinity leans over. "Let me try," she says. "I think I can grab it."

"What's it look like?"

"Flattened. Must have been stopped by the vest on this side."

I bite back a cliché about later and never, then clench every muscle. Infinity's nails deftly remove the bullet. It stings, but like pulling a tooth, it's better once it's free. But I bleed more.

"You stopped her takedown pretty well for someone in your condition."

"And your... bedside manner... is excellent," I grunt out.

"Infinity?" calls a voice, and my hand goes to the quiet pistol. Infinity's hand stops me. It's the vipe she called Deborah and, behind her, Morgan. His hospital gown is smeared with blood, and he's stumbling forward, carrying a bundle in his arms. With dread, I recognize it.

"Oh, Lord," Infinity says, "what happened?"

Morgan drops to his knees and puts one hand on the floor to balance himself. "Security," he says. "They shot her. I took care of it, but we have to get her out of here." He wipes his face with his hand, leaving behind a scarlet trail.

"What is this place?" asks Deborah, obviously in shock as well.

Infinity ignores her. "Jess? Is she alive?"

"No," Morgan says. "But if we leave her here, they'll dissect her. You know it."

While the vipes confer, I fumble with my stimweb, jabbing in tacks. Immediately, I know I'm in trouble. I'm used to my body's energy flow when the stimweb is dialed down and crackling with it when it's dialed up. Now, I can feel it skewed, like a bike tire that suddenly has some spokes shortened so the new shape will never roll.

The thought of Jessica on one of these slabs disgusts me, but I'm in little condition to help. I can walk—maybe—but like any good chess player, I have to plan several moves ahead.

I can probably run out of the building before feeling faint from blood loss, but a drive to some other hospital will leave me maybe twenty minutes in which I can pass out behind the wheel.

"I can't join you," I say. "I need to stop my bleeding."

"You can't stay," Deborah says. "Every city cop with a radio will be here."

"Come on," Infinity urges me. "Don't be an idiot and make me choose."

I shake my head. Trying to explain what's wrong in terms of meridians will just confuse them. I go for a more Western explanation. "I'm in hypovolemic shock," I say. "I can stop the bleeding, but I need to use qi now. Let me worry about how I'm getting out of here." I cover my entry and exit wounds with my hands.

Infinity meets my eyes for a few seconds, and I think I see pain in them. It might be from seeing her friend on the floor, but then again, it might not.

"Roland, if you get caught here, you're dead."

"Infinity," I say quietly, "I'm asking you to trust me. Have I earned that?"

Infinity doesn't answer, but Deborah steps forward. "I'll stay with him."

"What are you talking about?" Infinity says.

Deborah pulls a flat, little phone out of her pocket. "I'm saying if I can get five minutes in here uninterrupted, I can start an upload. And then, I can show this place to the entire world."

For a moment, none of us speaks. Then, I nod. "If radios are working, cells probably will."

Infinity looks skeptical. Deborah points at the phone. "One bar. See?"

Infinity turns away, and snakes an arm under Jessica. The part of my ego that wants to believe she needs rescuing takes another beating as she manhandles a sixty-kilo body, rifle slung. Blood drizzles on the floor, but even as she has Jess hoisted on her shoulders, she has less trouble walking than Morgan.

"Morgan," she says. "Door. Now."

I watch her vanish, running out of my life for the third time. You'd think I'd take the hint.

66 - INFINITY

I run.

I go as fast as I dare, terrified I'll twist an ankle or a knee under the strain, terrified I'll drop Jessica—even though nothing can hurt her now—and, most of all, terrified I will get caught.

Fini.

Morgan lopes along behind me. It's still a good pace. We reach a window, and I bust it with the chair again. When the laminate holds it, I snap open my knife and saw at the film. The glass cubes rain down, and my fingers get cut, but no one and nothing is going to keep me back this time. In moments, we can leap to the street. I stop looking back when we reach the entrance to the parking garage. Like a horse getting closer to home, I sprint. Cass's truck hums its electric whine. Ferrero jumps out of the driver's-side door to help relieve my burden.

You can't change, Fini.

"Where's Cass?" he asks.

You get yourself in trouble, and then you run.

"Front desk. He's got to be surrounded. Deborah's... staying."

"So this is... Jesus, this is it?" As Morgan catches up, the schoolteacher hugs him, then wrinkles his nose.

"Oh, man," he says. "They not give you toilet paper in there?"

"Hello to you, too."

"How bad are you hurt?"

"The blood, it's all Jess."

I pull down the truck's gate and slide Jessica's body onto it. By the time I'm done, Ferrero has gotten a blanket out.

"I'll do it," I say. "Morgan, get in the cab. There's clothes in the back."

Morgan climbs inside the running truck. Ferrero sees me hesitate with the blanket. He jumps in and tucks it under the body. It's soon wrapped.

"We need to look for a hospital," Ferrero says. "I'll drive."

"Listen to me very carefully," I say. "Get Morgan somewhere safe. Nothing else matters."

"She could be resuscitated. They have technology now—"

"Fer, no." I speak slowly and harshly. "Get Morgan somewhere safe."

The other vipe blinks first. "Then, we go," he says and leaps down.

The cab's rear window slides open. "Where's Ly?" asks Morgan.

He's dead already, Jess said once. I needed to believe it then.

I stare at my friend and silence all the explanations I want to say. I can run from Roland or I can run from Morgan. I owe them both. They both trust me. I eat regret for breakfast, but tomorrow morning, I'll choke either way. I couldn't protect Ly. Cass. Jess. Deborah.

You look back. That's the traitor's look.

"I need to go inside," I say.

"So, get in."

"Inside the *building*."

Fear grips Ferrero's eyes, then anger. "No, we are leaving. You put me in charge of the escape, I decide. You are coming with *us*."

He clambers inside the cab, and the truck takes off. The jolt makes me sway, but my balance is hardly taken even when Fer slams the accelerator as hard as he can. I wait as the truck tears through the parking garage, then choose my moment.

"Morgan," I say to him through the glass, "I don't deserve you."

The truck slows down to turn, and I hop over the side.

I hit the pavement evenly. The truck doesn't slow. Ferrero must not have been looking in the mirrors. I beeline for a door, hand on my slung rifle to keep it from jouncing. I burn across the sidewalk and hear sirens, more and more because it has been just too damned long.

There are two cops inside the door. One opens it for me, and it takes me an instant to figure out why: the uniform. While I'm alone, I can walk free.

I stride past them. "Olsen here," I say. "Going for the wounded."

And I'm not a traitor anymore.

I kneel on my coat among morgue tables, in the shadow of the gigantic drone. My hands cradle my wounds. Eyes closed. Lips pulled back as I push air past my teeth. Wounded people are supposed to lie down or stagger off if they can, but I can't think of myself in such mundane terms. To do so is to acknowledge that I am normal, and normal people in my situation have a very short time to live.

My first hypothesis is that my left kidney is holed. The drop in my water and yin qi is thorough. Without water qi, fire systems such as my heart will be unrestrained: it will beat like a triphammer and pump out blood until I lose consciousness. Western medicine would say it's adrenaline kicking my pulse into overdrive when I need it slow. Both are true simultaneously.

For an interminable time, I concentrate on losing my mind. My conscious thoughts will only get in the way, and no momentary impulses can worry me, or else I will be using the wrong tool for the job.

I did this.

The self, the ego and the *I* are weak little chisels compared to the hydraulic ram of the body's other organs, evolved over millions of years to survive, long before it needed to think about it afterwards.

"This is Deborah Shaw Hallet, beneath BRHI's Greenbriar Health in east D.C., and you can see here a number of vipe bodies."

Her voice is meek and far away, and I put it out of my mind. *Your concentration is everything,* a kung fu sifu told me once. *If an elephant walks in the room, you change nothing. You do not think. You concentrate.*

As I empty my mind, I feel my wound twinge with each heartbeat. The kidney's not hit. It's the renal artery, and the kidney is slowing its functions because it's starved of blood.

"I opened this body bag to show you the execution wounds. They're all like this. This is where they go, into the disposal. They have been disappeared, forgotten."

I register her words. Mistake.

Forced Protection was mine.

A yin organ is tricky to heal. Adding straight yin tends to weaken organs, and straight yang can overwhelm it. The solution is a yin-within-yang field that takes a half hour or more to apply, time I don't have. But an artery, that is possible.

They looked to me.

My hands hold back the red tide, and as power flows between them, the cells begin to change. First, the clots on either side of the artery, then a flush of the surrounding tissue in case the bullet punctured the intestine, which isn't that far away and can cause wicked infections.

I could die here, and it would be right.

The healing process starts to slip, my hands tingling as the energy meets resistance. But I don't make the mistake of tightening up and grasping at water.

Instead, I sink deeper, feeling for biofeedback that can guide me. I don't feel it but taste it—my saliva is foul and metallic. I amplify it, as much as I can stand.

I am the best magician left.

The qi between my hands lights up again, and some of the pain subsides. I don't know how long I heal. I know only that Deborah's phone vibrates, and she madly taps the screen.

I want to hear her voice.

"Did you get it?" I say quietly.

"Completely uploaded," she says. "Don't worry. I made sure you weren't in any shots. Least I could do, since you, uh...."

"I appreciate it," I say, with some effort. "You should run. I'll be here too long to be safe."

"Safe... is that a joke?"

"What I mean to say is you should try to catch up to Infinity."

"Okay," she says. "If we don't make it out... you were on the right side."

"That's kind," I say, and she disappears into the darkness.

I don't watch her go, intent on the heat building in my body, fusing me together like layers of steel. I will be well enough soon, if only I can finish it before the cops' backup—

"Yar? Olsen?"

My eyes snap open, and I put a bloody hand on the pistol. As long as I can still bite, I will fight back. The emerald laser dot aims up at where I hear the noise and fixes itself on the centerline of a very familiar doctor.

I freeze, clutching the cardboard-wrapped box. "Roland? What happened to you?"

"I get the feeling," Ranath says dryly, "that's not going to be your only question."

I see blood smears on the floor near him and no Yarborough or Olsen. Can I still turn and run? No—Ranath is too good a shot, stupid new haircut and all.

"Can you, uh... can you put the gun down?"

"First, why don't you put down that box?"

I hesitate.

"I see," Ranath says. "It's valuable to you."

Shit. I've got to move the conversation away from me, or everything will spill out in a rush. "You... did you cause all these alarms? There was this voice on the PA—"

"And now, you've waited until the shooting stopped to come find an F-prot escort," Ranath interrupts. "Now, what could motivate you more than survival?"

Time to defuse him. He's always been rational. I can use that. "Ranath, I realize you may be angry. But you should consider the proper target of that anger. I tried to protect you—"

"Put it down," Ranath orders, and I do so. The rodents inside scrabble.

"Mice," says Ranath. "Of course. Transgenics with human DNA to... let us see...."

He's thinking, not shooting. I can delay him. The police have to be on their way. Even if he takes me hostage, chances are good that he'll negotiate. He can go to prison or disappear for all I care—as long as he doesn't endanger the plan.

Ranath homes in. "Money got you up in the morning, but it was never your passion. I think those mice have some kind of potential. But you already have a vaccine. Is this a cure?"

He knows better. "Hardly."

"Interesting. That rings true. Elaborate."

"Ranath, you're a very intelligent person, but—and don't take this the wrong way—" His stare is as cold as the gun barrel. "You have the business acumen of a fifth-grader."

"Explain."

"No, you should know a cure isn't possible or profitable. You can figure the rest out."

No sooner are the words out of my mouth than I instantly regret them. The green targeting dot speeds upward, and it's shining in my right eye. I flinch—lasers can burn out a retina in seconds—and flail with my hand as Ranath keeps his aim true.

"Cut that out!"

"Explain," Ranath says again, but I turn at the sound of boots. An F-prot in uniform is here, but no shooting starts. I don't understand until the figure snaps its face shield up.

"Roland, time to go," says a woman's voice, and my hopes sink. It's Infinity. I drove those two together, of course, but that doesn't matter now. I have to deflect attention away, to make up something to try and occupy them, and where are the damned F-prots?

"We will not get this opportunity again," Ranath says, and I realize I'm going to be here for a whole freaking interrogation. "Dr. Kern is going to explain why he would risk his life for mice with a knockout gene."

Start with the truth. "The mice are expensive."

"Not that expensive," Ranath counters. "They have VIHPS?"

"Of course, they have VIHPS." I seize on the explanation to stall. "We can monitor their degeneration, their lapse into a coma when they can't be fed. They sometimes bite other mice, but they still fall apart without human blood."

"As fascinating as that is—" says Infinity.

"You're lying," says Ranath. "Infinity, pick up the mice. We're taking them."

"Wait!" I say, before I can stop myself. I have to keep Ranath and Infinity here, and I must keep them talking. "What do you care if VIHPS is cured?"

"Long story," sighs Infinity, but who cares what she thinks?

"I fell in love," snaps Ranath. "Now, explain the function of the mice before my trigger finger gets tense." The laser dot tracks down my body to settle on my knee.

I'm not sure what to say, thrown off by Ranath's off-the-cuff revelation. The Ranath I know doesn't date, mostly socializes with other men, keeps his mind in the lab and on the prey. As for the vipe, she looks confused, a sure sign he—

A bullet shatters my shin. The gunshot, the *zip* of the bullet after it exits my flesh, they echo endlessly as I go down in a heap. The pain blazes through me, and I writhe on the floor as if I'm paper curling in the flames. I'm screaming. I hold the wound with my hands, and oh, God, I feel bone fragments.

"You seem to be under the impression that our friendship has bought you time," Ranath says. "I have no time, but you have one more shin."

"It's a virus, damn it!" I yell, trying to take control of something, anything. "It's like any fucking virus."

"That tells me nothing."

"Viruses can be *edited*!"

I roll onto my side, holding the holes in my shin and calf. In my twisted position, I barely see Ranath and Infinity look at each other. If I don't talk, things will be worse.

"Its genome is short. You encode a couple of proteins, and the feedback loop does a spectacular dance. Say you eliminate the drawbacks. No dependence on blood, no saliva vector communicability. What do you have? You have a virus that grants bone ossification, proprioceptive neuromuscular facilitation, rerouting of neural pathways—"

"Slow down," says Infinity. "Or speak English."

"Healing!" I spit. "Healing goddamn everything and an immune system that would kick the ass of a sewer alligator's. That's not a curse. That's a *product*."

Neither of the pair moves. Ranath tries to be stone-faced, but I'm getting through.

"All this to make super soldiers—" starts Infinity.

"*Soldiers?* You think *that's* a market? Tell you what, you sell to every special ops outfit on the planet while I work on a VIHPS-delivered immune booster." I focus on getting one word out at a time, beating my way through the pain. "And when you're done... making some guy who can lift a rucksack better... I will kill more diseases than penicillin. Replacements for vaccines, from malaria to TB to mumps to... fuck knows what." My brain feels like someone is pressing down on it. It's the blood loss. "This is ten times... the qi healing revolution. We dissected vipes who partially repaired... muscular dystrophy. We had a stroke... victim... walk again."

"I don't care if it makes millions—"

"Girl, add eight zeroes. When we... put this in a syringe... it'll be ten years before *the rest of the health care industry goes out of business*. That's the endgame. Change the world, and own the rights. Monopoly. There will be us... and no one else."

The man and woman watching me just stare. In the distance, I hear many sirens, blurring together.

"You kidnapped my friend," says Infinity. I wish she'd shut up. I'm dizzy, which isn't a good sign when I'm already on the floor.

I close my eyes, but everything is still drifting. "We needed conscious minds. They were going to die anyway. It's not like I planned to exterminate them from the beginning."

Infinity looks like I slapped her. "Are we sparing him?"

"I used two rounds on Olsen," he says. "I'm out of ammo. Do what you want, but grab the mice."

Infinity walks toward me. Worried, I check for the look on her face. She could kick a hole in my head. I have to stay awake because if I can't talk, I can't stay alive.

"You—you two want to cooperate," I say, my breathing labored. "They're surrounding the building. You're both dead without me."

Infinity doesn't say a word but kneels next to me. I look at her eyes, and they are in shadow. I'm going to die.

"You want to put me in that fire, don't you?" I think maybe if I say it, she won't—

She spits in my face.

Strangely, her defiance prompts mine. Being an enemy is easy. "That's... original."

"That's half," she says and puts her fingers in the hole in my pants. She tears, revealing the angry entrance wound slathered in blood. Then, she touches the wetness on my face. I hold still, only realizing what she's doing when it's too late. Infinity wipes her sticky fingers in the wound and then stands, snatching up the box of mice.

"I'm ready," she says.

69 - RANATH

They are everywhere; that is clear.

I hobble as fast as I can. My injury has stopped bleeding, but the nearby tissue is tender, which is not what I want. Running involves core muscles just as much as my legs. Infinity easily sprints ahead of me. We get near windows but turn back when we see red-and-blue lights.

"Any ideas?" she says, after the second exit we try fails us.

"Can you hold a gun to my head, keep your face shield down and act convincing?"

"Probably not with a box of mice," Infinity says. I agree. If she doesn't have the confidence, it's a last-ditch gambit.

"How'd you get to me just now?"

"I came with cops who weren't cleared for the morgue. I changed our exit to avoid them. Where's Deborah?"

"You didn't see her on the way in?" Infinity shakes her head. "Hiding, I guess. You can't call her?" She winces, and I know she's kicking herself for not having a phone.

I triage. "I saw a glass walkway to the other building," I say. "Third floor, I think. Maybe they haven't surrounded the other one yet."

"Elevators are back there," she says, starting to go, but I grip her hand.

"Stairs." Soon we are pounding up the concrete flights to the third floor. I'll be in misery tomorrow morning, but for now, the adrenaline dulls the pain. We tear down hallways, deserted as far as I can tell—this is a lab, not a true hospital. Anyone still working here has bunkered down. Infinity runs past the skyway, confused in the twists of the building.

"This way!"

We dash across, and I get my first good look at the police cars. There are black-and-whites choking the street, unmarked cars from plainclothes officers, three ambulances disgorging paramedics and a green fire truck. Clearly, no cop in Prince George's County is about to let another cop die for lack of backup. Will fifty cops be enough? A hundred?

Then, it's all behind me, and we are into the heart of the next building. It's folly to think we're getting out of here by running one block over. We need another plan. Infinity is obviously thinking the same thing.

"That is some Bonnie and Clyde shit out there."

"Stairs," I say. "They'll be coming in from below." We go up three more flights, and my abdominal wound threatens permanent residence. I stop for breath in the stairwell, holding on to my injury like I'm holding my guts in.

"Tell me this is going somewhere," Infinity says. "You got magic the cops don't?"

"No other biomancer will have my locator function," I pant out. "They might have something similar, but I took out BRHI's magicians. That's the good news."

"If you want to pause between thoughts, now ain't the time."

"The bad news: they will search for us and cover every inch of the buildings, and they won't be gone 'til tomorrow. With us on security camera—"

"Now," she interrupts, "would be a great time for you to learn how to fly."

"I have one function I could use to conceal myself," I say.

"No, you don't. Its range sucks now. I could see you from the booth."

That's disturbing. I must adapt. "To extend it, I need a ring of living qi."

Her face falls. Then, she brightens. "Like human blood?"

"Blood, yogurt, plant matter—"

"Roof access." She points to the sign behind me. "Haven't seen a stairwell camera yet."

"They'll search there—"

"Yeah, but not more than once," she says and gets her shoulder under mine to lift me up. It doesn't help my injury to be half-pulled up the steps, but it keeps her from running out and inadvertently giving away our position. At the top landing, Infinity tries the door. It's locked. I bring out the burner phone.

"Are you authorized for this place?" Infinity asks.

"Disposable lockpick," I answer. The app fires its passcodes, then gives a warning burp.

"Just how disposable are we talking?" she asks. I shush her with a gesture, which she doesn't appreciate, but the cause is soon clear. We hear the blaring rotors of a helicopter outside.

"Ghetto bird," I say. "I like your plan less and less."

"It's far off, still," she protests.

I gauge the sound based on what I recall from Okinawa. I think she's right. "We still need blood. Are you planning a trip to the freezer?"

"Better," she says. Just then the phone chirps, and she opens the door into the night. The chopper's noise envelops us. The roof is covered in pebbles—probably for some insulation reason—and they crunch underfoot as we put the stairwell between us and the searchlight beam.

"We have no exit strategy," I say.

"Sit down," she shouts above the din. "I'm going to be your ring."

I kneel, tucking my legs under me Japanese-style. I puzzle out if what she's proposing could work. Her aura would be more complex than bacteria but not vastly different from blood. I've felt for it before, when trying to track her, so acquisition of her flow signature won't be new.

"I need skin-to-skin contact," I yell. "Circle me with your arms. Close the circuit with your palms. More surface area."

She peels off her armor and boots. She's doing her shirt when I stop her.

"We need as much skin as possible, right?" she asks.

I'm not sure. I usually don't touch the living ring for fear of breaking the circle. The danger is in how stable her signature will be with power coursing through it.

There's no time to dither. The helicopter is circling, its spotlight exposing all kinds of corners in the night. I take off my coat, then, hating it, my ballistic vest and my shirt. I put them on top of the mouse box to weigh it down. The useless, empty pistol goes on top of the coat.

Infinity scoots over to me. She wraps her bare legs around my torso, hooking her feet together, and does the same with her hands. I'm aware of how it looks. Will the helicopter spot us, only to pass it off as two thrill-seekers getting laid in the worst possible place? Unlikely. Kern is no doubt giving our descriptions to everyone with ears. We have one chance.

I dial the stimweb down. It's running full-bore stimulating healing points. Now, I need it to catch the proper signal before focusing outward. A subtle pain in my back reasserts itself.

I touch the two points beneath my eyes and straighten my spine. My torso muscles strain in protest. They've been hard at work trying to keep me upright, and some have locked up. But I retain enough control to align myself properly, and when I do, I can feel the start of the function I need. I adjust the stimweb's pulse, a gentle tap in rhythm with my heartbeat.

I begin with myself, the fewest number of variables. *Inside each of us is a transmitter*, a martial arts partner told me once. *It broadcasts exactly what we are thinking, what we are about to do.*

He meant it as a metaphor to describe the altered state of perception that allowed him to respond to opponents quickly, but in my case, it is far more literal. I begin to broadcast one signal, *ignore*, in an insinuating fashion that cuts right through human defenses.

I can tell it's working when Infinity's arms and legs relax. She's getting a headful being so close, and ardently, I work to incorporate her before she gives up entirely and breaks her circles.

I take her head in my hands and push the points beneath her eyes. Her qi is strong and panicked, like when I first laid hands on her. And here, now that I'm specifically looking for it, I sense the yin energy that never stops thirsting, the hungry heart of a vipe.

It's from there that I draw her signal, pure and easy to grasp. She has not fed in more than a week. It's wrapped around me, but though it occupies the same space as my own biological system, something is wrong. The two signals need to spin like wheels; instead, they grind against each other like a screeching brake pad.

She feels it and interrupts. "Are we good?"

"I haven't done this before," I say. "We need to be in lockstep."

"You need me to think about Bible verses again, just say so."

I wish. I try linking my signal with Infinity's. Impossible. I breathe in, breaking my concentration, and it's like throwing a grass stem in a river.

Infinity's qi is powerful, based in an urge somewhere to be ignored, to be lost. It's completely unlike the public face that she shows, and I can't help but wonder at this drive to hide and run, which is understandable—

Then, it hits me. She isn't the problem. I have a drive to hide and run, too, but hers whirls like a cyclone she has mastered, while I—

"Are you afraid of me?" I ask.

"No," she says flatly. "You?"

"A little bit."

"Come on, you're good at minds. Do it." Her disappointment pulls her energy away.

"It's slowing me down," I confess. "Not sure how to make the leap."

A strange thing happens. Her signal warms me, flowing around me more gently than before. "Here's a thought," she says. "Tell me your real name."

I tell her.

Infinity responds by squeezing me. Her skin is warm in the chilly blast churned up by the roaring helicopter. It's impossible not to think of its baleful eye searching the alleys and rooftops. But there is nothing to do but concentrate on the problem directly in front of me.

A bit of grit hits my left eye. I close both and rely on my nerves to feel my way through. I pull Infinity's signal into shape, from a cloak to a circle, radiating outward. It will have a weakened effect after about ten meters, and if she lets go, everything will skew off in unpredictable directions.

I hold my breath and draw the epicenter of my function out of my body, placing it between our chests. I lay Infinity's function over my own. My yang, her yin. No—there is no me, no her. She is no longer an *other*. The static was fear, and now I have none.

I can't see with my eyes closed, but my eyelids go red, and I know the searchlight is on us. Everything goes dark. Then, it all comes back in force. We've been spotted. My cybernetics trigger in reflex.

The two functions pulse in sync, washing through Infinity's arms and legs. There, they bend like light through a prism, shining out in waves that go on and on. The function screams *ignore* so hard, I'm surprised the chopper pilot doesn't fly into a chimney.

The light is off us once more. I open my right eye. The rotors keep beating the air, but the machine disappears from view.

"Are we a good team?" Infinity asks.

"The best."

"Is this going to work if they come up here to search?"

"It should. They will be turned away as well, provided we stay in position, until they leave in a few hours."

"I'm stuck here holding on to you?"

"It could be worse," I say. "You only have to talk to me for five minutes."

She leans in and brushes her lips against mine. Just as I'm starting to believe she means it, she squeezes me tighter, cheek to cheek, and her breath warms my ear. "You've got a lot of stories to tell," she says, "and I want to hear them all."

70 - BREUNIG

They find the mousy girl in the door-to-door sweep, not long after the police surround the area. The central command of BRHI is getting in their faces, simultaneously needing the police's help to clear the buildings but trying to keep the classified basement areas a secret. I don't give a damn about what happens—my job is to exact vengeance on the vipes for devastating my team.

I'm with three white-uniforms when we find the girl running for a back exit. If she gets to the end of the hall, the cruisers outside will cover her, but I'm not letting anyone get past me unchallenged.

"Freeze!" I shout.

"Don't shoot!" is the first thing she says, skidding to a stop. Her hands go up. One of them is clutching a phone.

"On the ground," I say.

"I just want to get out of here," she says, but something is off. She's calculating.

"We can't let anyone go without a check, ma'am. Now, get on the ground."

She sinks to one knee, then two, and looks over her shoulder. Her face is flushed, eyes puffy. The woman is easily winded, easily overlooked. I'm not in the mood to overlook anyone. And I just realized what's wrong.

"Ma'am, put the phone on the ground next to you." My voice carries the threat.

"Then I can't record you," she says and turns to face me.

All our weapons go up.

"There isn't anything to record." Maybe we can defuse this still.

"I've got a live streaming signal," she says, aiming it at me. "And now, you get to show the world what you do to vipes like me."

"Take her phone," I bark to Briar Team. "I don't know what you think you're d—"

She pulls a dull, black pistol. The security sees the movement. They know what it is, but in the video, it will be out of frame—

"No—" I shout, but they aren't my F-prots. Shotguns boom, and she rocks back. Her chest darkens with blood. Still, she stays up, but her pistol isn't aimed at us. The barrel lodges just above her own ear. She knows what awaits vipes when captured. I have a twisting, sick certainty that I can't argue the decision. Her other hand stops the video.

"You lose," the woman gasps and pulls the trigger.

71 - MORGAN

December 9th

I can't take care of Jess immediately. I stumble into the new rental house while Ferrero swaps the vehicles. We luck out: Infinity left her key to the Atlantis here, so the blood-spattered truck gets stored in the garage before anyone sees. I feed off Ferrero, and then we both pass out.

I wake first. With the feeling of starvation gone, I shower, dress, and shave, too beat to care about sculpting some new look. Only after I'm done do I think I'll need to blend again. I want to call Cho, but the police will be all over him and his voicemail. Bad idea. I watch the news, and there's Cass and Deborah. I will never see them again, in anything other than those damn security camera videos. Like they say in Hollywood, pix are forever.

I check the TV for messages and find there's one on the secure app. I stab at the icon and hear Infinity's voice:

"It's me. Just wanted to say I'm alive. Roland and I send our love. Give me a call when you've recovered. Interesting news."

I close my wet eyes. She made it. I don't know how. She is an invincible goddess.

That leaves Jess and what she'd want done with her body. By the time Ferrero gets up, I've found her phone, but I can't get at any of her contacts. He slips his fingers into a crack under a cabinet and pulls out a dusty slip of paper with numbers on it.

"We all wrote our passwords down," he explains. "They're hidden throughout the place." In an hour, he's talked with six vipes in New York who knew Jessica. In three hours, we've locked the place up, cleaned the vehicles and switched to the Atlantis.

We talk for the first hour, trying to keep it upbeat. I'm free. I can catch up on news, on sports, on the stupid bullshit that makes loss go away for a few seconds.

Then, we listen to Deborah's playlist, which is still stuck in the dash. There's Freddie Mercury and Lady Pang and half a dozen other soulful songs about regrets. I'm a wreck, but Ferrero soldiers on, driving through the tears because he can't hook us up to the grid and go autopilot. Even now, they're waiting for us to slip up.

And, from what I know, Ferrero's had to do something similar before. He's mentioned in my absence, they'd been forced to bury Ly.

I don't deserve you, Infinity had said. I piece that together. Fer explains what he can, and given my history with botched feedings, I hold off on the condemnation. I wanted Ly to last, to live. All of them should have.

It's four hours until we reach a funeral home in some suburb called Ardsley. I'm leery of talking to the staff because they're probably expecting the body to come from a hearse, not a trunk. But Fer says the director is infected. I numbly look on as specialists move the shrouded body into a simple pine box and close the lid.

"The others are in the reception room," says the director. She's said her name, but I haven't registered it. "I'll let you say goodbye. When you want to open this up for visitation, just ask." I nod. It's cold here. Jess's name isn't on anything, for secrecy. She won't have a headstone.

I thought I had cried out everything on the way up. I was wrong.

Ferrero squeezes my wrist. "I wish I knew what to say."

"Anything honest."

"I don't know, man," he says. "It feels like we did it wrong."

"It's the best we could manage."

"No, not this. You. You tried turning yourself in, staying legal, and it would have killed you. But then we tried everything to get you out, you know... Deborah being ten times braver than me... Cass bringing... everything—"

"Violence," I say. "Own it. You saved my ass with an active shooter."

"You mad at us?"

"Mostly at myself, but... then I think about it."

Ferrero rambles. "Yeah, you... you *had* something. I don't know what to call it, but us, we took that and we threw it all away. We got you free, but that's plus one, minus three. That math sucks."

I look at him point-blank. "So, you want out?"

"Out of what?"

"This war," I say harshly. "You know they'll never stop, right?"

Ferrero looks disgusted. "I remember you telling us we could do this. You were the one quoting MLK, and now you're telling me our life is war?"

"You fought to regain ground we lost, from an enemy who'd eliminate all of us if they could. That required the spirit of a war, like it or not. But how we fight it, we control that. We can try it like Cass or like Jessica and Deborah. We don't have much, but we have our entire lives to do things that honor them." I pause, out of words.

"I've never been in a war," Ferrero says. "I just know they go on longer than anyone wants them to."

He's right. "If you stick with me, I will make every effort to make it a clean one. I don't think any other vipe is going to give you a better offer. What do you think?"

Ferrero looks at the coffin and sniffs. Runny nose, no surprise. "I'm with you."

We embrace and then walk away out of the visitation room. In the doorway to the outside, there are a dozen people in varying shades of black. They're probably here for some other service, so I don't speak to them. But when I open the door to the reception hall, I can't pretend anymore.

There are a hundred faces in here.

The closest vipes give me passing glances. Then, they stop. Then, they glance again. "Are you..." asks one.

"Yes," I say.

"I heard you were dead. I gave up."

"Well," I say, "let that be a lesson to you."

72 - KERN

December 10th

For someone drifting in and out of consciousness, I'm concealing my infection well. The EMTs load me into one of the fire and rescue ambulances, and I wake up in a recovery room with a metal rod holding my shin together. A friendly-but-busy surgeon drops by with a plastic jar holding a bullet fragment that lodged in the meat of my calf. The wound is left to drain and heal—the full leg cast will go on soon enough. After the surgeon leaves, I get down to the serious business of freaking out.

They've put me on morphine, which solves a significant but small part of my problems. I can still feel the pain of my tibia, splintered like a plank of wood, but on the morph, I can somehow choose not to care and push it to the back of my mind. This is good because the front has no real estate left. I need an escape plan. It took me four hours to get into surgery, three to get it done. Sleep took up ten. That's all the incubation *it* needs.

My fever is at 38.4 C, and I've thrown up once already. That sealed my fate—the nurse suspected something. He took four vials of blood and saliva and skin samples, a flag that couldn't be redder if it had been made in a vat of maraschino cherries. Lyssaviruses are in saliva and skin. I'm within the window period, but they'll retest as long as I show symptoms. And when the results come back, the hospital will contact their security staff. I'll be in no condition to resist.

I ring for the nurse. It's fourteen long minutes before the man shows up, even though his station is maybe thirty feet away.

"What do you need, Mr. Kern?"

"Crutches," I say. "I need to be able to get to the bathroom."

The nurse taps the bedpan by the side of the bed. "Sorry. No walking. Until that cast goes on, it's Old Reliable here."

"I'm not shitting in a pan."

He's obviously heard this before. "Then I hope you don't have to go at all."

"If that's how we do this," I say, "please bring me a Discharge Against Medical Advice."

The nurse's face falls. I hold his gaze. That's right. You mess, I mess back. A DAMA isn't much, just a form stating I'm going to go home and live or die on my own dime, all hospital responsibility absolved. It's not anything a nurse should fear, but he'll need his supervisor and the attending to sign off: more work. More work is something people avoid like oncoming traffic.

"Mr. Kern, you are in no condition to get out of here."

"*Doctor* Kern."

The nurse compromises. "How about I get you a chair?" He leaves and returns with a wheelchair. I'm soon perched on the toilet, with the nurse outside the closed door, waiting.

The morphine's given me constipation, which is fine with me—I simply sit and use the time to plan.

I have to get out before the stuff wears off because when it does, I'll be useless. I need my clothes, I need to get past the desk, then out to a taxi because my car is still at Greenbriar. After that, what? My phone. I need to convert every asset I own to cash. If the police come knocking, I'd better be gone. They can take anything I own. They can take my life.

I flush the toilet for effect and shuffle into the wheelchair again. I roll out into my room. I feign compliance. The nurse lifts me into bed.

"You stay there, okay? Once they check the drainage and all that, someone will be in to put a cast on. We're not even supposed to let you use the bathroom."

"Look," I say, "I want a DAMA, but I guess explaining it to your boss could be annoying. If it's too much work for you, just print it out, and tell the next guy on shift to bring it to me."

That seems to mollify the man. "I'll see what I can do, all right?"

"Great."

I watch him go, consider waiting for all of a minute and decide to screw it. I unhook myself from the drips and make for the wheelchair again. I fall successfully into it and push myself over to the corner where my clothes are piled. The shirt and the underwear are done with some delicate maneuvering. But when it comes time for the slacks, they're rags. Dimly, I remember the EMTs cut them off me to see my leg. The slacks are shredded to the waist.

Waiting is death. I pull the one good pant leg on and let the chopped-up rags dangle. My wallet and keys are still in the pockets—excellent. I throw on my jacket and, within minutes, cautiously roll down the hall.

Avoiding notice isn't hard—there are tons of wounded officers from Greenbriar, as well as the usual ER patients. The nurse is on the phone. I roll through the double doors and then to an elevator. Five minutes later, I'm out by the parking lot, feeling cold wind and post-rain mist.

It takes me a few seconds to realize my victory is nothing of the kind. I need a ride but have no taxi and no phone. I roll into the parking lot, hoping some cab will swing around the corner and pull up right next to me. The road is dark, and the cars that come by are nothing good.

They're going to search for me. They have to. I push on to the main road. With no alternative, I stick out my arm, thumb extended. Cars pass me by, over and over, and every second I look back, waiting to see my captors. The mist turns to cold, small droplets of rain that sting me. If it weren't for the morphine, I'd lose it completely.

A black sport utility vehicle finally comes to a halt a little beyond me. A man gets out and throws open an umbrella. I roll toward the car, down an incline. I seize the wheels to avoid hurtling into him. I can barely control myself going ten fucking meters.

"Hell of a night, huh?" says the man, whose head is framed by long, gray braids and male pattern baldness. The bumper stickers plastering the back of the car were mostly catchy slogans about world peace and how the current occupant of the White House was a moron. He's a walking heartbrainer stereotype. That's normalcy, blessed normalcy.

I see an opening. "They kicked me out," I say. "No health insurance. I'm trying to get to Bethesda. Is that far out of your way?"

"Don't you worry about that," my savior says. "Let's get you in."

It's a struggle—the SUV is high, and as I clamber into the back, I bang my foot on the shotgun seat. I wince, less in agony, more afraid I've knocked something loose. The driver manhandles the wheelchair into the trunk, programs the drive, and in a minute, the SUV is doing its electric glide. I notice a distinct plastic smell.

"New car?" I ask.

"Four days," the man says proudly. "Just in time to lend a hand, right?"

"Right, thanks," I say distantly. Human interaction is more difficult than I imagined. Is the morph wearing off? I have meds in my house from the last time I pulled a muscle, but they can't be sufficient. I debate asking my savior to stop, but there are so many things to stop for, I don't know where to begin. I need pants, a phone, plaster so I can put on the cast myself and a crutch from a medical supply store so I can handle stairs. If I can just convert my stock to a cashiers' check, I'll be home free—

—except I won't be. I glance down at my wasted leg, still discolored from the iodine of the surgery, still wadded with dressing that will need to be changed. I'm supposed to heal fast now but if, and only if, I can get what I need.

Blood? That's so small, so petty, by comparison. The videos are everywhere. The F-prots will find out what I am. And Field can blame me for losing ENDGAME. But what was it that I said back at the trial? A vipe in a wheelchair. Still dangerous.

"You okay back there?" asks the driver.

"Yeah, it's nothing," I say. "I'm just hungry."

EPILOGUE

December 14th

Ena flexes her muscles one by one, peeling away a layer of white, dead skin and emerging with cool, gray scales that look young and a little bit beautiful. I watch as the snake finishes pulling her tail out of the sock-like skin. She doesn't mind my presence now that I sit obediently on the couch and make no sudden movements. I can't explain why, but I find the shed soothing to watch, at least from the safety of the other side of the glass.

I glance over to the cherry-wood god carving. He tried to return it, but I told him to keep it. He drilled in a hole and strung it on a leather thong. It's on the bed, now, just a little too awkward to wear when we make love. We've done a lot of that, slowly and carefully, since we made it to Atlanta. It beats grief.

Ranath is hanging up the phone as I come in.

"What did they say?"

"Nothing terrifying," he reports. "I still have the job, and a very nice intern is going to take us house-hunting in the suburbs. It will all be rather boring."

"Until the day you drop the mice on them," I say.

Ranath—it is strange to call him that but hardly the strangest thing I've ever done for a lover—scrubs a pot and puts it in the drying rack. "Well, legally the CDC can't do a thing with stolen research. But you never know. They may provide interesting answers."

"You don't think—I mean, Kern was talking like in ten years—"

He shuts off the sink and looks at me intently. "I can't promise a cure," he says. "I can't promise that we can create prey for you immune to the virus."

"You'll have a lot of nights where I come home from biting another man."

"I understand," Ranath says. "But I know we won't lie to each other."

I don't say anything but walk closer and embrace him. He squeezes back, and I try to come up with something good to say.

"Is it weird if that sounds very romantic to me?"

"Romance needs all kinds of weirdness." He brightens. "Come on, the news is almost tolerable tonight." He turns on the wallscreen and televised opinions blare.

I grimace. I guessed him for a bookworm, but no one is perfect. "Have they stopped showing Deborah?"

"Breunig's the story now. Charges against him were yesterday. The missing persons tied to him are today."

"He's going to rat out both of us."

"At the moment, just you. It's probably time for a change of name."

"Just how good are you at that?"

He gives me a smile. "I have practice in making things disappear. Now, fortunately, the news isn't all BRHI. Most of it is swallowed up by the election."

"I barely even know who's running," I say. "I mean, I know there's like twenty jokers who announced, but call me when there's a choice of four. Two, even."

He mutes the television. "Well, given the next president's ability to sign executive orders and the ages of the Supreme Court justices... I think we'd better get involved."

I stop. "Wait, we couldn't... I mean, they ruled no..."

"The world changed once," Ranath says. "It can change again." I look into his eyes, and for once, the cold sea-green is warm and inviting. He believes it.

I tune in a few seconds later to hear him saying something about scathing dissents and legislation in Congress. You can't take the D.C. out of him.

"Go back to the president thing," I say. "Is there good news or not?"

"This debate was last Thursday," he says. "From what I hear, the shocking impact of a video came up, and then, among other things, the candidates clarified their positions on VIHPS. I took the liberty of downloading it all for tonight."

I'm a little startled that he remembered to do all this in the midst of everything. But I'm not mad. I'm remembering Kern and his rant about affecting an election. The thought makes me mad enough to fight.

"Get out of here," I say. "Why do you sound like you're going to make me vote?"

"Because," he replies, "I like you."

Acknowledgements

Only after considerable time and effort did I realize that writers always mean it when they say, "no book is written alone." I would like to thank my initial beta readers, Anna Salonen, Mary Sexton, and the writer who goes by "Learned Foote." Adding expertise were Brian Joughin, who corrected my medical slip-ups; Ronald J. Allen, James Daily, and especially Carole Hirsch, who shot down the worst of my legal ridiculousness; and Philip Daay, who helped me jump into the world of self-promotion. Lindsay Mealing of Emerald City Literary offered encouragement over a long project when giving up was a tempting option. As for editing, Cameron Harris killed useless chapters with a tai chi sword and Sigrid Macdonald finalized the manuscript that, like a vampire, refused to die. Any mistakes that remain are mine.

Beverly and Shane, the kiddos, provided much-needed breaks and perspective, and my brother Brian is always up for talking about how to clear a house. My parents have displayed an unending patience with my choice of profession, and their optimism is always heartening.

Lastly, my wife Jennifer helped conceive *Lorenz v. BRHI* back in a Constitutional Law class when learning about a case similar to the fictional *Kelly v. Seven Star Health and Hospice*. I would not be the writer I am today without her, nor would this novel be what it is. Thank you, Jenny.

Dedication

For Sue Colton-Carey, who made me read *The Washington Post*

every morning of third grade.

It stuck.

Edited by Sigrid Macdonald.

Cover art by Jake Clark.

Print edition published in Foster City, CA, USA.

Library of Congress Control Number: 2018904598

Print edition ISBN **978-0-9996133-1-3**

Kindle Edition ISBN: **978-0-9996133-0-6**

Electronic Edition ISBN: **978-0-9996133-2-0**

Information about the author and the *Civil Blood* universe can be found at:

www.christopherhepler.com

12/18

CPSIA information can be obtained
at www.ICGtesting.com
Printed in the USA
LVHW092336051218
599434LV00001B/63/P

9 780999 613313